TETRASTATUM

TETRASTATUM
A NOVEL

TIM SMITH & DR. RICHARD

WARNING
Psychothotonix[SM]

*AN INTRODUCTION TO **PSYCHOTHOTONIX**[SM],*
THE DISCOVERY OF UNKNOWN UNIVERSES

Epigraph Books
Rhinebeck, New York

Paperback ISBN 978-1-948796-67-5
Hardcover ISBN 978-1-948796-68-2
eBook ISBN 978-1-948796-69-9

Cover and interior illustrations by Ken Krekeler
Book design by Colin Rolfe

Epigraph Books
22 East Market Street, Suite 304
Rhinebeck, New York 12572
(845) 876-4861
epigraphps.com

*IN MEMORIAM **RICHARD FEYNMAN** & **STEPHEN HAWKING** –*
INSPIRATIONAL TEACHERS OF DR. RICHARD.

|CONTENTS|

By that pure, holy, four lettered name on high,
nature's eternal fountain and supply,
the parent of all souls that living be,
by him, with faith find oath, I swear to thee.
PYTHAGOREAN OATH $\pm\infty$

I don't know how I got here, or where I came from, or where I am going. The small questions that I can answer only lead to other larger unanswerable questions. It is madness, total madness. My head is throbbing and I can't stop the buzzing, hissing noise in my head. Maybe I should stop asking the questions? "Make it stop," I cry out, but it won't. No matter how loud I yell, the noises only subside for a second as my lungs fill up with air and my vocal cords call out in anguish. It is my fault that they are dead. I should have been there. Now they are gone, and it is my fault. My naked body aches from the hard padding on the floor. I have been curled up in a ball for hours, maybe days, trying to stay warm as the vents flood the windowless room with dry, cold air. The fluorescent white light bounces off the four white walls, illuminating the faded white padding in waves. The light fixture above, like a beacon to the mad, makes an almost incomprehensible humming sound that is almost drowned out by the buzzing in my own head—yet is still audible if only to the truly insane.

No matter how loud I scream, no one answers. Only the humming, buzzing, hissing, white light continues into eternity, mocking my torment in an image that expands out into desolate space-time in perpetuity. The omnipresent, cosmic image processor passes no judgment, and only allows the images to unfold into the cosmos for all those who can see to interpret for themselves. I have failed them as I have failed myself. I can never bring them back…I can never bring myself back. Or maybe I can? Are you there? I can see you. I warn you, to continue this journey beyond this point is a grave decision. One should fully consider the consequences because the answers will come with larger questions, the humming, the buzzing. And nothing will ever be quite the same.

This manuscript, which accounts the details of my own quest for knowledge, is a perilous living journey that will perhaps answer your questions—but at an untold cost. If you must know the answers, they are here for those who absolutely must have them and can see. Wait, shhh, quiet—I hear something…. The barely audible sound of heels walking down the corridor can be heard approaching as well as muffled voices behind the padded door of confinement room number four.

"I think it's time, Nurse Nestpa, please prepare the patient for treatment."
"Are you sure that he's ready doctor?"
"It is his and our only hope, Nestpa, please prepare the patient."
Are you ready?

Psychothotonix is a new field created by Dr. Richard that is designed to maximize the immersive experience of the reader/viewer of a novel or motion picture, providing thought-provoking entertainment to a broad audience. The following brief interview with Dr. Richard discusses this method as it relates to the development of *Tetrastatum*.

Warning! Psychothotonix may cause you to have new interpretations of reality—clearly intended, as it is the essence of the methodology embedded in the novel itself!

INTERVIEWER. In your previous work you introduced the concept of Psychothotonix as a new form of space-time travel that manifests itself differently in each viewer's mind's eye. Please explain what that means as it relates to *Tetrastatum*.

DR. RICHARD. In the world of physics, the mathematical machinery and related technology are set up so that all events are moving forward in time. For example, if we view a quantum nano particle moving in a bubble chamber at close to the speed of light, it is moving forward in time, not backward, or in some sort of imaginary time universe. However, my detailed analysis has shown that our minds perceive events differently relative to the nature of space and time. For example, consider your own dreams. When you dream it is often in a place and time with people you don't know—it is a foreign space and time. In fact, time may not even be perceived in a dream state. When you awaken, you might say, "Where was I? Who are those people? I can't believe I only slept for five minutes! Was that all real somewhere, in some parallel universe, or is it just a figment of my imagination?" This can also be apparent in reading an engrossing book, or in watching a captivating movie—time and space can seem to evolve outside of the way we think in linear terms or in ordered events in physics. Part of the goal of *Tetrastatum* is to develop scenes that follow a different set of rules (in terms of how people interpret "reality") in a novel or a motion picture.

INTERVIEWER. Your basic model deals with a rather simple formula and evolves from there into other more advanced models of reality, first a basic and then a more advanced explanation in Appendices A and B. Please give us the nuts and bolts of the model with a few simple examples related to scenes in *Tetrastatum* that you and Marcus Rodriguez designed.

DR. RICHARD. I define Psychothotonix as an image-processing technique. It is the analysis of what I call thotonix and photonix images as they relate to reality. It is the process of interpretation of thotonix and photonix images in the mind of the viewer of the external event.

A photonix image is simply what a camera records and displays to other human observers. For example, a camera can take a picture of some piece of art with an extremely high degree of resolution—without distortions, noise, etc. Physically, the photons (light particles) scatter off the physical object and are collected by the camera's image-processing software and hardware, and display an image of the object. In this way, the image of the art, as seen by the camera, can be almost exactly the same as the details of the art piece itself. We say in photonics, the image is a photonics duplicate of the object. I use the word photonix instead of photonics because in our case the image can mean different things to different people. In fact, every person that views the piece of art will have a different interpretation of the actual physical object.

A thotonix image is simply the way the person captures the photonix image from the camera and processes it in terms of how they identify with it personally. One can say, how they relate the photonix image to their personal identity. The process of how all that happens is very complex. A simple explanation is: the photons from the camera image are translated into the "thotons" in the observer's brain (the person's image processor). But the thotons add emotional, ethical, historical meaning, and many other intangible characteristics to the photonix image in a way that provides meaning to the observer's internal identity of external events.

The Psychothotonix observer is an objective observer, like myself, who analyzes the differences between the photonix and thotonix images. I have developed a mathematical model that explains why this happens. The details are included in Appendices A and B.

INTERVIEWER. What would be a practical example of this process?

DR. RICHARD. In the above example, consider two observers of a perfect photonix image. This image was taken almost exactly by the camera (just as it was presented to the camera by the photons scattering off the art piece), then processed and displayed to observers "A" and "B." Let's say that observer "A" sees the artwork as a perfect photonix image of the piece of art—no physical distortions at all, but he/she sees the piece of art as a thotonix image as 100% unpleasing—it does not fit with his/her "identity" of what is important to the meaning of the art piece. But, observer "B" sees the artwork in a dual opposite thotonix state. It fits exactly the way he/she finds 100% pleasure in the meaning of the artwork. The independent observers each have dual opposite interpretations of what the art piece really means. My math model captures the natural phenomenon that all external photonix perfect images will always have dual opposite interpretations of the meaning of the photonix object.

The simple explanation of the equation I use to describe this natural phenomenon is that the observers' meaning of the piece of artwork is the sum of their photonix interpretations of the piece of artwork (in this case both "A" and "B" agree it is a perfect photonix image of the true physical object) and their differing thotonix interpretations. In this case, their thotonix images are 100% dual opposite to each other. "A" sees the work of art as having 100% no meaning to their internal world and "B" sees it as having 100% meaning to their internal thotonix image processing of "reality." My Psychothotonix interpretation is that they are both mathematically correct (to be objective) in their interpretations. As an objective observer of the interpretations of both "A" and "B" clearly, both "A" and "B" are "right" relative to their "choice" of meaning and identity of the piece of artwork.

INTERVIEWER. Can you give me a specific example of that as it relates to the flow of photonix and thotonix images in Tetrastatum.

DR. RICHARD. Yes, again let's consider "A" and "B" as readers of the book. In the novel, the main characters travel from Earth to Atlantis and are transformed into dualistic characters in Atlantis relative to the context of the book. In addition, the characters in Atlantis have their own photonix and thotonix interpretations of Atlantis as well.

Observer "A" might interpret all of this as Atlantis does not really exist as a photonix image because there are no real camera images of Atlantis. Observer "A" could conclude that the thotonix images of Atlantis are just purely imaginary—meaning that, since no photonix image with a camera of Atlantis actually exists, it must be just the author's manipulation of the meaning of objective reality. However, observer "B" might believe the photonix images might exist somewhere and have been lost in time, or have been buried for some reason. Observer "B" would believe that the scenes of Atlantis could be both real photonix and thotonix possibilities. The Psychothotonix writing of Marcus Rodriguez and Dr. Richard captures this in the novel—to allow different observers to have different photonix and thotonix image interpretations that are all correct and still fit with the basic equation described above. The book weaves places, history, current events, and personal identities into a complex blend to provide meaning and immersion to all people reading the book. The standard model of Psychothotonix is designed to maximize immersion and provide thought-provoking entertainment to a broad base of viewers.

As you read the book remember, the Psychothotonix equations are the driving force behind all of the scenes!

CHAPTER ONE

THE QUANTUM TELEPORTATION PROGRAM

"**G**OOD MORNING DR. SMITH,**"** mumbles the security guard at the DARPA entrance, which like so many other government office buildings is filled with conveyor belts, metal detectors and trays for keys, watches, and loose change. The building itself is a typical sprawling concrete edifice with a few small windows that barely let any natural light flow through the immense structure. Even if there were windows, it wouldn't matter. The section of the building where I work is subterranean, four stories below terra firma. Miles of fluorescent lights, illuminate the building complex. Once lost in the cavernous expanse of sub-four, time becomes imperceptible as day and night merge into one. It is always fluorescent white, work-time.

I empty my pockets and complete the first part of my morning ritual of walking through the metal detectors and collecting my trinkets from the plastic bucket. As I approach the oversized cargo elevator with my ID badge in hand, I am greeted with the nondescript yet familiar, "Good Morning, Dr. Smith." At least he didn't mumble it. The army soldier with a sense of urgent authority speaks, "Sir, please place your thumb on the pad and look directly into the scanner." Every morning, day after day, the only thing that is able to look into my eyes and see me with an absolute certainty of truth is DARPA's retina scanner. Other than that, I have been lying to my family, friends and just about everyone else outside of the project as to what I do every day, probably even myself. The project's cover story has me working at the National Institute of Standards and Technology, winding up Atomic Clocks. An undergraduate degree in Physics from Columbia, two PhD's from Harvard in Applied Physics and Mathematics—and the best I could do is become a glorified time-keeper? Oddly enough, nobody ever questions it. I guess people tend to like easy explanations and hate to probe too deep into things that can't be easily explained. People simply glance down at the hands of their watch for a split second, accepting the certainty which is reinforced by everyone else, and then move on with their day. I guess the brass at DARPA had it all figured out.

The soldier's voice startles me. "Sir, all clear, please proceed." The elevator doors open slowly as I approach. There are no buttons to push once inside. It knows where I am going and doesn't need any help from me to get there. The real action is in the basement, and it wasn't winding up the clocks—rather, tearing them apart. Clocks now appear to me as nothing more than an antiquated artifact in a museum explaining the primitive beliefs of an extinct civilization conquered by technologically superior beings. The brass understands what happens in sub-four, just like they did in Los Alamos. Upon witnessing the Trinity test of the first nuclear detonation, Oppenheimer quoted the Hindu, Bhagavad-Gita, "Now I have become death, the destroyer of worlds." Hinduism has a nonlinear concept of time that perceives the deity creator as also being the destroyer. I guess this big bang universe isn't good enough anymore for the brass, it is now "space-time universes."

As the dimly lit elevator descends, there are neither buttons, nor any indication of floor numbers. The only way to perceive where you are is the faint white light that intermittingly passes through the crack between the doors as you travel between floors. When the doors open on sub-four, the small plaque in the basement will tell you that the whole thing started from a bunch of Soviet scrap metal floating around the earth, emitting a pulsating radio signal on October 4, 1957. Shortly thereafter in 1958, the Advanced Research Projects Agency (ARPA) a division of the Department of Defense, was created to develop emerging technologies for the military. The Defense ("D" ARPA) was later added in 1972 and then removed, and then added back again, once the brass finally decided on the "D." But it all really started way before that. "Sub-Four," chimes the elevator. The doors open and the same two soldiers in a golf cart are there to greet me as they do every day, "Dr. Smith, how are you this morning? Sir, please get in."

We drive by a labyrinth of tunnels, passing various ongoing projects down the long corridor past the particle accelerator and quantum computers, and finally arrive at the Quantum Teleportation Project (QTP), my baby. "Here you are sir, have a blessed day." One soldier stands up and swipes an ID that opens the heavy vaulted automatic doors. Once inside, I am surrounded by rows of cubicles and whiteboards, illuminated by fluorescent light and the familiar smell of fresh coffee. I have been leading the QTP at DARPA for over four years now—with not much success. The brass is getting impatient. Today is the day, I tell myself.

"Good Morning, Dr. Smith. Are you ready for your coffee?"

"Yes, please bring it into my office, Janice."

"Mak is in there waiting for you."

"Great, thank you."

The last person I want to see this morning is Mak Naiyua, the head of DARPA. He couldn't wait a few hours to hear what I have to say in my presentation like everyone else? Mak is in his mid-fifties and served

an exemplary military career working his way up the corporation by sourcing academic talent capable of innovating technologies in both the private and public sectors for the military industrial complex. That is not to say he doesn't have his share of battle scars. Mak lost his hand in combat and replaced it with something that resembles a prosthetic iron claw that looks every bit as formidable as the man. Needless to say, he is very good at his job. Mak answers only to the Joint Chiefs of Staff. No wonder every time I see him, it is accompanied by an overwhelming feeling of uneasiness. As I approach my office, I can see his distinctive silhouette sitting on the couch in full military attire—metals shining, cap fastened tightly—poised to lecture me once again on the importance of the success and timely completion of the project. My stomach feels like it is taking a ride on a roller coaster at Coney Island, and I haven't even started drinking my coffee yet. Guess I already know how this is going to go.

"Tim—good morning. Do you have a few minutes before the presentation?"

"Sure Mak, what's on your mind?"

"As you know Tim, the Chinese have sent a quantum satellite called Micius into orbit and are correctly predicting the spin of entangled pairs of photons at distances of over 1,200 kilometers in separate receiving stations in Delingha and Lijiang. A system of those satellites could be used to network quantum computers in the future. The Russians aren't too far behind...and what have we done here with $1.4 billion? Nothing!"

"Mak, that's just not fair, I've been working with a team of some of the best minds in the country for over four years and, as I told you, we have the conceptual construct."

"Great Tim, the Chinese will be able to create secure encrypted photonic communication and maybe network their quantum computers—and all we have is a conceptual construct?"

"Yes Mak, but what we're doing here has far more significant implications and is a much more difficult task. Predicting the spin of an entangled pair of photons is a parlor trick, compared to QTP's final objective.... For God's sake Mak, you want us to teleport matter across space-time at a speed exceeding that of light—contrary to the basic tenants of known physics!"

"When I first found you languishing in the university getting soft, that's exactly what you signed up for Tim. Tenured professor? I'd say—an overpaid babysitter. You know you wanted to be here with all the resources I could offer. This is where the action is! Now produce, or you can go back to grading papers. I have some of the top brass from Washington coming to your presentation along with the congressmen who backed the bill allocating the funding for this snipe hunt. It better be good, or this project will be terminated—right along with you."

"Understood, Mak. But to close the QTP down after all of the work that's been done—while we're so close to proving the viability of the project—would be a huge mistake. You'll see, this afternoon."

"I hope so Tim, for all of our sakes," Mak says. He rises from his chair in a stately manner and walks out of my office, closing the door swiftly, almost slamming it as he departs.

An old picture of Kathy, Sarah, and Anny (my wife, daughter, and white Persian cat) sits on the corner of my desk, catching my eye the entire time Mak was speaking to me. They seemed to be saying, "Don't worry, Tim. Don't worry, daddy—it will all be okay. Purr." Of all three voices, my cat's purr was the most reassuring. I named Anny after Erwin Schrödinger's wife. It used to give me a way of connecting with my work while at home, because I couldn't talk to my family openly about my job. Anny, on the other hand, knew all my secrets. Schrödinger's probability wave function forms the basis of our hypothesis—and ultimately, the success of the project depends on it. So does my sanity. I stand up, close my blinds, and review the presentation for what seems like the hundredth time. I know we are right! The Quantum Teleportation Image Processor can be created and it will work! I can save them. My office wall clock keeps ticking. I am transfixed by the rhythmic sound of this imaginary metronome until a knock on the door brings me back from my trance.

Janice walks in. "Tim, they're ready for you in conference room 4D. Dr. Richard is waiting for you outside," she says.

"Thanks, Janice."

Conference room 4D is constructed in a manner resembling a Tesseract, a four-dimensional analog of a cube. The word Tesseract is derived from the Greek *téssereis aktines*—"four rays," as each of the four lines from each vertex connects to the other vertices, creating an inner cube that is unobservable in 3D space from the perspective of someone outside of the cube. Einstein and Murkowski's concept of space-time is derived from the 4D Euclidean space depicted by the Tesseract. The presentation room is shaped like a perfect square with a smaller suspended cube hanging exactly in the middle of the room, with a stage allowing the presenter to walk about and, from any direction, face the audience who are seated below at descending levels. The outer cube is designed similar to an amphitheater, except square in shape with terraced seating for roughly two hundred people. Seating slopes downward away from the suspended stage as opposed to the normal upward slope. The closer your seat is to the stage, the closer you approach the eye level of the presenter. The further away you are seated, the angle increases as you have to look up.

The focal point is the smaller, inner-suspended cubic stage, which has a glass floor illuminated with fluorescent white light. Presenters actually enter the stage from the fifth floor above and are lowered down from what appears below to be the glass ceiling from the fourth floor. The glass ceiling above actually becomes the stage floor as it is lowered, providing a magnificent entrance. Oversized monitors adorn the square outer walls on each of the four sides. It is reserved for only the biggest and best dog and pony shows. The stage design provides quite a dramatic effect and gives the presenter a feeling of immense, inexplicable power. The brass designed it that way, I guess. When the brass has to really impress the politicians to keep that money spigot flowing, it is in 4D. I grab my laptop computer and walk across the hall accompanied by Dr. Richard. Dr. Richard's work is the cornerstone for the QTP project. If anyone can deflect the heat from this crowd, he is the one to do it.

"Are you ready for this, Richard? The brass and politicos are going to have some pretty pointed questions when I get done with them."

"Nothing I can't handle Tim. If it gets too rough, I'm just going to teleport out of here."

"If you can do that, we're both sitting pretty!"

I turn on the microphone. "Excuse me, we'll be starting in a few minutes, if you can please take your seats now." Wow, no feedback on the microphone. I am used to hearing that awkward high pitch squeal in the other briefing rooms, but not in 4D. That's a good start. The hum dies down as everyone starts shuffling to their chairs. As the stage floor starts its descent, I can see most of my colleagues are already seated and are talking among themselves. After about thirty seconds, the floor completes its journey down, and the room grows quiet— all eyes transfixed upon us on the stage.

"My name is Dr. Tim Smith and I am the project manager of the Quantum Teleportation Program at DARPA." At least I am today, I think to myself after digesting Mak's morning pep talk.

"This is my colleague, Dr. Richard, who is the lead scientist of the Psychothotonix Quantum Image Processing laboratory. I would like to thank everyone for coming today to learn more about our team's progress in our work towards achieving the audacious goal of moving matter through space-time, quantum teleportation. We started this project over four years ago with the generous funding and patronage from those sitting with us today. I am proud to present the current findings and status of the project and to outline our future goals and objectives. Before we can begin, it is important that we address what we have learned of the space-time continuum itself. In order to have mastery of the ability to transport matter through space-time, we first have to have a fundamental understanding of its actual design. Currently, our views of the structure of space-time have been constrained by Einstein's theory of special relativity (STR) that applies to our big bang universe, whereby a universal speed limit is implied, suggesting that an infinite amount of energy would be required to accelerate an object with mass to the speed of light.

"It is our hypothesis from the research we have conducted which indicates that, within the context of space-time, there are universes that exist which do not consist of matter. The universes are connected by what we have called Space-Time Axons (STA) because they resemble the long threadlike portions of the body that carry impulses between nerve cells. Space-Time Axons can be thought of as fiber-like matterless cables that connect the multiverse of overlapping matter and non-matter universes across space-time. There are major STAs in the matter universe that extend for light years and minor STAs of less than a meter in length, while in the non-matter universes STA have no definable size. In order to accelerate an object at a speed that exceeds light c, an object must be scanned and photonically recorded in four-dimensional space utilizing an advanced crystallography process with Icosahedral Quasicrystal, (IQ).

"The IQ has a unique crystalline structure that contains a photonic band gap trapping light from all directions, providing the density required to store Yottabytes of photonic information in a holographic form. This is required for capturing the molecular structure of complex organic and inorganic objects. We are developing a prototype Quantum Teleportation Image Processor that utilizes a modified laser to read/write the digital data from the crystal converting it to photons, whereby the photons can be transferred instantaneously through STAs to matter or non-matter universes anywhere within the space-time continuum. Upon re-entry into a matter-based universe, the object is restored to its original form based on the transmitted holographic data.

"Our initial stage of the project involves the development of the crystallography media to facilitate complex organic and inorganic object photonic translation and the development of the QTIP. Upon successful completion of the prototype QTIP, we will begin mapping the STA universe by designing holographic probes, which will provide us temporal as well as geographic coordinates for matter universes. Once we have completed mapping, we will initially test with inorganic object teleportation, progressing to organic studies for the ultimate directive: human space-time teleportation! I would ask everyone to review Appendix A and Appendix B of the presentation as it contains the relevant notes and explanation of the formulas supporting our hypothesis of the new space-time continuum paradigm.

"Thank you. I am going to turn the mic over to Dr. Richard, who will be able to answer any questions, and then we'll proceed with the demonstration component of this presentation in the Psychothotonix lab for those of you who have the appropriate clearances."

One of the suits in the front, probably a congressman, raised his manicured hand. "Dr. Richard, has your team conducted any tests to provide data that supports your hypothesis of the existence of Space-Time Axons?"

"We have developed experiments using Cherenkov Radiation Detectors in a large vacuum, whereby the velocity of white light and photons are measured, indicating that some of the photons emitted from the modulated laser at random oscillation frequencies outside of the visible spectrum exceed that of white light—in other words, instantaneous movement through space-time. It is our belief that this is due to minor STAs traversing the path of the laser as we modulate the oscillation frequency of the wave. We are in the process of developing more elaborate tests and gathering more data," Dr. Richard responds.

In the third row, a hand goes up, catching Dr. Richard's eye as an older gentleman in a suit looks up quizzically.

"Yes, sir, what is your question?" Dr. Richard asks.

"I have reviewed Appendix B of the presentation outline and was wondering if you can explain your Dual Opposite Extension of Schrödinger's wave function equation and the applicability to quantum teleportation."

"Great question!" Dr. Richard says with enthusiasm. "The Dual Opposite Extension of Schrödinger's wave function equation is based upon the duality principle of quantum mechanics itself. My equation postulates that if the expected value of the Schrödinger's wave function is 0, the expected value of my extended equation is 1. For example, picture an electron bouncing between two positively charged mirrors, whereby Schrödinger's wave function would state that the probability of the electron being in the exact middle of the wave would be 0. My Dual Opposite Extension formula would result in an expected value of 1, indicating the electron exists in the exact middle of a wave in another universe. The Dual Opposite Extension equation expresses the fact that, at the precisely same moment in space-time, the electron would be exactly in the middle of the wave in the unobserved universe due to the fact that it can never be in the observed universe. With the certainty that Schrödinger's wave function predicts the impossibility of the electron occupying the space in the middle of the wave, the corollary predicts the certainty of the position of the electron, which is only possible if there is another unobserved universe. Applying the duality principal to Schrödinger's wave function and the corollary, Dual Opposite Extension of Schrödinger's wave function, the existence of other space-time universes is a certainty. This idea has formed the basis for the QTP."

"Thank you, Dr. Richard, I appreciate the thorough response."

"Well done Doc," I say to myself.

A curvy middle-aged blonde woman in the front row, wearing a tight-fitting military uniform with too many medals to count, smiles at Dr. Richard and slowly raises her hand, slightly exposing her bosom. She has been staring at him during the whole presentation while crossing her legs back and forth, fidgeting in her seat, and batting her eyelashes. Her name tag is written in oversized cursive—*Penny*. This is a no-brainer, I have no doubt who was getting called on next.

"Yes, ma'am in the front row, what is your question?" Dr. Richard asks sheepishly as he grins.

"Dr. Richard," she says in a seductive voice, pausing for an uncomfortably long time, "Do you have any hard evidence.....that supports QTP's theory of teleportation?"

"I sure do, but as we are running out of time, I would suggest, ahh— Penny—and the rest of the group, head over to the Psychothotonix Quantum Image Processing laboratory for the demonstration. Dr. Smith, do you have anything else to add?" he asks.

"No, the demonstration should speak for itself. I appreciate everyone's time and remind you that this briefing is Top Secret and Classified subject to Executive Order 13526 and 32 C.F.R. 2001, as amended. Have a good day. I'll see you at the lab in twenty minutes. Security will check clearances and escort you there." I pick up my laptop and start to exit the briefing room. I notice Mak seems somewhat pleased as we receive a fair amount of obligatory applause. He is shaking hands with the suits, who seem to be all smiles. As I am leaving, Mak looks up at me and seems to give me a nod of approval. "Maybe I'll live to see another day at DARPA. Not so fast—better wait and see how the Doc's magic show goes…." I tell myself. Dr. Richard and I grab a golf cart and head over to the lab.

The Psychothotonix Quantum Image Processing lab is the nerve center of the entire QTP, affectionately dubbed the Red Dungeon by those fortunate enough to work there. The room is illuminated with a low level of scarlet light providing a visitor with an immediate ominous feeling of danger yet, at the same time, excitement. This is where the magic happens, all of the senses come alive. The lab itself isn't terribly grand in scale, although it is large enough to house a D-Wave 2000Q quantum computer as well as a Cray XC30 whose liquid-cooled cabinets line the back wall and provide a soothing, low humming background noise. The humming contrasts perfectly with the frequent Miles Davis, "So What" piece and other cool jazz tunes that the good Doc usually plays over the lab speaker system in the wee hours of the morning. There is an assortment of specialized lasers and various electronic components on workbenches surrounded by whiteboards with varying calculations. My personal favorite is the wave function that graphs a probability density describing what time Dr. Richard will break the team for lunch on any given particular day. Special ventilation and climate control systems have been installed to maintain a constant, exact room temperature of sixty-nine degrees per Dr. Richard's specific request. I once inquired as to "Why sixty-nine?"

"I like the duality of the six and nine, Tim," he snapped back. "They make the perfect inverted pairs just like the Yin and Yang. It is just cold enough to keep me awake, but not too cold to cause discomfort. Duality, Tim, think cosmic duality!"

If it was the perfect temperature, I wonder why Dr. Richard is the only staff member that wears a heavy red lab coat that closer resembles Hugh Hefner's smoking jacket than the standard-issue, white technician's attire everyone else around here dons. I am not buying it or the whole red-dim-light business. The "red bulbs" cost the program three times as much as the regular, white fluorescent bulbs that adorn the other 1.4 million square feet of office space at DARPA. Of course, Dr. Richard had an answer for that one, too.

"Tim, in 1704 Newton, in his treatise on optics, devised a color circle consisting of a spectrum of seven colors—uhuhmm," Dr. Richard stated, clearing his throat. "Newton observed that certain colors were opposed to one another and provided the greatest contrast—red and green being one of these pairs. When we're using green lasers, the red lighting provides me with the ability to see what the hell I'm doing. Does that answer your question?"

"It sure does," I think to myself. Whatever else is left to my imagination I fill in with the closed circuit cameras Dr. Richard had installed in the lab to record experiments. He knows it too, adding a little edge to each performance. I find the good Doc's 1:00 a.m. sessions, accompanied by a superb single malt scotch, a relaxing ending to my fourteen-hour days in this madhouse.

A few eccentricities and some red lightbulbs are nothing compared to the imagination and creative genius that lurks in the Red Dungeon. If Mak had his way, they would never let the good Doc out of the dungeon. I really don't think he would care. Dr. Richard was originally recruited by Mak from the private sector, where he had finished developing a photonic naval warship missile-threat-assessment imaging system. Dr. Richard wanted to push the edge of the envelope further on the advanced interpretation of the imaging information beyond the established Johnson criteria, but it fell on deaf ears at corporate. An unlimited budget to buy all the toys he wanted for the dungeon, space-time teleportation, and free reign over his subterranean kingdom pretty much clinched it. Mak had his answer in less than an hour. The next day the construction of the dungeon commenced.

The group from 4D finally makes it to the lab as the soldiers drop them off in front of the vaulted door. Dr. Richard leans over and softly speaks, "Tim—looks like we have nine brass balls and a Penny." I shoot

him a quick glance, pleading for the good Doc to behave at least until he pulls the rabbit out of the magic hat and we send our friends from DC marching home.

"Welcome, welcome everyone, welcome! Please grab a pair of....*safety glasses*...and follow me into the lab. Don't touch anything. Only I am allowed to touch!" Dr. Richard says in a tone which gives even the brass a feeling of overwhelming trepidation as the lights dim and they pass through the doorway into the Red Dungeon. The group follows Dr. Richard to an eight-foot-long inverted table that houses the prototype Quantum Teleportation Image Processor, which is held in place with belted straps. A large canister containing an attosecond laser camera is pointed vertically upward toward a quartz crystal obtruding from the center of a modified computer, directly in the path of the laser.

Dr. Richard reaches into the pocket of his red lab coat and grabs a pair of safety glasses. He extends a long glance to Penny and says, "Why don't you come over here closer, where you can get a better view?" Penny smiles and walks over to where the good Doc is standing. "Glasses, everyone—glasses!" Dr. Richard motions to the lab tech. "Power it up!" The subtle humming noise in the background is quickly overtaken by the higher-tone pitch of a rapidly increasing frequency, which feels like a small ball-peen hammer striking in rapid repetition on a primal nerve. I didn't know if I should run or fight as the hairs stand up on the back of my neck. Even though I had experienced this before, the adrenaline flows with equal intensity each time.

Dr. Richard looks up at the lab tech and shouts, "turn cameras 2, 3, 5 and 7 on now! Ready 10, 9, 8, 7, 6, 5, 4, 3,...2,...1. NOW!" A burst of green concentrated light penetrates through the crystal, creating a perfect three-dimensional image of a rotating green apple five feet above the inverted table, which appears to be hovering in midair. The Doc is right about the red lighting as it enhances the holographic image creating a truly lifelike effect. Dr. Richard holds his arm in the air in a manner that reminds me of a conductor leading a symphony at Carnegie Hall. Looking at the lab techs, he shouts over the background noise, "Start the frequency modulation, NOW!" They comply. The green apple that appears solid in mass continues to hover as we all watch. Another minute elapses while everyone looks intensely at the holographic image. A lab tech raises his hand and signals to Dr. Richard. "Power it down!" he yells waving his arms in the air. The room becomes quiet, with only the soothing background noise of the Cray XC30 audible once again.

One of the brass looks up and speaks. "Dr. Richard, that was a fantastic hologram, but nothing that I haven't seen with my kids before at Disney. I don't understand what the hell does that image have to do with teleportation? As far as I can tell, all we have here is a billion dollar hologram of an apple!"

Dr. Richard doesn't react. He calmly looks over at the lab techs and says, "Playback the STA event on monitors one through four. Everyone looks up at the four monitors dangling from the ceiling, on the horizontal axis, time stamps are denoted in intervals of thousandths of a second. Cameras 2,3,5 and 7 are specialized equipment developed at MIT that can capture images at a trillion, 10^{-12} frames per second. "Disney doesn't have these babies," Dr. Richard tells himself.

Even at 10^{-12} frames per second, the MIT camera doesn't capture the true complexity of the STA event. The maximum speed images can exist in time per Schrödinger equation is defined as 10^{-34} frames per second in a matter universe. Dr. Richard refers to this as the "quantum shutter speed" of this big bang universe. Any images, which theoretically could exist at speeds in excess of 10^{-34} frames per second are outside of our known concept of reality. Image information consisting of non-photonic particles traveling faster than the quantum shutter speed would exceed the speed of light, resulting in a tunnel through time by which images of other universes could theoretically be visible.

The monitors display the holographic green apple in time lapse. The apple is there as clear as day, and then suddenly disappears on each of the monitors for what appears to the viewers to be at least thirty seconds in time-lapse, but is actually denoted as a period of ten milliseconds on the axes. The brilliant green apple than reappears out of thin air, back on each of the monitors. "The human brain can perceive images at a rate of approximately thirteen milliseconds," Dr. Richard mumbles to himself. Even the humming seems to fade out as silence overtakes the group, contemplating what they had just witnessed.

"Thank you. That concludes the demonstration." Dr. Richard says with finality.

I look at the brass to gauge their reaction, Penny is smiling and asking Dr. Richard questions. Some of them sit with a blank expression, and others have skepticism written all over their faces. Probably, most just want to move on to dinner and not give this much more thought. "After all, an apple a day keeps the doctor away. The brass just had their bite of the apple," I think. Mak ushers the group out of the room to the four-star dining experience only the DARPA chefs can provide. Penny and the good Doc continue on with their conversation in the lab. I am beat, and head back to my office. After the few minutes' walk, Janice is there to greet me. Good to be back. I rarely leave my office. I've seen Janice's face more often than Kathy's over the last five years.

"Dr. Smith, Kathy called wondering what time you would be coming home this evening."

"What did Janice just say?...she couldn't have...," I say to myself.

"What did you just say, Janice?"

"I said, you had a bunch of calls and I was wondering if you would be leaving late again this evening. If so, I can grab you something from the cafeteria. You need to eat, you know. Your messages are on your desk."

"Thank you, Janice. No I'm not hungry. You can take off for the evening. Good night."

"Good night, Dr. Smith."

I enter the familiar safe surroundings of my office, close the door to the world, and sit down in my Herman Miller chair, one of the nicer perks at DARPA. I hadn't been home early in the last five years, working nearly fourteen hours a day. If I had been home, things may have been different. After that presentation, I think I will call it an early day. I say that to myself every day, but it never comes to pass. DARPA is my home.

CHAPTER TWO

FIRE

THE LIGHTS OUTSIDE my office are turned off, which tells me that Janice and most of the other staff have left. It is the same routine every day. As soon as I hear the vacuum cleaners humming, like a Pavlovian dog, the neurons in my brain start firing in anticipation of escape. I lower my office blinds. Settling back in my chair, I reach over and open my favorite after-hours desk drawer. Between the accounts payable and receivable folders is the Macallan 18 single malt. It used to be for special occasions, now it is just there. That account is always past due. Better make it a double, today is a celebration. I find my glass in the usual spot and help myself to a liberal pour.

Finally, peace, quiet, and sedation. I untie my shoes and remove them, settling down at my desk, feeling a sense of illusory freedom as my toes move unconstrained. A pile of pink *While You Were Out* messages are neatly stacked up. "Somebody better let them know that I've been checked out for quite a while, no need to rub it in, but maybe out," I say to myself. I put on a good show, nobody has any idea. Not Janice, Mak, Richard—nobody knows how far down the rabbit hole I have already fallen. The burnt oak tingles in my nose as I wet my lips and feel that familiar burning sensation in my gullet. My senses are slowly dulled. Time to watch a little tube, the "Red Dungeon" channel is my favorite after hours.

I turn on my monitor and query the four observation cameras on the quadrants of my screen that capture every angle of the room. Looks like I am not going to be disappointed tonight, the Doctor is in! Observable on the first quadrant is a table with a military uniform, neatly folded slacks, and a jacket with metals shining in the dim red light. A black bra and white lacey panties sit on top of the pile. If I hadn't seen it before, I probably wouldn't believe it. When babies are born, they see images upside down because the brain hasn't assimilated enough data based on experience to invert the images in accordance with their new environment. It takes varying amounts of time for the brain to compensate.

Adults actually see inverted two-dimensional images in each retina in the eye, which the brain flips to create three-dimensional vision through unconscious inference. The images of the universe and the information contained in those images are simply raw photonic data that must be interpreted by an image processor to give it context and meaning. Dr. Richard calls this process Modular Image Translation, which can be simulated using semiconductor technology and A.I. software, or organically in an organism through a process developed through billions of years of evolution. In order for the QTIP to succeed, we need to simulate the brain translation process, interpreting existing image data that the brain has lost the ability to process. Either people lost the capability to process the exogenous image data through natural selection because the perception of the additional data wasn't tied to a survival trait, or it is altogether not possible to comprehend due to the physical limitations of the organic structure of the eye. A pretty tall order, in either case.

The brain adapts to its environment once enough data is assimilated, adjusting our perception without our conscious recognition. Our eyes don't see, our minds do. They say seeing is believing?

I think, how the hell do I know what unconscious inferences my brain is making to fine-tune my personal picture show?

Just to be sure, might as well turn on the audio feed too. I can hear Penny's subtle moaning, "Yes, Doctor!" and the crack of a riding crop against the backdrop of Miles Davis' cool jazz, "So What." I peer over at quadrant four and see an inverted table that is designed to strap in the laser setup for the QTIP. Dr. Richard's red lab coat and a riding crop appear to be his only attire for this evening's extended work session as he stands erect in front of the table. Penny's hands are strapped to opposite sides of the table with her legs spread apart and bound form-ing an X. The red light reflects off her naked body, creating a hue of foreboding scarlet pleasure as her plump thighs squirm in rhythm, with her back and buttocks firmly pressed up against the table. Her heavy bosom heaves as she struggles. "I've been a bad girl, Doctor, I have to be punished," she says in a soft whisper. The cool jazz echoes through the dungeon, Miles Davis's trumpet calls out to Penny, "So What."

Dr. Richard doesn't miss a beat. He slowly caresses her with the riding crop starting at her bound hands moving slowly down her body with anatomical precision. "Yes, you've been a very naughty girl." So What! The riding crop cracks as the good Doc looks straight up at the camera, Penny screams in pleasure, "Ahhh, yes, bad, very bad, Doc."

"I see," he replies in a casual tone. My focus returns as I regain my breath and look back up at the monitor, searching the images from each of the four quadrants. The "Red Dungeon" is empty, and the QTIP laser is mounted on the inverted table as it had been during the earlier presentation. The audio feed is silent except for the humming of the Cray XC30. I watch in disbelief as I rewind the video searching, nothing! It has to be there. Maybe it is just what I wanted to see? No, it was there, I saw it clear as day in my mind. Didn't you?

The optic disc, "blind spot," is the area in the retina where blood vessels and the optic nerve are attached, it is void of visual receptor cells in each eye, resulting in dots where there is no visual data. The brain fills in the blank spots. Whatever the cosmic image processor wants me to see defines the level of my cognitive visual perception. After working in this place for over four years, I can tell you with certainty there is a hell of a lot more out there that the brain is incapable of visually assimilating, yet exists. Even in the absence of photonic data, the brain is processing four-dimensional images, as well as other sensory perceptions linked to the image data—what Dr. Richard calls "thotons." (Even while you are reading my manuscript, two-dimensional characters on a page are transformed by your brain into four-dimensional visual images.)

I turn off the monitor and decide it is time to go back to the house. Although as I wrap up my evening ritual tonight, I am left with a sense of unusual uncertainty about the state of my own reality and mind. How are you doing?

With the same formality and security of entering the building, I exit, making my way out of the labyrinth of DARPA. It is more of a hassle leaving than coming to work because they have numerous measures in place to ensure that none of the classified information makes its way out of the building—my favorite being the last line of defense after the x-rays and scanner—the super high tech, late-night pat down. It doesn't make much sense to me as the "classified" information is *me*. Everything I work on is stored away safely in my brain, or maybe not. As soon as I drive off the lot, there isn't much anyone can do about it. I exit the building and make my way to the parking lot. It reminds me of the feeling you get when you arrive back home from a long trip, trying to remember where you parked in the long-term airport lot. I can remember the last bit of every classified detail of the QTP, but just don't ask me where I parked. DARPA's parking facility is immense. The only positive thing is that at this hour the lot had thinned out. Most people do their nine to five, cash their checks, and are out of here. No questions asked. I envy them because they have somewhere other than here to be, an alternative universe that doesn't revolve around work.

A slight creaking noise can be heard as I open the door of my 1973 AMC Gremlin X, which I've been driving since graduate school. I just can't let it go. I am like that, once I become attached, I can't part with people, places or things. I've had to have the engine rebuilt twice, but it was my Green Gremlin, after all. The Gremlin chokes as I turn the ignition key, sputtering until a small cloud of smoke erupts from the tailpipe with a bang, and the engine roars to life. The car has a slight vibration when driving over sixty mph. But other than that, the black interior is in great condition, and all the instruments are in perfect working order. The Gremlin is a living, breathing time capsule, reminding me of who I am, where I came from—but most importantly, where I am going home. I slowly pull out of the parking lot down a long winding road which goes on for miles leading to the entrance of DARPA's property. Once I leave the parking lot and travel about a quarter mile, if I turn off the Gremlin's headlamps, it is nearly pitch black. Mature oak trees and other vegetation line each side of the road, providing a canopy blocking out most of the moonlight. I've done it a few times, just to check and see how far I can drive before I lose my nerve and turn the lights back on. It drives the guard at the exit crazy. He usually asks before he opens the gate, "Dr. Smith, what happened to you, why are you driving with your lights off?"

"Just an electrical short!" I snap back. He looks at the age of the car. It makes perfect sense.

After a month or so the new ritual becomes, "Dr. Smith, haven't you gotten that short fixed yet? It's pretty dangerous driving out there without working headlights. You should take care of that."

"I've been meaning to, just haven't been able to find the time."

I literally mean it, as my job is to find "time." No wonder I am losing it, I am the first one to admit it. How can you ever find something you can't see? My Gremlin is real, I can see it. So far, I haven't crashed the car into the oak trees driving blind, so maybe I still have a chance to find "time" before I crack up? Maybe it's already too late—maybe "time" has already found me. Tonight, I am not in the mood. I keep the lights on and exit the gate, flashing a fake smile and a quick wave. I drive for forty minutes down the highway through all the other dots of quickly moving red and white lights to my exit through suburbia, past the small town, and finally to the outskirts of the country to Observatory Hill. Kathy and I had bought the house shortly after we were married, before Sarah was born. It is a historic Victorian with three stories and a basement. Plenty of room for the three of us and the cat.

The Queen-Anne style all brick house was originally built before the panic of 1893 by the local banker, George D. Crown. His bank was the only one within a hundred-mile radius, located in the small town of Fairview, not more than a few miles from the house. By 1895, the bank had shuttered its doors because its primary customers were local wheat farmers, whose crops eventually became virtually worthless. In the last years of his life, as his finances dwindled, G.D. kept himself busy with astronomy. Visitors frequently found him looking through his telescope, staring out of the third story cupola into the heavens, muttering incoherent, slurred profundities explaining God and the universe to anyone who had time for a drink and would listen. This accounted for a good part of the townspeople of Fairview, at least those that didn't hold a grudge against G.D. for calling in a loan or foreclosing on a family farm. The locals started referring to it as Observatory Hill, and the name stuck. So did the local phrase, "Did you enjoy your G.D. up on the hill?" G.D.'s name became synonymous with "God and Drinks" or "God Damned Crown," depending upon who you asked. General Dynamics is all that came to my mind when I first saw his initials carved into an elm tree in the front yard.

The house looks like a weathered Victorian birdcage perched above the countryside, peering out to the heavens above and Earth below, surrounded by hundred-year-old, knotted elm trees whose long branches extend out in every direction. When Sarah was little, Kathy and I built her a swing with an old tire. She loved to spend hours swinging and watching Anny, our white cat, playing on the manicured lawn. The swing is gone, but the elm tree stands defiantly, refusing to let go. Two leaning brick pillars covered in ivy greet me at the entrance, each adorned with an oversized cement pinecone at the pinnacle. They seem to defy gravity as they lean in opposite directions looking like they will collapse at any moment, with only the ivy holding them up. I don't have it in me to fix them, myself, or anything else around here anymore.

I approach slowly up the winding driveway, carefully negotiating large cracks and unfilled holes in the weathered concrete. I park the Gremlin outside under the portico, which is sloping in a lopsided manner as it extends from the side of the house, also badly in need of repair. It is an eerily still night as shadows are cast in all directions from the moonlight passing through the maze of tree branches above. The shadows hit the ground and form an intricate pattern of light and darkness around the house. Near the elm tree where Sarah's swing used to be, I catch the silhouette of a white cat out of the corner of my eye, slowly turning around to the other side of the tree trunk. "It can't be," I think.

"Anny…is that you? Anny," I call out into the darkness. I walk over to the elm to get a better look. Nothing is there. "My mind must be playing tricks on me," I say to myself. It is not possible. As I continue walking up the flagstone path to the front door, the porch lights are turned off. It doesn't look like anyone is home—all the lights are off, except a small table lamp in the cupola.

As I fumble with my keys in the darkness trying to fit the right one into the lock, I finally open the door and turn on the foyer lights. No expense had been spared when the house was originally constructed by G.D. It was obvious—when Kathy and I first walked in and saw the remains of the burled walnut wainscoting, remnants of the sconces, alabaster chandeliers, and millwork from a bygone era—that this place had once been something special. Even though, over the years—vandals, looters and squatters had left the once majestic manor in a state of utter disrepair, Kathy and I bought it. Both of us liked a challenge. We spent a good part of our savings and my salary restoring Observatory Hill to its former glory. G.D. would have been proud. The foyer provides a spectacular entrance. You can look up three stories as the staircase winds all the way up to the cupola. One of the previous owners converted the original alabaster, paraffin-lamp chandelier to electricity. It hangs all the way down from the highest mid-point of the ceiling on a heavy iron chain. Supposedly, that is where G.D. met his end. The townspeople found him dangling from the lit chandelier, with paraffin dripping onto the floor, leaving a permanent mark. When restoring the hardwood floors in the foyer, no amount of sanding could get the G.D. paraffin stain out.

As I enter the foyer, pictures of Kathy, Sarah, and me stand out on the accent table. More pictures line the walls up to the stairwell between the intricate moldings. I can't help but look at these images that provide the feeling of warmth that flows through the house. "I wonder where they are." I think to myself. I walk into the family room, turn on the lights, and help myself to a nightcap. Scotch neat does the trick. I head up the stairs to the cupola with my glass, thinking of Kathy and Sarah while I wait for their return. Old G.D. and I have shared a few in our time to make the waiting, bearable. After walking up the three flights of stairs and catching my breath, I sit down in the lounge chair next to my telescope. It is pointing out the large window in the center of the cupola, which I imagine to be the cyclopean eye of the house. Like G.D., I too enjoy star gazing.

It is fascinating to me that it takes about eight minutes for light from the sun to reach Earth. The light from the next closest star system Alpha Centauri, made up of three stars, takes more than four years to accomplish the same feat. The naked eye can see approximately six thousand stars without the aid of a telescope. Some of the stars we can see are nearly one thousand light years from our sun. We already have a doorway into the past because the oldest images seen with the naked eye are from light radiated by stars ten thousand years ago, which we are perceiving in the present. Images of light from the beginnings of our universe have been captured by satellite dating back to 13.7 billion years ago. Through the telescope, it is also possible to see "ghosts," blue stars from distant early-forming galaxies. Due to their extremely large size, blue stars have a short life span of only a few million years, smaller stars can exist for trillions of years. Blue stars have a flair for the dramatic, just like G.D. A spectacular increase in brightness is followed by a catastrophic explosion ejecting most, if not all, of the star's matter into the universe—a supernova. The orphaned light still traveling through space and observable to us is from a star that no longer exists, a ghost. As Neil Young proffered, "It's better to burn out than to fade away." Just like the stars, we are all dying from the moment we are born, our fate inevitable, with the only remaining questions being how bright we can burn prior to the dramatic explosion or the imperceptible breeze that extinguishes the light.

I take a quick look through the telescope. The lights of Fairview are visible on most nights. That is all I can see, the still clouds hover above, and no stars are visible. A soft, barely audible "meow" breaks the silence. My head snaps back around as I turn my gaze from the telescope to the ornate doorway and see a fluffy white tail crossing the threshold. "Anny?" I call out. I stand up and look out over the hallway and stair-well. Nothing. I hear the patter of soft footsteps heading to the second floor, toward my bedroom. I quickly follow, shuffling down the flight of stairs. Still, I can't see anything. I fumble for the switch, turning on the light as I walk into the master bedroom. Kathy had decorated the house true to the period. An oversized canopy bed is the focal point of the room, drawing the eye to an alabaster chandelier hanging below a gold leaf medallion set into the coffered mahogany adorning the ceiling. An oil painting of Kathy hangs above the mahogany mantelpiece that outlines the marble fireplace. Kathy seems happy in the painting. Her regal smile, flowing blonde hair, and blue eyes warm up the room. Anny is nowhere to be found.

It is the end of a long day. My glass is empty and I am too close to approaching the unconscious to walk all the way downstairs and pour another. I disrobe, hanging my suit on the wooden valet as I stagger to remove my trousers and crawl under the welcoming, warm quilted covers. I roll over and face the nightstand to turn off the light. A picture of Kathy, Sarah, and me on our trip to Maui catches my eye. It was my most fond memory of the three of us. Sarah had just turned ten and seen a surfing video that captured her imagination. She begged Kathy and me for a visit to Hawaii. Kathy and I had never been there. We had batted it around as a possible destination for a honeymoon that had never materialized. At this point, I was teaching physics at a university in California and had accrued some vacation time to get an early jump on the summer months. So we both got on the bandwagon and made arrangements. I will never forget Sarah's expression of disbelief and joy when she saw the sunrise on Mt. Haleakalā a dormant volcano on the island of Maui. "Daddy look. It looks like we're on the moon," she blurted out with excitement. The purple, red, and yellow hues in the clouds against the backdrop of the martian-like rock crater captivated Sarah, as she gazed in utter astonishment. "Is this where God lives, Daddy?" she asked, as serious as could be. The rays of the early morning sun reflecting against Sarah's face and her newfound look of amazement and wonder are something I will never forget and often wish I could experience again. I switch off the light. "Did I just travel back in time?…. Images are powerful, very powerful." I think before nodding off to sleep. Then I let dreams overtake my consciousness. They are all I have left.

The Green Gremlin jolts me awake as the vibration rattles the car. I am behind the wheel, rolling down what appears to be a blue road at over seventy mph, heading to work. The radio is blasting "My My, Hey Hey (Out of the Blue)." I quickly swerve as I see a white cat crossing the road, and barely miss her. It is Anny. How did she get all the way out here? I look over, and there is G.D. in the flesh, smiling at me— wearing his spectacles, dark three-piece suit, handlebar mustache, and banker's derby hat.

"That was a close call old boy!" G.D. says with a sadistic smile. "That cat just doesn't know where it belongs—alive, dead, neither dead nor alive, dead and alive. You tell me, Tim, where or when the hell is that cat going to show up?"

"I have no idea, it seems like it is everywhere lately," I reply as I try and understand my surroundings.

Once we had completed the renovation, Kathy and I went to the Fairview Library archives to piece together a scrapbook detailing the history of Observatory Hill. G.D. looks far better in person than the old black and white clippings I had seen in the newspaper.

"Love what you've done with the place, Tim," G.D. says coyly.

"I must really be losing it—might as well play along." I think. "It had good bones, G.D., good bones for Kathy and me to work with." I smile at him.

"You wouldn't have an early morning nip of sunshine for me, would you, son? It's been a long time," G.D. inquires with a sense of earnest immediacy.

I grab a silver flask from the driver-side door. "If you have a taste for a single malt, I'm more than happy to oblige." I hand him my flask and he takes a strong swallow, passing it back. I do the same. The way this ride is going, it can't hurt. The radio changes tunes abruptly as "Hey Hey, My My (Into the Black)" echoes through the airwaves, as Neil sings "There's more to the picture than meets the eye." Dr. Richard's voice echoes in my mind, "Damn right there is, Tim! Mr. Young obviously understands cosmic duality and Psychothotonix."

The Gremlin starts accelerating, and the speedometer increases from seventy to ninety in the blink of an eye while the mesmerizing blue surface of the road turns to regular black asphalt. The car races down the road through the curves in the countryside. My foot isn't even on the accelerator, and pressing on the brakes doesn't seem to do anything.

G.D. looks over at me, "It flies by son, and then the lights go out for good. Keep a firm grasp on the wheel, see where you're going and you'll be okay. By the way, where and when are we going?"

I look up, surprised by such a simple question, "We're headed to the office now."

"Are we?" G.D. grins. "What if I told you that you already have everything you need to travel in space-time faster than the speed of light? You are doing it right now!"

"I would tell you that you've already have had one too many. G.D. takes a swig from the flask. But who am I to judge. Let's hear it," I say reluctantly.

"Not hear it, Tim, SEE IT! You can see me—can't you?" G.D. asks.

"Clear as day in 3D, G.D.," I respond as he glances over from the passenger seat.

"Good. Close your eyes, Tim—don't worry about the Gremlin—it will steer itself. When you and Kathy searched the archives, do you remember the black and white photo of me dangling from the chandelier in the foyer? Not my best day—but you saw the image? I want you to picture it in your mind."

"Got it., G.D."

"Fantastic, Tim. You have just traveled through space-time at a speed faster than light! Open, your eyes."

I open my eyes and look up just in time as the Gremlin is about to veer off the road into a McDonald's billboard. "I thought you said the Gremlin would steer itself."

"It did. I'll let Dr. Richard explain this, so you can remember it in the morning," G.D. says as he turns the radio station dial to 96 FM.

Dr. Richard's voice carries out over the radio speakers as his theme song fades out, "GOOOD MORNING, TIM, the Doctor is in! As you already know, your brain is a modular image processor. It takes high-speed snapshots of photons and translates the two-dimensional wave images captured by the eye into a three-dimensional contextual image recording all the associated senses and feelings. The contextual images are stored in your brain as entangled elements. I call the stored waves "thotons" or anti-photons. Think duality—cosmic duality."

"When did the good Doc get his own radio show? I didn't know he had a theme song. Do the brass at DARPA know?" A visual image of

Dr. Richard in his red lab coat behind the recording studio glass window emerges in my mind.

"FOCUS, Tim," Dr. Richard's voice booms over the car speakers. "Photons form light energy waves—thotons form dark non-matter waves. Photons are constrained to the speed of light. Thotons are entangled and can travel instantaneously through non-matter channels in your brain, similar to STAs in the universes. As you probably are not aware, you are dreaming RIGHT NOW! Your eyes are closed and photonic imaging is impossible. You saw a three-dimensional instantaneous image of G.D. in the past as well as in the present and you now have an image of listening to my G.D. radio show as you drive to work. It is only possible with thotons. Want to take a crack at the future?" Dr. Richard asks as G.D. motions to me to pass the flask over.

I feel a pang in my stomach, and for a brief instant I can see myself waiting in line at the drive-through at McDonalds and then eating a Big Mac and large fries at my desk in the office. Must have been that stupid billboard.

G.D turns the radio off. "Congratulations, Tim you've traveled to the past, present, and future at a speed exceeding light through space-time and have never even stepped out of your bedroom. No QTIP or $1.4 billion budget required—not bad for a beginner."

I sit in the driver seat with a puzzled look on my face. "It couldn't really be that easy, could it? Occam's razor comes to mind—the simplest solution tends to be the best."

"Yes it is that simple. It doesn't require advanced degrees in anything, and all of us do it every day and all day long. And as you would put it, the brass knows," G.D. says with authority.

"G.D. is right, the complexities and powers of the human mind are still largely not understood by science," I say to myself.

G.D. continues speaking, "Images are the ultimate source of power in the universe, Tim. The ability to control images in space-time is the domain of the fourth state, *Tetrastatum*, as it shapes the past, present, and future. When one person visualizes an image of the future skipping ahead through space-time, it potentially has an impact on the outcome. Now, if they share their concept of the future image with other people via any medium of communication (speaking, writing, hand signals—it doesn't really matter how); as other people see the projected future image it becomes more powerful, shaping space-time itself through the fourth state (superposition), ultimately leading to the observable future outcome. The closer the image is to present space-time, the easier it is to impact the outcome based on Dr. Richard's probability image wave function. The further out in space-time, the more difficult it is to perceive and create. People who are extremely gifted and forward-thinking can see further out into the continuum and share these images, altering the destiny of mankind and shaping the future.

Tim, you're a 'Trekkie.' Think about Gene Roddenberry and his version of "Wagon Train to the Stars/Star Trek." The images he projected into the space-time continuum were intended to be more than three hundred years into the future from the original airing in 1966. Many of the images were futuristic and impossible based on the technology during the time the show was created. However, his vision of the future which he shared in the form of 4D images (video) shaped the minds of generations of scientists, engineers, mathematicians, and physicists— resulting in the space shuttle, cell phones, lasers, and countless other innovations closely resembling his images of the future. One of the last remaining final frontiers was human space-time teleportation, as Roddenberry's images portrayed in the transporter room on Star Trek. Once it is understood that we are all walking, talking time-traveling image processors that can influence the future on an individual as well as collective basis, the power of images can be used for both good, resulting in human innovation and advancement—or alternatively, political control and amassing of power by the privileged few—just like any other technology. Based on the history of mankind, my money is on the latter.

The brass has this matter universe contained via the fourth state, mainly using the media. The media controls the images people see in their minds through radio, television, newspapers, social media, and (of course) advertising. The media holds the cusp of image superposition in their hands. It is just another probability image wave function. Once images are projected to a large number of people, a statistically significant set of the population reach the same basic conclusions, perceiving the images in the same way, or are polarized by design. The fourth state can be measured statistically by calculating the probabilities of a large population's behavior of reacting in a predetermined, predictable manner to the image data projected into the universe. Thoton images ultimately dictate the course of future events, such as elections, economic behavior, wars....everything! Controlling the past is even easier, it is simply a matter of what has been recorded and who records it, creating the imaging people perceive and store in their brain and creating a context for future image creation and self-identity, typically in formalized educational settings."

"G.D. Orwellian," I think.

Right now you are traveling in a non-matter state through space-time via thotons, but your QTIP presents the possibility of transporting matter across space-time universes, which is the ultimate control of the past present and future of not just *this* universe, but *all* universes. The technology goes beyond shaping outcomes through imaging to being able to physically intervene across the timeline to alter events in other matter universes.

"I don't understand, G.D," I say, looking bewildered, "I'm just a scientist."

"Empires exist for one basic reason because they can dominate and control nature through technology, land-armies, sea-naval fleets, air/space-airplanes, satellites, space travel. The fourth and final empire will be whoever can dominate and control space-time. That is what the brass wants from you, Tim." G.D. smiles.

The Gremlin comes to a screeching halt at the end of the road—at the front security gate at DARPA. My stomach starts to feel queasy. The guard walks over to the driver side of the Gremlin, "Dr. Smith, are you okay? Dr. Smith, are you all right? Can you hear me?" He starts tapping the butt of his rifle against the Gremlin's window.

I wake up as my alarm goes off. The sheets are soaked in sweat and my stomach is upset. The morning light shines through the curtains as I grimace, opening my eyes slowly to the first images of a brand new day gradually coming into focus. A pile of clothes is strewn on the floor among the empty bottles, cobwebs, dust, and white fur scattered about the room. It looks like nobody has cleaned the room for several years. A large open bottle is suspended on a pile of socks and white pills are spread about everywhere in my nightstand drawer. I reach over and grab a handful of aspirin, carefully separating out the lint, before ingesting them. They only make the throbbing pain in my head more acute. I can hear Kathy's voice, "Tim this is a bloody mess, pick up after yourself, for God's sake." The house is in disarray that probably closely resembles the original state we purchased it in after the squatters had lived here for years. Based on years of experience, the throbbing in my head doesn't actually go away, no matter how many aspirins I take. But I still take them, hoping the result will be different this time. The only thing that makes it stop is the scotch. Thank G.D!

I can't find a robe, so I put on my white lab coat and walk down the stairs through the dust and fur, making my way to the kitchen. As the morning light passes through the windows, flooding the house, it is apparent that the kitchen, like the rest of the house, is neglected beyond the norms of even the sleaziest fraternity house. Pots, pans, empty pizza boxes, coffee grinds, eggshells, bottles and more bottles, and other residuals of my existence litter the counters and floors. I don't have it in me anymore to pick up myself or anything else around here. All my efforts are focused on developing the QTIP. I know I can do it. I know I can. I am going to save them. I remove my clothing from a chair next to the heavy oak table in the kitchen and throw it on a pile already accumulating on the floor. I pour myself a glass of morning sunshine. That is the only way I can get up and keep going anymore. I look over toward the front yard at the elm tree where Sarah's swing used to be and—as clear as day—Anny is sitting looking back at me through the window. This can't be. Anny is gone, dead, never coming back. I never should have bought the G.D. cat! I take a big gulp, rub my eyes, and she disappears.

It all happened so quickly. Sarah was ready for school, waiting for Kathy in the front yard, playing with Anny by the elm tree. I kissed her goodbye on her forehead. "Your mom will be down in a minute, sweetheart. Daddy has to go to work now."

"Love you, Daddy," Sarah said as she continued waving a small elm branch on the grass as Anny chased it back and forth, trying to catch it in her paws.

"See you this evening, buttercup," I said with a sense of mundane certainty.

I backed the Gremlin out of the driveway and headed off to work, just like any other day. But, it wasn't like any other day. I'd taken everything for granted, not realizing the fragile uncertainty of existence.

Regardless of our natural instincts to presume normalcy in the sequence of images that play over day after day with unwavering repetition, it is counterintuitive to understand that at any particular moment, the cycle of images can change dramatically. The images can cascade beyond our comprehension of contemplated outcomes, forever leaving a permanent, growing blemish on the film. The projector keeps playing the movie, but that white spot sits in the corner of the screen pulsating, growing, and eating away at the film. What is left of the good images, fades and is consumed until you can't see the picture at all anymore. Only a large white screen remains with remnants of the images on the outer corners of the screen and the eternal sound of the reel spinning in vain. It is too painful to keep watching. I learned on that day to not take anything for granted—every thought, image, action or inaction can potentially alter our 4D picture show forever. A dull drama can become a tragedy or horror in the blink of an eye. The QTIP and G.D. are the only reasons I am still barely hanging on. If I work harder, I will be able to rewind the film, reshoot the movie and bring Kathy and Sarah back. It is all my fault. I wasn't there. Even when I was there, I really wasn't. My body may have been, but my mind is and has always been at DARPA. And for what?

I still clearly remember Janice walking in my office, stricken pale with a look of sheer terror in her eyes. "Tim, State Trooper Todd is on the phone. You need to sit down and talk to him," Janice says. Her left hand is shaking and her voice is cracking. Seeing her in this state scares the hell out of me.

"What happened, Janice?" I ask.

"Tim, please sit down and talk to State Trooper Todd. He needs to speak with you," Janice says in a soft tone as she slowly turns away and closes my office door.

I sit down, pausing for a moment to compose myself, and pick up the receiver. "Mr. Smith, my name is State Trooper Todd, there has been a terrible accident out on Route 4 eastbound near the Fairview city limits. I regret to inform you that your wife Kathy and daughter Sarah are no longer with us, sir."

"Kathy and Sarah? Gone? That can't be. What happened?" I ask with a sense of trepidation as my heartbeat speeds up, yet time seems to slow down. My mind goes entirely blank and a sensation of numbness strikes me with the force of a sledgehammer. This can't be happening.

"Yes, sir. I am sorry Mr. Smith, I can't tell you anything else over the phone. You need to come to the Fairview hospital morgue for positive identification." Trooper Todd says in a sad and somber tone.

"Please, tell me they're okay. This has to be some kind of mistake," I plead into the receiver.

"No sir, Mr. Smith. Do you know where the Hospital is? Please go to the basement level and I will be waiting for you with the coroner. Do you understand, Mr. Smith?…Mr. Smith, are you there?"

About a minute elapses as my throat swells and choked-up tears run down my face before I can respond, "Yes… I know where it is…. I understand. I'm on my way."

Why did they even bother having me come down to identify Kathy and Sarah? Their remains are so badly charred, neither of them is recognizable—charred husks. I heave and can't look at them for more than a split second before I run out and throw up in the lavatory. Even though it was but for a split second, the images are burned into my brain, a white spot growing larger every day. Trooper Todd informs me that Kathy was headed to the veterinary in Fairview. Anny had been hit by a car in front of the house shortly after I had left for work. Kathy was headed over to the vet with Sarah, speeding down the two-lane road, racing to save the cat. She crossed into the oncoming lane and struck another vehicle. The car burst into flames, and they were both unable to get out. Kathy, Sarah, and Anny all died on Route 4 that day.

That was over three years ago. I take another gulp of scotch and look up across the kitchen table. In the doorway, that G.D. cat is sitting there on its haunches, completely still, just staring at me with her big black soulless eyes. "Get out of here!" I yell and pick up an empty bottle, throwing it in Anny's direction. Anny doesn't as much as flinch.

It was supposed to be me that day, I could clearly see it all, every detail in my mind, what should have been. I had forgotten my keys in the house and walked back inside. Sarah, screaming at me, "Daddy, come quickly Anny is hurt, Daddy." Kathy running out of the shower, grabbing her robe and taking Sarah into the house. Anny bleeding on the black interior of the Gremlin as I carefully placed her on the passenger seat. Glancing over for a split second as Anny shrieks in pain, the Gremlin swerving over the line—then the big bang. The darkness, flames, smell of burning flesh, and the white light. Forever. It was supposed to have been me, not them. But I hadn't forgotten my keys, they were in my jacket pocket. Why? Why? Six out of nine days, I would forget them and have to go back and Kathy would run around the house trying to find them for me. It should have been me. I guess God does play dice. It was a lousy roll.

The white spot kept growing, there is no more film left to watch—only the white light flickering. It is all clear to me now, I know how to find Kathy and Sarah. It has been in front of me all along, like Anny. I quickly scavenge through the piles of clothes in the kitchen and change into a button down shirt with dried sweat stains frozen in the blue fabric under the armpits and down the sides. A tattered three-piece suit—the trousers spotted with dry mustard and the vest missing a few buttons—has to do. I don't have time for this now. I put on an argyle sock and, unable to find its match, I quickly slip a black one over my foot. I grab my pocket watch and put it in my vest with a reinvigorated sense of purpose. I head out the front door toward the Gremlin parked on the side of the house. As I pass the stain on the hardwood floor in the foyer, I can't help but utter, "G.D., I get it." I open the driver side door of the Green Gremlin, "Come on Anny, let's go for a ride." Anny hops obediently into the Gremlin. The engine sputters to life and I head off to the Red Dungeon, alone.

CHAPTER THREE

SHOCK AND AWE THERAPY

I ARRIVE AT D.A.R.P.A.'S PARKING LOT in the early morning hours, well ahead of the pack. The passenger door eases slowly open as I stand up and look at Anny curled up in a pile of matted red fur and blood on the seat. After a split second, the image disappears. Anny is gone, I am gone, and they are all gone. It's going to be okay—they are all going to be okay. Looks like it is going to be a solo journey down to sub-four. I knew this instinctively before I even left the house. I have always known it is a solo journey. I slam the car door and trudge on with a sense of misguided urgency.

"Good Morning, Dr. Smith. You are in early this morning. Everything okay, sir?" the guard says in a wavering tone as he casually scans my disheveled attire.

"Yes, fine…. Everything is fine," I reply. After ten minutes, I finally make it through all the security checkpoints, elevators, golf carts, and to the vaulted door of the Red Dungeon. I open the door and walk in slowly as my eyes adjust to the low red lighting, I can see Dr. Richard sitting alone at a workstation in his red lab coat, typing. I wonder if he even ever went home last night. Taken by surprise, he abruptly looks up at me.

"Tim—good morning—you're up before the rooster crows, Wow! You look awful. Are you okay?"

"Yes, yes— fine….I finally figured it out, Doc. I know how it all works and we've been going about it all wrong….. I know how to travel through space-time. I can help them," I say as my hand starts shaking uncontrollably.

"Okay, let's hear it. What have you got?" Dr. Richard replies.

"I can't explain it, Doc. I'm going to have to show you…. Yes, you can only truly understand by seeing. You have to see it. An explanation simply won't make any sense. You won't believe me unless I show you."

"Tim, calm down…. Fine—you can show me your work—but take it easy."

"I have it all figured out now. You'll be amazed at how it's been right in front of us the whole time. Turn cameras 2, 3, 5 and 7 on," I demand.

"All right, Tim just take it easy. I'll turn them on for you. Take a deep breath—exhale."

"Good, just turn them on now, Doc! Okay…I'm going to do this," I say with a moment of hesitation.

"Do what?" Dr. Richard asks with concern.

"Travel through space-time! What else? I know it will work. Just turn the cameras on now and get out!"

"Tim, the cameras are on." Dr. Richard snaps. "What the hell are you going to do?"

"GET OUT! I need to do this alone. I need to find them."

"Tim if you don't calm down, I'm going to get security in here. Just tell me what you're going to do." Dr. Richard demands.

I pick up a workstation and hurl it in the direction of the good Doc. It smashes onto the floor with a thud, the case opening up and green circuit boards spilling out onto the otherwise spotless floor of the Red Dungeon. "GET OUT!"

"That's it, Tim, I am getting security." Dr. Richard stands up and heads toward the door to summon the guards outside. "Hey guys, we have a live one in here—need some help."

As Dr. Richard stands in the threshold of the doorway, I run up behind him, closing the heavy door, and he falls forward into the hallway. I quickly press the red "emergency" button, bolting the door shut from the inside, a function installed for lock-down procedures. A siren starts blaring, but I can still hear the rustling of feet and commotion outside in the hallway. The brass always designs things to keep people out, they never actually think someone would want to lock themselves in. "That should buy me at least twenty minutes," I say to myself. Now I just have to work up the nerve. How the hell am I going to do this? My mind starts racing, all I can think about is the brilliance of the circuit boards spilled out over the floor. Moore's Law comes to mind: "the number of transistors in an integrated circuit doubles approximately every two years." I was looking at the manifestation of exponential technology growth, an electrical engineering achievement spanning decades.

Based on Moore's Law, the circuit boards at my feet undoubtedly face inevitable obsolescence as progress and new circuit boards with a higher transistor capacity replace the older ones. Even silicon has its limitations, the laws of thermal dynamics and quantum mechanics will ultimately prevail and even the age of silicon will come to an inevitable close. I go to each of the desks and pull all of the workstations apart, placing the circuit boards in neat piles. I then proceed to borrow Dr. Richard's walking stick raising it above my head and smash the piles into tiny pieces—helping evolution out a bit, smiling at the cameras the whole time. It felt good. It felt really good. No telling when the age of Homo sapiens will come to an inevitable close, just like silicon. Everything has its day. Today is mine.

I know by now that Dr. Richard has probably gotten Mak involved. If he wasn't already on the base, he will be soon. I'm sure that they have the monitors up and are watching my 4D picture show. "The best part is yet to come, the 4D Grand Finale," I think. Corinthians 4:16–5:8 raced through my mind. Not that I am particularly religious—agnostic on a good day and atheist the rest of the time. The words still struck me, "…..while we do not look at the things which are seen, but at the things which are not seen. For the things which are seen are temporary, but the things which are not seen are eternal." "Time to put that theory to the test, Old Boy," G.D.'s voice beckons.

All of this military technology lying around and there doesn't appear to be a blunt instrument capable of completing the job in the lab. Just need to be more creative. Think, G.D., think. Of course. I slowly walk over to the inverted table and remove the laser and mounted equipment. A power cord from one of the workstations should do the trick. I can hear the drilling at the vaulted door as I tie the cord into a noose, securing it to the top of the inverted table. I roll a chair over and adjust it to the lowest position. I stand up gingerly, my legs shaking— trying to maintain my balance as I place the looped cord around my neck. I look up at the cameras and say, "You'll understand when you watch the time-lapse footage, Doc." One, two…. I kick the chair out and dangle as the cord tightly claws into the skin around my neck, causing a burning sensation as the air in my lungs grows stale. I can no longer breathe. Time slows down as all of the details of the dungeon glare at me in a red brilliance. My face starts swelling as I feel an immense pressure in my head squeezing my eyeballs, pressuring them out of the socket. My vision starts to fade into the white, as the noise of the film reel in my head ceases. The last sensation I feel is the warm urine running down my leg and the sound of it dripping as it flows unto the floor below.

And then—nothing.

With a loud bang, my ears start ringing and I perceive a flash of brilliant white light. I start crying like a newborn trying to take oxygen into his lungs for the first time as my image processor begins adjusting and the waves of consciousness start to flow. The first thing that hits me is the pain. My naked body aches from the hard padding on the floor. I've been curled up in a ball for hours, maybe days. I really can't say. I have no idea how long I've been here. I try to stay warm as the vents flood the windowless room with dry, cold air. The fluorescent white light bounces off the four white walls, illuminating the faded white padding in waves. The light fixture above, like a beacon to the mad, makes an almost incomprehensible humming sound that is almost drowned out by the buzzing in my own head. The barely audible sound of heels walking down the corridor can be heard approaching. Muffled voices behind the padded door of confine-

ment room number four are barely audible. What are they saying?

"I think it is time, Nurse Nestpa. Please prepare the patient for treatment."

"Are you sure that he's ready, doctor?" "It is his and our only hope, Nestpa. Please prepare the patient."

I can hear the bolt slide as the heavy metal door opens slowly. I look up. My mind slowly begins to comprehend the image as my gaze ascends from the white patent leather high heels to the shapely calves and legs clad in white stockings, and the uniform hugging her firm buttocks.

The angelic face of a woman with flowing auburn hair and dark eyes exuding warmth and kindness wrapped in pure sexuality stands in front of me in an all-white nurse's uniform. It is too tight around the bosom and unbuttoned, revealing her hefty cleavage. It is completely surreal. Her red lipstick and auburn hair, neatly tucked in a nurse's cap, contrast with the entirely white room and her white outfit. She radiates life. Her name tag comes into view: *Nestpa Yumain.* She speaks softly in a sultry, rhythmic tone. "Dr. Smith, my name is Nurse Nestpa. I work with Dr. Udaza. We are here to help you. Everything is okay. You had a close call, but you are alive. You are going to be fine." Her penetrating dark eyes meet my gaze. I am totally absorbed and unable to look away—feeling a brief moment of comfort as the noises in my head cease, granting me a sense of momentary peace. "She is right," I think to myself, "for the first time in a long time, I actually feel alive."

"Cosmic duality, Tim." Dr. Richard's voice echoes, "Birth, death—are one and the same. If you are dead in one universe, you must be alive in another. Energy cannot be created/born nor destroyed/die. It is only altered from one form to another in perpetuity. Conservation of Cosmic Duality. Your thotons are alive and well, buzzing and humming."

"That is all hunky-dory, Doc, but I am still sitting here in the loony bin," I mutter. After the stunt I pulled at DARPA, who could blame Mak and the brass for committing me, I probably belong here.

"Excuse me, Dr. Smith, what did you say?" asks Nurse Nestpa.

"Nothing, nurse, just having a hard time getting up," I retorted in an effort to at least appear that I still have some semblance of sanity left as opposed to letting the naughty nurse in on the full-blown conversation I am having with Dr. Richard, who is standing in front of me in his red bathrobe/lab coat and.... For God's sake—I am in a padded room in an asylum after trying to off myself. I'm pretty sure she already knows that I'm bat-shit crazy. Well, no harm in trying to keep up appearances.

Dr. Richard couldn't let it go. He had to chime in again, "Tim, how do you know she's a naughty nurse?"

Of course, that's what Dr. Richard is most concerned about right now? This time I whisper barely moving my lips, so as to not draw attention, "Must be the heels and lipstick, Doc. Who the hell wears that in an asylum?"

"Sanitarium," Dr. Richard snaps back.

"Did you look at the dungeon footage? Where the hell am I really?" I speak out.

"You know where you are Tim." Nestpa firmly responds.

Her gaze turns toward me as she slowly scans my body, I become acutely aware of my nakedness and the outwardly visible signs of excitement I display. "Here Dr. Smith, please put these on. You must be frozen stiff. When you first came in, you were in a horrible state. It is protocol to strip our patients of anything that may be harmful to them." Nurse Nestpa hands me a pair of briefs, a white robe, socks and slippers—standard loony bin issue. "If they are harmful, why are they giving them to me now?" I think to myself. I proceed to get up slowly.

"Please go ahead and get dressed," Nestpa says with a lack of enthusiasm. As I stand up her dark eyes briefly follow mine, and before she completely turns around a faint smile appears on her sultry red lips. "Let me know when you are decent, Dr. Smith," she says dryly. I really don't know if I was ever decent, but I am willing to try.

"All done, nurse."

Nestpa turns back around and says, "Excellent, let's not waste any more time, I have someone who wants to meet you." She calmly walks over and, much to my surprise, grabs my hand and holds it firmly with familiarity as she guides me out of the padded room through the doorway into the long, white corridor. We stroll down the hallway holding hands until we come to a large wooden door with a frosted glass window on the upper half. *Dr. Haram Udaza, MD* is stenciled on the glass in large, black letters. Nestpa knocks loudly four times with her free hand while still clutching my other with ferocity. There is no immediate answer. My hand is starting to perspire as her grasp tightens.

"Yes…yes—hold on a minute. Who is it?" Haram calls out.

"It's Dr. Smith and me," Nestpa responds. Nestpa releases my hand, and the door opens. We walk past the threshold of the doorway into Haram's office. Haram is a dignified gentleman in his early sixties. I can see his piercing blue eyes beneath his tortoiseshell-rimmed, round spectacles. It looks like he means business. A well-kept white beard and mustache cover the weathered skin on his face. Haram wears a buttoned-down, white shirt with a green sweater-vest and a brown tweed suit that seems to fit his personality.

"Ooh, good— good. Come right in, Tim. I've been eager to meet you—didn't expect you this soon," Haram says with genuineness. He extends his hand, "I am Dr. Udaza, but please call me Haram. I am the senior psychiatrist at the Aduat Asylum, your new home."

"I don't know about this 'new home' business, but Haram looks like an okay fellow," I say to Dr. Richard. I try to speak to him, barely moving my lips. I can see him peering in through the frosted glass behind Haram's door. I clearly see the outline of his red lab coat through the glass, so I know he is there listening.

"Excuse me, Tim, did you say something? Who are you speaking with?" Haram asks.

"Ahh, nobody. It's a pleasure meeting you, Haram. I hope we can work through this and help me to get better and out of here as soon as you feel I am ready," I say with the utmost enthusiasm and conviction, even though in the back of my mind I feel like I am never going to get out of this place—just move on to another 4D picture show in a different wing of the building—same old circus, same ringmaster, same clowns, elephants, acrobats—all of it the same, just under a new tent.

"Yes, Tim I am here to help you. It's going to take a lot of hard work on both our parts, and a lot of time before I can even contemplate authorizing your departure from Aduat—for your and everyone else's safety. You understand, of course?" Haram says.

Ooh yeah—boy, did I ever understand how screwed I am. "Yes, I completely understand, Haram," I say while nodding my head in agreement.

"Good. Then we will get started right away," Haram says looking directly at me and then turns to face Nurse Nestpa. "Thank you Nurse Nestpa. When the patient is ready to return to his room, I will page you. That is all," Haram says as he opens the door and motions for Nestpa to leave. I wonder where Dr. Richard went. He isn't outside anymore. Probably getting a closet ready for a quick roll with the naughty nurse.

Haram's office is tidy, with neat piles of paper stacked in an orderly fashion and manila folders organized by what appears to be patients' last names sitting on his large mahogany desk. There are two matching

49

mahogany claw-foot wingback chairs upholstered in red leather and a green glass ashtray full of cigar butts on a small, round table situated between the chairs. An intricate Victorian-era wallpaper made up of abstract tan, brown and green patterns contrast well with the hardwood floors and rich wool Persian rugs. One chair faces the cliché psychiatrist's couch in the dark corner of the room. I am pretty sure that is where I am headed. Haram casually strolls over to the wingback chair and motions for me to have a seat on the couch. He takes out a cigar from his breast pocket, cuts off the end and rotates it in his mouth as he holds a blue butane flame up to it until the end is glowing red. I take my shoes off and lay down fully reclined on the red velvet couch. The velvet is not very comfortable as it scratches the back of my neck.

A plume of smoke rises up to the ceiling, whisked away by the fan. As Haram's gaze meets mine he says, "Tim, let me give you a little background about Aduat, our methods and what we hope to achieve in helping you recover from your illness, so you may rejoin society as a normal, happy, functioning adult."

"A normal, happy, functioning adult? This doesn't sound like a Dr. Richard pep talk. Can I at least have a G.D. scotch to take the edge off the Aduat induction ceremony?" I think, as my hand starts to quiver. Haram looks directly into my eyes like he's reading my mind.

"Tim, would you care for a single-malt? I believe I have an 18-year-old Highland here somewhere."

"Please, that would hit the spot, Haram," I say as my facial muscles ease into a faint smile and a sense of relief pours over my being. How did he know I'm a scotch drinker? Haram opens up the large globe behind the mahogany desk, revealing an assortment of liquor bottles. As he sorts through the bottles, a clanking can be heard as he searches for the single malts. I eagerly anticipate wetting my whistle. "Ah here it is, Tim," Haram says casually. He pours me a glass, neat. I think, "This place isn't that bad." Haram continues his orientation lecture as I enjoy the privileges of institutionalized insanity.

"Tim, Aduat is built on the foundation that there is no judgment passed and everything we talk about is held in confidence and subject to the moral and ethical standards of the patient-doctor relationship. The sooner you open up and explain your innermost thoughts, feelings, perceptions, and dreams in the most honest unfiltered manner possible, the better I'll be able to understand what ails you. We will work together to overcome your demons. The way we take away the power of demons at Aduat is simply by naming them. Once you have named them, you have acknowledged your ills and they can be vanquished from your psyche forever as we confront your true inner pain. As I am going to explain to you, there are four states of transformative behavior that govern our interpretation of external realities, including the most common modes of social interaction. I want you to visualize which state you are in as you contemplate your external traumas."

I say to myself, "Yeah, sounds fascinating, I didn't just get off the banana boat, Haram. I too studied Egyptology, buddy. What kind of rinky-dink outfit is this place?" I remember Duat from ancient Egyptian mythology and the hieroglyphs depicting it in the various scrolls collectively referred to as *Book of the Dead*. Duat is the underworld, or realm of the dead, where souls went for judgment. I know Haram is judging me. This is one big charade! The Egyptian name for the text is translated as *Book of Emerging Forth into the Light*. The various scrolls were written by Egyptian priests over a period of a thousand years to provide guidance in preparation for death and journeying through Duat to achieve eternal life, living among the gods. The book contains supposed spells to overcome the various demons on the deceased's journey to Anubis, the god of the dead, who after hearing your negative confession, would weigh your heart against the goddess Maat, usually depicted as an ostrich feather on a scale of justice. Just to make sure nobody cheated, Osiris, lord of the underworld, witnessed the entire affair.

The average human heart weighs about eleven ounces. Not good odds, if you ask me. The best part is if you lie in your negative confession (you said you didn't do it, but you know you really did), and your heart doesn't balance with the feather, your soul gets eternally devoured by a demoness named Ammit (part lion, hippo and crocodile). But don't worry—if you have a spell from your personal, very expensive copy of the *Book of The Dead*, you can fool the gods of the underworld (you could do it and say you didn't) and still pass through to the heavenly fields. It could cost anywhere from six months to a year's wages, still a more affordable option than a Papal indulgence. I will just have to play along with Haram's little Egyptology complex. But, if Haram thinks I'm going to give my negative confession, he is surely going to be disappointed, since there isn't much I haven't done. But I am good on the biggies. I am sure that I never.....

"Excuse me, Tim, are you listening?" Haram inquires politely.

My eyes are glazed over into a blank, fixed stare as I ponder Ammit devouring my soul. "Sorry, Haram, I'm a bit tired, given everything I've been through. I wasn't paying attention. Please continue," I say apologetically.

"As I was saying, Tim, there are four transformative states of behavior 'Resisting,' 'Controlling,' 'Accepting,' and 'Flowing.' When you perceive an image and interpret an external reality as a perceived threat, the most primitive responses that are hard-wired through our nervous system first trigger a physiological response, secreting hormones, including adrenaline, increasing the flow of blood to the muscles. The adrenaline facilitates either Controlling or Resisting the situation commonly referred to as 'Fight or Flight.' Picture yourself walking in the jungle and encountering an ambush of tigers. Your image processor will immediately assess the threat to your wellbeing by perceiving the tigers and, for simplicity's sake, presume that two primary images are created in your mind in a state of superposition. The first image consists of Controlling by overcoming the tigers with force—fighting—beating the tigers into submission with a club, for example. The second image is Resisting, due to an inability to control. Perhaps running—fleeing while throwing rocks at the tigers. The other images in superposition would consist of Accepting—climbing a tree, accepting them as an element of your environment; and Flowing—putting leashes on the tigers and making them your new pets. Notice, Tim, the duality of states as Accepting and Controlling are opposite pairs, as are Resisting and Flowing."

"Sounds like Dr. Richard all over again. All right. The scotch is finished, hopefully. Haram wraps up the show, and now I can proceed to my evening sponge bath courtesy of Nurse Nestpa," I think. "Yes, very interesting, Haram," I say with sincerity. "Are we about done here, for today?"

Haram looks at me, tilting his tortoiseshell glasses down, "Yes, Tim, but I detect you are Resisting. It doesn't matter, for now there is plenty for you to ponder. I don't think you are going to try and do harm to yourself or others in Aduat, so I am going to give you this notepad and pen. Please, only write down answers to the questions I give you after each session, as well as anything pertaining to completion of your work on the QTP, if you wish. I think it will be constructive when you are ready to return to your duties at DARPA."

I take the notepad and pen from his extended hand. "Great. Thank you, Haram. I look forward to our first session—and when exactly will that be?" I ask with hesitation.

"Tomorrow morning at 4:00 am Nurse Nestpa will wake you up and escort you to my office and make sure you are on time. We will meet every other day—Monday, Wednesday, Friday, and Sunday for four-hour sessions until you are well. Your first assignment is easy, Tim. Just write down a list of your demons. I must warn you that each question I pose to you should be considered and answered with the utmost gravity. Failure to answer truthfully or incompletely will result in more drastic treatments to secure your long-term state of mental wellbeing. I hope you understand."

"Yep, I think I basically got it, Haram is running his own little Milgram experiment, but for real, and I am the Guinea pig. From the looks of Aduat, I am pretty sure that neither Nurse Nestpa, nor anyone else working here, has ever disobeyed a single, solitary order. For that matter, I don't think I have either? I am screwed." I admit to myself. Stanley Milgram was a Yale University psychologist who conducted a social psychology experiment in the 1960s examining the habit of obedience by studying the willingness of the test subject to obey an authority figure in contravention of basic moral behavior. An authority figure would order a test subject to administer an electric shock to another knowing participant when the other participant intentionally answered the test subject's question incorrectly. The voltage is gradually increased to the point that the test subject believes that the shock he/she is being told to administer will be fatal. The test subject has to decide to either obey or disobey the authority figure as to administering a fatal shock to another human being. A high proportion of men would fully comply, albeit with reluctance. When the tests were repeated in other studies around the world, the conclusions were always nearly the same. The compliance rate hits the high 90% range if all of the day's test subjects watch the experiment room on closed-circuit TV and the authority figure carries a visible revolver. Next, nearly 100% compliance rates are achieved if the future test subjects in the waiting room view the outcome of any refusal to throw the switch being met with a swift gunshot to the head—a little televised "Shock and Awe." The brass has this down—Resisting is futile. Throw the switch, collect your paycheck, and hope the world will be a better place in the morning. Go with the Flow that seems the best way to survive in Aduat.

"I fully understand, Haram," I reply.

Haram picks up the phone and pages Nurse Nestpa, who promptly shows up at the door with a wheelchair. He smiles. "Nestpa, that won't be required today, we had quite a productive orientation. Did you provide Dr. Smith with a desk, chair and cot for the remainder of his stay?"

"Yes, Dr. Udaza, everything has been set up per your specifications. Dr. Smith will feel as snug as a bug in a rug in his room." Nestpa leaves the wheelchair in the hallway and firmly grabs my hand as we stroll out of the office down the corridor. As I look up, Mak is walking straight toward us in full military uniform.

Mak grabs my shoulder, while Nestpa is still holding my hand. Mak looks at me straight in the eyes and says, "Looks like you found yourself a new friend, Dr. Smith. That was a close call. Dr. Richard and I got to you just in time. How are you feeling, son?"

"Better, Mak, much better," I retort.

"Just take all the time you need to sort things out here and you will be up and at 'em in no time. Nothing to be ashamed of— happens to the best of us, the better angels of our nature don't always prevail. You will be fine and back to work in no time. Just a speed bump, Tim. You and Dr. Richard are very close, months— even weeks, maybe. Keep it together, son."

"Thanks, Mak I am grateful for your and Dr. Richard's intervention. Did Dr. Richard come with you?" I ask. "I think I saw him outside Dr. Udaza's office earlier."

"No, he's been in the lab all day cleaning up your mess, but I'm sure he'll come to visit once he cools off. Hold your head up high, son. Hang in there—no pun intended," Mak says as he continues walking and warmly greets Dr. Udaza. They go into Dr. Udaza's office and quickly close the door. The red circle around my neck where the cord tore into my flesh itches terribly.

"Come on Tim," Nurse Nestpa says as she swings my arm forward, still hand-in-hand down the corridor. "Time for your bath, dinner, and beddy-bye. I just love baths, don't you, Tim?"

We walk down the corridor until Nestpa stops in front of a double door. The plaque on the wall reads "Cleansing Room." Nestpa swings the galley doors open and pulls me by the hand through the doorway. Shiny, white, ceramic tile lines the walls and ceiling of a square room that is roughly forty feet long and wide. Floodlights from above illuminate the white space, blinding me momentarily until my eyes adjust. I don't see a bathtub or any showers, only a drain in the middle of the tiled floor. "That's strange," I think. I lose my balance for a split second, almost slipping as I walk into the room. The wet floor is noticeably slanted from each of the four walls to slope inward toward the drain. I notice beads of water slowly dripping from the tiled ceiling. The room is quiet. Only the slow drip can be heard as the beads of water fall from above, then silence. The silence is quickly broken by the crisp clicking of Nestpa's heels echoing off the walls and ceiling in the barren room. The cleansing room is humid, with a slight smell of eucalyptus that pleasantly engages the nostrils while titillating the senses.

She leads me to a wooden bench in the far corner. A solitary bar of green glycerin soap is sitting on the bench on top of a white washcloth and towel. A large, red standpipe that extends up the entire height of the twenty-foot ceiling is adjacent to the bench. A pressure gauge protrudes from the side of the pipe next to a large brass fitting that connects a twelve-inch-diameter red iron circular valve handle with a metal cross emanating from the center. "Looks like someone can get a good grip on that," I think. I start to speak, but before I can get any words out, Nestpa lets go of my hand. She puts her index finger to her lips and quietly whispers, "Shhh, no talking, Tim, disrobe and put your clothes on the bench."

As I start to take off my clothes, Nestpa sits down on the bench and removes her white heels. I become acutely aware of the red circle around my neck as the torn skin throbs in pain as I remove my robe. I stand naked in front of Nestpa while she rolls her white stockings off each leg, one at a time, revealing her alabaster skin and pedicured feet with red-polished toenails popping against the white tile. Barefoot, Nestpa stands up and removes her nurse's cap, freeing her auburn hair to flow down her shoulders. She hands me the washcloth and soap. Quietly, she whispers, "Tim, stand over by the drain—and no matter what happens, do not make a single noise until we are done bathing. Otherwise you will leave me no choice, I will have to inform Dr. Udaza that you are uncleansed and not ready to proceed with your treatment—in which case you may never be able to leave Aduat. You need to prepare to transcend the matter universe to non-matter, photon to thoton—the higher state. Do you understand, Tim?" Nestpa proceeds to unbutton her nurse's uniform. Her cleavage protrudes, exposing her white lace bra and her hardened nipples.

"As far as I am concerned at that moment, regardless if I understand or not, I am definitely replying in the affirmative. I am pretty sure I can keep the noise to a minimum," I think as I respond in a whisper, "Yes, I get it, Nestpa. I will keep it down." I quickly walk over to the center of the room in a state of excited anticipation. I stand directly over the large metallic drain, waiting for Nestpa to remove her remaining clothes and join me.

Nestpa opens the bench and takes out what resembles a coiled fire hose and attaches it to the valve on the standpipe. "Initiating cleansing sequence," Nestpa says while looking up at the ceiling. The lights turn off as I wait for what seems like an eternity in total darkness. Suddenly, the strobe light comes on, modulating in various frequencies. I can see Nestpa standing in the corner by the bench turning the valve. I hear the sound of pressure building, then nothing—only darkness. Suddenly, I can see Nestpa is standing pointing the hose toward me as a wave of freezing water hits me, knocking me off of my feet.

The stream knocks the wind out of me as I fall to the ground. Otherwise, I probably would have yelled. My muscles tense up and my body starts to shiver as Nestpa relentlessly focuses the stream of freezing water directly on me. I cover my face with my arms, and my legs are curled up protecting my groin. The cold water accumulates on the ground around me as the drain fails to accommodate the unwavering flow. Nestpa continues to relentlessly pound my body with the stream of water in an ever-increasing rhythmic intensity. At first, rage hits me. All I can think about is taking the hose from her and giving her a "cleansing" bath to see how she likes it. I must take control. I look up briefly, seeing her white teeth behind her parted red lips as she smiles, straddling the hose between her legs—moving it back and forth, her eyeballs rolling back in her head as she delivers each fluid blow with a sense of ecstasy.

It's pretty clear to me at this point that Nestpa is actually enjoying this, which is even more infuriating. I stand up quickly and run at her to try and take the hose from her. Nestpa just laughs as she aims the hose, striking me in the groin as I fall back on the tile floor into the pool of freezing water. My circumstance is abundantly clear to me, even in a state of shock. "Resisting is pointless, just take the pain until Nestpa finishes and ACCEPT everything," I say to myself. At that very moment, the cold water became warm and the stream diffuses into a circular spray. The strobe light ceases and the lights come back on.

"Pick up your washcloth and soap from the floor and finish cleansing yourself, Tim," Nestpa says in a relaxed, satisfied tone. I proceed exactly as she instructs. The flow of the warm spray feels pleasurable as the lather is washed away from my body and flows down the drain. Nestpa turns off the hose and puts it away. "You are now clean, Tim," she says as she picks up the towel and motions for me to approach. I walk over, and with the greatest care and affection, Nestpa dries me and wraps me in the towel. "There we go, that wasn't so bad. All done, Tim. Welcome to the fourth state. Dr. Udaza will be able to begin your treatments in the morning. Now let's get you back to your room for dinner. Chicken, peas, and carrots tonight—yum." Nestpa smiles as she grabs my hand and walks me out of the cleansing room and down the corridor back to confinement room number four.

CHAPTER FOUR

A BITE
OF THE APPLE

NESTPA OPENS THE DOOR and walks into my cell. Exactly as Haram had requested, a desk and chair have been brought in to accommodate my needs for the remainder of my stay. How long is that going to be? I still have no idea. In Aduat, not only do the patients not seem to have any sense of time, neither does anyone else. Watches aren't worn and there are no clocks anywhere. Nestpa looks over at the corner of the desk, picks up a black leather-clad book, and thumbs through the pages. I can barely see the worn gold leaf lettering on the cover, *King James Bible*. Must be standard issue in Aduat, although I was rather expecting an Egyptian *Book of the Dead*. "Dr. Smith, I will be back to check on you in a few hours with your dinner. Oops, almost forgot—here are your notebook and pen. Don't forget to do your first assignment. Oodelly, doodly," Nestpa says as she places them on the white desk next to the bible and walks out of the room. The door shuts with a heavy thud and a clang as I hear the locking mechanism engage. Back to my white, padded room and acceptance. I am starting to feel better. The stream is flowing in my head. In hindsight, the shock may have been worth it, because the cool, cleansing water is refreshing. My mind feels clear and a sense of newfound focus is apparent. I sit down behind the desk and open the notebook. Demons, hmmm, what are mine?

After staring at the blank, white page for a few minutes contemplating my negative confession, none of my demons come to mind—but another unshakeable thought hits with a momentary jolt of subconscious recognition. It keeps repeating in my head. I can hear Dr. Richard say it over and over again as clear as day. I can see him and hear his voice repeating, "Tim, it is all about the thoton from Croton, the thoton from Croton." I can't shake it. What the hell is Dr. Richard talking about? I know that modern-day Crotone is a city in southern Italy where the first Pythagorean community was founded around 518 BC. Croton was one of the most flourishing cities of Magna Graecia, with a population of roughly fifty to eighty thousand. Pythagoras traveled there himself and founded a school called "the semicircle." It was Pythagoras's second go at it. He had originally founded a school by the same name in the city of Samos, which still exists today. His teaching methods were looked down upon and he was treated rudely by the Samians. Eventually, most of his time was spent teaching select students in isolation in a cave outside the city, rather than at the school. One day he had enough, so he picked up the whole show and moved it to Croton. The semicircle he established in Croton is more akin to a cult than an institution of higher learning.

Sworn to secrecy, initiates lived in a communal setting exploring the mysteries of the universe under the strict guidance of their master and the motto, "number rules the universe." Pythagoras of Croton actually created the term "philosophy" from the Greek (*philos*) a love and (*sophia*) of wisdom. The overriding philosophy of Pythagoreanism is that "All or God is number." The members were divided into two groups: the *mathematikoi*, referred to as "learners," who worked on the mathematical and scientific works Pythagoras initiated; and the *akousmatikoi,* the "listeners," who focused on the spiritual aspects of Pythagoras's teaching. Even in ancient Greece, religion and science were divided. Pythagoras's students learned the earliest ideas concerning the spherical shape of the Earth, metempsychosis, a philosophical term describing the transmigration of the soul, as well as the advanced mathematics of the age. Pythagoreans crafted the Theory of Opposites. The Pythagorean Table of Opposites represents a philosophical systematization of the very ancient mythological concept of binary opposites. There were ten basic pairs of opposites: limit (the finite) and the unlimited (infinite), odd and even, one and many, right and left, male and female, rest and motion, straight and curved, light and darkness, good and evil, square and oblong. The Pythagorean Theory of Opposites is the basis of the principle of Cosmic Duality and the extended quantum equations derived by Dr. Richard. Who knows what else? Why all the secrecy?

In the end, much still remains a secret as the Pythagorean sect in Croton was attacked due to political disputes with neighboring communities around 510 BC. Meeting houses were torched and cult members killed, including possibly Pythagoras. It isn't known whether he survived or not based on various conflicting accounts. It is interesting how time changes ideas: the Pythagoreans were attacked for their socialist ideology in ancient times; yet Pythagoras's ideas would return to twentieth-century Greece much later and be embraced. Again, in 460 BC, the cult's reclusive and eccentric behavior threatened the outside community, which led to all of the Pythagorean meeting places being burned and more than fifty members being killed—perhaps the end of the semicircle. There are no surviving writings by Pythagoras. Much of what is known today about the Pythagoreans is based upon the much later writing of Aristotle and Plato from accounts passed down over the years from Pythagoras's followers.

I look over at my cot, and see Dr. Richard sitting on top of the blanket in his red lab jacket, thumbing through a pin-up calendar with a big grin on his face. It appears our very own Nurse Nestpa made the cover. I just knew he couldn't miss out on this conversation. "So Doc, why all the secrecy in Croton?" I ask.

"Tim, I would be glad to explain the mysteries of the Pythagorean semicircle cult, but then I would have to kill you. But don't worry, we can test this whole transmigration of your soul business—you are not really going to die," he says as he put the calendar down and props himself up on the pillow trying to get comfortable. "In death, once the body shuts down, the photons slowly stop being processed by the brain. But the thotons are still there humming and buzzing as Pythagoras, himself, said, 'There is geometry in the humming of the strings, there is music in the spacing of the spheres.' Einstein also came to the conclusion that it is probable that our three-dimensional space is approximately spherical. The strings are the Space-Time Axons, matterless channels connecting spherical big bang universes! Your photon processing days may be over in this universe, but your thotons are already entangled with another universe. Based upon the principle of duality, your thotons can travel through non-matter channels across space-time instantaneously in a manner similar to the way the Pythagoreans perceived transmigration of the soul. These images are powerful.

"Whoever has control of the perception of the afterlife image can assert direct political control of populations such is the case in theocracies or wield indirect control of other governing structures through the power and wealth amassed from the "believers" in organized religions. The religious institutions ultimately garner their power from the proposed afterlife image. Any perceived threat to the images concerning the afterlife directly threaten the power structure of the existing religious and political institutions. That is why the Pythagoreans demanded secrecy of their members. It has even been said that Hippasus a Pythagorean was killed for simply revealing the existence of imaginary numbers. That is a shame, as imaginary numbers open the door to reality.

"Pythagoras had it all figured out in the sixth century BC—the Egyptians, a millennia before. The most likely origin of the Pythagorean concept of transmigration of the soul originated in Egypt. Pythagoras learned the Egyptian concept of the afterlife during his own travels there. Egyptian ideas also were commonly passed along the trade routes of the ancient Greeks and Phoenicians to Croton in Magna Graecia, which at that time was a cauldron of mixed civilizations bubbling with the different philosophies of the known world. As Pythagoras and the Egyptians figured out, we are all walking, talking time-traveling image processors. Transmigration of the soul, or thotonic space-time travel, at its simplest form is the idea of eternal life. Whatever you want to call it, they are all shades of the same underlying natural phenomena." Dr. Richard is right, the brass couldn't let that genie out of the bottle, neither in the sixth century BC, nor today. It appears that the knowledge was forever lost or destroyed with the school in Croton and the end of Pythagoras. Or was it? How much survived? The most famous theorem which bears Pythagoras's name (although really not directly attributable to him, because the sect worked as a collective) is later used by Einstein in his 1905 and 1915 Special and General Theories of Relativity. Einstein's metric equation is simply Pythagoras's theorem applied to spherical coordinates equated to the displacement of light. Einstein states in his own words, "The defining equation of the metric is then nothing but the Pythagorean Theorem applied to the differentials of the coordinates."

I look over at the empty cot and speak to Dr. Richard for no other reason than to reinforce the idea that the images I am seeing are real. "Thanks for clearing that up Doc. If that is only the semicircle, imagine what the full circle looks like. And why didn't I get an Aduat calendar?" It would sure help pass the time away—better than the water cannon treatment or pondering my transgrecians.

Oh well, back to my demons. The bible is usually good at this kind of thing, I shall not this and that. Flip right through to the Old Testament, throw an "I never" in front of a commandment, whichever is false—and bingo, I found my demons. Sounds like a plan. I reach over to grab the *King James* and notice that Nestpa has left it open to Genesis 2:10–14. The Garden of Eden, a regular paradise of pleasure, sounds just about what I need right now. Where is it? When is it? And most importantly, how do I get out of Aduat and there? Looks like I need to find the mouth of the four rivers Pishon, Gihon, Chidekel (Tigris) and Phirat (Euphrates). Why Four? It struck me at this very moment, and I looked at my notepad. I'd been doodling a line along the horizontal axis of the page and a compass on the top with the four cardinal points. My head starts spinning—four, four, four is everywhere. Why four?

The first evenly even number—the Pythagorean holy number symbolizing justice? I keep scribbling:

Four Cardinal Points – North, South, East, and West

Four Seasons – Spring, Summer, Autumn, and Winter

Four Classical Elements – Air, Fire, Water, and Earth

Four States of Matter – Liquid, Solid, Gas, and Plasma

The Pythagoreans believe God is number and swore the oath "By that pure, holy *four*-lettered name on high."

For that matter, the idea of "GOD" in most religions past or present is expressed as a Tetragrammaton (consisting of four letters):

God of Israel—IHIH (to be), AHIH (existence)/YHWH or YHVH in Latin script

English—LORD, Assyrian—ADAD, Egyptian—AMUN, Greek—THEO or ZEUS,

Latin—DEUS, German—GOTT, French—DIEU, Turkish—ESAR, Tartar—ITGA,

Arabian—ALLH, Samaritan—JABE, Kabbalist—IHVH.

I wrote Time on the horizontal line and began drawing a Tetractys, which is a triangle consisting of four evenly spaced rows descending from one point at the apex to four points at the base. I place it on top of the horizontal timeline. The Tetractys is a mystical symbol integral to the secret teachings of Pythagoreanism, whereby each row represents a dimension in space-time. The Pythagoreans took this stuff pretty seriously and even had a prayer to the Tetractys:

"Bless us, divine number, thou who generates gods and men! O holy, holy Tetractys, through that contains the root and the source of the eternally flowing creation! For the divine number begins with the profound, pure unity until it comes to the holy four; then it begets the mother of all, the all-compromising, the all-bounding, the first-born, the never-swerving, the never-tiring holy ten, the key-holder of all." {1 0}

I guess if you perceived God as a number, it makes as much sense to pray to a geometrical shape as it does to a sculpture, a four-letter Tetragrammaton or any other symbol? Humans throughout the ages have tried all of the above. It is probably a basic human instinct to wrap the inexplicable complexities of existence into an objectified symbolic form and then worship it as divinity. I guess it is better than doing nothing because it makes one feel less helpless in the process of acceptance and the flow of nature, a form of resistance. Maybe I'll give praying a whirl, since I still haven't found my demons. If they turn the white lights off in this place, I would probably already be asleep. I still can't get the number four out of my mind. I wildly continue to scribble as sweat begins to pour down my brow and my eyes remain open but red from rubbing. I wish they would turn off the damn, fluorescent light and stop the buzzing and humming. I can't think about demons. I can't think about anything but being stuck in Aduat as my hand keeps shakily writing. Four…four…jars.

The ancient Egyptians used four canopic jars as part of their transmigration of the soul ceremony. They would remove the liver, stomach, lungs, and intestines of the deceased and safely store them in canopic jars because they believed that they would be required in the after-life. The heart was left in the body to be weighed by Anubis, the god of the dead in Duat. What four more? The fourth most abundant element in our big bang universe by mass is carbon. Carbon is the basis for the chemistry of life. What makes carbon so special? FOUR, of course! It is Tetravalent whereby four electrons are available to form covalent chemical bonds. It has four valence bonds that require just the right amount of energy to break them for building molecules that are both stable and reactive. Carbon is the backbone of the organic molecules that form living matter, DNA. The blueprint of all life, DNA is a carbon-based molecule that is made up of two chains twisted around each other to form a helix carrying the genetic instructions for growth, development, functioning, and reproduction of all known living organisms in this big bang universe. DNA is composed of—you guessed it—four bases. Adenine (A) and guanine (G) are the larger purines. Cytosine (C) and thymine (T) are the smaller pyrimidines. RNA also contains four different bases.

The four quantum logical states are conveyed as sets in the following expression:

$[<> \{0,1\}], [1], [0], [\{0,1\}] = \pm\infty$. The first state being neither 0,1, the second 1, the third 0, and the fourth state both 0,1. The fourth state is representative of quantum superposition. All of the states combined represent plus and minus infinity, defining all of space-time. My hand is cramping as I continue writing on the notebook page. I draw a line dividing the Tetractys into three sections with a fourth connecting triangle below the timeline assigning the states to the life cycle of a living organism. This is the way Pythagoras must have had it. The Pythagoreans perceive 1 simply as being alive and 0 as death. The first state [<> {0,1}] is neither being alive nor dead, unborn. The second state [1] commences at birth, being alive. The third state begins at death [0]. The fourth state [{0,1}] encompasses all other states extending from the apex of the Tetractys downward. I don't know how I know, but I do. It has sunk into my core in Aduat. The fourth state is Pythagoras's doorway, an open door, transmigration of the soul. The big secret. A D...D...D...Doorway? Why D? D is the fourth letter of the Roman alphabet. Where did the letter D come from? I remember it came from the Dalet (dāleth, also spelled Daleth or Daled). It is the fourth letter of the Semitic abjads, including Phoenician Dālet. The Phoenician Dālet gave rise to the Greek delta (Δ), and the Latin D—each the fourth letter in the respective alphabets. The Greek delta is commonly used in science as a symbol signifying change or transformation. Where did the Dālet come from? Of course, right where Pythagoras found it, back to Egypt. The letter is based on a glyph of the Middle Bronze Age alphabets, derived from an Egyptian hieroglyph depicting an open door. The door to the fourth state is open! I will rewind the film and find a way to save Kathy and Sarah.

I hear footsteps outside the door and quickly tear out the page from my notebook and place it in between the mattress and slats in the cot. The door opens, "Here you are, Tim, the best chicken, peas, and carrots under the sun. Make sure you eat all your veggies and then night-night."

"Roger that, umm, Nestpa. What time do you turn off the lights in Aduat?" I ask as the constant illumination is becoming unbearable.

Nestpa looks at me quizzically, "Why Tim, the lights are always on. It's for your own safety." She puts a glass of water on the desk and exits confinement room four. How the hell am I going to get any sleep? I eat the asylum food and must say that Nestpa didn't exaggerate—the food in this place is terrific. I don't know about the glass of water. They could have served a stronger beverage. I need it. I quickly scribble in Haram's notebook, "I never made an idol." There done. I slip under the covers put the pillow over my face and do my best to get some shut-eye.

I toss and turn as the pillow does little to temper the harsh white light. My eyes finally close and my stream of consciousness fades until I am standing in Hawaii overlooking the sunrise with Kathy and Sarah. I feel the warmth of their love, cascading all over my spirit. Sarah looks up at me and as she is about to speak.

Nestpa starts shaking me. "Time to get up Tim, it's your big day, your first session with Dr. Haram. Wakey-wakey, let's go," she insists. I'm feeling dazed—it seems like Nestpa left just a few minutes ago. It can't already be time to wake up. I see a wheelchair with restraints for the arms and legs sitting at the end of the cot. Nestpa grabs me by the arm and walks me over and sits me down in the chair. "Where's your notebook, Tim? Dr. Haram is going to want to see your work," she says sternly.

"Why are there restraints on the wheelchair, why can't I just walk?" I ask.

"Oooh, those aren't for you silly, they're for our mentally disturbed long-term residents. You're going to need all of your strength today, Tim. You are a very special patient. Don't worry, I don't mind wheeling you around," Nestpa says with a smile. "Ahh, there it is," she says as she picks the notebook up off of the desk, "and away we go!" Nestpa wheels me down the expansive corridor at a speed that seems excessive—almost running, heels clicking, and bosom flopping up and down, panting for breath. She abruptly stops in front of an empty lavatory and waits patiently as I shower, occasionally peering in the curtainless stall. "You okay in there, Tim? You need my help to get all your little nooks and crannies cleany-weeny?" she asks with sincerity.

"No, I think I can handle it, Nestpa," I say, remembering our last bathing experience together. At least I didn't get the firehose treatment this time. I don't think I could handle it this early in the morning—hell, that is if it is even morning. I have no idea. Once I put my robe on, Nestpa sits me back down in the chair and snuggly fastens the restraints. "Hey, what are you doing? I thought you said that those are for the long-term, mentally disturbed patients?" I ask nervously.

"Yes, Tim that's exactly what I said. Dr. Haram is very excited to treat his number one patient," Nestpa smartly snaps back. We are off again running down the corridor until she stops in front of a swinging set of green double doors. There are no markings. Nestpa forcefully pushes the chair through the entryway. Once inside, it appears to be an operating room of some sort. There are no windows. The walls and ceiling are painted green, with hanging plants flowing from the ceiling and potted shrubs lining the walls. What appears to be a steel operating table with restraints is in the center of the room, surrounded by magnifying lamps on rollers. Two orderlies stand at attention at one end of the room. Next to the lamps are a series of trays on rollers with various medical instruments: scalpels, knives, scissors, and long metal needles. A serious of electrodes protrude from what appears to be a headband and an ankle bracelet attached to an electrical panel under a utility cart that is plugged into a 220V outlet in the wall. A ventilator is on the last mobile cart. There are rows of earthen jars with hieroglyphic inscriptions and different faces adorning the lids lined up against the wall. It can't be. "Canopic jars?" I blurt out.

"Good morning, Tim. Yes, you are quite correct—no worries. They make exquisite decorations," Haram says curtly. "Has the patient been cleansed, Nurse Nestpa?" Haram asks.

"Yes Doctor, he did very well last night. He accepted the stream and flow very quickly—no problems," she replies.

"Excellent, and his notebook?"

"Right here doctor," Nestpsa says as she hands the notebook over to him. Haram opens it up with a sigh as he looks at the first page, reads the one line that I wrote, and flips through the empty pages.

"I see, Tim, that you only have only one demon. It doesn't look like you gave this much thought. Very disappointing," Haram says condescendingly. "Did you write anything else in your notebook, Tim?" he asks in a solemn tone.

"No, I didn't, Haram, but I did give my demons some pretty serious thought. I've been through a lot in the last few days, Haram. Can you cut me some slack? I can go back to my room right now, and I'm sure I can think of more demons," I reply.

"You wouldn't lie to me, would you, Tim? I'm here for your benefit to help you. Lying to me will only prolong your recovery. It's pointless," Haram says, with the level of his frustration evident in his tone. "I will ask you again for the last time—did you write anything else down in the notebook?"

"No, I did just what you asked. I only wrote down my demon, Haram," I say as this whole notebook nonsense is starting to agitate me.

"Hmm, you are not a very convincing liar, Tim. I can plainly see the imprint from the ballpoint pen on the page beneath the one you must have removed. It is of no consequence. We will proceed with your treatment as planned. Please prepare the ventilator and the suxamethonium injection," Haram says in a monotone voice that makes the hairs stand up on the back of my neck.

"Wait, Haram, please let me explain. What are you doing? What the hell is a treatment and why do I need an injection? SUX, I know it. Stop!" I cry out.

"Hmm, so you know it, SUX? The injection will induce a state of paralysis while you are conscious whereby you won't be able to feel anything or have any muscular control but will be cognizant of your surroundings during the therapy. It will make it easier for us to root out your demons, the ones you chose not to confess. We will get you better in no time at all. I know it's not your fault, Tim. Don't worry. Everyone in Aduat is here to help you recover," Haram says as Nurse Nestpa wheels me closer to the operating table.

"Nurse, please proceed with phase one, and administer the SUX," Haram orders.

Nurse Nestpa walks over to the tray and picks up a large metal syringe. The needle extends five inches beyond the metal casing. She holds it up in the air gingerly, pressing down as a bead of liquid trickles down the sharpened point. She looks at me with a cool smile and says, "We are all set, Tim. This will only hurt a teeny little bit. You may feel a little pinch, stinging, nothing more than a baby bee. In a few minutes you won't feel anything after one little stingy-wingy, that's all." I struggle in the wheelchair, but the restraints hold my arms firmly in place, bound to the handrails. My legs can't move because they are strapped into the metal frame around the footrest. Nestpa walks over and wipes a swab that smells like rubbing alcohol around my neck. She probes my neck with her cold fingers as she stands behind me, her warm breath condensing on the back of my neck. Suddenly, I feel a sharp pain followed by a burning sensation as she jabs the syringe into the back of my neck, injecting the SUX. Then slowly—a tingling feeling all over my body until I lose all sensation. I can't move my arms or my legs. It feels like I am suffocating as I try harder to gasp for air. It is pointless—I can no longer draw air into my lungs. "Quickly, get the patient onto the ventilator," Haram barks out.

The orderlies remove the restraints and pick me up, placing me roughly on the table. Nestpa grabs a tube from the ventilator, opens my mouth, and shoves the tube down my windpipe, then starts running another one through my nose all the way down to my stomach. I have no feeling. There is no pain, but I try to close my eyes so I don't have to watch any more of this. The images are too much. I can't. My eyelids will not respond. "Make it stop," I say to myself. I can't even yell. I can't feel my tongue or vocal cords. I am suspended in a state of sublime acceptance. Resistance is not even a concept, an impossibility. "Accept," I think to myself. The only resistance left is my thotonic world. It too will yield. I must accept and just give them every last one of my thotons. I can feel oxygen flowing again as the ventilator pump moves rhythmically up and down, pushing air in and out of my limp body. The orderlies strap my arms and legs to the table as Nestpa pulls a straight razor from the tool cart. I can see her inches away from me as I stare directly into her eyes when her face nears mine. She leans over with the razor, rubbing her hands through my hair. "You just need a quick trim, Tim, nothing to be worried about," she says in a sweet reassuring voice. She shaves off all the hair around my temples and then moves down to my left ankle.

Then Nestpa takes a blue bottle of conductivity gel off one of the carts and rubs it all over my temples and left ankle. Not exactly the rub-down I had pictured with the naughty nurse. She takes the headband off the cart and places it over my head, aligning the electrodes directly on my temples. Finally, she slips the ankle bracelet over my foot and adjusts the electrode to make contact. "There you are Tim, all set for your little trip. Dr. Udaza the patient is prepped," she says with a sense of pride.

"Excellent. Charge the unit up to 2000 volts," Haram says to one of the orderlies. Haram walks over to the machine as it starts to hum with increasing fervor and places his hand on the lever. I still have no sense of feeling, but in the back of my mind I am still thinking that this is going to hurt. The indicator light on the machine changes color, from a red, to a yellow and finally a green. Haram pulls the switch. My body is jolted back and forth, held in place only by the restraints as the charge involuntarily contracts every muscle fiber in my body. I can smell my flesh burning. I probably would have bitten my tongue off if it hadn't been for the tube running down my throat. I continue to convulse until it is too much. My eyelids finally close.

And then—nothing.

Curled up in a ball on the ground of what appears to be a parking lot, I can feel the cold, hard asphalt on my side. I look up and can see stars, tons of stars in the heavens above. There are four moons, but none of the recognizable planets I am accustomed to seeing in the night sky. I slowly stand up as my head starts to throb in horrific pain. I become aware that I am wearing a flowing white Grecian toga and brown leather sandals. The pulsating stinging runs through my temples down my spinal cord, causing me to grimace. Other than the stars, the only other light is emanating from an enormous sign that is flickering on and off in large letters. *UNIVERSAL DEPOT*, it beckons.

The building is gigantic, stretching nearly as far as I can see across the horizon. It appears that they are closed, because the parking lot is empty. There are many doors. I happen to be closest to the contractors' entrance. I decide to give it a try to get out of the cold night air. The sliding glass door is slightly ajar, so I am able to squeeze in between the frame and make my way past the cashiers' counters to the main aisle. It looks like the aisle goes on for miles: electrical, plumbing, lighting, cooling, heating, windows, doors, hardware, tools, and of course Lawn & Garden, as well as many other aisles too distant to see. I'm startled to hear the sound of soft laughter as I turn. Out of the corner of my eye, I catch the outline of a nude female figure scurrying through the aisles.

I give chase, turning down the appliance section in pursuit. I finally catch up to the young maiden, sitting on top of a washing machine with her smooth, petite legs dangling over the side, swinging to and fro. She is smiling and looking directly at me. Her long flowing brown hair cascades down over her small firm breasts.

In a flirtatious voice, the maiden says, "Welcome, Time Smith. We've been expecting you."

"She must have me confused with someone else," I think.

"No, my name is *Tim* Smith. What is your name?" I ask.

"Eve, of course. I am not the one confused, you are the *Time* Smith Ahura Mazda told us you would come to the Garden. We've been expecting you," Eve says confidently.

"Who is Ahura?" I ask.

"Ahura is the omnipotent creator, mighty wisdom, all that is good, the essence of morality, the cosmic image processor. All that your thotons perceive is his will. He is the manager of Lawn & Garden. Botany is his true passion. He told us you would come to the Garden one day," Eve replies solemnly.

"Is he here now, Eve?" I ask.

"Ahura is everywhere, but he manifests in physical form to prune the trees in the garden from time to time as it suits him. Would you like to go to the garden and wait for him? I am sure he will want to see you," Eve asks.

"Lead the way," I reply.

This couldn't get any more bizarre, could it? Eve jumps off of the washing machine and scampers down the aisles—almost skipping, her firm buttocks moving to and fro, arousing my carnal senses as well as my curiosity as to the answers that lay in the Garden. I follow her through the maze of aisles until we arrive at a large glass dome, the Lawn & Garden section of Universal Depot. The automatic sliding glass doors open, and we walk in. The first thing that strikes me is the sheer size of the glass dome that must extend five full stories into the sky. The stars are shining down on rows of plants, trees, flowers and shrubs of just about every variety one has seen or could imagine. The ground is covered in AstroTurf. As we walk in I see a large waterfall fountain spilling into a koi pond that is surrounded by cypress trees in wooden buckets. Next to the pond is a large, bubbling hot tub. Much to my disbelief, Dr. Richard's red robe is hung neatly from a hook, and he is sitting in the tub with a young man, carrying on a conversation.

Dr. Richard looks up, flashes a quick smile, and waves. As we approach the hot tub, Eve stops next to a large apple tree planted in a huge resin bucket that must have been over five feet in diameter. The tree is truly astonishing, over twenty feet tall with the greenest leaves and countless Red Delicious apples hanging in bunches. Two white wooden Adirondack chairs sit beneath the tree's branches. Eve notices me staring at the size of the apples in utter disbelief. "The apples are only for visitors. They are forbidden to us. It is too cold, Time Smith. I am going to jump back in the hot tub. You are welcome to join Adam, Dr. Richard, and I—or enjoy an apple and wait here for Ahura—no telling when he will manifest," she says. I haven't eaten breakfast yet, and four is usually a crowd. I decide to have a seat and enjoy a Red Delicious.

"Thanks, Eve, I'll catch up with you, Adam, and the good Doc in a bit," I say as I pick a grapefruit-sized apple and sit down in the comfortable chair. Eve skips back over to the cypress trees and jumps into the tub, picking up where the three had left off.

Over the frolicking and hum of the jets, I hear Dr. Richard carrying on about the miraculous mini big bang bubbles of the universes floating through the infinite void in a synchronized cosmic progression of time curvature in perfect harmony with each other. Adam listens intently, while Eve seems to like the explanation, as she smiles and, splashes away, pointing toward the heavens. Wow! This apple is out of this world, the flesh just dissolves on the tongue into a sweet sensuous liquid, leaving no hint of an aftertaste, demanding another bite. I oblige. As soon as I had swallowed the sweet nectar of the gods, a brilliant ball of fire descends towards the dome. It becomes the figure of a man riding a phoenix composed of yellow and red flames that irradiate light as brilliant as the sun is visible. The illumination remains outside the dome as the doors fly open. An old man with piercing blue eyes, a flowing white beard, and a mustache covering the weathered skin on his face appears. He is wearing a red tunic and carries a staff.

"I am and will always be Ahura Mazda, the source of all good, evil, and everything in the universes. Kneel before me, Time Smith." His voice echoes throughout the dome. I throw the apple core in the resin bucket and take a knee to learn my fate. "Rise, Time Smith, there is much to talk about," Ahura says.

I stand up, surprised at the height and imposing image. As Ahura approaches it appears he must be nearly ten feet tall. He walks over to the Tree of Knowledge, picks an apple and devours it in a few large bites, core and all. Ahura sits down in the large Adirondack chair, lays his staff on the ground, and motions for me to sit next to him. "Time Smith, the spheres are sacred. Pythagoras's sphere, Einstein's sphere, and the nameless other visionaries in other universes, who have seen the same image. The sphere is the building block of the universe. Dr. Richard was sent by me to prepare you so that you have a chance to seek out your destiny and preserve the continuum before it is seized by Angra Mainyu and lost to good forever, the end of all universes. Apparently, Dr. Richard has been preoccupied with other worldly desires and seems to have neglected his duties, which is evident as you and I are having this conversation at Universal Depot. I hate having to come here other than to tend to the garden." Ahura says. I look up in utter astonishment, unable to fully comprehend what Ahura is talking about. "Dr. Richard, get out of the hot tub. Quit playing around with Eve and come over here for a minute and explain to Time Smith the space-time paradigm once and for all so I can fill him in on the rest of his fate and turn my full attention back to universal thotonic image processing," Ahura barks. Dr. Richard obediently climbs out of the hot tub, puts on his red robe and strolls over to the tree.

Dr. Richard stands in front of me, still dripping wet and begins to speak, "It is beyond most people's comprehension to imagine a void consisting of positive and negative infinity, everything and nothing—but you must do so, Time Smith. Picture an infinite number of mini big bang universes contained in floating spheres traversing the void on one Universal Cosmic Time curve. Picture our universe as the Earth floating in a balloon with an infinite number of other balloons filled with matter and non-matter universes. All of the balloons are tethered by Universal Cosmic Time. Within each of the mini big bang universes (balloons), there is an infinite number of time curves relative to each observer, particle, or anything in motion for that matter inside the balloon. It is as if each observer in each universe carries their own personal time clock, ticking as they are all moving at different velocity levels relative to each other. When you travel through space-time at a speed exceeding light, perhaps thotonically in a dream state to another matter or non-matter universe (balloon), you are now on a different time curve. You have traveled outside of your universe's light cone. Additionally, the special and general theories of relativity not only apply to the mini big bang universes, but they also extend to the Universal Cosmic Time of the Master Universe, the collection of infinite balloons floating through the cosmos."

"Okay, I got that down. Now what does that have to do with anything?" I think. "What does Dr. Richard mean by....," Tim stammers. Ahura interrupts, "Atlantis is one of the first mini big bang universes created at a point in space-time that is both the beginning and end, truly in a state of superposition. Atlantis is the gateway to all space-time universes. The Atlanteans successfully completed building what you call a QTIP. With a crystal device called the Chronos, the Atlanteans can teleport matter to any universe at any point in space-time. At the beginning or end of creation or both the beginning and end, near the time Atlantis was formed the cosmic principle of duality had to be upheld. Angra Mainyu was created by me and is my antithesis, pure evil destined to crawl through the universe in eternal blindness surrounded by those who lurk behind his shadow. He had to exist, but I banished him to the planet Atlantis as I foresaw he would have a son, Aka, and daughter, Spenta. In my stream of consciousness, I perceived Spenta, who embodies goodness, ruling the planet wisely with her brother Aka, overseeing the safekeeping of the Chronos and protecting the universes from Angra. It didn't happen. Somehow I misjudged the spherical probability function because it is autonomous and once created beyond my control, independently dictating the course of future events.

Angra turned Aka against his sister and began a brutal civil war. The rebellion led by Spenta was almost entirely wiped out. Spenta used the QTIP to flee Atlantis to your universe and the planet Earth, taking the Chronos with her, making the QTIP virtually worthless and protecting everyone from Angra. Spenta and what was left of the rebellion joined a small community in Croton with Pythagoras and the semicircle. Spenta and the Atlantean survivors of the rebellion make up the other half of the circle, the Atlantean ouroboros. The full circle is the symbol of the order. The circle pledged to keep the mysteries of Atlantis and space-time travel secret and protect the universes from Angra. Time Smith, you are the last human descendant of the community of Croton. An Atlantean prophecy foretells your coming and freeing the Atlanteans from the bondage of Angra. Your lineage has pledged allegiance to me as the sacred keepers of space-time. Anrga and Aka have been able to locate the rebellion on Earth in Egypt before the full circle forms in Croton. They have developed a limited crystal based on the original Chronos, which is destroyed after it is used to send another through space-time after Spenta, the Chronos, and you. You must help Spenta overthrow Angra, restore peace to Atlantis, and secure the space-time continuum.

"Ahura, I don't understand. I am in Aduat, restrained to an operating table, undergoing shock treatments. How can I do anything to help Spenta? Are you sure I am the Time Smith you are looking for? My name is Tim Smith. I don't know how I got this toga. I have never been to Egypt, and I am not even Greek!" I say emphatically.

"Time Smith, in the end good always prevails. The cost is tragedy and sacrifice. You are the instrument of my choosing, and you will fulfill your destiny," Ahura assures me.

"What about Kathy and Sarah? Can I use the Chronos to bring them back?" I ask the omnipotent creator.

"The technology you are seeking on Earth, Time Smith, which the Atlanteans possess is the beginning and end. The laws of causality are ingrained in the fabric of space-time, whereby even the best intentions can lead to unintended catastrophic consequences. The past was, the present is, and the future will be," Ahura says in a thunderous voice.

"How can I save Kathy and Sarah?" I ask again, unable to take a hint.

"It is not for men to bear the responsibility and wield a tool this powerful. Every day your planet sits on the cusp of total destruction, constrained by the meager tools you presently have at your disposal. The universes shall not be subjected to the frivolity of the whims of mankind. Every tool mankind has created, it has used. Angra does not yet exist in your universe, but evil does. The great power of the technology you seek for mankind, no matter that your intentions are to use it with the utmost wisdom for the purpose of good, will inevitably be overcome by corruptness and evil. Accept your fate and flow. Kathy and Sarah exist forever in the images of space-time, their thotons buzzing and humming in the universes. Let it be, Time Smith. Fulfill your......." Ahura's voice begins to fade.

My temples start to throb again as the pain runs down my spine, the images of Ahura, Dr. Richard, and the Garden started to fade in and out. "I am not the one, Ahura! You are mistaken!" I yell as the images I see turn into the nothingness of white. All I can see is the fluorescent light above, and I can hear Nestpa's voice.

"Dr. Udaza, the patient has regained consciousness," Nestpa says with alarm.

"Quickly, recharge the unit up to 2200 volts, and stand clear," Haram orders.

I look down over my naked body and see two large incisions on my left and right sides and a series of steel staples holding the skin together where the precise cuts must have been made. Red stains cover the white sheets of the operating table with drips of blood scattered on the floor. I glance over, following the drips to the canopic jars and notice two are full with my blood on the edges. "Dr. Udaza, the unit is charged and ready. Clear!" Nestpa says. "Decorations, my a...!"

And then—nothing.

CHAPTER FIVE

THE RIDDLE
OF THE SPHINX

*T*HE DESERT AIR FILLS MY LUNGS* as I gasp, breathing in a gulp of warm, dry air. I am lying on the ground under a palm tree in the evening darkness. My senses are slowly restored. As I stand up I can see a vast pyramid with a shining light shooting up through its zenith into the evening sky, splitting the heavens. The sky is familiar, the moon and North Star are recognizable to me. The noises in the background are deafening, a cacophony of man and machine—car horns, sirens, garbage trucks, people's voices laughing, shouting, sobbing, and yelling. "Toga, Toga, Toga, Where's the party?" an inebriated stranger staggering down the street asks as he looks at my outfit. The sidewalk is packed with a stream of all walks of life— men, women,

tall, short, fat, skinny—wandering through the carnival of the de-bauched. A heavy voice booms out, "Time Smith, I have been waiting for you. The oldest riddle awaits your answer, and ye shall be granted entrance to Luxor or perish." Who said that? I look around and there is nobody— Luxor? I walk about twenty paces back and I can see a hundred-foot-tall sphinx hovering above with the face of a man on the body of a lion, sitting on all fours, guarding the entrance to the pyramid of Luxor. "I don't have all evening, Time Smith, are you prepared to answer my riddle?" says the Sphinx.

"This is not good," I think to myself. The Sphinx of Giza is one of the oldest, most recognizable symbols on earth, dating back to roughly 2500 BC, capturing the imagination of poets, scholars, and adventurers for millennia. Although this sphinx is clearly a newer reproduction built in the early 1990s, it does not make him any less formidable. From the looks of him, he's a pretty accurate replica. He faces directly from West to East, is proportionately correct and massive in scale, nearly two stories taller than his cousin in Egypt. Hopefully, he doesn't possess the ferocity of his Greek ancestors. As far as I recall, the Egyptian Sphinx didn't get nasty until the Greeks decided to perform a gender bender and turned him into her. The Greeks resurrected a mythical female version of the Egyptian Sphinx to guard the entrance to the city of Thebes in Greece. The Greek Sphinx devoured those who couldn't answer her riddle.

She was believed to have been sent by the displeased gods to prey upon the children of Thebes as a punishment for an ancient trans-gression. In Greek mythology, Oedipus vanquishes her by guessing her riddle, whereby she ends her own life. The first surviving written records of the Greek Sphinx are found in a few verses on a vase dat-ing back to 470–460 BC, derived from *Oedipodea*, a lost poem from 764 BC credited to Cinaethon. Around 430 BC, the myth is retold in Sophocles's quintessential Greek tragedy *Oedipus Tyrannus* (Rex), although Sophocles never discloses the actual riddle. In the third century AD, Athenaeus puts the written riddle forth in the form of dactylic hexameter in the *Deipnosophistae*, crediting it to the Greek historian Asclepiades (140-129 BC). This leads many scholars to believe that this may be the oldest version of the riddle known. In any case, it is a no win. If I don't answer the riddle, I am devoured. And if I do, I am reminded of the fate of Oedipus— killing his father, marrying his mother, gashing his eyes out—all sorts of unpleasantness.

Perhaps it is sometimes better to leave riddles unanswered.

"Enough. I pose my riddle, Time Smith":

ἔστι δίπουν ἐπὶ γῆς καὶ τετράπον, οὗ μία φωνή,

καὶ τρίπον, ἀλλάσσει δὲ **φύσιν** μόνον ὅσσ’ ἐπὶ γαῖαν

ἑρπετὰ γίνονται καὶ ἀν’ αἰθέρα καὶ κατὰ πόντον

ἀλλ’ ὁπόταν **πλείστοισιν** ἐρειδόμενον ποσὶ βαίνῃ,

ἔνθα **τάχος** γυίοισιν ἀφαυρότατον πέλει αὐτοῦ.

"Oh wise gatekeeper of the pyramid, my ancient Greek is lacking. Is there any chance you can repeat it in English? By the way, why are you letting all those other people through the doors to the pyramid without answering your riddle?" I ask as he seems to already be treating me rather unfairly.

"They have a player's card. It is of no consequence. You still don't have the wisdom to answer correctly, Time Smith."

A thing there is whose voice is one;
Whose feet are four and two and three.
So mutable a thing is none
That moves in earth or sky or sea.
When on most feet this thing doth go,
Its strength is weakest and its pace most slow.

Dr. Richard's four behavioral states come to mind as I can hear him saying, "You can resist or control the Sphinx by playing the riddle guessing game or you can accept and flow, make him your new pet." The guessing game didn't work out so well for Oedipus. "Well at least Oedipus became King of Thebes and wasn't devoured outside the Vegas strip," I think to myself.

"What is your answer Time Smith?" the Sphinx asks in an impatient tone.

"Give me a minute, my four-pawed friend," I say in order to buy some time to figure this out. Well, at least I didn't get the very ancient two sisters' riddle, which is also known to have been asked of travelers at the gate of Thebes by the ancestor of my new feline friend.

There are two sisters, one gives birth to the other and she, in turn, gives birth to the first.

Who are the two sisters?

The answer is: day and night. I could hear Dr. Richard chiming in, "Think Cosmic Duality, Tim, day and night." That isn't going to help me this time, or is it?

Let me think. Freud loved this Greek stuff! A little cocaine, a terra-cotta sphinx and a copy of *Oedipus Rex* to curl up next to and you're in business. I am sure his answer is spot on the money. The Oedipus myth provided the foundation for Freud's development of psychoanalysis. He wrote, "A single idea of general value dawned on me. I have found, in my own case too (the phenomenon of) being in love with my mother and jealous of my father, and I now consider it a universal event in early childhood." He believed this instinctual urge formed the sexual identity in both men and women. Psychoanalysis is based upon the interpretation of thoton images or what Freud perceived as a dream state, communication with the subconscious. Perhaps what Freud perceived to be the subconscious is nothing more than our comprehensive thoton image library? The image of the Sphinx and Oedipus ultimately led to one of the most important breakthroughs in psychology, the understanding of identity (a thotonic image of self) as well as the related idea of inter-preting images to obtain a better understanding of one's nature.

Who would have a better answer to the riddle than Sigmund? He was an obsessive collector of Greek antiquities, buying the little terra-cotta sphinx buggers as well as other artifacts in an effort to constantly decorate his office. It was like a revolving museum collection, underscor-ing his fascination with the myth, and probably a manifestation of his own obsessive-compulsive disorder. Freud described the riddle as "the question of where babies come from." Hmm— let me think about that one for a moment. Ancient Greek riddles are known to have a straight-forward answer and a bawdy subtext providing an alternative solution. I am sure it didn't take Freud too long to figure it out. The solution Oedipus is said to have given is "man." For as a babe he is four-footed, going along on four limbs; as an adult he is two-footed; and as an old man, he walks with a third support staff. That would be the straight-forward answer, because it alludes to man's progression through time.

Dr. Freud's baby answer suggests the solution of the riddle being a couple having intercourse. As the moaning becomes one voice, two feet per couple while copulating equals four. Two feet alludes to the woman and three feet to the man (two feet and a phallus). The word "phallus" in Latin is borrowed from a Greek word that is ultimately a derivation of the Proto-Indo European root $b^h el$- "to inflate or swell." "Oedipus" is de-rived from the Greek term for "swollen foot." The ancient Greek word for foot also often has a sexual connotation referring to a phallus or gland. So my answer is either "man" or the union of "man and woman by intercourse." The first answer is an allusion to time expressed as the aging of man, and the second is an allusion to creation communicated as the act of procreation itself, underscoring the nature of cosmic dual-ity, yin, and yang. The complete answers to the Sphinx's riddle capture the imagination because, ultimately, the answers to the riddle are really the veiled questions man has been trying to explain since the beginning of time through myth, religion, science, and philosophy. What is man's fate after death (i.e., progression through time) and the source of our ultimate origin or creation?

Ironically, even the answers to the riddle can be summed up in dualistic terms (e.g., Life/Death) toward seeking an understanding of the ultimate origin of life and of our fate after death—the two elusive questions that float through the infinite void forever unanswerable. Dr. Richard's extended equations may help answer the Sphinx's larger questions because the key to the space-time paradigm is the integration of the concept of time and cosmic duality to complete the current quantum equations, which currently only capture half of the mechanics of the universe. It is interesting that the riddle also contains the Tetractys in number (1, 2, 3, 4), the Pythagorean representation of space-time as well as their numerical representation of God the Creator, which would have been the Pythagorean's symbolic answer to the Sphinx's larger questions. Perhaps I have the answers and questions, but as Dr. Richard suggests, not playing the Sphinx's game may help me look at this in a different way.

"O' Ye Master of Riddles of the ages, I pose the question to you, why does the camel have a hump on its back?" I query to avoid my foreseeable fate of having to answer his riddle.

"It is not your place to pose the questions, Time Smith. Now answer my riddle, or perish like those before you," the Sphinx says with indignation.

"Why should I answer yours if you, mighty Sphinx, can't even answer my simple question? Let me tell you the answer, and if it puts a smile on your face, let me pass."

"As you wish, Time Smith, but I haven't smiled since my creation. If I do, you may pass. If not, you shall perish. Why does the camel have a hump on its back?" says the Sphinx as he looks set on devouring me.

"Oh, wise Sphinx,":

The sexual life of the camel

Is stranger than anyone thinks.

In moments of amorous passion,

He frequently buggers the Sphinx.

But the Sphinx's posterior passage

Is clogged with the sands of the Nile,

Which accounts for the hump on the camel,

And the Sphinx's inscrutable smile."

The Sphinx maintains its solemn crouched stance guarding the entrance, as it has since its identity was first perceived in antiquity. Its mouth remains closed, and it just stands there looking into the vastness of space-time in silence. It is amazing that this mythical creature, existing only as a five-thousand-year-old thoton image in man's mind has survived the passage of time, as immortal as my own thoton identity in the universes. Maybe the thotonic image of the Sphinx has always been suspended in an archetypical form waiting for an image processor to perceive it and bring forth its thotonic image into a photonic image in this universe. Images form identities. Identities are truly powerful. Analogous to the law of the Conservation of Energy, thotonic identity can neither be created nor destroyed. It only changes form, swirling around in infinity. Just as I am traveling through space-time as I record my experiences in this manuscript, I am subtly changing as I travel. But in essence I have the same identity, whether working in the basement of DARPA, confined to my room in Aduat, standing in front of this pyramid in Las Vegas, or wherever, whenever I have yet to go.

The Pythagoreans understood the Conservation of Identity principle as it is integral to their perception of the transmigration of the soul. All thotonic identity simply just is, just as the universes are spiraling through the infinite void with no beginning, no end. A similar concept exists in Zoroastrianism, the first monotheistic religion originating between 10,000 and 7000 BC. The idea is called *Fravashi* in the Avestan language. Pythagoras encountered Zoroastrianism when Cambyses II conquered Egypt in 525 BC. While studying in Egypt Pythagoras was taken prisoner as a slave and brought to Babylonia. Under the tutelage of Zarudas, Pythagoras was taught Zoroastrianism beliefs, which later played an important role in the development of Pythagorean ideology, specifically duality and the development of the Theory of Opposites. My four-legged friend no longer stands in my way, because in my mind I can see an image of him smiling and laughing at the silly humped-back camel.

I walk underneath him through the tunnel and hear his faint whisper as I pass, "Well done, Time Smith. You may know the solutions to my riddle but still have not answered. We shall meet again, entangled forever in our high-stakes game of chance. Such are the games of the universes, a series of spherical probabilities. Welcome to Luxor Be forewarned, as the name suggests, it has broken stronger men than you." I walk through the tunnel under the Sphinx's belly. What does he mean—Luxor? It seems like a harmless enough name. I remember that the Luxor pyramid in Las Vegas ultimately derives its name from the Arabic *al-Uqsur*, translated as "the palaces." When Cambyses II, the oldest son of Cyrus the Great, the founder of the first Persian Empire, conquered Egypt the Persians were astounded by the size and magnificence of the temples—incorrectly assuming that they were palaces (or al-Uqsur) where the King dwelled. The Arabic term al-Uqsur phonetically evolved into "Luxor." In ancient Thebes in Egypt, the temple of Karnak lies across from the Temple of Luxor, the "Ipet-Resyt," which is the southern sanctuary or harem situated across from the Nile River.

The Opet Feast derives its name from "Ipet-Sut," the temple complex around Karnak and the "Ipet-Resyt," the Temple of Luxor. The Opet Feast's core element focused on the ancient Egyptians' ceremonious procession of moving the idol representing the embodiment of their god, Amun, in an annual procession from Karnak through the Avenue of the Sphinxes to the temple of Luxor. Amun was moved from Karnak to the Temple of Luxor to have carnal union with his wife, Mut, and concubines in an act of symbolic rejuvenation coinciding with the flooding of the Nile River. At the time of the ceremony, the mortal Pharaoh would partake in secretive rituals to be reconsecrated as the son of Amun, restoring his divine nature. Ceremoniously, the pharaoh would also perform as a stand-in for the son of Amun to reconsecrate the union with the queen in the birth chamber of Luxor, witnessed by the priests in the seclusion of the holy of holies. The carnal ceremonies and the various images associated with Luxor flow through time, linguistically evolving into a word we know today. In Latin, "luxuria" means rankness or offensiveness, which morphed into the French "luxure" (unrestrained sexual pursuits, lasciviousness, debauchery, and perversity). In old English "luxurie" originally meant adultery, finally giving way to the modern term luxury, ultimately associated with the meaning of opulence. Even Cambyses II, wasn't immune to luxure as he married his half-sisters in Egypt. It didn't end well for Cambyses II. Herodotus chronicles that he died from gangrene due to a self-inflicted wound on his thigh from his own sword as he mounted his horse.

As I approach the entrance to Luxor, the magnificent modern structure appears to be living up to the enigmatic derivation of its name. A series of glass doors magically open releasing the cool air into the warm desert night as I walk through the threshold. The splendor of the inside of the pyramid lies before me—a vision of bright, flashing brilliance in a huge hall that rises more than twenty stories. Buzzers, bells, whistles, and jingles create a hodgepodge of grotesque noise that creates a feeling of inexplicable excitement and arousal. Mysterious Egyptian hieroglyphs adorn the walls and numerous obelisks are spread symmetrically on the sides of a palm tree-lined waterway that runs down the center of the grand atrium. A sarcophagus stands menacingly between each obelisk. The casino floor is relatively empty given the late hour, as several women of the evening stroll around looking for a quick fare.

As I walk through the casino floor I can see an elevated and roped off area with high-limit slot machines. The ropes suggest that this section is off-limits, forbidden, which intrigues me even more. What can be off-limits in the Luxor? As I walk up the steps to the cordoned-off entrance, I am met by a man with a dark complexion wearing a black suit. "Your player's card sir?" he requests as he says something inaudible into the microphone on his lapel, which is met with a nod as he tugs on his earpiece. "I'm sorry, I must have left it in my jacket pocket. I just returned from a costume party," I reply in a conciliatory tone. As he unhooks the red velvet rope from the chrome fitting to grant me entrance, he smiles and says, "It is no matter, Mr. Smith, we have been expecting you. We have been trying to reach you. You forgot your player's card in the slot machine in the corner. We have not let anyone else play. It is just as you left it." I thank him and walk to the back corner of the room. "That's strange," I think. I don't remember ever being here before.

The high-limit room is illuminated only by a gas-lamp torchiere and the luminous glow of the slot machines themselves. There is an empty bar in the center tended by a lone female bartender who is preoccupied polishing crystal glasses with a rag. As I approach, she sees me and smiles. The bartender is dressed in a long, white, tube-shaped, linen gown that hugs her shapely figure. She isn't wearing a bra; her dark pointed nipples are visibly protruding through the white woven linen fabric. She wears a decorative shoulder strap with a matching golden arm bracelet that extends midway up her forearm. Her black hair is neatly braided with golden beads, resembling Cleopatra—at least the Hollywood versions I have seen on television. The bar is surrounded on four sides by large sandstone pillars inscribed with hieroglyphics that rise up to the ceiling, culminating in lotus flowers painted in vibrant blue and yellow hues. The bar is a smooth, black obsidian surface resting on a sandstone base surrounded by inverted pyramid stools with square red cushions. A nip of scotch should take the edge off as I try and figure out what the hell is going on. I walk up to the bar.

"Good evening Mr. Smith, will you be having the usual, Macallan 18, neat?" the barmaid asks in a familiar tone. "Atossa and Roxane are waiting for you by your favorite slot machine. Will they be joining you this evening as usual—should I add them to your tab, sir?" she asks in a tone that implies familiarity.

"Who are Atossa and Roxane? My tab?" I ponder. I am not in the habit to turn down female company or decline credit extended at a bar. Oddly enough, I peer down at the name tag on the bartender's dress and, sure enough, in black and white it says, "Cleopatra." Maybe I've been here before.

"Absolutely. Please put the lovely ladies on my tab—and yes to the Macallan neat—a liberal pour, please." Cleopatra seems amused at my response, giggling as she reaches over to the top shelf and pours the Highland scotch. "What does she know that I don't," I think.

"Yes, of course, Mr. Smith. Good luck this evening, sir," she says as she carefully places a cocktail napkin under the crystal glass tinted with the amber nectar and hands it to me with ceremonial precision.

I take a quick sip, and the liquid eases down my throat and warms my gullet. I walk past several banks of slot machines to the farthest corner. As I walk down the row of slot machines there aren't any more gas lamps, only the glow from the machines' lighting making a path like a runway leading straight to the sisters. I see two female shapes hold-ing v-stemmed cocktails, laughing as they converse. They are sitting on opposite stools with a towering, illuminated slot machine situated in between. I could hear the machine beckon in a familiar voice, "Can you guess my riddle?" As I approach, I clearly see the outline of the machine and moniker. "It can't be," I say to myself. I guess my four-legged friend isn't going to let it go. Atossa and Roxane are sitting opposite the Sphinx 4D slot. The flashing lights from the display gradually provide clarity as I near. I can't believe the similarity. The sisters look virtually identical. Their skin is fair, with long, dark eyebrows framing mesmerizing brown eyes. The sisters are wearing gold loop earrings and simple bronze tiaras with a single leaf extending downward to the bridge of the nose. Their heads are wrapped in rich, scarlet scarves which flow down to their matching red and turquoise beaded gowns. I greet them. However, they hardly seem to notice as I sit down between them facing the Sphinx 4D slot. The sisters continue speaking to each other as each places a hand on one of my legs. After an awkward few minutes, Atossa looks up.

"Time Smith, we are so glad you finally came back. We have been waiting for what seems like an eternity for you to continue playing our game. We always play together, but never alone," Atossa says as she looks directly at Roxane, smiling.

"Yes, Time Smith, we were so worried that you might have forgotten all about Luxor and our pleasures. We thought that you were never coming back." Roxane chimes in as she strengthens her grip on my right leg and slowly sips her cocktail.

"Oh, our dear brother has probably been worried sick wondering where we are. We were having so much fun, we had to wait for you to return to finish the game," Atossa says with a smirk.

"Forget our dear brother and husband, Atossa. He is such a bore. The King is always too busy to satisfy us both. I doubt he has even realized we are missing from the southern sanctuary," Roxane says as she continues stroking my thigh in rhythm with Atossa.

Atossa reaches over and grabs her sister's hand by the wrist and draws a circle in midair, changing the digital 3D screen from day to night. The sisters then draw a heart together in front of the screen, which appears on the display, as both smile and turn toward me, blowing me a simultaneous kiss. "Tonight is your lucky night, Time Smith," they say in unison. Their hands part, each finding a place on my bare inner thigh that they caress in harmony. The Sphinx isn't amused, and is maybe even a little jealous, as he calls out again in a monotone voice, still prodding me for an answer, "Can you guess my riddle?"

I glance at my player's card snuggly inserted in the machine. Sure enough, the black card has gold lettering with "Time Smith" embossed on the outer edge. The bottom corner of the screen shows my remaining credits from whenever I was last here or there, or anywhere, or nowhere. "Ladies, would you mind doing the honors?" I ask, looking up at each of the sisters. Atossa takes Roxane's hand from my thigh and together they press the spin button. The machine whirls as the spheres and symbols dance across the lines to the mysterious music that booms out of the speakers. My excitement grows. The music stops—and then abrupt silence. The sisters keep pressing the button, bringing the Sphinx back to life, while intently looking at me and the screen. I look down for but a brief moment as I take a sip of my drink and then, suddenly, the noise is deafening as the light flashes on top of the slot machine. The sisters jump up and down in excitement. It looks like they hit a jackpot, or maybe I did. Who knows?

The sisters hug and kiss each other for an uncomfortably long time, seeming to forget all about the jackpot and me. After a few minutes, the man in the dark suit who greeted me at the high-limit entrance walks over. He inserts a key into the machine, resetting it. The light stops flashing and the noise subsides. "Congratulations, Mr. Smith, you hit the Pharaoh's Jackpot." He pauses for a moment, listening intently as he tugs on his earpiece and says, "Roger that," as he hands me a pen and clipboard with a form. "Please fill this out and sign this for tax reporting, Mr. Smith." I take the pen and fill in my particulars, signing the document in a robotic trance without reading it as the thrill overtakes me. "I have never won anything in my life," I say to myself as I hand the clipboard back. I suddenly realize that they will be sending my 1099-Misc. tax form to Time Smith c/o Dr. Haram Udaza, Aduat Asylum, Confinement RM#4. The casino didn't seem to mind. "Excellent. Your winnings may be picked up at the cage at your leisure, Mr. Smith. I am also pleased to inform you that the hotel is comping you a two-night stay in the Pharaoh's Suite. Here is your room key, sir. The elevator bank to the luxury suites in the south sanctuary tower is located behind the bar," the man in the dark suit says as he hands me the black plastic room key.

I thank him and look over at Atossa and Roxane, who appear to be stimulated from the celebration, impatiently staring at me as a desired instrument to help carry on their intimate soiree. "Ladies, shall we have a nightcap in the Pharaoh's suite?" I ask, already knowing the answer. Atossa and Roxane each put an arm around my waist. As we meander past the bar, looking for the elevators, Cleopatra's eyes meet mine. I could barely hear her voice as we pass. She mutters, "Heavy is the heart of the self-indulgent, Mr. Smith." What kind of bartender advice is that anyway? "Well, this isn't Weight Watchers," I snap back. Atossa and Roxane reply in unison as their hands move lower, firmly squeezing my buttocks, "No, it isn't, Time Smith." After stumbling down the hall, we arrive at the elevator and walk in. My room key fits nicely in the slot as the "PH" lights up on the panel and the elevator doors close. The elevator ascends swiftly, and as we rise I feel the pit of my stomach dropping.

Atossa and Roxane kneel down, kissing each other on the mouth with fervor while stroking me as the floors pass by until a chime rings out and the doors open. Atossa and Roxane stand up, and we walk into the darkness, together.

The top floor of the south sanctuary seems to extend beyond the blackness into a vast open space. The Pharaoh's suite appears to encompass the entire floor. The room is divided by a series of three massive Nubian-sandstone pillars resting on hand-cut stone tile, offset in a staggered pattern throughout the entire room. The walls are also made of beige sandstone with reliefs depicting ancient Egyptian mythology, including the divine birth of Amenhotep III. The hieroglyphs explain how the finger of god touched the queen, filling her body with dew, memorializing the moment of Amenhotep's divine conception in 1386 BC. Divine conception seems to be quite the rage in antiquity but hasn't caught on yet in the modern age. I guess the brass is still working on it. The other reliefs depict the divine filiation of the Pharaohs. Leave it to Vegas—looks like an exact replica of the Birth Chamber located in the Egyptian Temple of Luxor. This is the innermost chamber, the holiest of holies, the only reason Luxor was built in the first place. A sacred room for carnal unification of the divine and mortal, where you walk in a mere mortal king or queen and leave as a god or goddess claiming dominion over all of the known world. "Sounds grand, but at this moment I would settle for the company of the sisters and a free breakfast buffet in the morning," I think. I told Ahura he had the wrong guy in Lawn & Garden.

The entire walls are filled with hieroglyphic carvings, most too faded or cracked to read. There is no visible ceiling. Only darkness overhangs above the top of the pillars. As a slight breeze drifts down from above, fresh air swirls through the room, causing the gas lamps to flicker and cast uneven, swaying shadows on the walls. The light from the lamps reveals an oversized circular raised wooden bed in the center of the room. The ebony frame is covered in gold and decorated with ornate patterns of jewels. It is fitted with a large round mattress covered in silk linen. Oversized feather-filled pillows lay on top of the mattress—truly an alter fit for the gods. Atossa and Roxane waste no time disrobing each other. The nude outline of their firm forms is visible on the walls as they scuttle across the room and embrace on the alter moaning as they seek a reaffirmation of their own divinity. I guess there isn't a mini-bar or a telephone to call room service to get a drink before rejuvenating my own divinity. Didn't they mention their brother, ahh… husband, is roaming around the southern sanctuary somewhere? "Time Smith, come. We long for the touch of a man," Atossa says, and Roxane sighs in agreement. "Be there in a jiff," I reply as I decide to think this one through for a moment.

According to Ahura, I am supposed to be trying to find Spenta to help her and the Atlantean rebellion rise up against Angra and her brother Aka to secure space-time and bring peace back to Atlantis. Ahura never mentioned anything about the killer Sphinx, Vegas or the X-rated Bobbsey twins. Neither did he specify a deadline, nor even tell me how to find Spenta. Perhaps I have ample time for an abbreviated carnal rejuvenation ceremony, a few games of Pai Gow, and the buffet? What about Kathy and Sarah? Ahura said they exist forever in the images of space-time, their thotons buzzing and humming in the univers-es. If I can get the Chronos, maybe I can still go back and save them, even though Ahura said it wasn't a good idea.

Kathy would definitely not be on board with this god/goddess, car-nal-reunification thing. However, it could be perceived as a sort of an-thropological study lending insight into achieving a better understand-ing of ancient ritual. Good luck selling that idea to Kathy. How the hell would I explain this to Sarah, if they can see me wherever they are buzzing and humming? What happens in Vegas stays in Vegas…Oh, never mind, that is just a thoton image created by R&R Partners.

"Ladies—ummuhm… I'm not feeling terribly well. Why don't you continue without me. I'm going to go back down to the bar for a drink," I stutter.

Atossa and Roxane immediately stop and stand up. "Time Smith, get over here now! You will satisfy the sisters. We have been waiting for you such a long time to fulfill the prophecy," Atossa says as she and Roxane start slinking toward me. "We shall never be free of our brother until you lay with us," Roxane says indignantly. "You must sleep with us," they clamor together.

Atossa walks behind me, pushing as Roxane grabs my arm, pulling me onto the silk alter. The sisters are stronger than their petite feminine figures suggest, catching me by surprise. I am thrown down on the bed, landing on my back with a thud. Roxane quickly straddles my lower extremities while Atossa lays on top of my chest, holding me down, and reaches for a pillow to cover my face. I do my best to resist as Roxane pushes my toga aside and squirms on top of me, seeking a mount. I look over to the wall and can see an oddly shaped shadow appear. It looks like a cross with two semicircles suspended on either side. The horizontal line of the cross teeters up and down, seemingly trying to balance the black semicircles. It looks like a scale. Roxane moans, and I can feel the wet warmth as she lands squarely on her perch. I can feel my heart racing and beating faster as she rhythmically grinds back and forth.

What is that on the wall? I can hear my heartbeat pounding in my head louder and louder until the noise is almost unbearable. I can't catch my breath. Time seems to stop as I gasp for air. A red beating heart appears in flames, resting on one of the dark semicircles on the image of the shadow scale, tipping it out of balance. Ostrich feathers fly into the air as I continue to struggle with Atossa, trying to remove the pillow from my face. I can feel Roxane nearing climax as her muscles convulse around me. I can't breathe. I have to get Atossa off of me. I briefly see the shadow of a feather floating down onto the semicircle opposite my beating heart and the scale tilting towards equilibrium. I can't breathe as Atossa more forcefully pushes the pillow down. There is no more air in my lungs as I suffocate, gasping in futility. As I release, Roxane shrieks, "Yes!" her voice echoing through the chamber. Atossa relaxes her arms and tosses the pillow aside. As I look up, the last thing I see as my eyes roll back is a green man with a beard dressed in cloth bandages wrapped around his legs. He stands tall, intermingled with the shadows on the wall wearing a white crown decorated in ostrich feathers and holding a crook and flail—Osiris. He looks directly at me, "So it is Time Smith. You are forever judged."

My temples throb as a sharp pain runs down my spine, I can hear the constant tone ringing in my head. Nestpa's voice calls out, "Dr. Udaza we are losing him. He is flatlining." I look over briefly at the wall and observe a fleeting, blurry image of the four canopic jars. They are all full, and my blood stains the edges of each jar.

"It is of no consequence, the procedure is complete. It is an astounding success. We have captured his thotonic image library prior to natural transmigration and extracted it onto the crystal. Mak will be pleased, I will call him and let him know. Nestpa, please prepare the crystal for delivery along with Dr. Smith's notes," Haram says with a sense of contentment and pride. The voices fade into oblivion as they continue their banter.

And then—nothing.

I can feel the damp air rush back into my lungs. As my vision is slowly restored, a hazy image of the three pillars rising in the Birth Chamber of Luxor reemerges. I am lying on the wet ebony bed surrounded by a group of ten monks. Half are wearing black, hooded robes and the others are wearing white. Each has a sheathed sword at his side. They are standing at the foot of the bed, forming a semicircle. None of them make eye contact as they stare at the stone floor and chant in unison. The low, methodical tone of a forgotten language echoes in the chamber, raising the hair on the back of my neck. The gas lamps are no longer present. Oil lamps burn instead, hurling dark smoke into the upper recess of the chamber. The sisters are gone. As I throw my legs over the edge of the bed to stand, a female figure approaches from behind the hooded cluster. The woman is wearing a flowing white toga that exposes a green ouroboros tattoo encircling her navel. Her long auburn hair cascades down from a golden headband, gracefully covering her shoulders and muscular back. She is brandishing a shiny sword with an emerald-laden handle. Her dark eyes meet my gaze.

"Time Smith arise. I am Spenta Mainyu, the harbinger of all that is good—daughter of Angra, sister to Aka, Princess and true heir to the Atlantean throne," she calls out as she beckons me to come closer. I stand up and slowly walk over to where she is standing. "We have been in Egypt far too long awaiting your arrival in Luxor on this promised day, as foretold. We don't have much time. We must get you to the sacred Hall of Records, and you must retrieve the Chronos, because that is your destiny. Cambyses's soldiers are everywhere. My father and brother have sent the Interloper to this

time to kill you and put an end to the prophecy that is the last vestige of my people's hope of freedom from Angra's tyranny. There is great peril. We must move swiftly." she says in a foreboding tone. What is this prophecy? It would be nice if someone let me in on it. I seem to be doing pretty well without this Chronos thing that everyone keeps talking about. If you think about it, I hit the Pharaoh's jackpot, ditched the oversexed psycho sisters (avoiding death by erotic asphyxiation), had my heart weighed after dying on the underworld's operating table, traveled over twenty-five hundred years into the past—and am still here to talk about it. Why press my luck? If I can only figure out a way to zap myself out of here, the only Atlantis I care about right now is the resort in the Bahamas. Maybe if I think hard enough of images of beach, sand, and sun....

"Move, Time Smith!" Spenta orders as she raises her sword above her head. Looks like I don't have much of a choice. I can either end up a shish kabob at the end of Spenta's blade or get filleted by one of Cambyses's soldiers. Wait till he finds out about his sisters, uhh...wives. Atossa and Roxane didn't seem like the kind that keep secrets. The sisters are probably having dinner with Cambyses right now, telling the story of their Las Vegas Luxor romp just to get a rise out of him. If that doesn't get me on the most-wanted list in Egypt, desecrating the Pharaoh's personal pleasure palace probably will. Clearly, my thotonic image is still swirling away, so Osiris evidently didn't seem to have any issues with my unintended, pseudo-sexual, anthropological experiment. To be honest, since the ceremony I've been feeling rather rejuvenated, immortal, and godlike. Maybe the Pharaohs were onto something. "Move!" Spenta insists again. I follow her out of the Birth Chamber and through the doorway into the hall. The entourage of monks follows closely behind. So much for trying to ditch the lot of them.

Spenta moves swiftly through the temple compound, avoiding the soldiers, as I follow closely behind. The unlucky few that cross our path, Spenta makes quick work of—slicing and dicing with her Atlantean blade. We finally arrive at an opening to the outside of the Luxor Temple complex. I can see the pale moon and stars in the night sky above the tall palm trees that sway in the gentle breeze. The Nile River flows on my left. I stop and stare in utter disbelief. Not again— he is just not going to let this whole riddle business go. Over a thousand sphinxes line the miles of road between Luxor and the Temple of Karnak. If each has a riddle, I'll be here forever. A vision of the future unfolds in my mind as I see the green and white street sign announcing "The Avenue of the Sphinxes" and the tourists lined up to look at the Pharaoh's statuary zoo while buying trinkets and shish kebabs from the street vendors. Spenta continues moving stealthily into the night with purpose, appearing to have a final destination in mind.

"Where are we going?" I ask, as if I actually expect a comprehensible response.

"The Hall of Records, Time Smith," she says quietly in an exasperated tone. "Keep quiet until we get there." We continue bobbing and weaving past each of the sphinx statues until we stop at one as we near Karnak. The sphinxes that line the road are much smaller than their father in Giza and quieter than their cousin in Vegas. They are nearly twelve feet high from the pedestal base to the apex of their heads and fifteen feet in length. Some have the head of a ram, a symbol of Amun instead the head of a man. Spenta places the palm of her hand methodically on the middle of the pedestal until she locates a slot and then quickly thrusts her sword all the way into the base of the statue. Using the handle of the sword, she bends over and with both hands pushes on the hilt with all her strength. Her well-developed arms flex as she grunts and heaves. The statue slowly rotates, revealing an underground stairwell. "Welcome to the Hall of Records. After you, Time Smith," Spenta says while drawing her sword out of the stone.

CHAPTER SIX

ATLANTIS

*T*HE NARROW ENTRYWAY IS ILLUMINATED by only the moon. I follow the steps downward, feeling my way through the twists and turns of the stairwell. As I descend, the moonlight vanishes entirely, and it is pitch dark. The walls are cool and damp as I slowly climb down, feeling the smooth stone with my outreached hands. I can hear Spenta and the monks' footsteps paces behind me. "Quicker, we must hurry Time Smith, it will be light in a few hours and you have much to learn," Spenta says in a maternal tone. The steps are unevenly carved in the sandstone so that I must find my footing, cautious not to fall and plummet into the darkness. After walking down what feels like several stories below ground, the descent ends as the stairway yields to a flat path covered with what I assume to be pebbles. The crunching noise of the procession trudging through the cavern is unnerving. After what seems like an eternity in the dark, I can see a faint, colored light shining through the entryway ahead.

As I approach the opening, my eyes adjust to the light and I can see the pathway below. What I thought were pebbles are actually bones, piles of them. Before I can open my mouth to speak, Spenta's voice fills my head, "These are the remains of the Pharaoh's workers who constructed Karnak and Luxor; many have been lost building monuments to kings and gods, all eventually fated to disappear in the sands of time." "Telepathy," I say to myself—or did I imagine hearing that? Dr. Richard's voice also chimes in, filling my head, "Man fears time and time fears the pyramids. The Pharaohs were stuck in the first two behavioral states—controlling and resisting, resurrecting the Pyramids in a misguided, vain effort to outlast time itself. Unlike the Pharaohs, you must not perceive time in the first or second behavioral states View time in the fourth state—flowing. Do not resist it. Make it your pet, like the Sphinx. Let time carry you on its thotonic waves to whatever distant shore you want to visit."

Their answers are truly enlightening. I just wish Dr. Richard and Spenta would ask before popping into my stream of consciousness. My attention shifts to a partially mummified figure that becomes visible standing on the right side of the opening. His two green hands extend outward from the bandages, holding onto a crook, a flail, and a scepter. A menat necklace made of beads dangles over his chest and onto his back. He wears a side lock of hair and a beard. "Spenta, who or what is that?" I ask. "His name is Khonsu. He is the son of Amun and Mat, the third part of the trinity. He is the god of the moon. His name is translated in your tongue as the 'Traveler.'" The ancient Atlanteans placed him here to guard the Hall of Records. All humans and Atlanteans of impure spirit are forbidden entrance because he only allows those worthy of dreaming to pass. You have nothing to worry about, Time Smith, because you have Atlantean blood in your veins. You are a descendent of both sides of the semicircle," Spenta says. I hope Spenta is right—this Khonsu fellow doesn't look very friendly as I approach. I walk right past the sedentary statue, ignoring its ghoulish, frozen stare.

As I leave the narrow passage, the path opens up into an expansive, cavernous dome naturally formed out of sandstone, the result of water erosion over time and what remains of an ancient Egyptian quarry. The pathway ends at the edge of a plateau overlooking a deep pool of opaque, dark-blue water that abruptly turns into a clear turquoise in the shallows on the opposite shore. Because there is no other apparent origin, the water appears to be fed from an underground spring . The natural luminescence that is the source of the light is a cluster of hundreds of crystals in the shallow section on the far side of the pool—each a different color, shape and size. Spenta nears and whispers to me, "Behold the sacred Pool of Dreams, Time Smith, it requires only a small push and a leap to wade in its waters." Before I have time to internalize Spenta's words and the images I am seeing, I can feel her muscular hands on my back as she shoves me off the ledge. Looks like I am getting the full spa treatment today, whether I want it or not. The water is deep. My feet do not touch the bottom of the pool as I torpedo downward. The cold water shocks for but a moment as I am fully submerged and slowly float back to the top. A second splash echoes in the hall as Spenta jumps off the ledge into the dark-blue waters. The monks remain at the plateau, standing guard and methodically chanting in the same strange tongue that I had heard before at Luxor. Their song fills the cavern as the crystals react to the harmonic sound by glowing even brighter. The colored light dances on the domed ceiling and sandstone walls as the waves ripple through the pool while Spenta and I swim toward the distant crystal-lined shore.

I can feel the sandstone floor under my feet as the ground rises. The water recedes just below my knees as I stand. The crystals range in size from a few feet, up to perhaps twenty or thirty feet tall. The circumference of the larger crystals matches that of a mature redwood tree—the smaller ones I can easily grasp in my hand. The largest of the crystals is a translucent amethyst obelisk situated in the center of the cluster. I am stricken with awe at the natural beauty of the underground crystal garden. I look over to Spenta to ask how this is possible. Before I can open my mouth to form the question, Spenta looks at me and says, "Yes, it is beautiful, Time Smith, but more importantly, you are looking at the entire thotonic image history of the Atlantean race from past to present. As new thotonic images emerge, the crystals in the garden grow. The planet Atlantis is the first in the oldest universe created by Ahura Mazda, both the beginning and end of space-time." That is a lot to digest. "How did the crystals end up under the Sphinx in Egypt?" I think.

Spenta, looks at me with an eerie sense of understanding and continues to explain, "In order to colonize, our scientists developed the Chronos—what you would call a QTIP with a mandate to seek out other intelligent life forms in other carbon-based universes capable of sustaining life. Atlantis intended to provide other planets with our technology to facilitate the harmonization of existence in the everlasting thoton image Ahura, first conceived. Angra, my father, grew enraged because he wanted to use the power of the Chronos to conquer all other known worlds to make them subservient to the technologically-superior, Atlantean-universal Empire. Atlas, the most prominent Atlantean scientist, searched all of the universes that are capable of supporting carbon-based life. The first one he found was yours. Of all the galaxies in your universe, the planet Earth of the Milky Way appeared to be a nearly identical blue sphere with a chemical and biological makeup similar to the planet Atlantis. It has nearly the same mass, comparable gravity, and a similar atmosphere; and it circles a single yellow sun. The planet was the ideal choice to develop the universal colonization program.

So it came to pass over nine thousand seventy-five Earth years ago that a small group led by Atlas was sent to Earth. Because his scientific research led to the development of the Chronos, Atlas reminds me very much of you. He was a great Atlantean scientist. The island colony on Earth, your Atlantic ocean, and the Atlas Mountains—all bear his name and the name of our planet, his namesake. In your planet's mythology, Atlas is depicted as holding up the celestial heavens for eternity as he is spared by the Olympians when the Titans fell in the Battle of the Gods. In antiquity, he was credited with inventing the first celestial sphere. The colony he founded flourished for many millennia, growing powerful until contact was lost and it simply disappeared." "Where did the Atlantis colony go? What happened?" I wonder.

Spenta pauses for a brief moment, probably reading my thoughts, and after a brief pause, speaks, "When the rebellion against Angra broke out, my brother Aka shared the same thotonic image of the future as my father and decided to join him rather than support the rebellion against his imperialistic ambitions. Aka and my father intended to use the technological power of the Chronos to achieve Atlantean-universal domination. I led the rebellion against Angra and Aka to no avail. When it appeared all was lost, I used the Chronos to flee Atlantis with the remnants of the rebellion, only ten warrior monks remaining from an army of thousands, and the crystals that contain all recorded history of the planet Atlantis and foretell its emerging thotonic future. I brought them here to protect the thoton images that collectively constitute our civilization's identity. If I had left them, Angra would be able to corrupt the thoton images, thereby distorting history and forever changing the Atlantean people's self-identity to serve his evil purpose. I hid them here with the Chronos and the original Ancient crystals from the lost Atlantis Earth colony. The rest you can see for yourself, Time Smith. Simply think of what you wish to learn and the crystal will call to you. Just touch it and the thoton image will appear to you. Be warned that we have only a few hours, but in order to retrieve the Chronos, you must see the past to create the future. Hurry!"

"What do I already know about Atlantis?" I think to myself. Pretty much anything and everything there is to know comes from the ancient

Greek philosopher, Plato. He references Atlantis in what was intended to be a triad of dialogues: the first *Timaeus* written circa 360 BC,
which is later followed by *Critias* and the ill-fated dialogue, *Hermocrates*.
Hermocrates was never started and *Critias* was never completed by Plato
prior to his death. I always presumed that the fictional dialogues were
intended to explore the interaction of ancient Athens with other nation
states. The dialogues are a unique treatise on international relations
and political philosophy from antiquity. They are also the only original
written references to the lost city of Atlantis that are known to exist
in historical documents. I always presumed, until my bizarre encoun-
ters with Ahura and Spenta that the story of Atlantis is nothing more
than a parable created by Plato to illustrate the hazards of moral decline combined with imperialistic military ambitions (nation-building).
Plato creates and destroys the entire thotonic Atlantean civilization just
to make this very point. Aristotle is said to have joked that Plato con-
jures nations out of thin air and then destroys them.

Plato also uses the Atlantis parable to further examine the idea of
the deteriorating life cycle of the nation-state that he proposes in *The
Republic*. In the story presented by Plato, Atlantis is an aggressor of
ancient Athens. As punishment for its imperialistic ambitions after a
thwarted invasion, the gods destroy the island nation, sinking it to the
bottom of the sea to disappear from history forever. Not quite. The
thoton image Plato created of Atlantis is still buzzing and humming—
capturing the imagination thousands of years after he forged it, the rele-
vance of the image unwavering throughout time. I would be completely
unfamiliar with the subject of Atlantis had I not stumbled upon Plato's
dialogues due to the exquisite early explanation of photonics he provides in 360 BC. Dr. Richard calls it "the embryo of illumination." Dr.
Richard regularly quotes the dialogues in the Red Dungeon, astounded
by Plato's innate ability to perceive the mysteries of the universe without

the aid of the modern scientific tools and technology we have at our disposal at DARPA. Like Pythagoras and Einstein, Plato also perceives our big bang universe to be spherical in shape, which he states in the dialogues. How did Plato, like Pythagoras, intuitively understand this more than two millennia ago?

In the *Timaeus* dialogue Plato says, "First, then, the gods, imitating the spherical shape of the universe, enclosed the two divine courses in a spherical body," making reference to the eyes in the head. His detailed description of photonics, associating light with fire (energy) and the understanding that the nature of images is external and internal is truly remarkable: "And of the organs they first contrived the eyes to give light, and the principle according to which they were inserted was as follows: So much of fire as would not burn, but gave a gentle light, they formed into a substance akin to the *light of every-day life*; and the *pure fire* which is within us and related thereto they made to flow through the eyes in a stream smooth and dense, compressing the whole eye, and especially the center part, so that it kept out everything of a coarser nature, and allowed to pass only this pure element. When the light of day surrounds the stream of vision, then like falls upon like, and they coalesce, and one body is formed by natural affinity in the line of vision, wherever the light that falls from within meets with an external object. And the whole stream of vision, being similarly affected in virtue of similarity, diffuses the motions of what it touches or what touches it over the whole body, until they reach the soul, causing that perception which we call sight."

Dr. Richard is amazed that Plato perceived internal thotonic images, as well as external photon image processing, as continuous (contrary to the current understanding of Quantum Mechanics that limits quantum action to $\hbar$ [h-bar], Plank's constant divided by 2π). The value of h-bar is determined by the finite difference in energy levels in atoms. Its value is this energy divided by the emitted photon's temporal frequency.

It is also equal to the energy uncertainty multiplied by the temporal uncertainty in a quantum-squeezing experiment involving pixel values. In fact, some researchers say that it may not be an absolute value in the universe. Dr. Richard explained to me that h-bar can be related to the absolute minimum shutter speed between images that some futuristic image processing machine might be able to achieve. Dr. Richard calls this the "shutter speed of the universe." In his work at DARPA, he expands the concepts of quantum mechanics by changing the wave function to a more expanded image wave function. In this way, we can relate external image pixels to internal (brain) image processing, which he calls thotonic image tixel processing. Dr. Richard also describes the probability that h-bar could be zero, at least in a fictional universe.

Plato's light of every-day life (the photonic external image) and the "pure fire" (thotonic internal image) he references in his dialogue appeared to him as continuous because he had no knowledge of h-bar. The duality that Plato perceived in the differentiation of the internal and external images is paramount to Dr. Richard's work on the QTP at DARPA. Dr. Richard theorized that Schrödinger's equations of probability amplitude waves could be interpreted as probability amplitude image waves and applied to external photonic images, as well as extended to describing internal thotonic probability amplitude image waves. Dr. Richard's extended equations based on his theory operate dualistically. The intertwining of the external photonic and internal thotonic images capture the totality of consciousness, the interaction of at a minimum one photonic and one thotonic probability amplitude image wave. The interaction of the image waves creates our sense of reality, consciousness. The duality Plato perceived based on his current reality at the time he wrote *Timaeus* was possibly influenced by his perception of the thotonic image of the Pythagorean Theory of Opposites. Or could it simply be a photonic image that forged the document?

Why did Plato choose Atlantis as his doomed, fictional nation-state—a thoton image floating around ancient Greece waiting to be perceived? Perhaps, he just made it up. Maybe he got it from someone else? Maybe the answer is in the story itself. In Plato's dialogues, Critias says that he had heard the story of Atlantis from his grandfather, who had learned it from the Athenian statesman Solon, who lived between 638 and 558 BC, nearly three centuries prior to Plato's lifetime. Solon supposedly learned it from an ancient Egyptian priest who claimed that it occurred nine thousand years prior to the time he relayed the tale to Solon. The provenance of the tale leaves much to be desired. Why did Plato go through all the trouble to include such detail regarding the origin of the story? One of the smallest crystals in the garden starts glowing with a blue intensity. The images it has to convey must not be from that long ago. I kneel to touch it and give the thoton image garden a whirl. "Start small," I think, kneeling down in the water and placing my hand around the tiny obelisk. I can clearly see the image of an Egyptian priest, seated with Pythagoras and Solon in the company of Pharaoh Amasis II, carrying on a conversation regarding the Island of Atlantis. Pythagoras is listening intently. He writes on the papyrus with a reed brush dipped in a red solution as the priest relays his account of the history of the island of Atlantis. The thoton image quickly fades as I release my grasp. I can't understand the spoken tongue, yet I can capture the meaning of the conversation. "Not bad for my first try," I think as I look at Spenta, who nods in agreement.

It is recorded by Antiphon, that the Pharoah Amasis II was so intrigued by Pythagoras that he taught him to speak Egyptian. Pythagoras was allowed to study with the priests in the ancient city of Thebes in Egypt, and was the only foreigner ever allowed the honor of participating in the ancient Egyptian worship ceremonies. If Solon had been the primary source of the Atlantis story recorded in the *Timaeus* and *Critias* dialogues, he would've had to have recounted it to Critias's grandfather prior to his death in 558 BC. Critias died in 403 BC, nearly forty-three years before Plato wrote *Timaeus* and the even older, un-completed *Critias* dialogue. If in his youth Plato had heard such a fantastic tale directly from Critias, it is surprising that he chose not to write about it earlier. Plato would have been in his early twenties at the time Critias died at the age of fifty-seven. Plato waited over forty years to recount the Atlantean tale, one of the greatest mysteries in all recorded history. Perhaps he wasn't the original author of the *Timaeus* and *Critias*. There are many similarities to Pythagorean ideas in Plato's writings, so many—that some of the Pythagoreans claimed that Plato had plagiarized documents.

The answer may be found with the successor to Pythagoras—Philolaus of Croton, a Greek philosopher and scientist who lived from 470 to 385 BC (born a hundred years after Pythagoras), a contemporary of Socrates. He is the first Pythagorean credited with writing a book, *On Nature*, which was the primary source for Aristotle's description of Pythagorean philosophy. Perhaps he had other Pythagorean works in his possession that were destroyed. In a letter, Plato instructed Dion to purchase the Pythagorean books (plural). Hermippus recounts that, according to one writer, Plato went to the court of Dionysius in Sicily and acquired the Pythagorean books from Philolaus's relatives for forty Alexandrian minae, and from them copied the *Timaeus*. There are other claims that Plato secured the release of one of Philolaus's pupils in exchange for the book. There are multiple conflicting thoton images of the origination of the *Timaeus* dialogue. Plato also may have appropriated the Pythagorean ideas concerning transmigration of the soul. In his "Seventh Letter," Plato mentions Archytas, a student of Philolaus and an influential Pythagorean scholar, as a friend who could have been the source of many of his seemingly Pythagorean ideas. In the end, who painted the picture is irrelevant. Everything is after all a copy of a copy; photonic and thotonic images meshed together, spinning throughout space-time, creating our perceptions. Regardless of whether the retelling of the Egyptian priest's story (if there even was an Egyptian priest) originated from Pythagoras or Solon, or was simply created by Plato's imagination—the thotonic image of the lost island of Atlantis stands unblemished through the waves of time for all to see, wonder about, and learn her lessons.

If the veracity of the Egyptian priest's story is to be believed, the *Timaeus* and *Critias* provide specific references to the lost island's geographical location. Given Ahura's story in the garden, my Atlantean traveling companions, and my recent blue crystal experience, I am inclined to take it all at face value (at least in this thotonic universe). Where was the lost island of Atlantis located? The *Timaeus* and *Critias* dialogues give us several clues. The *Critias* states, "And he named them all; the eldest, who was the first king, he named Atlas, and after him, the whole island and the ocean were called Atlantic. To his twin brother, who was born after him, and obtained as his lot the extremity of the island towards the Pillars of Heracles, facing the country which is now called the region of Gades in that part of the world, he gave the name which in the Hellenic language is Eumelus, in the language of the country which is named after him, Gadeirus."

Gadir, which is considered by many to be the oldest inhabited city in Western Europe, was founded by the Phoenicians. Archaeological evidence of the Phoenicians' existence in Gadir dates back to 3,100 BC. The ancient city was located on the island of Erytheia, northwest of Gibraltar, at the top of the Iberian Peninsula. In ancient Greek, the land was called Gádeira. In Latin, the city was known as Gādēs and is the current location of modern-day Cádiz. According to Plato, Gadir is named after Atlas's twin brother. The *Critias* alludes to the Pillars of Hercules as a landmark and describes the island's land mass: "This great island lay over against the Pillars of Heracles, in extent greater than Libya and Asia put together, and was the passage to other islands and to a great ocean of which the Mediterranean sea was only the harbor; and within the Pillars the empire of Atlantis reached in Europe to Tyrrhenia and in Libya to Egypt. This mighty power was arrayed against Egypt and Hellas and all the countries bordering on the Mediterranean." Most of the ancient Greek writers would have placed the Pillars of Hercules at the Straits of Gibraltar, but the Iberians and Libyans held that the true Pillars of Hercules were at Cadiz, as the ancient Greek poet Pindar agrees. A lost passage is quoted by Strabo in which Pindar refers to the Pillars of Hercules as the "Gates of Gades."

Another reference in the *Critias* dialogue also lends potential insight into the possible geographic location of the island, "There were bulls who had the range of the temple of Poseidon; and the ten kings, being left alone in the temple, after they had offered prayers to the god that they might capture the victim which was acceptable to him, hunted the bulls, without weapons but with staves and nooses; and the bull which they caught they led up to the pillar and cut its throat over the top of it so that the blood fell upon the sacred inscription." The thoton images conveyed by Plato in the description describe a precursor to modern-day bullfighting in Spain, whose origin is traced back to the Iberian Peninsula.

Another relevant fact that lends credence to the conceivable location of the island of Atlantis in the modern-day Gulf of Cadiz is the existence of the Azores-Gibraltar plate boundary. The plate boundary is a potential source of devastating earthquakes and tsunamis. The Gulf of Cadiz is known to be the area of origination for the 1755 earthquake and tsunami that affected Portugal, southwestern Spain, and northern Morocco with an estimated moment magnitude of 8.7 Mw, which would have placed it in the top ten most powerful earthquakes in recorded history, had it occurred in recent times. There appears to be a long seismic cycle over millennia associated with these extreme geological events in this region. As a result of the potential for massive destruction in this region, many high-quality, multi-channel, seismic surveys were conducted, which revealed numerous still-active faults: the Tagus Abyssal Plain, the Marquês de Pombal, the Horseshoe, the Gorringe Bank and the Portimão Bank. This area is recognized as the main source of major earthquakes that can generate destructive tsunamis capable of affecting the northeast Atlantic.

The *Timaeus* describes such an event: "But afterwards there occurred violent earthquakes and floods; and in a single day and night of misfortune all your warlike men in a body sank into the earth, and the island of Atlantis in like manner disappeared in the depths of the sea. For which reason the sea in those parts is impassable and impenetrable, because there is a shoal of mud in the way; and this was caused by the subsidence of the island." Given the numerous faults and geological structure of the Gulf of Cadiz, it is not unthinkable that a devastating earthquake and tsunami could have destroyed an entire island off the coastline of the Iberian Peninsula, sinking the land mass. Rising sea levels would have increased the depth by 350–400 feet over the last ten millennia, covering it completely.

A medium-green crystal begins to shine brightly, catching my attention. As I kneel beside it I put my hand on it, and the pulsating light jolts my being with a feeling of inexplicable horror. I see a city walled in shiny concentric circles, each coated with a different metallic substance glimmering in the sun, leading the eye to a majestic citadel with a glimmering center. The structures, some simple and others intricate, are constructed of white, black, and red stone. The earth is shaking as women run through the streets sobbing and carrying babies, men push each other over trying to climb up the towers, and a variety of animals run amok in sheer terror. As the earthquake continues its intensity increases, causing large chasms to open up in the earth, buildings to topple, and the concentric walls to crumble into dust in an instant. Screams are heard emanating from under the rubble. The island is cut to pieces as the earth opens up and the ocean swallows it whole. No land mass remains visible—just the debris of the Atlantean civilization floating everywhere. Then for a moment the water subsides and the broken land mass reappears as a huge wave forms on the horizon. It swiftly approaches, crashing onto the sunken remnants—and Atlantis is no more. All that is left are seagulls circling above the floating wreckage.

I look over at Spenta as she solemnly looks down into the shallow pool, "So it was, Time Smith, that the colony was lost forever." Perhaps Plato was right; it was the will of Ahura as he saw the corrupting power of the Chronos and Atlas's hubris and foresaw Angra's evil intentions for Earth and all universes. Why is the story of Atlantis such a compelling tale, capturing the imagination of people for thousands of years? What makes this thoton image so enthralling that it surpasses the photonic image (if one even ever existed)? Maybe it is the parable itself that strikes a nerve, sending out a timeless warning that is understood at a primal level regardless of the civilization or time period. People are compelled to look at accidents. This is one of the greatest accidents in history that may not have occurred, yet people still turn their heads to stare at the thotonic skeletons of our past.

Even Adolph Hitler couldn't resist the pull of the Atlantis thotonic image as Heinrich Himmler undertook a decade-long project to locate the lost island, claiming it as the origin point of the "pure Aryans" from whom the Germans were supposedly descended. No archaeological evidence of an Aryan civilization had ever been found. An isolated island that was virtually wiped out fit the twisted Nazi ideology perfectly. The

Nazis believed that the Aryans lived as a homogeneous society that survived a cataclysmic natural disaster resulting in a long migration of survivors to Germany, which they tried to tie into the Atlantis myth. If proof of the "pure Aryan" Atlantis was found, the Nazis could potentially replace Christianity with their own religion, even further tightening their control over their own population by propagating their own afterlife image. The discovery would also be used to affirm the existing propaganda of Aryan racial superiority and the justification for the war which would break out in 1939 shortly after Himmler claimed proof of the discovery of Atlantis.

An SS unit called the Ahnenerbe (Ancestral Heritage), made up of scientists and archaeologists, was formed to search all corners of the globe for proof of the existence of Atlantis. This discovery would bolster the Nazis' immoral ideology and provide a rationalization for their institutionalized evil by molding Germany's thotonic identity to suit these nefarious purposes. Their ill-intentioned expeditions led them to Sweden, Scotland, Iceland, France, and ultimately Tibet, where (based on a peculiar theory of skull measurements) Himmler believed the evidence of the migration of the Atlantean race could be found. The Nazis' propaganda machine, largely a product of Joseph Goebbels' design, understood the power of thotonic image creation. Thoton images in themselves are devoid of morality, yet they can be used to provide a rationalization of immoral acts. The ministry of propaganda, under Goebbels's control, quickly took over thotonic image modulation sources—news media, arts, radio, film, and television—to shape the identity of a future nation through their perverse ideology. Thoton images are the higher order that ultimately takes form in the material world and relies on the hearts and minds of men and women to move them from a state of superposition to material reality—the future. Ironically, the true meaning of the Atlantis parable was lost upon the Nazis. Because they failed to comprehend the ancient thotonic warnings that bubble upward from the depths of the Atlantic Ocean into eternity, they suffered virtually the same fate as the island.

"Time Smith, the hour is growing on us and the sun will rise soon. You must hurry and find the Chronos before the Interloper finds us and play your part to fulfill the prophecy," Spenta's concerned voice echoes in my mind. I am sick of hearing about this Atlantean prophecy. Isn't it about time someone should clue me in? As soon as the thought entered my mind, I could hear Spenta's voice calmly reciting the following verse in unison with the ensemble of warrior monks:

Unheeded a tale Atlantis will be, overlooked by many
from beneath the sea, in the sands of time, Atlantis will rise
the phoenix flies west underneath clear skies, eternal the hope
the Time Smith prevails, Atlantean's freedom won from that which ails
Angra's grip shall be held on thee no more, Atlantis rising
on distant a shore, peace, harmony takes hold, so it is foretold.

ANCIENT ATLANTEAN PROPHECY

A third yellow crystal's luminosity catches my eye as its glow increases with my own curiosity. Kneeling down, I lean over, feeling the rigid texture in my hand as the images start to form in my mind. I see an old man sitting in a wheeled-chair with flowing white hair, wearing a soiled toga. He has eyes with no pupils, only solid red eyeballs. He is staring inanely at a crystal ball hovering suspended in a liquid solution in the middle of a white marble room. He appears to be blind, unable to perceive any precise point on the crystal sphere, yet his gaze is transfixed on it. A large black crow on his shoulder flies to the crystal ball. As Angra sightlessly gestures towards various points on the rotating sphere the crow pecks on them, and images of different times, places, and peoples emerge on the marble walls of the hall. Angra seems to be searching for something or someone. His head jerks up suddenly and the crow squawks ceaselessly—almost as though they can feel my presence as I watch. Then I see it. There is an image on the wall of me in the garden clenching the yellow crystal in my hand. A smile appears on Angra's lips, exposing the rotted remains of the nearly toothless cavity of his mouth.

"Aka, come here, NOW!" Angra calls out in a crackling voice with an echo that reverberates through the marble halls. A man wearing a red tunic, body armor, and a warrior's metal mask storms into the room, saluting Angra and raising a golden trident in the air, "Yes my lord—what is your bidding, father?" Aka says in a stoic tone. I can't place it, but I feel as if I know Aka or had met him somewhere before.

"We have found the Time Smith, Aka. Prepare the Interloper and program him for immediate eradication of the Time Smith as the primary objective. We will end this silly prophecy once and for all and quash any remaining hope that the agitators and rebellion have by killing the Time Smith, recovering the Chronos, and retrieving the Atlantean thoton crystals. We can resume Atlantean colonization and the conquest of Earth as soon as it is accomplished. Make it so," Angra orders.

"Yes, father, but what about violating causality? We vowed to only use the crystal ball and Chronos for thotonic intervention in material universes after the failure of the Atlantis colony and unforeseen repercussions," Aka asks.

"We have no choice. Our sun shall soon burn no more and we must find another host planet. Now do it, AKA!" Angra barks back.

"Come forward soldier. Your time has come— the fate of Atlantis rests on your shoulders," Aka says as he motions to the doorway with his trident. The Interloper walks into the marble chamber. My hand starts to burn because the crystal is now too hot to grasp. I let go, and the images quickly fade from my mind. A sense of uneasiness overtakes me as I picture Angra's plans for Earth and his discovery of my location.

My thoughts drift to October 30, 1938. Orson Welles's voice calmly floes across radio waves all over America. "With infinite complacence people went to and fro over the earth about their little affairs, serene in the assurance of their dominion over this small spinning fragment of solar driftwood which by chance or design man has inherited out of the dark mystery of Time and Space. Yet across an immense ethereal gulf, minds that to our minds as ours are to the beasts in the jungle, intellects vast, cool and unsympathetic, regarded this earth with envious eyes and slowly and surely drew their plans against us." The thoton images created by Orson Welles from his radio adaptation of H.G. Wells, *War of the Worlds* allegedly caused a panic as his mock Martian invasion of Earth was broadcast. The broadcast occurred after the Nazi army had started its military aggression earlier in the same month, marching into the Sudetenland in Czechoslovakia, a precursor that built up to the beginning of World War II. Perhaps it is part of our human makeup to have a primordial instinct to fear an unknown superior intellect destined to invade our world, enslaving or eradicating mankind forever—a thotonic image forever suspended in superposition.

The unknown, unsympathetic intellect that we potentially subconsciously fear is really our own, hidden behind the mask of imaginary villains. As history has shown, mankind is more than capable of the contrived atrocities committed by Martian invaders from other planets or Atlantean tyrants from other universes. One needs to look no further than our own universe, galaxy, and lonely planet to find the terror of evil. Ironically, it is disputed whether Welles's radio broadcast ever even caused a panic, or whether it simply was a thotonic image created by the newspaper industry, which ran numerous front-page stories after the airing to undermine the credibility of the relatively new medium of radio, which was siphoning off advertising revenue from the entrenched print media. The thotonic image of the broadcast and alleged panic even reached across the Atlantic to Nazi Germany. Hitler commented that the panic was "evidence of the decadence and corrupt condition of democracy." The broadcast and thotonic image of panic inspired by the invented Martian invasion may have been prophetic, preparing America for the true panic and atrocities which were to follow in the real war of the worlds.

A thunderous clap of metal striking echoes through the sandstone cavern as the monks' chanting ceases and they draw their swords. My eyes follow the clamor and look up to the entrance of the cavern as the once-sedentary statue of Khonsu comes to life. His sharpened scepter clashes with the sword of a tall, dark figure wearing a black metal mask with only two glowing red eyes visible beneath the helmet. Spenta unsheathes her sword, "Retrieve the Chronos now, Time Smith, or we all shall have seen the last of our days. The Interloper will stop at nothing until you are dead." The largest of the crystals, an amethyst roughly thirty feet tall, large enough for me to walk inside, beckons as its light fills the entire cavern. I walk over and place both hands on its exterior. I can feel the massive crystal oscillate. Wavelets manifest in concentric rings of small circular ripples that move outward across the water. The energy pulses through my body—at first gentle, then increasing in intensity and pain. The Interloper takes notice as he is knocked off balance by Khonsu. His red eyes meet my gaze as he peers over at the intensifying illumination from the crystal. My fingers are numb as the pain runs down the back of my spine. My hands are frozen in place, and I am unable to remove them from the crystal. They are being pulled into the crystal as my forearms and the rest of my body follow. The purple glow is unbearable as the light overtakes all other images in my mind as my head seamlessly moves through the crystalline structure like it is water.

And then—nothing.

I no longer have any physical form. I do not breathe. My heart does not beat, and I cannot feel or see any of my appendages. There is only the blackness of infinite space. I am cognizant of another presence in the crystal void. Ahura Mazda's voice booms out, "Time Smith, you who have traveled through the Red Dungeon, thrice died to self, releasing you from your mind, flesh, and past in your journey through the Underworld and have been judged pure of heart—what makes you worthy to bear the burden and wield the power of the Chronos, guardian of all space-time?"

I'm going to need a few minutes to answer this one. I'm still getting used to the Atlantean telepathy; speaking without physical form in a thotonic universe to its creator is just another challenge of illumination. Three images materialize in spherical bubbles as I ponder the question: one of the Tree of Knowledge in Universal Depot's Lawn & Garden section, my riddling friend the Sphinx guarding the Luxor, and the lost island of Atlantis floating in the waves of the past. What the hell can these have in common? Without further thought, the following response flows out as a thotonic image into the void, "Ahura, all of the knowledge of the physical universe men possess through science ultimately leads to the larger questions of the unanswerable riddles of the origin of creation and the afterlife, which men have attempted to answer through mythology or religion. The past creates a flowing doorway to the future beholden to neither science nor myth, one that is swept down the flowing river of the totality of consciousness from the waves of external photonic and internal thotonic images of all of time, capturing the essence of those both living and dead forever held in balance by the nature of duality itself."

I no longer sense Ahura's presence. My thotonic image consciousness is now alone in the emptiness of the void. I can feel the crystal oscillating as the pain runs down my spine again and my physical body begins to take form as I walk backward into the waters of the Pool of Dreams, stumbling and almost falling as I materialize. Something is different. I am aware of a heavy weight around my neck, which feels like it is pulling me toward the ground with all the might of Atlas. A gold chain hangs around my neck, suspending a bronze pocket watch soiled with a faded green patina. The unusually cold metal dangles against my chest as I struggle to lift it to my line of vision. The pocket watch is made of the finest craftsmanship with an inscribed image of the Ankh on the front cover and the Tetractys on the back. I open it, and I am struck by a mesmerizing, hazy, amethyst crystal face. I peer into the crystal, which is constantly changing subtly into different, smoky shades of purple—providing a never-ending window with a view into infinity. The pocket watch has no numerals or hands, only the four cardinal points engraved on the inside cover.

"Well done, Time Smith. Hurry—we must get back to Atlantis," Spenta says as she swings her sword against the heavy weapon wielded by the Interloper. The statue of Khonsu lays in pieces at the entrance, and the pool is filled with the floating crimson stain of the monks' blood as only four remain battling the Interloper with Spenta. The Interloper's red eyes catch mine as he swings his sword furiously in the air shrieking and trudging forward nearer to where I stand. The monks fall back to surround me, each placing a hand on me as Spenta continues fighting the Interloper, slowing his progress as he gains ground.

"Quickly, Time Smith, use the Chronos to return us to the planet Atlantis," Spenta says in a hurried breadth as she strikes the Interloper on the leg. He stumbles and his blood spills into the waters. Spenta retreats and grabs onto me with the monks. "Now! Time Smith," Spenta yells as the Interloper regains his footing and approaches the huddle.

"You will die today, Time Smith," the Interloper says as he swings his sword, slicing into one of the monks' arms as he approaches.

The Chronos isn't exactly the most user-friendly QTIP. There is no instruction booklet. How the hell am I supposed to get this thing to work? Dr. Richard's words come to mind, "We are all time travelers and all of us have the ability to create an infinite number of thotonic universes." I gaze into the Chronos, thinking of an image of the planet Atlantis. As the hazy crystal starts to clear, a bright light grows more intense, culminating in a blinding flash.

And then—nothing.

CHAPTER SEVEN

CAPTURED

*I*N THE TIMELESS VOID, as everything turns black, all I can picture in my mind is bottlenose dolphins swimming in the confining, cold, industrial glass and steel-riveted tanks in the subterranean level at DARPA. Dr. Richard and I wander down the hallway on our way to lunch and stop to speak with an attractive woman standing down the hall from the Red Dungeon. She explains that she is a marine biologist working on the development of technology for submarines and new underwater weapon systems based on dolphins. She introduces herself as Candice, extending long, sensual fingers adorned in crimson red polish. Candice's dark eyes are transfixed by Dr. Richard's gaze as they exchange pleasantries. Her long, brown hair flows over her shoulders, creating a striking contrast with the snug, white, lab coat that reveals a slender, statuesque figure.

Dr. Richard is captivated. Looks like I'll be skipping lunch today. I wander through the open doorway to the Marine Biology Technology lab almost in a trance as I can hear the dolphins splashing and calling out playfully in a high-pitched, rhythmic banter that draws me closer. Two grey bottlenose dolphins swim up to the glass wall of the tank as I approach. A bucket of fish sits next to the tank. I can't resist, even though the sign next to the tank warns in big red letters, "DO NOT FEED THE CETACEANS." There are plenty of warning signs that no one ever observes at DARPA. Why should I start now? At least my seafaring friends are going to enjoy a lunch today.

The adaptation of marine mammals for military use, specifically the bottlenose dolphin, started in the United States in the 1960s. Dolphin deployment in US Navy operations soon followed. Dolphins are still used in combat as recently as in the first and second Gulf Wars at the end of the second and beginning of the third millennium. Bottlenose dolphins are highly intelligent, easily trained, and have highly-evolved bio-sonar, making them ideal for locating underwater mines and as biological test subjects used to innovate new technologies. I couldn't help feel sorry for them as they swim back and forth in the small tanks with electrodes attached to their smooth grey skin. The dolphins are captive to the poking and prodding of their terrestrial masters, perhaps destined one day to being blown to pieces by discovering an underwater mine, or simply dying of old age and boredom while being studied in their confining tanks. The Dolphins don't seem to mind as they swallow the fresh mackerel whole, bobbing their heads to ask for more—just like most of us working here.

"Hey, cut that out, Zooey and Franny already ate," Candice says as she and Dr. Richard walk into the aquatic research lab. I awkwardly put the bucket of fish down.

"Tim, come here. You have to hear this—it's absolutely fascinating," Dr. Richard says as he motions me to join the conversation. "Candice, please repeat what you told me regarding your findings with respect to your ongoing studies concerning hemispheric brain independence of bottlenose dolphins," Dr. Richard asks with surprising enthusiasm. Why is Dr. Richard interested in marine biology? He is a hardcore physicist. A pretty smile, stunning figure, and I guess he's all ears.

Candice doesn't miss a beat and starts to explain, "Sure Doc, my research indicates that dolphins have shown slow wave sleep (SWS) electroencephalograms (EEGs) in one brain hemisphere while produc-ing waking EEGs in the other. Several physiological and anatomical observations suggest a degree of dolphin brain hemispheric indepen-dence." What the hell does that mean? I know dolphins have larger brains by mass than humans—a highly developed neocortex, the part of the brain that is largely associated with various traits of human intel-ligence, including problem solving and self-awareness. Dolphins' brains also contain Von Economo neurons, which are related to the higher functions in humans, including emotions, social cognition, and even Theory of Mind (the ability to ascertain mental and emotional states in other cognizant beings). It has even been shown that dolphins can recognize their own image in a mirror.

"Do you understand what this means, Tim?" Dr. Richard asks, inter-rupting my train of thought. Dr. Richard is clearly in a state of height-ened excitement, which is rare for him outside of the Red Dungeon. Before I can answer Dr. Richard explains, "In the open sea, dolphins are exposed to predators continuously. In the beginning, it deprived them of the ability to sleep. Those that slept perished as the others evolved—Darwinian natural selection, the end-all-and-be-all of tho-tonic determinism in any given photonic material universe. The dol-phins that evolved hemispheric brain independence multiplied as a re-sult of the survival trait. The dolphins that couldn't adapt perished over generations, ending up as fodder for the higher-evolved bits and pieces of genetic code swimming around in the spinning, spherical, floating fishbowl of Earth. The bottlenose dolphin is the surviving biological masterpiece of evolution. It can function in a conscious state in one hemisphere of the brain, processing photonic images while simultane-ously processing thotonic images in a state of sleep in its other hemi-sphere. The dolphin is conscious of material photonic space-time while simultaneously perceiving thotonic images across nonlinear matterless universes. To put it simply, dolphins are awake and sleeping in a dream state at the same time—the pure evolution of biological dualistic totality of consciousness!"

Candice, looks over at Dr. Richard, "Fascinating. If you want to borrow Zooey and Franny for further study, let me know. I am very interested in your theory and would love to see the data," Candice says as she glances over at her cetacean friends swimming in the glass tank, viewing them in a new light.

I can see the wheels turning in Dr. Richard's brain as he contemplates the infinite possibilities. "Thank you, Candice. I may just take you up on your offer."

My head is starting to ache with an intense throbbing emanating from my forehead, causing my vision to become blurry. As my focus begins to sharpen, revealing my present reality, the brief images of DARPA's Marine Biology Technology lab, Candice, and the dolphins fade as I now see that I am in the marble halls of Atlantis with Spenta and the four warrior monks, surrounded by hundreds of the elite Atlantean Guard. As Spenta and the monks quickly regain their senses, they draw their swords in a feeble attempt to ward off our potential captors. A wheeled-chair slowly rolls past the circle of enveloping soldiers. "Daughter, I am so glad that you have traveled from so far to visit your poor old father. What a surprise," Angra stammers.

"It is of no use, Angra. Whatever happens here today, Ahura will prevail and the Time Smith will stand with Atlantis when it rises up again as is foretold," Spenta feistily replies.

"Fortune-telling is for fools, daughter. The future is what I make of it in these marble halls here and now! Lay down your weapons, or this shall be your last day," Angra demands. "I only spare you, daughter, because you are of my own blood and there is still hope you will someday truly see my reality."

Spenta glances over at me briefly, her usually erect posture slouching in submission. Her face loses all expression, reminding me of the dolphins swimming in the tank at DARPA. She slowly kneels and drops her sword. The monks follow her lead, relinquishing their weapons. It sure would be as good a time as any to use the Chronos to whiz-bang us somewhere other than here. I look into the Chronos dangling around my neck, but all that appears in the hazy crystal is a reflection of the marble halls of the Atlantean chamber where I stand.

Angra quickly turns his blind gaze to mine, "It is no use, Time Smith, apparently nobody explained to you that you only have half of what you call a Quantum Teleportation Image Processor or Chronos. The crystal ball is the navigational unit which allows one to select a single point on the sphere representing any photonic material universe and synchronize along linear space-time where and when you wish to travel with the Chronos. The crystal ball may also be used to locate and communicate in thotonic non-matter universes. The part of the Chronos you wear around your neck houses the crystal that opens up the space-time axons to the coordinates provided by the crystal ball and returns the traveler to the point of origin, here, the hall of the crystal ball. This is where both the crystal ball and device you wear around your neck, the Chronos, were designed and built by Atlas many millennia ago in Earth years. I thank you for returning it. My daughter's impudence has kept it from its proper place for far too long, delaying our efforts. Now give it to me!"

Aka advances past the group of encircling Atlantean soldiers, past Angra, and straight toward me. He points his trident at my neck. "This is who you think will save Atlantis?" Aka says to his sister. His towering figure looms above me, causing my stomach to tie up in knots. All my muscles freeze, leaving me utterly paralyzed in his shadow. He slides the trident across my neck, catching the gold chain tethered to

the Chronos, and pulls the loop over my head. Then he slides the handle of the trident down through his hands, grabbing the pocket watch firmly in his opposite steel claw, holding it triumphantly up in the air for all to see. As soon as Aka removes the Chronos from my neck, I feel as if a burden is lifted and the weight of the universes is no longer on my shoulders. For but a moment, I am simply Tim Smith again, a physicist and mathematician. The identity of the Time Smith is gone as quickly as it had emerged, until I realize that nothing has changed—my thotonic identity is intact, whether or not I wield the power of the Chronos. If I am not the Time Smith foretold by the prophecy, as soon as I awake with my Atlantean brethren, the dream will be over, and this thotonic universe will be destroyed and a new reality will take hold, one forged by the image of Angra. The story will be told by him and the thotonic identity of a planet carved into stone for eons until it too is beaten down by the sun, washed away by the rain, and simply fades into another thotonic reality created by a new empire. Those who lurk behind the curtain will become nothing more than a shadow of the former.

"Aka, bring me the Chronos," Angra demands. Aka walks to Angra's wheeled-chair and places the Chronos in his hands.

"Shall I finish the Time Smith, father?" Aka asks as he turns back and heads toward me. Angra is staring into the Chronos, ignoring Aka's question until he slowly lifts his head and his red glaring eyes look in my direction.

"No, of course not, Aka. Why would I strengthen his thotonic identity now that we have the Chronos? To dispose of him in another time in another universe at the hand of the Interloper or an arranged accident on Earth would go ignored by Atlanteans. But to make a martyr of him here in the great marble halls of Atlantis would only ensure that the strength of his thotonic identity would grow among the people as they speak of his inevitable resurrection, the prophecy, and other such nonsense that inspires hope. That is the kind of hope that feeds rebellions," Angra says with a sadistic grin. "I've planned something that is a fate far worse than death for both Spenta and the Time Smith. They shall both walk the same path," Angra bellows.

"What can be worse than death? An arranged accident on Earth?" I think.

"Patience, Time Smith—you will find out the truth and your fate soon enough," Angra says with a sense of satisfaction. "Aka, dispose of the monks and escort Spenta and the Time Smith to the T.I.R.E chamber and begin the procedure forthwith," Angra commands as he turns his wheeled-chair and rolls past the encircling elite guard and out of the hall, with his crow still perched on his shoulder. "It shall be so, father," Aka says as he gestures to the guards. The monks each fall to the floor in a circle of blood as they are quickly skewered by the Atlantean guard's blades.

Spenta sobs uncontrollably, her tears welling up and cascading down her reddened cheeks. "How could you be a part of this evil, dear brother?"

Aka looks at her coldly, "It is not your place to question sister, you are a traitor to Atlantis. Your actions may be responsible for the eradication of our entire race if we cannot resume Earth colonization with the Chronos before it is too late. You and the rebellion are the true evil that plagues Atlantis. I would not have shown you the kindness that father did—and spared your life, sister," Aka retorts.

"Kindness? I don't think so, dear brother," Spenta mocks.

Aka points his trident at us as we are herded through a maze of marble corridors into a room that reminds me of a beauty salon on Earth. There are several chairs lining the wall with devices that look similar to cylindrical hairdryers, designed to fit over one's head, mounted above a row of black chairs. A large machine sits between them against the wall with a sign that says, *Thotonic Identity Removal and Evisceration*. A room behind the wall is equipped with a one-way mirror that provides a view into what appears to be a captivity cell. The cell has a white line painted squarely in the middle. Two sofas are sitting back-to-back on each side of the line, facing two large monitors hanging on the walls opposite one another. Sweat seeps from my pores and stains the back of my toga. Spenta can tell I am nervous. "Do not worry, Time Smith, we are captured for but a brief moment. We all inevitably find our freedom from that which binds us one way or another. You can only capture an image for an instant, and then it always escapes its captors, forever moving on its own destined path through the universes," Spenta says in a reassuring tone.

It's the "one way or another" part that makes me nervous. Capture images? What is she talking about? How can we capture images? A camera comes to mind. Photons, individual particles of light, flow in waves and interact with external objects—changing their frequency, resulting in variations of color and form when perceived by an image processor. The photons flow through the lens of a camera, which focuses them on the aperture, a tiny opening behind the lens. The shutter covers the aperture, which is opened at a particular rate—the "shutter speed," which allows the focused photons to pass through film, imprinting the image in layers of red, green, and blue (or black and white) on film. The image is captured in space-time in material form and can be reproduced from the film. When someone views the photonic image a corresponding unique thotonic image evolves for each individual observer, evoking a psychophysical response. How does an image escape and have its own destiny? Let me think about this one.

The picture "V-J Day in Times Square" was taken by Alfred Eisenstaedt on August 14, 1945, coinciding with the announcement of Japan's surrender ending World War II. The image has endured as an iconic photonic and thotonic image. The black and white image captures a handsome young sailor in the middle of Times Square kissing an attractive nurse in a white uniform. He holds her around the waist and dips her gracefully as she extends her leg. On one pole of the thotonic sphere, one could perceive a sailor returning home from Europe—victorious after a long, brutal struggle against Nazi tyranny—reuniting with his girlfriend, celebrating Japan's surrender because he would not be redeployed in the Pacific Theater. A romantic image evoking strong feelings of victory, patriotism, and hopefulness for the future....

On the opposite pole, the sailor could have been seen wandering inebriated through the crowd indiscriminately groping and kissing various women. In 2005, Greta Friedman (the nurse, who actually was a dental assistant in Manhattan) stated, "It wasn't my choice to be kissed. The guy just came over and kissed or grabbed." An image of sexual assault, on the other pole of the sphere.... Regardless of one's thotonic interpretation of the image of V-J Day in Times Square, the image escaped August 14, 1945 and swirls through time down its destined path to our present reality, creating ever-evolving thotonic images as it travels. We are all cameras, shooting a continuous picture show that runs in an endless loop, processing our thotonic images and storing them away in our own personal library. As such, all of us are captured within the confines of our own thotonic spheres, perceiving the external light based on our own experiences (thotonic image library), education, and understanding. The only potential for escape is in the pursuit of expanding our perceptions by considering all of the dualistic points of thotonic spheres in an effort to better understand how others perceive what we contrarily believe to be absolute.

"Enough, both of you. Sit down so we can engage the T.I.R.E. machine and be done with you once and for all," Aka says as he points to the chairs. Spenta sits down, and I cautiously follow. The machine operator clamps our wrists down, using the metal restraints on the arms, and pushes the hairdryer units down over our heads. The head units extend downward to the brow, leaving our eyes uncovered.

"Aka, I understand what thotonic identity removal is, but what exactly does evisceration entail?" I ask just to clarify. "I am sure that it is not covered under my insurance plan."

"Time Smith, does it matter? Once your thoton identity has been removed it won't be a concern because you will no longer know who you are and will simply be a matter image wandering the material world in a state of continual confusion and fear, consuming food and water and whatever else in a never-ending attempt to fill the missing void of identity—a zombie, a ward of the state," Aka says with a sense of satisfaction.

"I am absolutely positive that my insurance doesn't cover thoton identity removal or evisceration. It definitely sounds like an elective surgery!"

"Don't worry, Time Smith, the state is paying for the procedure. No insurance is required," Aka says, laughing as he exits the room.

"Hey, buddy what's your name?" I ask as the machine operator, who is dressed in an odd-looking, black toga and looks preoccupied with the task at hand.

"I am Klementos. I have been working in the palace since Spenta was a baby. This whole thing is very upsetting for me," he says with a frazzled look. I look up at Spenta, as this might be an opportune moment for her to have a heart-to-heart with Klementos. Spenta looks back at me with sullen eyes, overcome with the loss of her monk friends, having to hand the Chronos over to Angra, and the state of our current predicament—too devastated to say anything. If she isn't going to jump in, I will buy some time and give Spenta some much-needed motivation.

"So...ahh... Klementos, what exactly is evisceration?" I ask reluctantly while this hairdryer gadget starts to warm up on my head.

"You really don't want to know, Time Smith. It is rather unpleasant, but don't worry—it is painless and will be over before you know it. I am very proficient at my job and have done this procedure hundreds of times." Klementos says with a sigh.

"Humor me Klementos, what the hell is it?" I ask, frustrated by my inability to get an answer from anyone.

"If you must know, a laser cuts a circle around the sclera, the white outer layer of the eyeball, then the scleral rim (which is attached to the cornea) is held back with forceps while I use a small evisceration spoon to remove the intraocular contents (cornea, iris, lens, vitreous, and retina), rendering the condemned blind and unable to process photonic images—but with the white of their eyeball and muscle intact post-procedure. It is usually done as an act of mercy to ease the burden of those whose thotonic identity has been removed to eliminate photonic image shock. Photonic images may be a disturbing source of thotonic image creation—causing anxiety, depression, and extreme mental disorder once your thoton identity is removed," Klementos explains as he quickly flips through pages on a clip-board. "Uh-oh—it looks like you and Spenta have not been approved for evisceration. You must have really upset the big man. You are only receiving thoton identity removal. This will be far more difficult for Spenta than you because at this point the human brain hasn't yet evolved thotonic hemispheric brain independence, like Atlanteans. Humans can shut out photonic imaging when they sleep, Spenta will be subjected to a constant state of photonic and thotonic image processing, without being grounded by a concept of her own thotonic identity. I could bend the rules and perform the evisceration, which is a far more merciful fate, but it is your decision," Klementos says looking at me.

I don't know about Spenta, but I like the idea of having my intraocular contents intact, regardless of suffering from a little anxiety and mental disorder. Hopefully, they have a decent pharmacy on the planet. "No, that's okay, Klementos, let's just follow the rule book," I reply as Spenta consents by her silence.

"Very well, Time Smith, you are a braver man than I. Then let's begin," Klementos stammers as he retrieves two baseball-shaped crystal spheres from a cabinet and inserts them in the T.I.R.E. machine. "Your thotonic identities are now being removed and captured in the crystal spheres," he informs us casually as he flips the switch.

My head grows warmer, my eyelids grow heavy as I fight to keep them open, maintaining an attachment to photonic reality as long as I can. It is of no use. Darkness and then images flash by in my mind, first from my earliest biological moments to the present and then in no apparent order. It feels like I've been watching for days, maybe weeks. Then other images appear that have no context or bearing on any known reality that I have ever experienced consciously—but they are in there, and I see them until they are also gone. The summation of my entire existence fades, leaving an emptiness which I can no longer even comprehend, but my body remains. The humming of the machine stops and I am left sitting in the chair, surrounded by strangers in a place I have never seen before, unaware how I got here.

A man in a black toga walks over and releases the arm restraints and raises the apparatus around my head. "Prisoner X, follow me please," he says as he guides me through a door marked *Reality Room*. "Please have a seat, Prisoner X." He points to a sofa on one side of the room delineated by a white line.

"Who am I? Where am I?" I ask.

"It is not of any importance. Now you are Prisoner X of the State. Here is the remote control for the monitors to entertain you. Meals are served three times daily. The only rule is that you must never cross the white line into Prisoner Y's cell, or you will be immediately terminated. Do you understand?" he asks.

"Yes, pretty simple. I got it," I reply.

Prisoner Y, a muscular female with dark eyes and long auburn hair, is escorted to the sofa on the opposite side of the room and appears to be given the same induction speech, although I cannot hear what the man in black is saying to her. All I know for certain is that I have the remote! Let's get to it—click. "Welcome to the Atlantis News Network—the truth, the whole truth, and nothing but the truth—twenty-eight hours, nine days a week." I look over my shoulder and realize that my remote also turns on the monitor on the opposite wall that Prisoner Y is now watching. Although I can't hear the broadcast, I can see the Sphinx News Channel moniker on the bottom half of the screen with the epithet, "Real News for Real Atlanteans." I click on the up arrow to change the channel and nothing happens. I guess it is ANN for me, and Sphinx for her, all day long. I luck out—for some reason I find the image of the Sphinx discomforting.

"This just in. BREAKING NEWS! Angra and his east wing supporters have failed to pass a funding bill to keep the government open. Angra is unable to secure allocated funding for building a galactic barrier to prevent Trotants from illegally landing on the planet. We turn to the Overlord in the marble hall of the palace."

A close up image of Angra emerges on the monitor as he speaks in a solemn tone. "My fellow Atlanteans, we were unable to find a compromise with the west wing in order to finalize a budget today. Trotants that ignore intergalactic borders in contravention of the established treaties and come here illegally in violation of Atlantean law pose a serious threat to our society because they cost Atlantean taxpayers thousands of throngin each year in social services they receive, while taking good Atlantean jobs and not paying any taxes. Trotants bring duppers into our schools and sell them to Atlantean children while farungging Atlantean females without government consent. They are unevolved beasts. That is not to say that there are not good Trotants, but they need to follow our laws and come to our planet lawfully. Until we receive funding for the galactic barrier, I vow to keep the government closed."

An image of the ANN studio appears, and the commentators (seeming overtly angered by Overlord Angra's comments) retort, "This galactic barrier is pure fantasy. Angra is simply placating the far-east wing of the party that got him elected. This fantasy is now having real implications because it's affecting millions of government employees and the entire Atlantean economy, not to mention the Atlantitarian issues raised by the horrific treatment of Trotants in the detention centers. Trade agreements with Trotan and other strategic allies are also being jeopardized. Most Trotants are hard-working and take jobs that most resident Atlanteans wouldn't consider doing and pay their taxes and get government permission before farungging anyone. Trotants are simply looking for opportunities that aren't available on their home planet. They come to Atlantis to find a better life for themselves and their families through hard work, as many of our ancestors did. Atlantis was a planet built on accepting aliens from all galaxies, thriving on diversity. What happened to Trotan paying for the galactic barrier? Now it is the Atlantean taxpayer that will bear the burden of Angra's folly.... Reporting from ANN."

I turn my head to look over at Prisoner Y, who is intently watching the Sphinx broadcast. "Wow—can you believe this Angra character. He is out of control. I wonder how he was elected as Overlord in the first place. He didn't get the popular vote, you know. The Princess should be Overlady," I say, expecting some semblance of agreement.

"What do you mean? Angra is just trying to protect the lawful citizens of Atlantis from the awful Trotants. I am proud to have him as my leader. You should be too," Prisoner Y says with a sense of unwavering sincerity. I quickly discover that the off button on the remote control doesn't work, so we are stuck with ANN and Sphinx News forever. The days went by—the food tasteless, providing little nourishment—as Prisoner Y and I continue our ongoing dialogue, which quickly digresses into daily screaming and yelling matches as my politics shift to the far-west and she inevitably succumbs to Sphinx News, a full supporter of the far-east. We are both consumed by our new thotonic programming, unable to do anything else all day and night but argue. If the white line hadn't been there, our exchanges would most likely turn into physical altercations. It is pure torture, I can no longer bear it and am considering walking across the white line to end it all.

"Pssst, Time Smith," Dr. Richard's voice echoes in my head. Who is that? Great, now I'm hearing things. The black toga man warned us of photonic image shock and mental disorder. "Time Smith, it's me, Dr. Richard. Well never mind—you won't know who I am, but trust me, I'm trying to help get you out of here," his voice again reverberates through my consciousness.

"Okay, Dr. Strangelove or whoever you are, anywhere is better than here as long as they have ANN, so what do I need to do?" I say out loud.

Patient Y looks over. "Are you talking to me you far-west fruitcake?"

"No. Shhh—I'm trying to get out of here," I respond.

"Well, I don't want to leave, I can't miss the next segment of Sphinx news, Angra just chittered, so keep it down over there," says Patient Y as she turns back to the regularly scheduled programming.

"Close your eyes and clear your mind, and I will try to share a thotonic image. That should clear things up for you. Focus, Time Smith," says Dr. Richard.

I close my eyes and put my fingers in my ears to drown out ANN. An image of the other side of the wall, behind the curtain, starts to form, I can see Angra with a group of distinguished-looking Atlantean men peering through the one-way mirror with Aka pointing at prisoner Y and me laughing.

"I told you, the thotonic polarization programming would work, Aka, just as it has with all of the population of Atlantis. Spenta and the Time Smith have been completely neutralized, consumed by the thotonic images created from the photonic broadcast, each on opposite ends of the thotonic sphere. Without Spenta and the Time Smith there is no rebellion and we can move forward with Earth colonization," Angra says gleefully as he squeezes the Chronos he wears around his neck.

The thotonic image fades as I hear Dr. Richard's voice again. "You and Prisoner Y have to get out of the Reality Room as soon as possible before it is too late. Your thotonic identities are stored on the crystal spheres in the cabinet in the T.I.R.E chamber. The door in your cell is unlocked. All you have to do is get up off the sofa, open it, and walk out. You don't have much time." Sure, I guess I could do that, but I would miss ANN's afternoon roundtable and have no idea what is going on in the world. I sit back down on the sofa, grab the remote, and turn the volume higher—transfixed and content in a state of induced thotonic polarity as Dr. Richard's voice is no more.

"You are watching ANN. It's time for out afternoon roundtable with our panel of experts to dissect the daily happenings in the marble halls of Atlantis. Our guests today...." Wait a minute—I'm supposed to be doing something. The thought fades as the guest lineup is announced. Suddenly, the monitors turn off and the door swings open. A bevy of hooded monks, some dressed in white and others in black robes walks into the room with swords drawn.

"Hey—put Sphinx News Channel back on right now! Angra is going to declare a state of emergency and build the galactic barrier," Prisoner Y demands.

"What's all this commotion about—you're not authorized to turn the State monitors off," I say to a tall muscular bearded monk without a hood, who appears to be the leader of these outlaws. Like Prisoner Y, I also want to get back to ANN's afternoon programming without delay.

"Do not be alarmed, I am Sebastos, a friend, let's get you both out of here," he says while helping Prisoner Y up off the sofa with his extended hand. Prisoner Y pulls back, refusing to go.

"I will only go with you if you promise to fix the monitor so I can finish watching my show," she insists.

"Of course my dear, follow me and we will have Sphinx News Channel back on in no time at all," Sebastos says with feigned sincerity. Looks like Prisoner Y bought it. I am sure that he is going to put ANN back on, not Sphinx. Sebastos leads us out of the Reality Room back to the T.I.R.E. chamber, where he instructs Prisoner Y and me to sit in the black chairs while he lowers the cylindrical hoods and clasps the arm restraints. "Sphinx and ANN will be back on the air in a moment, sit still."

"Got 'em," one of the monk says as he tosses the crystal spheres to Sebastos.

"Looks like this one, Prisoner Y, is Spenta's thotonic identity," Sebastos says after a few seconds of studying them. How long is this going to take? It really doesn't matter to me whose sphere is whose as long as he gets ANN back on, right now. Sebastos places the crystal spheres in the T.I.R.E machine and flips the lever. Wham! All of a sudden I feel a rush of energy as my mind clears and I can see images, unknown yet familiar, passing through my mind, restoring my thotonic image library to its former self. "Looks like it worked," Sebastos says as he releases the arm restraints.

Spenta looks up at Sebastos, dazed. "Who are you?" she asks as she slowly rises to her feet.

"I am Sebastos, the leader of the rebellion. When you traveled from Atlantis to Earth, I was but a boy in the monastery of the full-circle." Sebastos pulls up his sleeve to reveal the green ouroboros tattoo.

"Of course, I remember you, Sebastos," Spenta says with fondness.

Sebastos continues to explain. "Once news of your return with the Time Smith and Chronos reached us, I came right away, Princess. There is not much time. Angra is preparing for the full invasion of Earth. We must get the Time Smith and Dr. Osenstardt to the palace press-room so Atlanteans can learn the truth about Angra's deception.

"Who is Dr. Osenstardt?" Spenta asks.

"Bring Osenstardt forward," Sebastos orders. Two monks walk toward us, holding a middle-aged man by both arms. His beady brown eyes are barely visible under his long, unkempt, dusty-blond hair. He is wearing a white lab coat and horned rim glasses. "Tell the Princess what you told us, Osenstardt," Sebastos demands.

"I had nothing to do with it, Princess It was all Angra's idea. He threatened to harm my wife and son if I didn't follow their instructions," Osenstardt mumbles, with his head down, sobbing.

"What did you do, Osenstardt?" Spenta asks with fiery intensity.

He slowly looks up at Spenta, avoiding eye contact, and says, "Angra, asked me to falsify data to show that the core of the Atlantean sun was running out of hydrogen fuel and was going to turn into a red giant in forty to fifty years. This inevitably would destroy the planet Atlantis as the sun's radius increases, leaving Atlanteans little choice but to colonize Earth. Angra had me make these false claims in order to gain public support for what really was his intended invasion to plunder Earth's vast resources and enrich those that lurk behind the curtain. I changed the data and made the public announcement as he asked. Angra was going to kill my family. I am so sorry, Princess. I didn't have a choice."

Spenta looks pensively at her empty scabbard for a moment then speaks, "It is not too late for you yet, Osenstardt, you still have the opportunity to right your wrong."

"Give me the Princess's sword," Sebastos calls out. The monks quickly comply. "You will need this Princess, we found it in the cabinet with the thotonic crystal spheres," he says as he hands over her emerald-laden blade. "Because we are no more than fifty warriors strong, our only chance is that the truth, along with the appearance of the Time Smith as told by the prophecy, inspires a populous uprising. We have enough men to overrun the press-briefing room and hold the Atlantean guard off long enough for a few minutes' broadcast. But after that, we are all dead if the thotonic image doesn't inspire the spirit of righteous revolt and capture the hearts and minds of Atlanteans."

Spenta raises her sword, looking right at me, "Than let's not waste time—onward to the future of a free Atlantis and fulfillment of the prophecy!" The procession exits the T.I.R.E chamber, winding through the hallways and meeting little resistance until they reach the palace press briefing room. After making quick work of the handful of posted Atlantean guards, Sebastos, Spenta, Osenstardt, and I enter while the monks remain to guard the doorway.

The cameramen and reporters for Sphinx News and ANN stand in the corner of the briefing room with a look of shock and terror as they hear the commotion in the hallway and see us enter the room. The room is compact, with a large marble desk, where Angra usually wheels up for a bust shot when he addresses the Atlantean people. Behind the desk is a marble backdrop with the Atlantean planetary symbol of two golden dolphins overlapping in a circle embossed into the marble stone. Spenta grabs Osenstardt by the collar and walks him to the desk, sitting him down to her left in one of the four chairs facing the cameras. "Time Smith, come here and sit next to me on my right. Sebastos, convince our media friends to go live," Princess Spenta says as she looks at the cameras with a newfound sense of determination. I walk over to the desk and sit down as I hear Sebastos say to the camera crew and reporters as he draws his sword that they will be no more if the networks don't air the Princess's impromptu news conference. Two small monitors in the back of the room display the live feed of Sphinx News and ANN. Although there is no sound, I can see the BREAKING NEWS moniker on both networks with headlines about a terrorist incident at the marble palace. Not exactly the coverage Spenta is expecting. Looks like the crews convince the networks to switch coverage as I can see myself on both monitors along with the Princess and Osenstardt. Spenta turns on the microphone.

"Atlanteans, I have returned from my distant travels through space and time, from my perilous journey to Earth as your Princess and protector, defending the Chronos and thotonic records of our people from the tyranny of my father, Angra. I have learned much since my return of the deceit willfully woven by Angra and cast out as a net of fear over Atlantis. Angra's net of fear is nothing more than an attempt to blind you while he enriches himself and those who lurk behind the curtain at the expense of the Atlantean people. I have proof of Angra's treachery. Sitting next to me is Dr. Osenstardt, who Angra extorted to mislead you in order to spread the panic and blind you to his true motives, greed, and corruption. Dr. Osenstardt, please tell the people of Atlantis the truth," Spenta says as she turns her head to look at him.

Osenstardt faces the camera and solemnly speaks, "The sun's core has enough hydrogen to continue burning for millions of more years. I falsified the data and made the claims based upon Angra's threats. I am truly sorry, and ask you all for your forgiveness."

Spenta looks back out towards the cameras, "During my journey to Earth, I found the Time Smith. He has come to Atlantis just as the prophecy foretold. Spenta looks over at me and pauses.

I look into the camera. "I came to Atlantis wielding the unimaginable power of the Chronos, having dominion over all space-time universes, a Time Smith. The Chronos is gone, fallen to Angra and those who lurk behind the curtain. My power is seemingly gone. But I have come to realize, that the power of the Chronos pales in comparison to the true power to shape the future. It doesn't lie with any advanced technology; rather, it exists in each Atlantean's heart and mind as thotonic spheres suspended in superposition, ultimately determining the future of your world and the world you will leave to your children. Atlantis is in a polarized state by design because the thotonic images have been manipulated by Angra and those who lurk behind the curtain to maintain power for the few at the expense of the many. It is your duty as an Atlantean to tune out the noise and develop your own thotonic images with prudence. For as they emerge in totality, they become your thotonic identity—who you are. Everyone is a Time Smith. As your thotonic images grow in strength, finding overlap with other's images, they will manifest into material reality and shape the future of your world. Material reality is nothing more than a physical representation of who we collectively are—a shadow of our thotonic universes, the higher order. The power lies in each of us. Wield it free from fear and define a future that reflects the freedom and miraculous wonder of creation itself."

CHAPTER EIGHT

VENGEANCE

"To me belongeth vengeance, and recompence; their
foot shall slide in due time: for the day of their calamity is at
hand, and the things that shall come upon them make haste."
THE HOLY BIBLE (KING JAMES VERSION), *DEUT 32:35*

SPENTA AND I RISE UP from the table as the press cameras are turned off and walk down toward the exit into the hallway to meet our fate. As we near, the clamor from the hallway ceases. "Look, Princess," Sebastos says as he points to the live news feeds. The images on the screen depict a mob rushing the marble palace and other imperial buildings all across the planet. The Atlantean guard is throwing down their weapons and joining the revolt. "Princess, we must get to the Hall of the Crystal Ball before Angra does and flees with the Chronos," Sebastos insists as the warrior monks enter the press room.

Spenta nods her head in agreement. "Lead the way."

"What about Osenstardt, Princess?"

"Let him be. He has atoned for his transgressions and has to live with his actions for the remainder of his days," Spenta says as we exit the pressroom. I follow as Sebastos, Spenta, and the warrior monks ramble through a maze of corridors, fighting off the remnants of Angra's loyal troops until we arrive at the Hall of the Crystal Ball.

Aka is kneeling on the floor in front of the crystal ball, his helmet removed, sobbing. Purple blood seeps out from a fresh wound on his face, staining the white marble floor. He is surrounded at sword-point by the elite Atlantean guard. Holding the Chronos in his hand, he turns toward Spenta, "Sister, I am sorry for my blindness in betraying you, Atlantis, and myself. Father has fled with those who slithered in his shadow on the space shuttle Atlantis, heading towards the planet Trotan. I confronted him over his deceit and treachery. All he said was, 'The cloak has been lifted for but a brief moment, Aka. As surely as Ahura's identity rises with the light of the sun, so shall mine persist. The cloak descends softly, fading the brightness of the light until the darkness reemerges subtly, beyond perception. Whether in Atlantis, Troton, or in another universe, I am forever entangled with Ahura. Join me, all is not lost.' I rebuffed his overtures and fought through his security forces. I was able to retrieve the Chronos from him as he fled but was struck down as I gave chase. Please forgive me, sister."

Spenta collects her thoughts for a moment before responding. "Brother, our feud need not continue, as you have seen through father's treachery. Atlantis has already experienced too much strife and bloodshed for far too long. Rise up and give the Chronos to him whose destiny it is entangled with for eternity, the Time Smith."

Aka stands and walks over to me and places the gold chain once again around my neck; the burden of the weight is no less than before. "Time Smith, you must also know the truth. Angra used the crystal ball to reach into your world through thotonic intervention to eliminate you in order to prevent this very day and the fulfillment of the prophecy. *You*, not your wife and daughter, were supposed to be driving the car that was struck on Earth. Angra is responsible for their deaths in your world. I am sorry." My temples began to throb as my face turns red with anger. If I had forgotten my car keys that day, it would have been me driving Anny to the vet.

Spenta grabs my arm, "Time Smith, let it pass. Vengeance is born only in the hearts and minds of men. Atlanteans have evolved beyond retribution because it only yields temporary solace. It is only Ahura's will that rights inequities. Strike the thotonic image of vengeance from your being. There is no need to harden your own heart. Reach down into that part of you that is from Atlantis and find peace. It is a time of celebration because Angra is vanquished."

"Princess, Atlanteans have gathered below the palace in droves awaiting your first appearance as Overlady. You must address them," Sebastos says.

"Come with me, Time Smith," Spenta says as she grabs my hand and leads me down the corridor. We come to a large, open balcony that overlooks the manicured grounds of the Palace below. The blue grass is barely visible, with every inch of the grounds occupied by revelers. The gates have been overrun, and a crowd of thousands congregates around a massive fountain rising three stories into the sky in the gardens below. Two bronze dolphin statues hover suspended in air with water flowing around them in a perfect circle. The crowd chants, *Princess*, in unison. As the Atlantean people see us, the intensity of the chanting increases to a deafening pitch. Spenta takes my hand as we walk out onto the balcony and raises it in the air with her own as she waves to the onlookers below. The crowd roars! Sphinx News and ANN camera crews are below, broadcasting our appearance to the entire planet. Spenta releases my hand and motions for the crowd to become silent.

After several minutes, the chanting and cheering subside and she is able to speak, "My dear Atlanteans, today is the day that the prophecy has been fulfilled. After a long, tumultuous battle, many Atlanteans have given the ultimate sacrifice to sow the seeds that sprout up this very day. Angra has been vanquished, and peace and order have been restored to the planet. I will lead you down a road covered with the wreckage of Angra's past that was unable to be breached until the arrival of the Time Smith and the fulfillment of the prophecy cleared the way. The people of Atlantis will know the taste of freedom and prosperity once again. This is the dawning of a new age of peace, acceptance, and free love." Wow, I knew it all the time that—deep down beneath the hard, exterior warrior-façade—Spenta is really a hippie at heart. Spenta continues, "A celebration is in order. The next five days shall be proclaimed a government holiday to commemorate the overthrow of the Overlord Angra in preparation for the new world order. The government will run the sextroscopy brewing machines for a week and provide all the nubile nectar Atlanteans can drink in honor of this momentous occasion. Celebrate the beginning of the new era and what is to be the restoration of that which existed before the evil shadow of Angra poisoned our planet." The crowd roars in approval, chanting, *Hail Overlady Spenta—Hail Spenta!* After a few minutes of waving at the crowd, the newly self-proclaimed Overlady of Atlantis takes my hand, and we walk back inside the marble palace together.

"Spenta, what exactly is nubile nectar and a sextroscopy brewing machine?" I ask confused. Whatever it is, the Atlantean's reaction to a week of it gives me the impression that it must be grand.

"Follow me, Time Smith, and I will show you," she says as she leads me down several flights of stairs into the basement of the palace.

"Sounds, like a week of drunken debauchery to me," I stammer out in my Earthly ignorance.

"Nothing of the sort, Time Smith, Atlanteans do not ingest any substances that alter their perceptions of photonic reality. Nor do Atlanteans share physical intimacy as a means of procreation or pleasure. We have evolved from the old barbaric ways, which haven't been practiced on the planet for millennia. On Atlantis, farungging without obtaining government permission, which hasn't been granted for several thousand years, is a crime. In order to procreate a partner is selected based on the principle of duality, choosing the genetic code that is in the maximum complimentary range within the legal limit set by our scientists. Our computers maintain a database of all Atlanteans' genetic information from birth. When an Atlantean woman turns eighty years old, she selects a mate from the database, and their offspring is created in the laboratory. The optimal offspring of the pair is reared by the couple until it reaches the age of maturation. It is a very efficient process, maximizing the use of our technology to maintain interplanetary evolutionary primacy." Wow, I sure as hell wouldn't want to end up in their octogenarian computer catalog of procreation. Leave it to the Atlanteans to bureaucratize nature's oldest propagation tool, removing all the magic of good, old-fashioned romance. No wonder they all seem so high-strung and serious around here.

Look, Time Smith, this is a sextroscopy brewing machine which produces the nubile nectar," Spenta says, pointing to hundreds of massive brass cylindrical vats with a slew of wires and gauges connecting them. "Place your hand on the pad," Spenta says. I look down at a computer that has a grey silicone mat with an outline of the shape of a hand etched into it. I do as instructed, and Spenta presses a button on the instrumentation panel. Ouch—a pin pricks my finger, and a small sample of blood is drawn. The machine starts to whir, filling a glass with different colors of stratified liquids. A laser shoots through to a receptor on the opposite side, displaying a rainbow of colors. The machine arranges what appears to be a random spectrum as the liquid contents are poured in the glass. Spenta hands me the perplexing cocktail and provides a mixing stick, inscribed with "don't forget to stir."

The Overlady makes one for herself, and we head back up the stairs with our nubile nectar cocktails. It's not a Highland scotch, but it smells rather potent and should do the trick. I take a small sip from the edge of the glass. "Yuck—this stuff is absolutely horrible, Spenta." It has the consistency of maple syrup and tastes like tabasco and pineapple, burning the throat as it sticks, slowly dripping down the gullet.

"It is not a pleasant taste, Time Smith, but the sextrascopy process uses the DNA taken from the blood sample from your finger to optimize the potency of the nubile nectar to heighten thoton receptors to provide the optimal orbatronix orgasm, OOO. It takes about an hour for the nectar to circulate through the system Warm water accelerates the process.

"Where are we headed, Spenta?"

"The public baths fed by a hot spring, of course, to join the others until the nectar reaches peak potency," she says, grabbing my hand and leading me up the staircase. We walk outside through an arched doorway that reveals a clear, cool, evening sky filled with stars. I feel unusually at peace with this universe.

The moonlight shines down on the blue grass surrounding the courtyard and marble stone pathway. The pathway is lit by a strange hedge that lines both sides, casting a glowing red bioluminescence. We continue down the path until we reach a massive grotto with a sign carved into the marble structure: "Vera Libertas." Rows of marble steps, unevenly worn from the passage of time lead two stories down into the bottom of the grotto, which contains a colossal rectangular pool. Steam rises from the black water into the crisp evening air. The floor of the pool is delineated by golden decorative tiles that divide the black bottom into multiple quadrants. Marble statues and benches are scattered around the edges, illuminated by the moonlight and bioluminescent shrubbery, providing an alluring glow. Hundreds of Atlantean men and women relax in the warm waters, conversing as they sip their nubile nectar. Spenta walks over to the nearest bench and removes her toga, exposing her muscular feminine form. "Come, Time Smith, sample the pleasures of Atlantis," she says as she descends into the waters up to her waist.

As I survey my surroundings, it is readily apparent that the Atlanteans, a shapely lot, haven't discovered fast food yet. Maybe there is something to the genetic-geriatric-gerrymandering procreation thing. Anyway, I have no idea how the whole bunch of them don't end up being charged with farungging. (The mere sight of the after-hours skinny-dipping party is already straining *my* manhood as I stand, fully erect.) I remove my toga and wade into the warm clear water. Spenta takes my hand as we walk by various couples with whom she exchanges pleasantries until we stop at the centric-most quadrant by ourselves. "Why are we stopping here, Spenta? Don't you want to mingle with your friends?" I ask.

"It is forbidden Time Smith. Atlantis is democratized, but each of the classes must stay within their own quadrant. As the Overlady, I am permitted only in the middle quadrant by myself and with my chosen mate."

Well that sounds the alarm bells in my head. "Chosen mate?" I am already accounted for, I have an Earth wife whom I love and have been searching for endlessly through space-time. Although the whole thing sounds rather harmless given the Atlantean "no farungging" policy, Spenta is tantalizing me as she swishes around naked in the water. I did fulfill the prophecy, so perhaps I'm entitled to a little rest and relaxation. I take a strong gulp of nectar to give this some further thought. All of a sudden, I hear the low deep primal moaning of multiple women in no particular sequence. I look up, and everyone is simply conversing, keeping their distance from one another. Where did that noise come from? It can't be…I clearly see the red robe near the edge of the pool and Dr. Richard waving at me. He is politely sipping from his glass as he talks to four Atlantean women of the aristocratic strata who appear to be giggling and pointing at me. I take another strong drink from my glass, finishing it off. How the hell did he get here? He always shows up when things get interesting.

I hear Dr. Richard's voice as he shouts across the pool, "Tim, this nubile nectar really gets the thotonic juices flowing. You absolutely must get the design specs from Spenta for the sextrascopy brewing machine before Atlantis implodes into nothingness." A few of the couples near him turn their heads and look at him quizzically. Atlantis destroyed? How does he know that? For God's sake, don't tell them that, Doc. I guess he's using history as his guide. In the end, Atlantis is always destroyed, rebuilt, and called something else. Lessons unheeded, right now I just want to relax and enjoy myself. Thank God he has to stay in his quadrant of the pool. The sound of the moaning around me intensifies—the rhythm moving faster, the water lapping over the edge of the pool. The moaning becomes so loud that it drowns out my train of thought. I peer up and everyone in the pool—all different shapes, sizes, and positions are one huge mass of flesh, moving together in a wave of underwater pleasure. Even Dr. Richard seems to be partaking with his four companions, which now number only two—the other two having disappeared under the water. What they are doing I can't say for sure, but he is smiling in approval.

I look up at Spenta in alarm, "What's going on? How did we end up in a floating orgy? I thought you said farungging is illegal in Atlantis?"

"Of course it is, Time Smith. The nubile nectar must be peaking. It may be too strong for the primitive human part of your brain," she says as she leads me by the hand out of the pool. As we are leaving I casually glance around. Everyone is just sipping their cocktails and chatting the night away. I must be losing it. "No, Time Smith, the nectar enhances your thotonic imaging capabilities in order to be able to see through to the multitude of thotonic image universes. The image you saw is the one you chose to perceive."

We walk back into the palace, following a winding staircase up several stories. "Where are we going, Spenta?" I ask as the walk up the stairs is becoming difficult.

"The royal bedchamber—we are almost there, Time Smith," she says, not the least bit winded.

After our ascent, we arrive in front of two enormous bronze doors. The door handles resembles dolphins with eyes made of turquoise stones. The door's intricate inlaid castings depict various scenes in Atlantean history. Two guards stand at attention, greeting us. "Overlady, your chamber is prepared. The orbatronix spheres are charged, entangled, and ready as you requested." The guards open the doors, grimacing as the weight of the bronze casting proves challenging. The moment I walk in the room, I am overtaken by the curved exterior wall made entirely of glass that overlooks the capital city of Atlantis. The stream of flashing colors and buildings flows till the end of the horizon, leaving me nearly breathless, or maybe it is the ten flights of stairs I walked up. The city is built upon a body of water. Concentric channels surround the vast network of golden streets. Four maidens stand ready to serve at the Overlady's beckon-command.

I see two bulky, circular, foam structures that must be the Atlantean version of beds resting on opposite sides of the large slabs of white marble flooring. A silver sphere the size of a basketball hovers at arm's length above each of the beds. Ornate silken tapestries hang from the marble walls, depicting Atlantis's history. A table in the middle of the room is the resting place for various platters filled with fruit and unusual local delicacies as well as a bevy of unfamiliar colored beverages in crystal flutes. Two of the maidens lead me to one of the beds as the others walk with Spenta to her resting place, removing her toga, and she reclines nude under the hovering sphere. The maidens also disrobe me, laying me down onto the comfortable foam surface. "Try the plikaleys," Spenta says from across the room as the maidens return with silver trays of varying fruits. The plikaley looks like an Earth cucumber but is orange. It tastes sour when I bite into it, then grows sweet as the enzymes interact, causing a sizzling sensation on the tongue. After the full ten-course tasting, Spenta dismisses the maidens, instructing them that we are not to be bothered. I can hear the bronze doors closing as their weight collides with the frame, causing a distinctive echo that reverberates through the sparsely decorated royal bedchamber. We are all alone.

"Time Smith, lay back and take hold of the orbatronix sphere so our thotonic images can be entangled, perfecting each of our thotonic carnal desires," Spenta says. As she reaches out to grab it, her eyes roll back and her eyelids shut. I reach out and grab it, my hands squeezing the warm, round sphere as I pull it down closer to my chest. The moment my hands make contact, I am lying on a blanket at the beach, the warmth of the sun cascading over my naked form. Spenta is in my arms, and I feel her solid body against mine. My lips gently touch hers as we embrace. The waves roll in an out as the surf's hypnotic sounds weave in and out of my consciousness, interrupted only by the distant screech of seagulls flying above the deep blue waters. For what seems like hours we roll around on every inch of our blanket, oblivious to the universe. The sand beneath provides a warm, firm foundation, which helps us fully explore the sacred likenesses and subtle differences of each other's bodies, fully entangled in the ritualistic mystery of creation. As the waves crash into the shore, so do our pleasures proceed—measured until all control is lost and consciousness has gone in a brief moment, only to return completely exhausted yet spiritually replenished. We repeat the ritual over and over until neither of us can take any more. These are the most intense orgasms I have ever experienced.

I gently release the orb, feeling invigorated. Spenta is propped up on her elbows, smiling at me, "That was wonderful, Time Smith, you did great for a first time orbatronix orgasm."

"The beach felt so real. It is amazing how advanced virtual reality technology is on Atlantis—far more evolved than on earth," I say as I stand up erect, apparently still excited.

"You mean the hot spring in the snow-covered mountains," Spenta laughs. "The orbatronix machine harnesses our thotonic imaging processing capability to provide us each with our optimal environment for relaxation and stimulation. I was in the mountains and you perceived the beach, but our thotonic identities shared a union, regardless of our perception of the setting. Each of our thotonic images of our love-making is captured in space-time and real, the orbatronix is not a virtual reality simulation. The thotonic union is actually of a higher order than the material and quite real," Spenta says as she stares for an uncomfortably long time below my mid-section. After the spin on the orbatronix, I am rather worked up, feeling a desire for some old-fashioned, barbarous farungging.

I walk over to the bed where Spenta is sitting, shove the orbatronix machine to the other side of the room, and roll Spenta over, mounting her from above while holding her arms down. "Time Smith, you must stop! This is prohibited. I command you as Overlady of the planet Atlantis," she says playfully. As we kiss passionately Spenta's feigned objections subside. I caress her as I had on the beach, mountain, or wherever we are right now; it doesn't really matter, we were both lost in a moment, within each other. I don't know, but the old-fashioned way still has its appeal to me.

Suddenly, the bronze doors open and Aka is standing staring at our tangled naked bodies in utter disbelief. "Sister, what is the meaning of this? How dare you desecrate our laws, farungging with the Earthborn half breed! Is it of no consequence that right now there are more urgent matters that you must address? Get over to the Hall of the Crystal Ball immediately. There is an emergency. We are under attack. I will deal with you later, half breed," Aka says as he storms out of the royal bedchamber, pointing his trident at me. Before I have time to fully comprehend what Aka has said, an alarm sounds and red lights flash across the marble halls of the palace. Spenta and I dress quickly and run over to figure out what on Atlantis is going on.

"Princess, look up at the monitors," Sebastos yells as we enter the room. The monitors display a time clock counting backward, with a repeating message flashing *Imminent Missile Threat Detected.*

Spenta turns to the minister of defense, "What is happening?"

The Atlantean defense minister studies his handheld device for a few moments. "Princess, Trotan has launched a full scale nuclear missile attack targeting our plasma fusion generator grid. Upon detonation, the nuclear reaction will overload the plasma fusion reactors, causing a chain reaction instantaneously converting all of the matter of the planet to light."

"Why would Trotan attack us?" Spenta asks.

"Perhaps Angra gave them the coordinates of our plasma fusion reactors in exchange for asylum, or they could be monitoring the current upheaval and trying to take advantage of the chaos created by the regime change," Aka responds.

"Princess, we have a five-minute window to launch a retaliatory counterattack, striking their plasma fusion grid," says the minister of defense. The photonic image warning continues flashing on the screen as my mind begins to wander back to planet Earth.

It is early in the morning on November 9, 1979 at the North American Air Defense Command (NORAD) located in the Cheyenne Mountain Complex in unincorporated El Paso County, Colorado (next to Colorado Springs). The mountain complex is a veritable fortress capable of withstanding the unthinkable. More than 693,000 tons of granite was excavated from the mountain to build the facility. Geopolitical tensions had escalated from the period following World War II between the remaining superpowers, the USSR and the United States, morphing into the "cold war." Both nations were relying upon their vast nuclear arsenals, built up lock-step over the decades, to create a thotonic image of mutually assured destruction (MAD) providing a deterrent to a full-scale nuclear conflict. By their very matterless nature, thotonic images reside in the fourth state, in a state of flux susceptible to change, slowly evolving into material reality. If the thotonic images of MAD were to be altered, the consequences would be devastating. While intact, the thotonic images of MAD anchored the possibilities of annihilation. It also emboldened each nation to fan the flames of rhetoric, which at any time could ignite the fuse and bring Oppenheimer's thotonic image of self to fruition—a destroyer of worlds. November 9, 1979 was such a day.

The United States relied on a nuclear triad consisting of Intercontinental Ballistic Missiles (ICBMs), Submarine Launched Ballistic Missiles (SLBMs), and strategic aircraft capable of dropping bombs (BOMBs) or launching missiles. The US had a more robust submarine and air capability, while the Soviets had more than double the number of long-range ballistic missiles. On November 9, 1979 the US had an estimated 2,251 ICBMs, 5,712 SLBMs, and 6,264 BOMBs. The Soviet Union had 4,833 ICBMs, 1,605 SLBMs, and 596 BOMBs. Combined, the potential energy of the nuclear arsenals could destroy a good portion of the entire land mass of the planet Earth. However, even given the massive size of the combined destructive force sitting at the fingertips of the superpowers, it pales in comparison to a single large Asteroid striking the Earth.

There is evidence that such a cosmic annihilation occurred about sixty-six million years ago when an asteroid roughly 6.2 miles in diameter struck what is now southern Mexico in the Yucatan peninsula, creating the Chicxulub crater. It is widely accepted that the asteroid strike was the catalyst for the Cretaceous-Paleogene extinction, virtually wiping out 75% of plant and animal species on Earth, including the non-avian dinosaurs. The destructive force of the extinction event exceeded two million Tsar Bomba, the largest nuclear test blast in the history of Earth, conducted by the Soviets with a yield of approximately fifty to fifty-eight megatons. There are fifteen thousand near-Earth asteroids (or "Earth Crossers") which have orbits that pass close by in astronomical terms, roughly 121 miles from the sun. Approximately 861 asteroids are known to exceed over a half-mile in diameter, with 1,409 classified as potentially hazardous. At some point in time over the next one hundred million years, when another large impact event occurs—if mankind still inhabits this floating sphere, at least there is solace in the fact that eradication is the result of cosmic probabilities, a roll of the dice as opposed to stunted thotonic evolution.

In the belly of the mountain—past the two twenty-five-ton blast doors, a steel structure enclosing the entire complex built on thirteen hundred steel springs (each one weighing over a half-ton), principally a steel faraday cage that can move twelve inches in each direction, further sealed behind two thousand feet of natural granite—at the end of a mile-long tunnel sits a 427M computer purring quietly. The photonic images the 427M will project determine the fate of the world. At approximately 3:00 a.m. the evening tech might have forgotten to pull out the nuclear war simulation tape from the reels before clocking out, spilled a cup of coffee, or just felt like ending it all because his girl-friend left him. The reason why isn't important, but what happened is illuminating. No matter how many safeguards or fail-safes are in place, systems tend toward entropy.

Maxwell's demon thotonically emerged that evening, taking the form of the president's national security advisor, who received the 3:00 a.m. call from a military assistant informing him that the Soviets had launched 250 missiles at the United States. The national security advi-sor understood that the president's response time was a window of two to seven minutes. The national security advisor, convinced that the US needed to retaliate, stood by waiting for another call confirming the Soviet launch and the intended targets before alerting the president. The call came a few minutes later, but it was far worse than expected: 2,200 missiles, nearly half of the ICBMs in the Soviet arsenal had been launched according to the photonic-generated computer images on the screens at NORAD.

The images created on the computer monitors that early morn-ing lasted for over eight minutes, a solid 100% in accordance with the Johnson criteria. The thotonic image of a Soviet-initiated nuclear war was just as real in the president's national security advisor's thotonic reality as he confirmed that the Strategic Air Command was launching planes in preparation for retaliation because SAC had also received the same images from NORAD as did the National Military Command Center. The national security advisor didn't bother waking his wife as he figured that everyone was going to perish in half-an-hour anyhow. Given the size of the perceived Soviet launch and time elapsed, a coun-terstrike would only be purely retaliatory because the United States would most likely no longer exist, but the 427M computer responsible would still be purring away under the mountain. A minute before the national security advisor intended to notify the president, he received a third call from the military assistant indicating that no other systems detected a Soviet missile launch, so it was a false alarm. NORAD's commander-in-chief later acknowledged that the "precise mode of failure could not be replicated." A green gremlin in the machine....

My thoughts turn back to Atlantis as the time clock shows less than ten minutes until expected impact, and the red warning flashing "Imminent Missile Threat Detected" on the monitor is only slightly less annoying than the siren blaring. I would have hoped that at least my last ten minutes on the planet Atlantis could be peaceful or at least hook me up to the orbatronix for one last thotanic hurrah.

"Overlady, the window for retaliation will pass in one minute, do you want to launch a full-scale retaliatory strike, wiping out the planet of Trotan?" asks the minister of defense.

"It is of no use. We do not know why Trotan launched the attack or what treacherous role Angra played in this apocalypse, but whatever we do it is not going to save the people of Atlantis from inevitable destruction. By retaliating, the only thing we would accomplish is subjecting the people of Trotan to the same annihilation that is our destiny—murderers no better than those that orchestrated this tragedy. Our days are over. I will not sentence the population of Trotan to a similar fate. We are not mass murderers. Everyone is dismissed. Aka, go inform Sphinx News and ANN so that our people may spend the last moments making peace with Ahura," Spenta says.

Aka looks at me as he walks out of the hall headed to the pressroom, "I have not forgotten you, you farungging half-breed—our score is far from settled."

The hall empties, leaving Spenta and me by ourselves. "Don't worry about Aka, he will be vaporized in a few minutes," she says while pointing to the Chronos around my neck. "Save yourself. Go to the crystal ball and travel to another time and place, but never forget the beauty and wonders of Atlantis, or its immutable message," Spenta says as she embraces and kisses me with a sense of finality.

"I can't leave you here to die Spenta. Come with me—we can travel back to Earth together," I say to her, already knowing that it is not possible.

"Go now, Time Smith. You waste your words and precious minutes. You know as well as I, that I belong with the people of Atlantis. My fate is forever tied to theirs. I am their leader. I will always love you, whenever or wherever your travels take you. Do not forget me, Time Smith," she says as she turns her back and watches the countdown on the monitors.

I walk slowly over to the crystal ball to see if I can figure out how this whole thing works. The unnatural luminescence of the crystal becomes clearer as I approach. If Angra can do it, I am sure that it can't be that difficult. Just point and click my way out of here, before this place lights up like a Christmas tree. Maybe, if I can change the timeline and save Kathy and Sarah that will also ultimately save Atlantis and the Princess, because Angra will still be Overlord. At least Spenta and the people of Atlantis will still be alive. Ahura warned me about causality and altering timelines, maybe I should just use the Chronos and teleport back to Earth. If it doesn't work and I am still here in two minutes, I will implode right along with Atlantis. The pressure is too much—my head starts throbbing. I am mesmerized by the images in the crystal as they take form, forever lost in the alluring glow of its power. I lose myself. Gazing into the sphere, staring into the vastness of space and time, I behold everything and nothing.

CHAPTER NINE

THE
VISITATION

And nine is one,
And ten is none.
This is the witch's One Time's One!
...Science is light!
But from the sight.
GOETHE, *FAUST*

ERO IS SYMBOLIZED BY A CIRCLE representing the set of numbers zero through nine (Hindu-Arabic), which make up the entire set of integers in the base ten number system when it is used as a placeholder representing everything in the set. It also may be perceived simply as the empty set—nothing. Duality is maintained due to the fact that zero may be both representative of everything and nothing, both a real and imaginary number. Symbolically, the dualistic concept of zero, everything and nothing, may be found as early as the thirteenth–fourteenth century BC. On the gilded shrine of Tutankhamun, the ouroboros symbol is carved: a snake eating its own tail, forming a circle that may be interpreted symbolically as a form of zero. The adoption of zero by the West was hindered by the church, as Goethe alludes in his description of zero as a place-holder in *Faust*, referring to it as witch's multiplication. In Europe, the zero was at odds with the Western Christian ideology that God is in everything. A symbol that represents nothing was perceived to be satanic.

The modern concept of zero is documented in India as early as the third or fourth century in the Bhakshali manuscript, which shows a placeholder using a dot symbol. The mathematical expression Shunya in Sanskrit is connected to the Buddhist doctrine of Sunyata, or emptying the mind of thoughts and impressions. The origination of the earliest concepts of zero is most likely tied to Buddhist and Hindu teachings, which both have deep-rooted ideology connected to the idea of a void, nothingness. It is said, while in India during the fourth century, Alexander the Great encountered a naked yogi. Alexander asked him, "What are you doing?"

The yogi replied, "Contemplating absolutely nothing, and you?"

"Conquering the world!" Alexander responded. And they both burst out laughing, each thinking the other a fool. Without zero the modern world comes to a screeching halt. Everything—accounting, computers, engineering, physics, and calculus—is dependent on that which is both real and imaginary, zero. So it is the same with modeling reality—only observing the photonic physical observables without taking into consideration the correlated non-material thotonic images provides no more than a partial understanding of what makes the universes tick. Such is the case in the "Miracle of the Sun."

As I look into the crystal ball, an image begins to form of a massive crowd of people assembled at Cova da Iria, in Fatima, Portugal. It is October 13, 1917. Their umbrellas dotting the countryside, people anxiously talk amongst themselves while looking at the rolling hills in the distant skyline. Perhaps thirty to a hundred thousand onlookers wait as three children look up to the heavens for a sign promised to them by the Virgin Mary. Ironically, the site chosen by Mary for her visitation,

Fatima, is named after a Moorish princess whose namesake is Fatimah bint Muhammad, the daughter of the prophet of Islam, Muhammad. The story of the Moorish Princess Fatimah, who was carried off by the knight, Gonçalo Hermigues is the direct source of the origin of the name of the parish. Two thotonic images emerge, one in accordance with the Western Catholic perception whereby Fatimah is said to have fallen in love with her kidnapper, converted to Christianity, and consented to be baptized and given the new Christian name of Oureana. The opposing thotonic image—that of Fatimah being held against her will, sexually assaulted, and forced into conversion—is consistent with the history of the Iberian Peninsula during the Reconquista (the reconquest: AD 711–AD 1492). In either case, the Arabic name "Fatima" was selected, and that is where the Virgin Mary chose to appear—a place mired in centuries of bloodshed across two opposing poles of the thotonic religious sphere—to foretell what was to become of mankind. Coincidently, Fatima is roughly 350 miles north of Cadiz, perhaps where one could have seen the lost island colony of Atlantis off of the coast if they looked hard enough 11,500 years ago. The Iberian Peninsula is a thotonic hotspot!

Maryam, the Arabic name for Mary is mentioned thirty-four times in thirty-two verses in the Quran. Additionally, she is mentioned eleven times without a connection to her son Jesus. Maryam is the only woman in the Quran that is explicitly mentioned by name. The Quran usually reserves the mention of names of individuals unless they are prophets. When a name is mentioned, it is meant to honor the person and show their great status. The Quran also declares Maryam is the best of all women. As such, it may not be surprising that Fatima was the chosen place of visitation. The thotonic journey started with three children in 1917, moving through space-time to a local Bishop da Silva, who organized a commission to study the miracle in 1930, declaring the event "worthy of belief." The thotonic image didn't end there. It traveled from the parish of Fatima all the way to the halls of power in the Vatican, influencing five Popes until as recently as 2017 and capturing the imagination of the world. Millions of pilgrims visit the site on the anniversary of the visitation, May 13 and October 13 of each year.

It all started in the spring of 1916 when Lucia, who was nine and her younger cousins, Francisco and Jacinta, were herding sheep at the Cova da Iria fields in Fatima and saw an apparition that identified itself as the "Angel of Peace" and "Guardian Angel of Portugal." The children recounted that they saw the apparition three times and were provided with instruction on how to pray, make sacrifices, and worship the lord. On May 13, 1917 the children saw a different apparition, "a Lady more brilliant than the sun," the Virgin Mary. The Virgin appeared to the children on various occasions, asking them to say the rosary prayer daily to bring peace and an end to World War I (the Great War). The month before, in April of 1917, the first Portuguese soldiers had made their way to the front lines of the conflict. The children were also entrusted with three secrets, one which was to be kept from the world and revealed only at the proper time. Lucia later wrote this down in a sealed envelope, which found its way to the Vatican and was passed down to each Pope, who read its contents and decided whether the world was ready for the third and final prophecy.

The first secret recounted by the children was the thotonic image of hell. Mary informed them that there are many souls perishing in hell because nobody is praying or making sacrifices for them. Mary also prophesized that Jacinta and Francisco would not live long lives, and she would take them to heaven soon; Lucia would live longer because Jesus wished her to make the Virgin known and loved on Earth, spreading devotion for the immaculate heart. Jacinta and Francisco died in the 1918 flu pandemic at the ages of nine and ten, as foretold. The second secret foretold a greater war than World War I, in the event that mankind continued to displease the Creator. The sign of such displeasure was to take the form of unusual light illuminating the evening sky, a precursor to imminent punishment in the form of another world war. In order to prevent such a conflict, Mary instructed the Papacy to consecrate Russia to the immaculate heart and institute the First Saturdays Devotion.

Such a light as prophesized by the Virgin appeared in 1938, an unusual aurora borealis hovering over the Northern Hemisphere a month before Hitler annexed Austria. Unfortunately, the Papacy didn't get around to the consecration business (not that Stalin would probably care one way or another) until Pope Pius XII, in his Apostolic Letter, Sacro Vergente Anno, of July, 7 1952, consecrated Russia to the Blessed Virgin Mary. There were other attempts of consecration after that, as well. The third secret, which Lucia insisted be released in 1960 after several requests were denied by the Vatican, would remain unknown for another forty years. The official position of the Papacy at the time was that it was most likely "the secret would remain forever under absolute seal." This created more speculation as to its actual contents. The Virgin Mary told the children that on October 13 she would reveal herself performing a miracle "so that all may believe." This is why everyone is standing around with umbrellas in the rain on October 13, 1917 in the fields of Cova da Iria in the parish of Fatima, Portugal.

Without warning, the rain stops falling as the clouds are pushed aside to reveal a brilliant sun radiating the full spectrum of the visible colors of light. The revelers stare directly at it as it dances in the heavens. The banter of the thousands of people subsides, and there is a somber silence unbroken by words. Only the sound of gasping astonishment reverberates through the crowd. The umbrellas close one by one as the dark clouds give way to the sun and the ground dries, as does people's clothing. Onlookers' shoes are radiated by the miraculous light that gives life to the planet, drying them. Lucia, Francisco, and Jacinta each see different visions of Mary, Jesus, and Saint Joseph blessing the unsuspecting onlookers below. After it is over, the sun simply is the sun. Many people leave—their lives changed forever as the thotonic images they perceive are nothing short of the "miracle of the sun." Others lack the thotonic evolution required to fully grasp the event and go home with wet clothes and soaked umbrellas, but still appreciate the sun's mass and the gravitational force that keeps the Earth in orbit and from veering off into the vast, cold emptiness of space. The only photonic evidence, a surviving picture, does not capture anything out of the ordinary. Scientists did not report any unusual solar activity that particular day. The Johnson criteria scale of the photonic image related to "capturing a miracle" is an absolute 0, 0%, but the thotonic image is a solid 1, 100%—off the charts. The thotonic miracle thrives, gaining strength until this very day and will exist till the end of recorded history as perhaps revealed in the third secret.

On June 26, 2000, the Vatican published the third secret of Fatima after Pope John Paul II authorized the release. Pope John Paul's connection to Fatima intensified after he survived an assassination attempt on his life on May 13, 1981. He believed that the Virgin Mary intervened, because May 13 corresponds to a Fatima visitation date. Additionally, the four-page handwritten text discusses the Holy Father ("Bishop in White") being killed by bullets, which also intensified Pope John Paul's connection to Fatima due to the failed assassination attempt. An interpretation of the letter also suggests that the Virgin Mary saved the world from the potentially disastrous outcome of the Cuban missile crisis in the 1960s, when Sister Lucia had originally requested that the letter be made public.

The fifth page of the letter remains filed away somewhere in the fifty miles of subterranean shelving in the Vatican Secret (but not so secret)

Archives, between "End Times" and "Papal Indulgencies." Regardless of whether it exists or not, or where it may be located, like the other prophecies, it describes the Creator's growing anger and need to punish the inhabitants of Earth yet again—but this time for good. Maybe Atlantis will take the brunt of the Creator's ire and Earth will be left alone for a few more millennia. The third secret talks about the lights dancing through the skies at night, right before the sea of mushroom clouds start to rain down. Maybe it's worth a shot to give praying a whirl, but it looks like it's already too late as the images in the crystal ball move forward in time, following my train of thought to the future planet Earth.

From above, I can see what appears to be Earth in time-lapse as the mushroom clouds pop up all over the globe—brilliant flashes of light one after another—thousands of them. The atmosphere grows dark as hundreds of megatons of black carbon residue from the blasts rise to form a black ring around the planet, cutting off the light from the sun. As the carbon clears, blue oceans are no longer visible—only white, because the Earth is covered in ice from pole to pole around the entire sphere. The temperatures must have fallen a hundred degrees or more as the black carbon cut off sunlight, killing a majority of plant life. The entire land mass is frozen solid. There is no rain. The food chain is broken, with nothing left to sustain the scattered populations, if any survived the initial blasts, freezing cold, and radiation.

The ozone layer is nearly wiped out as the ultraviolet rays of the sun destabilize the DNA of anything still living, perhaps a few cockroach colonies. All that remains of civilization is the metal rubble of man-made structures barely poking above the layers of ice, mass gravestones. Some space junk still orbits the planet. The satellites also eventually disappear, plummeting into the planet's frozen surface—no longer a beacon of man's technological innovation. Finally, in a brilliant flash it is all gone. The entire sphere vanishes into an enormous stream of blinding light and the third planet from the sun is no more. All that remains is the thotonic images and identities from the past. Earth's future doesn't look that much different from Atlantis. Maybe I should just live out my final minutes here in Spenta's arms. How could it all end like that?

As I ponder the question, the crystal ball starts to display an image of me floating in a tank filled with water. Mak and Dr. Richard are looking up and pointing at monitors on the wall. Somehow, the same images I am seeing in the crystal ball of a laboratory in China are also being displayed on their screen on Earth. The scientists are celebrating with each other because they have assembled a device similar to the QTIP and teleported matter successfully with a design that is similar to our initial prototypes. This shifts the balance of power to China, as the first nation on Earth to control the fourth state, space-time. How did the Chinese technology evolve so quickly to become so similar to our own design? An image of Dr. Richard sitting in a hot tub on a rooftop balcony in the city appears in the crystal. An open bottle of champagne in a steel ice bucket sits on the edge of the tub. Dr. Richard watches the tiny bubbles racing to the top of the bottle as he anxiously awaits his evening companion, slowly sipping from his crystal flute.

"Why are you taking so long? Dingbang, are you coming out? It's an absolutely gorgeous evening," Dr. Richard calls out impatiently.

"Yes, Dr. Dickey, I be there in a moment. We have lotsa fun. Be patient for a few more minutes, sugar cakes," Dingbang responds.

"Okay, but hurry up!" Dr. Richard sighs impatiently. Dingbang is inside Dr. Richard's apartment. The silhouette of her naked body shines against the wall as she hovers intently over Dr. Richard's laptop. After a few moments, she removes a small portable device from the computer, places it in her purse, and walks out onto the balcony. Her short, black hair and dark eyes compliment her buttery skin and slender feminine figure—truly a beauty. I understand why Dr. Richard is obviously infatuated with her. She slowly wades into the bubbling, hot water.

"I miss you Dr. Dickey—we have a good time tonight," she says as she climbs onto his lap, straddling him in the water as she passionately kisses him.

Well, that pretty much explains why the world is going to end. It is only fitting, because it probably explains how it all started. The brass isn't going to let the balance of power shift, they would rather have everyone end up floating through the universe entombed in a rotating snowball, as long as it is their snowball. Maybe I shouldn't even bother to try and bring Kathy and Sarah back if that's the future that awaits them. Nothing can be set in stone; even the visions of the future I've seen in the crystal ball must be malleable and infinite, just by virtue of the crystal ball's own existence creating the possibility of an infinite number of universes with infinite timelines. My mind quickly wanders back to Earth, Kathy, and Sarah as I feel the crystal ball guiding my thoughts toward images that it somehow perceives I need or want to see.

An image of Observatory Hill materializes—then one of our house, and finally Sarah's bedroom as she lies asleep, her suitcase still on the floor yet to be unpacked from our trip to Hawaii. She is out cold. It appears to be the day we came back home with everyone exhausted from travel.

All of a sudden, I am standing next to Sarah, enjoying the sunrise on Mt. Haleakalā. "Daddy look—it looks like we're on the moon," she blurts out with excitement. The purple, red, and yellow hues in the clouds against the backdrop of the Martian-like rock crater captivate Sarah, as she gazes in utter astonishment. "Is this where God lives, Daddy?" she inquires. The rays of the early morning sun are reflected on her face, which glows with amazement and wonder. I must be in her dream, I know it. I have been here before. This is what Aka meant by thotonic intervention.

"Sarah, can you hear me?" I ask, not sure if I am able to communicate with her.

"Yes, of course, Daddy," she replies.

"I have something very important to tell you. You must promise me that you will not forget. When you wake up in the morning you must remember. Do you understand?" I ask as I put my arm around her.

"Of course I understand. What is so important, Daddy?"

"You know how you have always wanted a cat? Well, it cannot happen. You can get any other pet you want, but not a cat. You must promise me this. Do you understand, squirrel?" I ask.

"Yes, I can get any pet except a cat. I can't wait—when are we going to the pet shop? I want a parakeet, Daddy."

"We'll go soon, squirrel. Yes, you can get a parakeet. I love you, squirrel," I say as the images start to fade, and I hear Sarah's voice waning, "Love you too…."

I am back in Atlantis looking into the crystal ball as Spenta kneels praying to Ahura as the final minute counts down on the monitor.

I don't understand how, with all the knowledge, advanced science, and technology at its disposal, Atlantis is standing on the precipice of destruction. Maybe the technology isn't the problem; rather, it is the method by which the understanding of the universes is being pursued. Perhaps to unravel the physical universes one stone, atom, or photon at a time gives the scientist a rudimentary understanding of the mechanisms of the clock, creating the illusion of mastery of what makes the hands turn. Meanwhile, the corresponding unseen thotonic data is ignored. The thotonic data would explain how time is perceived by an observer upon viewing the working clock in its totality, the summation of its parts. Capturing the essence and truth of what time is—is not how it is technologically measured. The scientific methodology that is most widely used today, Instrumentalism, is predominately concerned with how useful a model is in creating predictions and in confirming those predictions with observable photonic data that explores the mechanisms of the universes. Instrumentalism is a form of antirealism.

Since the very beginning of the thotonic creation of the image of the scientific method, it has been constantly evolving from the ancient world, underpinned by the duality of philosophy itself. On one pole of the thotonic sphere is realism and the other opposite pole is antirealism. This also might be simply perceived as photonic (realism) and thotonic (antirealism) image processing. Realism is rooted in the belief that the photonic images we perceive exist outside of our minds in an independent external reality. Antirealism is the dual opposite, whereby the thotonic images we perceive exists solely in our minds, whereby any perception of external reality is really our internal projection of a thoton image. Antirealism suggests that the external photonic universe we perceive only exists in our minds as a thoton image.

In order to truly capture meaningful information corresponding to the essence of reality, both realism and antirealism must be incorporated into the scientific method. The combination of photonic and thotonic images together form the complete stream of the individual as well as a collective consciousness, creating a reality that is ever changing as it reveals itself. Relying solely upon either photonic or thotonic image data can provide results which may have unintended consequences as the mysteries of the universes are slowly unraveled. The vast power of nuclear fusion—a particle accelerator creating an unintended black hole that can't be contained, quantum teleportation destroying the timeline and collapsing a universe, nuclear war annihilating a planet because the technology is ahead of the thotonic evolution of those who wield its power—all illustrate the unintended consequences of unbalanced

scientific discovery ending in disaster. The universes are clearly created in duality. Therefore, in order to truly understand the essence of
existence, duality must be used as the basis for the scientific method
to safely explore the world we inhabit—a miraculous combination of
both that which is real and that which is imaginary. To proceed blindly,
tethered only by photonic data and the ambition to evolve technology
before completely understanding the larger thotonic truths underlying
it, can have lasting repercussions.

I glance back down at the crystal ball. As the haze begins to lift,
another image appears. It is July 1959. I am in the hills of Simi Valley
California, about thirty-five miles outside of Los Angeles on a 2,800-
acre facility, the Santa Susana Field Laboratory. It is a clear evening,
with a gentle breeze blowing from a southwest direction. I can see the
scattered lights from houses in the town of Moorpark, below. The sign
on the barbwire fence outside the massive facility says, *Private Property,
Atomic International, DANGER KEEP OUT*. This is the Sodium
Reactor Experiment, the first nuclear reactor in the United States
to connect to a commercial power grid. Moorpark, the unsuspecting
Guinea pig, is oblivious to the unique source of its electricity. The site,
among other things, was a collaboration between the US Government
and the private sector to gather experimental data on nuclear energy.

Over decades, more than ten reactors of varying design were built
and tested in Area IV up until the last reactor was shut down in 1980.
The site also houses a plutonium fuel fabrication facility, a uranium fuel
facility, and a "hot lab" that can cut radioactive materials. In addition to
building and testing the nuclear reactors, research was conducted on
futuristic weapons and advanced rocket propulsion systems, helping secure America's future dominance in the Space and Arms race with the
Soviet Union. The research conducted also helped further develop nuclear reactor technology and provide data as it relates to nuclear energy

being a viable sustainable source of energy, potentially lessening dependence on limited fossil fuels. Unfortunately, government lies, a cesspool of toxic and radioactive materials left behind, and the unknown human cost paid by a population that relied on its government to keep them safe are also part of the legacy of the Santa Susana Field Laboratory. But it could have been far worse.

It is like any other night in the control room, the nerve center of the reactor. The faded green instrumentation panel is illuminated by various gauges measuring the core temperature, energy output, and other readings. The panel is full of switches, dials, and a big red button labeled *Emergency* standing out among the others. The control room is manned by a team of four technicians, who at the moment are busy eating their cheeseburgers and reflecting on the Dodgers' game from the night before. "I told you, the way Koufax was pitching last night, we are going to win the pennant—guaranteed," Jim says as he wolfs his burger down.

"I don't doubt it, buddy. Just hope they let us out of this monkey cage long enough to take in a few more games before the season is over," Randy says as he dips his fries in ketchup.

"Hey, guys look at that core temperature. Doesn't that look like she is running a little hot tonight?" Jim asks, throwing the paper wrapper in the wastebasket as he finishes his burger.

"It spiked a couple of nights in a row—been running hot for a while after they cracked her open for a look. I wouldn't worry too much about it," Randy says. He turns on the radio, and the sounds of the ballgame fill the control center.

"Holy shit, look at the joule's reading—the core temperature is also rising! We're going to fry the core, and this thing is going to blow sky high!" Jim shouts across the room.

"Take it easy, Jim. Let me have a look at that," Randy says as he jumps up from his chair and walks over to the instrument panel. "The sodium isn't cooling the reactor down. Maybe there's an issue with the fuel rods. We're going to melt the grid if we don't get this fixed or offline ASAP. Call the big boss, Jim, and tell him what's going on."

"He's at the ballgame, Randy."

"Well, I'm sure as hell not going to be the one responsible for a total reactor meltdown. Disconnect us from the grid and push the emergency button, numbnuts," Randy says.

"You know, if I do that, the radioactive particles from the core will be released into the air and blow all over the place, Randy. There's no way I'm going to be responsible for a radioactive cloud floating over Los Angeles," Jim says, infuriated with the mere idea that he would be asked to do such a thing.

"Well, if we don't do it, this whole reactor is going to blow—and a much bigger cloud will be headed to Los Angeles—and we won't be here to see it. Get out of the way," Randy says. Jim moves aside and Randy pushes the red button. A siren erupts into the evening night as the lights in Moorpark disappear into the blackness. The radioactive dust rises up the stack into the heavens, floating to unknown destinations as the core temperature gradually decreases, a major disaster averted for most, but the others won't know for decades what happened. The Sodium Reactor Experiment is the worst nuclear accident to occur in the United States, an estimated 240x larger scale event than the Three Mile Island incident, and kept secret for decades. The image slowly fades back to the Hall of the Crystal Ball.

I take the Chronos from around my neck and lay it at the foot of the crystal ball. I look up at the monitor as I walk over to Spenta, realizing these are my and her last thirty seconds in at least this universe. Spenta stands up, surprised, as I interrupt her prayer. "What are you still doing here, Time Smith? I told you to use the crystal ball to teleport back to your own universe and planet Earth. Now, as Overlady of the Planet Atlantis, I order you to get out of here! You don't have much time."

I grab Spenta in my arms. "I will stay with you and share the fate of Atlantis, Earth is destined to be no more. My final moments belong with you because it is you who have revived my spirit and brought life back to my heart. I love you across all time and universes and will be with you here, in the now, in the end, and in the new beginning." "I love you, too," she says as the monitor reaches zero and the sound of distant explosions can be heard. A momentary sensation of vibration hits as the palace walls rock back and forth. Spenta kisses me softly, tightening her embrace in the last moments. Then a white light flashes, blinding all of the senses, Atlantis is once again, no more.

And then—nothing.

CHAPTER TEN

THE RESURRECTION
OF REALITY

Few people have the imagination for reality.
GOETHE

Everything you can imagine is real.
PICASSO

*T*HE COLD WATER SPLASHES against my face as I awaken. I perceive the sensation that I am floating as I feel the subtle waves moving up and down while I lay in the supine position with my arms extended outward. The fluorescent white lights from the high ceiling above become visible as my eyes open, and I can see that I am strapped to a floating table immersed in a pool of water, surrounded by two dolphins swimming around me in the tank. I hear a woman's voice in the background, "Dr. Smith is regaining consciousness—his vital signs have stabilized and are normal. The synchronization link has been terminated successfully," Nurse Nestpa says in a relieved tone.

Dr. Richard removes his red robe, wearing only his black Speedo, and dangles his feet over the edge of the tank. As he jumps in, the dolphins swim playfully around him. I can hear a familiar voice greeting me, "Tim are you okay? Can you hear me?"

"I'm fine Doc, just a little groggy. My head is killing me—feels like a hangover from a two-bottle night. Where the hell am I, and what happened?" I ask as I regain my senses.

"Easy, buddy, take it one step at a time, I'll answer all your questions, but first let's get you unhooked from the Biological Quantum Teleportation Image Processor (BQTIP) and out of this tank," Dr. Richard says as he removes the ankle bracelet and the electrodes from both my temples. As he releases the restraints, I emerge with a new sense of freedom.

Candice looks over the edge of the tank, calling Zooey and Franny over and removing their wireless electrodes as she feeds them some fish. "Good girls, you did just great!" Candice strokes the smooth grey skin on the top of their heads, feeling the slippery flesh to make sure the electrodes didn't harm them. Their flippers splash in the water as they bob their heads up and down, relishing the praise and asking for more fish. I feel a strange connection to the dolphins as I jump off the floating table and Dr. Richard helps me climb up the ladder and exit the tank. Nurse Nestpa wraps me in a towel as I land on my feet on terra firma.

Dr. Udaza calmly walks over, "How are you feeling Tim? You've experienced severe psychological and physiological stress as a result of your thotonic journey." Thotonic journey, what is Udaza talking about? Haram holds up his finger in front of my face, asking me to follow it with my eyes, while shining the light from a small flashlight pen to track the movement as he shifts his finger slowly from side to side. "What is your name?" Dr. Udaza asks. "Time, I mean Tim, Smith," I reply. "Where do you work and what is your job function?" Udaza asks. "I work at DARPA as head of the Quantum Teleportation Program," I answer. "Where were you earlier today, Tim?" It is the oddest thing—before my mind catches up with processing Dr. Udaza's question, I have already replied "the planet Atlantis."

I look over at Candice, Dr. Richard, Nurse Nestpa, and Dr. Udaza. None of them seem surprised by my response. I am more alarmed then they are. My hand begins to tremble uncontrollably. Dr. Richard looks over at Dr. Udaza. "Haram, that's enough for now. Let's get Tim dried off, into a fresh pair of clothes, and rested up for tomorrow's debriefing."

"Fine. Tim's cognition appears to be intact; however, I will require numerous sessions to evaluate the psychological impact of photonic and thotonic space-time integration in order to document them for the program, as this is the first known human trial. Dr. Smith, I'll see you soon, and we can further discuss your experiences," Dr. Udaza says as he exits the Marine Biology Technology lab.

"Tim, come on—I have fresh clothes laid out for you in the men's room," Dr. Richard says. I follow Dr. Richard into the hallway of the sub-four basement at DARPA, past the Red Dungeon, and to the washroom. "I'll be next door in the dungeon. If you need anything, come talk to me when you're tidied up, and I'll answer all the many questions you must have," says Dr. Richard. I walk into the restroom as the lights automatically turn on. On the far side of the sink a tee shirt, sweat pants, and jacket are neatly folded next to a razor, shaving cream, toothbrush, and toothpaste. As I walk across the room, I notice my image in the mirror. Wow, look at all that stubble. I wonder how long I've been in the tank. Looks like at least a week's growth, and my skin feels like a prune.

I turn the faucet on slowly. The flowing water falls into the basin, and the soothing sound relaxes me as I splash the warm liquid on my face. I am startled when, glancing at the mirror, I catch a fleeting image out of the corner of my eye. A strange pocket watch floats in a marble hall with an old man in a wheeled-chair chasing it while looking directly at me through beady red eyes. I rub my eyes, and the image vanishes. Haram is going to have a field day with this. A close shave, fresh breath, and a warm set of new clothes do wonders toward making me feel much better. I open the heavy vaulted door to the Red Dungeon and sit down next to Dr. Richard. The dungeon makes me feel unusually uneasy, as an eerie sense of dread subconsciously permeates my being.

"You look much better Tim," Dr. Richard comments.

"Feel better, too, Doc. Now what the hell was I doing playing with the dolphins at Sea World for a week?" I ask, trying to put the pieces together because my own recollection of recent events is completely insane. Haram will probably have me locked up for a long time, if not permanently, if I give him the full scoop.

Dr. Richard looks at me—barely able to contain his excitement. "It all started after the presentation we gave to the brass to secure further funding for the Quantum Teleportation Program. They weren't very impressed with our disappearing-apple trick or the progress we've made so far. Penny gave me a head's up that Mak slated the QTP for termination. Our only hope to continue our work relied upon providing definitive proof of space-time travel, by actually teleporting a human being. After our chance meeting with Candice, and the introduction to her research concerning hemispheric brain independence of dolphins, we postulated a new space-time diagram for material and non-material universes based upon the dolphins' simultaneous perception of photonic and thotonic reality. I calculated (based on the current state of our quantum computing power, existing lasers, crystal data recording capabilities, and processing speed of our current supercomputers) that it would take at least a millennia to create the technology needed to teleport matter. Is any of this jogging your memory, Tim?"

"No Doc, I remember meeting Candice briefly in the Marine Biology Technology lab, but that's it. I have no recollection of anything you're talking about."

Dr. Richard continues explaining, "It's not surprising—once you were linked to the dolphins, your memories and sense of reality most likely were scrambled. After we realized that the technological barriers were insurmountable, we concluded that a biological solution would be feasible given the data from our work with Zooey and Franny. You volunteered and became the first documented human teleportation machine in history. Tim, our theory worked! We hooked you up to the dolphins' brains, electronically taking advantage of their unique evolutionary development, and provided you with the ability to utilize their hemispheric brain independence—overlaying your photonic and thotonic realities into our newly conceived space-time diagram, fully capturing all states of reality. The image data of your enhanced perception of reality, thotonic time travel, was captured. We have it all starting from the Red Dungeon, Aduat, Universal Depot, Luxor in Vegas, and Luxor in Egypt—all the way to the newly discovered universe and planet Atlantis. You became the project. You have had one hell of a thotonic ride in just one week!"

As I begin to digest what Dr. Richard is telling me, one thought quickly ascends to the cusp of my consciousness, and I interrupt Dr. Richard as he is about to speak, blurting out, "Hold on Doc, let me ask you one question. Are Kathy and Sarah alive?"

Dr. Richard looks at me quizzically, "Why, yes of course, Tim. They're fine as far as I know. Why wouldn't they be?"

Having heard enough, I jump up and fumble in my jacket pocket for my keys. "Keys, Doc. Where are the keys to my Gremlin?"

Dr. Richard opens his desk drawer and hands them to me, "Tim, you should be very careful while you're still absorbing your new state of reality. Go get some rest and be back here tomorrow by 8:00 a.m. sharp. We need to talk before the debriefing at 9:00. Excellent work! Say hi to Kathy for me."

As soon as Dr. Richard informed me of the existence of my wife and daughter in this big bang universe, an emotional cloud of darkness lifted, giving me a long-forgotten sense of wholeness and purpose. The edges of the film started to fill in as the emptiness of the white light came into focus, creating meaningful full-color images forever attached to all of my senses. It felt like I hadn't seen Kathy and Sarah for many years. It makes sense, because thotonic universes are non-matter, each having their own time curve. Or perhaps I *did* alter this timeline through thotonic intervention. Maybe my consciousness returned to another big bang universe with a different timeline. I really don't care how or why, the only thing that matters is that I found them, and they are real, and they are here—and I will be able to hold them in my arms and tell them I love them.

I rush out of the Red Dungeon, maneuvering my way skillfully through the corridors, elevator, and checkpoints as quickly as possible. On most days, it would have taken me a good while to find the Gremlin in the lot, but not today. The green paint catches my eye as soon as I exit the building. The engine turns over with its familiar sputter, and I am off to Observatory Hill. The distant jumbled memories of the Sphinx, Luxor, and Atlantis playback in my mind as the white lines zoom by until I reach the turnoff to the entrance of G.D.'s old estate. The brick pillars at the driveway entrance are restored—standing straight up, erect, with cement pinecone finials shining in the fading evening sun. The intricate brickwork of the pillars and the entrance to our Victorian home are no longer hidden by ivy. The driveway is repaved, and the black asphalt shows no sign of wear. The cracks are all filled in. The portico is squarely attached to the house, no longer sagging. I can see the warm glow of lights shining out the windows of the stately looking home.

I walk up to the front door, taking a deep breath as I am overcome with a sense of excitement and joy. I slowly open the door, wary of anything that I might encounter that would shatter my hopes. I look down at the hardwood floor as I walk across the threshold. It is no longer there—that G.D. stain is finally gone.

Walking toward the kitchen, I turn and see her. I see the long, flowing, blond hair and familiar figure of Kathy leaning over the stove as she stirs a pot with a wooden spoon. Her blue eyes look up, catching my gaze, "Hi honey, I didn't expect you back so soon. Dr. Richard said your business trip had been extended a few more days." I walk over as the smell of a home-cooked meal fills my nostrils—a dish she used to make that I vaguely recall from years gone by. I throw my arms around her and embrace her with all my strength. Tears well up in my eyes and cascade down my cheek. "It was only a week, Tim. What did you do wrong? I have a good idea about those business trips with you and… uhum… Dr. Richard." Kathy says in a sassy tone as she smacks my buttock with the spoon in her hand. I tilt her head back with my arms coiled around her waist, kissing her lips and mouth passionately.

"Ooh, gross," Sarah says as she walks into the kitchen.

I release Kathy from my embrace. "Come here, squirrel, give daddy a hug."

Sarah runs across the floor and jumps into my arms. "I'm glad you're finally home Daddy," she says as she squeezes me.

I notice a bird chirping in a small cage hanging near the window. "Who is that, Sarah?" I ask, pointing at the birdcage.

"Why that's Anny, Daddy Why are you being silly," she says as she hugs me tighter.

"Should I fetch you a neat scotch, Tim?" Kathy asks as she pulls a dock glass from the cabinet.

"No, I'll just have a water tonight," I reply.

"Wow, you and Dr. Richard must really have had a good time on your…um…business trip. Still hungover, Tim?" she asks jokingly.

"No, my dear, I just want to take it all in tonight—nothing to dull my senses."

We eat together at the oak table as we have many times before, but tonight it is different. It reminds me of the small things that I had missed most—the dimple on Kathy's chin, Sarah's never-ending energy and inquisitiveness, the simple pleasures of a family meal one takes for granted. As quickly as it began, with the same lightness of being, the meal ends and the evening comes to a close. I walk Sarah up to bed and read to her while Kathy does the dishes. I kiss Sarah on the forehead as she nods off to sleep and join Kathy in the master bedroom. I climb into bed, feeling the smooth sheets against my skin holding, her tight in my arms as I had done so many times in the past. My conscience begins to weigh on me as my evening with Atossa and Roxane at Luxor nags at my inner being along with the sextrascopy brew and orbatronix session with the Princess. I have always been faithful to Kathy. Does a mere couple of thotonic transgressions induced unknowingly upon me in another non-matter, thotonic universe constitute a repudiation of my marriage vows? Hell, I didn't even know that Kathy was alive when I was with the sisters. And how can you say no to royalty? "Kathy, while I was on my business trip to Vegas, something happened that I have to explain to you, it will not be easy for you to understand because I may have been unfaithful."

Her gaze grows intense as she looks at me with her pure blue eyes, touching her finger to her red lips. "Shh, Tim, I don't care and don't want to know. You're here with me now. I know you are a good man." I feel a sense of relief and closer to her at that moment than I ever have been. "Kathy, with all the noise out there in the world—our mortgage, bills, work—do you ever think about what is real?"

"All I know about reality, Tim, is when you hold me in your arms every night, and I see our daughter grow up every day. That's the only "real" I care about. I love you."

"Love you too," I say as I snuggle up closer to her and fondle her well-formed breasts. Time escapes us as we make love into the early morning hours. I have the most wonderful, vivid dreams of the lost planet Atlantis and dolphins swimming around me, until the sunlight pierces through the blinds, waking me from a deep, hypnotic sleep. I can't believe it's already morning, yet I feel a sense of peace and better-rested than I have in years.

I look over at the clock. It is already 7:05 a.m. I give Kathy a peck on the cheek as she turns over, mumbling, "Is it already time for you to go, love?" I really didn't want to go back to DARPA, but the images of the future earth, which I saw in Atlantis leave me little choice given the role our little aquarium experiment plays.

"I am afraid so, sweetheart, I'll put the coffee on for you," I say as I tie my robe. Kathy rolls over and falls back to sleep. It isn't really about me anymore or even Sarah, or Sarah's children, or their children. It is about the thotonic legacy of the entire planet. Dr. Richard and I are going to have to make this right. I fall back easily into my regular morning routine—drinking my coffee, reading the newspaper, rushing through a shower, dressing, and head out the door to work. As I open the door I realize I've forgotten my keys.

Kathy walks down the stairs in her bathrobe, "You aren't going to get very far without these, Tim." she says as she hands them to me. "You also received a package while you were gone. It's on the table in the foyer. Love you."

I look down and see a small, square box wrapped in unassuming brown paper. "Love you too. Be home early for dinner," I say as I close the door behind me. I walk under the portico where the Gremlin is parked, admiring the landscaped yard. I open the car door, placing the box in my jacket pocket quickly and glancing at the sender's address: "Atlantis, Paradise Island, Bahamas." That's strange, I think as I rush off to DARPA to meet with Dr. Richard and get the debriefing over with.

I work my way through the labyrinth of security until I arrive at the dungeon. Dr. Richard is sitting at his desk reviewing the BQTIP project data. "Tim, glad you made it…we still have time before the de-briefing…to discuss what I think is on both of our minds," Dr. Richard says, intermittingly sipping from his coffee mug.

"You saw it as clearly as I did, Doc. Did everyone else see the future images of Earth in the hall of the crystal ball in Atlantis?"

"No. I pulled the feed to the broadcast monitors before the images of the frozen future-disappearing Earth and my little hot tub adventure with Dingbang were streamed and deleted the segments from the master data recorder. I told everyone that there was a technical glitch. I couldn't remove the images of the Chinese lab because Mak walked in the room and was watching me. Only you and I know the ultimate consequences of the extension of our work on the QTIP. The brass must react with a preemptive strike, or perhaps there is an issue of interpreting a photonic image using the Johnson criteria, similar to the 1979 incident. Whatever the case, the outcome is clear. Apparently, whatever we do, it is of no consequence—this matter big bang universe is doomed," Dr. Richard says in a defeatist tone.

"There has to be some way to alter the timeline, Doc, something we can do?" I ask while the weight of the small box in my pocket becomes heavier.

"Those who lurk behind the curtain probably already know most of the concepts we've discovered. This debriefing is just a big show to see how we were able to circumvent their thotonic image cloaking in order to prevent it from ever happening again. Penny told me that Hoover, himself, is going to be here today."

"I've heard that name before, but I can't place it. What agency is he with?"

"The director of the Image Cloaking Agency?"

"What on earth is the Image Cloaking Agency, Doc? I've never heard of them."

Dr. Richard explains, "It's above your security clearance level, Tim. I wouldn't have heard of them either except for work I was involved with that successfully developed uncloaking technology. The implications are far-reaching when you think about it, which is why the ICA knocked on my door. Cloaking is their business. The project I was working on created a technique capturing an image by shooting a slow light laser through a phase-conjugate mirror, basically a crystal sphere capturing electromagnetic waves (EMW) emitted by an object in the past and translating it to present time, actually reversing time. The technology uncloaks an image that is obstructed by clouds or other physical objects, making it visible by capturing the original EMW it emitted in the past and "uncloaking" them in the present. Do you understand, Tim?"

"Absolutely. I get it, Doc, but what does that have to do with our dolphin show?"

"Think about two different observers: one that views the photonic, matter image of an approaching missile behind dense cloud cover using the uncloaking technology; and another whose camera does not have it. They both are looking at the same photonic, matter image, yet the correlated thotonic, non-matter images are completely different. Both perceive the same photonic image, but their perceptions are altered by technology giving the technologically superior observer a truer picture of reality. One observer shoots the missile down, and the other is no longer in this matter universe. Interestingly enough, the Johnson criteria, which is the current standard used by US military intelligence to validate a photonic image threat, would be 1 in both scenarios, indicating that the photonic images are both 100% accurate based on the available technology—yet the results are drastically different. A

Psychothotonix interpretation would be most valuable because it would indicate that, even though the image is 100% accurate, a cloaked object could be hiding behind the clouds. Ultimately, it is the correct thotonic interpretation that determines everything. If you can alter thotonic perceptions (regardless of physical photonic observables) you control everything! Thotonic cloaking utilizing photonic imaging techniques is the business of the ICA. The science of cloaking thotonic images was perfected by them but developed for human brains. They didn't count on the evolution of our dolphin friends giving us the means to lift the cloak for but a brief moment. The implications of uncloaking non-matter thotonic universes are by far the greatest threat to the entire power structure because it is the door to the fourth state of thotonic superposition, creating the material photonic future. That is why the director is here, himself, for the debriefing, Tim."

"Sounds like we're in this deep, Doc," I say as my hand fumbles on the small, brown package in my pocket.

"Whatever we've accomplished here in the last week has hit a nerve far above the brass ceiling, perhaps even lifting the curtain for a brief moment in order for those who lurk behind it to peer out long enough to identify that which they wish to quash forever. The inalienable freedoms, a legacy from our thotonic past replaced with a whiff of democracy that carries the stench of the most horrific lies. The thotonic sphere of infinite perceptions is by its very nature the foundational piece of pure democracy, that which they fear most. Entropy exists as long as the thotonic universe is cloaked. Once this cloak is removed, a natural equilibrium of social order will assert itself as thotonic awareness energizes the system, restoring freedom. Those who lurk behind the curtain will do everything possible to never let this happen!"

The door to the Red Dungeon opens slowly as Janice emerges in the scarlet light. "I thought I would find you two down here. It's already

8:50 a.m., gentlemen. The panel is assembling shortly. Mak is already in the Tribunal Hall. He sent these men to escort you to the proceeding," Janice says as two MPs walk in behind her. This looks a lot more formal than I had expected. After Dr. Richard's explanation, it appears that this is going to be more than just a debriefing. Dr. Richard and I follow the MPs down the corridor and take the elevator down to sub-ten. This can't be good, I have never been lower than sub-four. The elevator chimes and the doors open. The MPs escort us down the hallway through a set of enormous, ornately carved wooden doors into a room with an equally intimidating mahogany dais that rises above the cordoned-off section delineating a partition with two chairs for Dr. Richard and myself. My good friends Zooey and Franny decide to join us, as they swim in circles around the portable tank. A series of black monitors line the wall behind us, as requested by Dr. Richard to facilitate his presentation.

Embossed brass nameplates adorn the dais from left to right: *Mr. Farma, Reserved, Mr. Fed., Mr. Church, Mr. Naiyua, Mr. State, Press* and *Mr. Petrahl.* Behind them all, Mr. Hoover sits in a small, retractable chair. As we walk in, Mak turns around and Hoover whispers something inaudible to him. Mak appears to be nodding his head in agreement. "Doc, who the hell are all of these people? Why are they here?" I ask in a state of confusion.

"These men control the entities that collectively are the cloak, Tim. Mr. Farma represents the interests of the large drug manufacturers, the last line of defense to cloak thotonic reality. Mr. Farma's network of entities create mind-altering prescription drugs—for example, opioids which are given to the masses, typically the thotonically-disadvantaged who are less susceptible to traditional forms of cloaking. If Psychothotonix dispensed via the Press in various photonic mediums isn't effective enough to alter people's perceptions neutralizing them as a threat, thotonic images are cloaked by Mr. Pharma. Drugs always do the trick!

"Who is this Fed guy? It looks like his spot is reserved but he isn't showing up," I ask.

"Tim, he's the lynchpin to the whole thing, the ultimate chief of all thotonic cloaking and the master of illusion. It's his illusion that all the others chase. He's far too important to bother with this proceeding, yet in deference to his power, his seat is reserved. Although Mr. Fed's name implies a connection to government, there actually is none. He represents a cartel of banks, a central bank, and is responsible for creating the thotonic image of the medium of exchange itself—a nation's currency and the economic driver of the world, as long as he does his job. If Mr. Fed fails, then it is just a green piece of paper in your wallet—the illusion the others chase disappears and another thotonic image emerges dominant, a new empire. Mr. Fed is far more effective at achieving global domination than any weapon we could ever create at DARPA."

"What is Mr. Church's role in cloaking?" I ask the good Doc.

"Mr. Church's thotonic cloaking has pitted mankind against each other for millennia over trivial differences of arcane mythology. As the gatekeeper of the after-life image, Mr. Church purports to be the sole master of the dominion of immortality and the self-proclaimed emissary of the Creator. You already are familiar with Mak and our own role in the development of the military industrial complex. The thotonic and photonic images we cloak create the warfare state—one pitted perpetually against its adversaries (whether the perceived threat is real or not), ensuring the perpetuation and growth of the complex. The brass already knows that thotonic warfare is actually more effective than the photonic, matter physical use of force. The thotonic warfare state is at constant odds with the dual-opposite thotonic welfare state, opposing dualistic positions on a thotonic sphere dictating the expenditure of finite resources as doled out by Mr. State.

"What about this Mr. State guy, Doc?"

"Mr. State's thotonic cloaking is simple, perpetuate the legitimacy of the governing body. Mr. State has worked with Mr. Church to cloak a leader's claims of rule by divinity. He also has worked with Kings and Queens to perpetuate the legitimacy of the lineage of a monarch attaining power by the claim of his or her birth rite. Mr. State can even help to perpetuate the thotonic image of a democracy, kept in check by balanced branches of government and a free press. At the end of the day, the only thing Mr. State cares about is the strength of the thotonic image that creates the validity of the governance structure, protecting those wrapped around it who are lurking behind the curtain of power. The Press is the thotonic imaging distributer that reaches the masses through print, radio, television, movies, social media, streaming online content, or any other form of mass communication. The Press weaves the fabric and pulls an invisible mask over our eyes, guided by their paymasters.

"Mr. Petrahl is a slippery one, Tim. He's the juggernaut of all industrialization. Without him, Mr. Fed's thotonic cloak collapses and all of us are back in the Stone Age. Mr. Fed and Mak ensure that Mr. Petrahl stands ready with his product to readily exchange it for Mr. Fed's national currency. But it is not without a cost. Mr. Petrahl's cloak hides the impact of fossil fuels, carbon emissions, greenhouse gases and, ultimately, global warming—shifting the environmental balance of the first sphere all of us come to know at birth, the planet Earth. Mr. Petrahl does not want anyone to know that other sustainable, environmentally safe, alternative sources of energy already exist that can scale-up immediately to replace fossil fuels. The thotonic cloak is extended by Mr. Petrahl until those who lurk behind the curtain have

maximized their profit, depleted the existing reserves of foreign nations, and finalized seizing control of the alternative energy sources.
All of the men seated here today collectively *make* reality as we perceive it, Tim. What is on trial today is not really our brief incursion
into thotonic universes and (by virtue of our accidental discovery)
the attempted annihilation of cloaked reality. This is the very trial of
reality, itself!"

A gavel strikes on the mahogany table as Mak looks up and turns
to the clerk, "Let the record show that Dr. Richard and Dr. Smith are
present. Gentlemen, you are advised that you are both being charged
as enemy combatants by this military tribunal in accordance with the
Military Commissions Act of 2019. You have a right to counsel ap-
pointed by this tribunal or the right to represent yourselves or designate anyone who is a party to this proceeding to represent you."

"This is going downhill, quicker than I could have guessed, Doc. An
enemy combatant? All I did was float with flipper. Any ideas, Doc?"

"I have this under control, Tim. Not a big deal—this kind of thing
happens at Gitmo all the time. You definitely do not want the tribu-
nal-appointed counsel, they will sandbag you every time. I'll handle it.
Just tell them that I'll be your counsel."

Mak looks up, irritated at our speaking with each other, and interrupts. "Gentlemen there will be no cross-talk during this proceeding.
Please state your names and positions at DARPA, and designate who
will represent you. Then be seated for the formal reading of the charges
against you.

"My name is Dr. Tim Smith, head of the Quantum Teleportation
Program. Dr. Richard will serve as my counsel for this proceeding."

Dr. Richard clears his throat and looks up at the panel. "Go fuck yourselves, you hypocritical, war-mongering, money-hungry, blood-sucking
parasites in suits."

"Ahh…umm…excuse me, Mak. After further consideration, I think I will take the representation provided by the tribunal," I say as Mak's glares at Dr. Richard.

"Dr. Richard, one more utterance of profanity and you will be restrained for the remainder of the proceeding. Dr. Smith, your request for alternative representation is denied. Now take your seats, so you can be formally charged," Mak says with authority.

Dr. Richard and I sit down in the ceremoniously uncomfortable chairs. "Doc, any chance you can tone it down a bit?"

"Don't worry about it Tim, I have the panel right where I want them. You'll see," he says as he looks over, smiling at Zooey and Franny.

"Dr. Smith, you are charged with three counts of involuntarily attempting to annihilate reality. Counsel, how does your client plead?" Mak asks, looking straight at Dr. Richard.

Dr. Richard glances over at me and gives me a thumbs up. "Mak, in order to truly imagine reality, you first must annihilate it. My client is guilty as charged."

"Wait a minute—hold on there, Mak. I'm innocent. I don't know what Dr. Richard is talking about," I shout up at the dais.

"Dr. Smith, you have had the opportunity to choose counsel. Please refrain from addressing this tribunal directly. Any further outbursts and you will be removed from this hearing." Mak informs me, smiling.

"Dr. Richard, you are charged with three counts of voluntarily attempting to annihilate reality and a count of sexual harassment and inappropriate relations with a co-worker in a thotonic universe. How do you plead?"

"I will have the tribunal know that I plead guilty to the attempted annihilation charge, but the sexual harassment charge is absolutely outlandish! This must be about the alleged quick roll in the closet at the Aduat Asylum with Nurse Nestpa. Preposterous! It is purely hearsay, because the only mention of my dalliance with the naughty nurse is from Dr. Smith's recorded thoughts in Aduat. I am not guilty of sexual anything," Dr. Richard says with conviction.

"Gentlemen, because you have both pled guilty to the attempted annihilation of reality, all that is left for this panel is to consider sentencing and to weigh Dr. Richard's defense of the allegations of inappropriate sexual conduct in a thotonic universe. Dr. Richard, the panel is ready to hear your arguments. The dolphins and monitors have been provided as you requested," Mak says as the lights in the room are dimmed.

Dr. Richard clears his throat and speaks to the panel. "It is the standard conception that there is only one big bang universe. There is no evidence of other universes, especially a thotonic universe—specifically 'Aduat' in which you have accused me of having inappropriate relations with Nurse Nestpa. With the exception of the experimental data collected from Dr. Smith's dolphin foray into thotonic worlds, there is no other data that substantiates the existence of Aduat. However, what people believe is rarely based on scientific thought. For example, the ancient Egyptians believed in Duat (another thotonic universe) for millennia, without a shred of supporting data. Did their shared collective non-matter thotonic image exist? Absolutely! Mak, as you are aware, the big bang model that is based on Einstein's theory has accumulated vast experimental data since its introduction validating his image of the physical construct of space- time. However, the evidence against me is based upon the digital recording of Dr. Smith's experiences in another thotonic universe, which creates my possible state of guilt. In order for the allegations of the tribunal to be possible one must conceptualize reality, including the possibility of another thotonic universe. If I may address the panel— does the panel concede that non-matter thotonic universes exist?"

I can see Hoover conferring with Mak as Dr. Richard seems to have stumped them for a moment. After a minute Mak turns back to Dr.

Richard. "Dr. Richard, the panel neither confirms nor denies the existence of non-matter thotonic universes. Please continue and enlighten us on your position." Looks like the Doc is going to have to do this the hard way. I just hope he isn't going to have me float with flipper again. I didn't bring a bathing suit.

Dr. Richard continues, "Many great philosophers and scientists (like Newton and Steven Hawking) have suggested that we live in a giant sphere-shaped universe (like a crystal ball) filled with all the planets, stars, black holes, particles, people, etc."

Mak interrupts at the urging of Hoover. "So, Dr. Richard, if the universe is this huge sphere, then is it finite in physical size as experimental data has basically suggested?"

Dr. Richard takes a deep breath, "Yes it is, but it is really big! It takes photons emitted from stars at the edge of this giant sphere billions of years to get to us! However, this still translates into a finite, physical-size universe. As you know, Mak, that is the party line at DARPA. There are other models suggesting the big bang universe is not a sphere, but our data shows otherwise. This is why I am focusing on spheres as the basic nature of universes in general."

Mak covers the microphone as Hoover whispers something in his ear and then removes his hand from the mic. "Then, Dr. Richard, you must think that there is something outside this big bang sphere?"

Dr. Richard responds, "As you know, Mak, many scientists have been speculating about this for years. Einstein developed his general relativity equations based on the assumption that this universe is a sphere of finite size, called a big bang universe. But others have said since that because the total universe itself could be infinite in size, there could be other big bang universes floating outside this one in some sea of endless size. That's where the term mini big bang universes comes from. Intuitively, these giant spheres would also be moving at different speeds relative to each other."

Mak quickly retorts, "Is there any evidence of such mini big bang universes, Dr. Richard? Have you conducted any experiments other than the dolphin incursion with Dr. Smith that can substantiate the existence of other mini big bang universes?"

"Yes, of course, Mak. It was actually part of a fully funded experiment which you signed off on. The experiment was designed to find a method of taking an image with a camera/detector to determine the validity of Schrödinger's equations. I proposed that Schrödinger's equations imply that images can travel at infinite speed, which if proven by some device, could lead to developing better ways to work with our quantum bit computer, which is currently used in our space satellite experiments to improve the transference of secured data. For example, if we found a better way to interpret the meaning of some of the existing validated experiments, then we could possibly discover that particles or images can travel instantly from one point to another. Then, as I said above, it would automatically imply an infinite universe that by definition would further imply that other mini big bang universes exist.

Quantum mechanics has some very strange effects that are counterintuitive. One of these is that a particle can go from one point in space-time to another via an infinite number of possible paths! We can't see this with a camera (a photonic device that takes matter images in space-time). But the quantum mathematical machinery says that all paths between two points in space-time need to be part of the final destiny of the particle in space-time. You can view this in your mind as a point in time. Say, at exactly twelve noon a quantum particle (an electron or anti-electron, it's dual opposite) is fired from an electron gun and we have an advanced detector that sees the particle hit a screen. If we solve the Schrödinger equation of space-time motion (which is the key equation of quantum mechanics), we have to consider that the particle did not go in a straight line of a "space-time diagram"—but in any one of an infinite number of curved lines that stretch from the space-time point at the gun's exit to the final entrance into the detector. To provide further illumination, I would ask the tribunal permission to call Erwin Schrödinger as a witness."

Hoover blurts out, "This is preposterous!" He talks with Mak for several minutes. "Dr. Richard, you may bring Schrödinger forth from a thotonic universe. However, the panel will add an additional count of attempted annihilation of reality to each of Dr. Smith's and your sentences. Do you wish to proceed?"

"Come on Doc, haven't we already racked up enough time?" I say to myself.

Dr. Richard doesn't take long to consider. "Tim, take off your clothes and get into the tank with Zooey and Franny."

Reluctantly, I jump in the tank. The cold water shocks me for a brief moment. Nurse Nestpa hooks me up to the floating table, securing the electrodes. "Tim, I want you to focus on everything you know about Schrödinger," Dr. Richard says as he turns on the machine and types feverishly away at his laptop keyboard. The monitors turn on, displaying only a blank screen. Several minutes go by as the image of the room starts to fade. I am sitting in a red, leather, wingback chair in Haram Udaza's office in the Aduat Asylum, next to a man wearing a bow tie with circular black glasses and a receding hairline. He doesn't seem to be too interested in me as he casually reads a newspaper. "Out of nowhere, I hear Dr. Richard's voice. "Tim, excellent job, introduce yourself to Erwin. I have a few questions for you to ask him."

As Erwin, folds the page of the newspaper, I peer over and introduce myself. "Excuse me, sir. Are you Erwin Schrödinger?"

"Why yes. Whom do I have the privilege of speaking with?" Schrödinger asks.

"My name is Dr. Smith. I have been following your work closely and have a few questions for you if you have time?" I politely inquire.

"Dr. Smith—all that I have now is time. Please proceed. I would be delighted to entertain any inquiries you have concerning my work."

"My colleague, Dr. Richard, expanded your equations and realized that the meaning of the wave function is really just images on a matter or non-matter sphere. The spheres interact with each other through matter and non-matter waves. The wave function captures the progression of matter (photonic) and imaginary (thotonic) images through time, combining to create reality. As you know, in order to create your equations an imaginary component, "i," is required to create a wave. The way that Dr. Richard recalculated your equations is by retaining the imaginary solution that is typically truncated. The imaginary solution actually represents the non-matter images that constitute the thotonic universe (ix, iy, iz). The imaginary number solutions are points on the thotonic sphere. The real number solution represents points on the photonic sphere, matter images (x, y, z). Dr. Richard is able to capture the (ix, iy, iz) images of our current conversation in a thotonic universe and display them in another matter big bang universe using dolphins to consciously overlay the photonic and thotonic waves, bridging matter and non-matter universes. What are your thoughts, Erwin?"

"Well, Dr. Smith, your colleague…uhm, whom you claim is watching us on some monitor-type device, has quite an imagination. Images, imagination, create that which brings wonder into the realm of understanding. I concede that I didn't contemplate the idea of two spheres and two sets of waves when I derived my equations. I missed the duality, nature's constant. But I confirm that this appears to be mathematically accurate and a plausible theory as to the nature of reality, itself. I would like to ponder this before I formally respond to you and…uhm…your friend, Dr. Richard. I am sorry, but I am short on time right now, but I will write to you and your friend. Would it be best to address future correspondence regarding this matter to you care of Dr. Udaza at the Aduat Asylum?"

"Yes, that will be fine. It's been a pleasure meeting you, Erwin," I say as I stand up and shake his hand.

As he leaves the room I hear Dr. Richard say, "Tim, good job. While you're in Aduat, see if you can find Nurse Nestpa. Her statement should clear up this whole sexual harassment nonsense."

I walk over to the phone on Haram's desk and page her. "Nurse Nestpa, you are needed in Dr. Udaza's office ASAP." This ventriloquist bit is getting old. Next time Dr. Richard is going to have to swim with flipper, himself. The door slowly opens. "Dr. Smith, what are you doing in here all by yourself? You should be back in confinement room four," Nurse Nestpa says.

"Nestpa, I just have one quick question and then I'll go back to my room. Did Dr. Richard have inappropriate contact with you in the broom closet or elsewhere in Aduat?"

"Why, of course not, Tim. Dr. Richard is and always has been a perfect gentleman. Why would you ask such a silly question? Let's get you off to dinner—peas, and carrots tonight—yum," she says as she grabs my hand.

All of a sudden, with a jolt I can feel the cold water and see Zooey and Franny munching their mackerel treat. My head is splitting in pain. Thotonic-universe-hopping is for the birds. I hear Dr. Richard's voice, "I rest my case."

I look up as Mak is conferring with the other members of the panel. He slams the gavel down. "Gentlemen, in accordance with the Military Commissions Act of 2019, this tribunal finds Dr. Smith guilty on all four counts of involuntary annihilation of reality, and Dr. Richard guilty of all four counts of voluntary annihilation of reality and not guilty of one count of sexual harassment and inappropriate relations with a co-worker in a thotonic universe. You are hereby sentenced to an indeterminable number of years in a maximum security detention center. MPs—take the enemy combatants into custody." The pain in my head intensifies as I am jolted by a sudden flash of white light.

And then—nothing.

I don't know how I got here, or where I came from, or where I am going. The small questions that I can answer only lead to other, larger, unanswerable questions. It is madness, total madness. My head is throbbing and I can't stop the buzzing hissing noise in my head. My naked body aches from the hard padding on the floor. I have been curled up in a ball for hours, maybe days, trying to stay warm as the vents flood the windowless room with dry cold air. The fluorescent white light bounces off the four white walls, illuminating the faded white padding in waves. The light fixture above, like a beacon to the mad, makes an almost incomprehensible humming sound that is almost drowned out by the buzzing in my own head, yet still audible to only the truly insane.

I can hear Dr. Richard's voice, barely audible in the cell next to mine. "I think it is time, Nurse Nestpa. Get up off your knees and fix your lipstick, for God's sake. The patient has finally thotonically evolved to where he may be able to alter the timeline and shift us all back to our matter universe."

"Yes, of course, Doctor. Are you sure he's ready?" "It is his and our only hope, Nestpa, please prepare the patient. It's been far too long since the Earth was destroyed that all of us have been stuck in this thotonic hell. He is ready."

"Doc, is that you? Get me out of here. I have to get back home. Doc—answer me, dammit. Something is horribly wrong." A small brown package sits on my cot, unopened. I carefully un-wrap the paper and open the small box. A gold chain is coiled in the box attached to a bronze pocket watch soiled with a faded green patina and inscribed with an image of the Ankh on the front cover and the Tetractys on the back. A note inside the box reads, "E=imc², Love always, Spenta." What on Earth does that mean? I open the pocket watch and am struck by a mesmerizing hazy amethyst crystal face. My memories flow back as I realize that I am a Time Smith, capable of shaping my own future.

Whether woman or man, creator or destroyer—regardless of whether one relies on myth, religion, or science to contextualize one's existence in the flowing consciousness of this big bang universe or another—in the end, it doesn't really matter. We each inherently play our own role and dance upon the stardust stage of the cosmos for but a brief time as our individual dramas, romances, tragedies, and comedies unfold. What each of us gives and receives as part of the individual, as well as the collective experience of being alive, is up to us. We are all part of a timeless theatre company. There are no surprises—every role has already been played, every story has already been written, and nothing has come to pass before that will not unfold again. Our film loops on in perpetuity in the cosmic theatre as our images fill the void of endless space-time along with each of our hopes, fears, desires, and dreams. The stories that have yet to be told lie in the undiscovered thotonic universes woven into the fabric of space-time, dangling within the grasp of our own imaginations, waiting to be found and sewn into material reality by our own hand.

PSYCHOTHOTONIX^{SM}: AN INTRODUCTION AND INTERVIEW WITH DR. RICHARD

*I*MAGES ARE POWERFUL. They shape the future. In all mediums—art, television, film, advertising, video games, novels, and screenplays, images are the building blocks of communication. Images create brands, determine the outcome of elections, shape economic behavior of consumers, and impact our lives in almost every facet of existence.

> **Psychothotonix^{sm}** = The measurement and control of human perceptions and related human behavior patterns based on space-time imaging.

> **Photonics** = The physical science of light (photons) generation, detection, and manipulation through emission, transmission, modulation, signal processing, switching, amplification, and sensing.

OVERVIEW OF PSYCHOTHOTONIX^{SM}

Psychothotonix^{SM} is a new field of image creation and interpretation invented by Dr. Richard in his PhD dissertations. Senior-level people from many top-level universities and other photonics organizations have reviewed the technical content (physics equations and concepts) of his work and agree that it is relatively consistent with photonics equations and technology. His extensions to special effects in entertainment media are also consistent with a plausible new actual reality. Dr. Richard is presenting the following ideas to help the reader of the main part of this book to better understand the fictional concepts.

Dr. Richard has developed international award-winning related products and applications in many industries, including defense, biomedical, and entertainment. Psychothotonix^{SM} technology is the driving force behind Dr. Richard's most recent entertainment project, this fictional novel, *Tetrastatum*. Dr. Richard believes that the proposed new space-time paradigm and field of Psychothotonix^{SM} have significant philosophical and societal implications that should be available to everyone, not just academia. He is undertaking the project to explain the theory in an easily understandable format combining metaphysics and science to present concepts that are accessible to anyone desirous of a better understanding of the universes we live in. Dr. Richard describes below a Systems model, Math model, Movie Special FX model, and Psychothotonix^{SM} Image Processing, "PIP" model. These models are integral to the conceptual construct and illustrated by example throughout the novel, creating a truly immersive experience:

THE SYSTEMS MODEL expands typical photonics image processing methods to include Psychothotonix^{SM} imaging methods in various application areas including: hyperspectral, quantum-optical, light-scattering, computer-generated, psychophysical, nonlinear laser speckle interferometry/holographic, and movie special effects. It is geared for advanced technology experts to bolster their thinking about new innovative applications.

THE MATHEMATICAL MODEL expands upon the logic of the modulation transfer function and quantum mechanics to unravel the conundrum of duality (for the first time in history), which Dr. Richard has termed the "duality space-time for physical and psychophysical observables." It is written for advanced technology experts who want to learn alternative ways to describe quantum physics and laser and electro-optical measurement techniques.

THE MOVIE SPECIAL EFFECTS MODEL expands upon current-day methods used in the movie industry to create advanced technology scenes to immerse the audience into "new universes" using I* methodology. Fictional FX examples include: Matter-non-matter/7 dimensional holographic universes; thotonic time travel with crystal balls and non-matter tunnels linking an infinite number of mini big bang universes instantaneously; the cosmic duality image processor that can mastermind the crystal ball travel; light matter space-time fountains using slow laser light; virtual non-matter quantum relativistic particle/antiparticle creation and annihilation. Non-fictional examples include: object trajectories using laser-driven cameras to illuminate the travel in space-time and display different physics solutions like time of flight, forces of impact, and uncertainties in performance. It is geared for the general public to enhance their knowledge of physics in new and interesting ways as well as provide maximum entertainment stimulation.

PSYCHOTHOTONIX^{SM} IMAGE PROCESSING IN DUALITY SPACE-TIME (PIP)

PIP media development as an industry standard is concomitant to the media optimally fitting with the bigger picture of reality created in the PIP model. PIP media development for books, movies, VR, AR, MR, laptop apps, creates an endless variety of new ways to view reality. The following topics highlight the essential concepts to successfully deploy PIP:

PHOTONIX IMAGES

A camera/laser image of any physical entity. We use the word photonix instead of photonics (which is a multibillion-dollar camera/laser marketplace) to distinguish that our primary function is to interpret camera/laser images (not create the camera/laser images). A photonix image can be classified on a scale of 100% perfect (no distortion of the physical objects) down to 100% imperfect (100% distortion of the physical object, with no meaningful data). This scale is an industry standard called the Johnson criteria.

THOTONIX IMAGES

The brain's interpretation of any natural image captured by camera/laser images. The interpretation provides meaning to the camera/laser image (thoughts, emotions, values...). In other words, the interpretation adds new dimensions to the photonix image. There are an infinite number of categories of thotonix images. For example, there is the thotonix image of someone else's thotonix image; there is a thotonix image of some possible entity, world, universe...that has no current photonix image (i.e., the image of the planet Atlantis created in the novel). This is the brain's interpretation of a possible physical reality that could (if the technology existed) be created by a camera/laser.

All photonix images in any industry need detailed thotonix image interpretation for the functionality of the application. For example, camera-inspected parts with close to perfect photonics images need further thotonix interpretation due to the fact that human inspectors may make a false positive or negative identification based on their thotonix interpretation; the image of the parts that are rejected need to be analyzed by the engineering/business team to determine the next steps toward improving the system's performance.

A PIP IMAGE

An objective view of the combination of the photonix image and the thotonix image. This is based on the Dr. Richard criterion (a new standard) where the PIP classification is based on a scale of 100% perfect (100% objective view of the images) down to 100% imperfect (100% non-objective view of the images).

PHOTONIX IMAGE DUALITY

Every photonix image has a dual opposite possible image—an image of a healthy cell means that an image of a diseased cell is possible.

Every thotonix image has a dual opposite possible image—an image of love means that an image of hate exists; life and death images, beauty and ugly, guilt and innocence are dual opposites.

A PSYCHOTHTONIX IMAGE

Every PIP image has a dual possible opposite—a 100% objective interpretation of photonix and thotonix images is important, but there is always a possible dual opposite non-objective view. It is essential that any PIP media product have the right combination of duality to maximize audience immersion.

PIP INDENTITY

The sum total of all of one's photonix and thotonix images over time defines one's way of identifying with the external world via their internal PIP. Consequently, this is a person's thotonix identity. One's identity therefore evolves over time. For example, one has thotonix images of their body as it ages as part of their identity, but as the body grows weaker one's identity grows stronger (as defined by the number of images over time).

PIP LAPTOP

A computer program that allows the user to create their own interpretation of any camera image. A computer program that collects data about how people interpret images in any social scenario.

MATHEMATICAL MACHINERY OF PIP

For photonics experts, the details are included in Appendix B.

PHOTONIX SPHERE

Each point of a photonix sphere represents some physical event and its duality.

THOTONIX SPHERE

The brain's interpretation of the photonix images.

Examples include:

Example 1.0 Defective Part Decisions

PIP North Pole: A part is perfect and accepted—not a false positive or negative.

PIP South Pole: A part is perfect and rejected for some human factor reason—a false positive or negative. This a dual opposite in terms of a perfect part being accepted or rejected.

PIP East Pole: A part is not perfect but is rejected—not a false positive or negative.

PIP West Pole: A part is not perfect and is accepted (dual opposite to the PIP East Pole interpretation).

Example 2.0 Court Case

PIP North Pole: The defendant is interpreted as 100% guilty and judged to serve the maximum time.

PIP South Pole: The defendant is interpreted as 100% guilty and judged to serve no time because it is perceived that the social system is 100% at fault. To make a dual opposite there must be dual opposites of the same state (example dual opposites of 100% innocent). That is how the mathematical basis that explains the natural phenomenon must work out.

PIP East Pole: The defendant is interpreted as 100% innocent and judged not be paid for his time in court because it was part of his social duty to prove his innocence.

PIP West Pole: The defendant is interpreted as 100% innocent and judged to be paid for his time in court as it is society's duty to support him for lost time.

A thotonix sphere can be created on a computer. The sphere has an image pointer from the origin of the sphere to any point on the surface of the sphere. Each point on the sphere can pop out an image on the PIP laptop display for any contemplated scenario that is modeled.

THOTONIX WAVE ACTION

Consider a full cycle of duality. The observer in the court case starts out at the PIP North Pole (at the initial time), which is shown on the laptop screen as a pointer, pointing to the North Pole. Then he/she changes his perception to the East Pole later in time, continuing back to the

North Pole interpretation—he/she has moved one full cycle around the sphere of images. The final displayed image is a wave that connects the initial North Pole of one sphere (at the initial time) with the final North Pole of another sphere (as the final time). This is just a sine wave. The same can be shown for the cosine wave. In general, there can be infinite waves for each person. Thus, the image data can be analyzed in terms of wave action. This is called a PIP space-time diagram. This forms the basis for a new type of math where the images that people record can be statistically calculated for any number of reasons—social, political, marketing, security—anything.

Each wave is a set of points, and each point pops out a thotonix image. Thus, we can create a wave equation (that resembles Schrödinger's wave equation), but it has the visual effect of being just a set of images evolving in time. The wave equation is just the second derivative of the thotonix image wave in physical space minus the velocity of propagation squared of the wave (typically the speed of light in free space) times the second derivative of the thotonix image wave in time—all set equal to zero in most cases.

THOTONIX SHUTTER SPEED

A camera can take photonix images at a speed of billions of images per second. The brain can interpret these just as quickly. The images can be sent via the internet at the speed of light. As a special effect, the images can be sent at infinite speed through an axon (a hole in physical space-time, as illustrated in the novel). Notice that as the image pointer moves in time it changes in angle. The change of the angle is just a measure of the shutter speed of the brain image processing.

Technical Note: Mathematically, that is, $\Delta w \Delta t = \Delta I$ divided by h-barΔt—where ΔI is defined to be the influence of the change of the image in time and h-bar is the fastest possible shutter speed limit. In quantum mechanics there is a similar term where ΔI is replaced with the change of the energy. But there is no interpretation that is visual. Therefore, it makes the Schrödinger wave function uninterpretable because it is not mathematically modeled as a wave of visual images—just some abstract wave of unknown origin.

AN INTERVIEW WITH DR. RICHARD

Dialogues expanded from the book *Tetrastatum* (general audience—no need for a math or scientific background, but those that do have a math or scientific background will want to read this information as well, because it introduces the basic concepts of Psychothotonix[SM] and the corresponding proposed new Space-Time Diagram):

INTERVIEWER. In the last chapter of the novel, The Resurrection of Reality, Dr. Smith has a thotonic dialogue with Dr. Schrödinger exploring the possibility of a new space-time paradigm based on your extension of his equations. Can you elaborate on the proposed model?

DR. RICHARD. The image depicted in (figure 1.0, below) is Erwin Schrödinger's probability wave from his master quantum equation that he created in 1925:

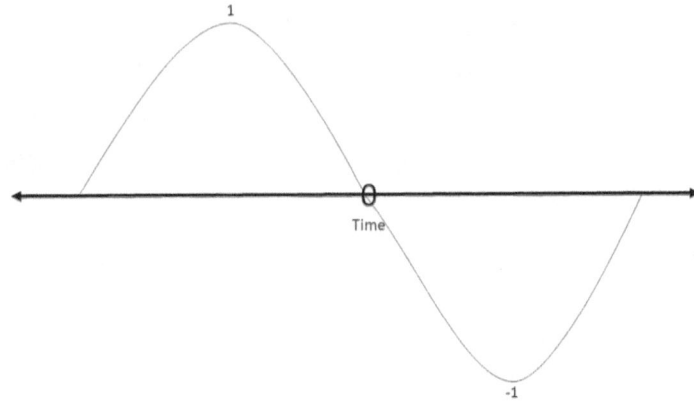

It is still the only wave solution type that is used by all quantum physicists to define the meaning of the nanoscopic interaction of light with matter. Even though most quantum waves are very complex, they are always built on the sum of many of the Schrödinger fundamental building block waves. The Schrödinger approach does not use images from cameras to interpret the events of the underlying quantum behavior, just the wave-particle duality concept imbedded in the meaning of the wave itself. For example, physicists would say that the peak of the wave represents 100% probability that an electron exists in some sort of spin state at that moment along its time line without having to see the state of the electron (because they do not have cameras with enough resolution to take a picture of an electron). The trough of the wave also represents the 100% existence of the electron in the same spin state at a later point along its time line. The other parts of the wave represent different probabilities of the electron's position in space-time. For example, at a time half way between the two points of 100% existence the electron is said to have 0% probability of being there.

INTERVIEWER. It appears that the electron in (figure 1) went from one point in time to another but never went through the middle. How is that possible?

DR. RICHARD. It is complicated and the current body of scientific knowledge never comes to any definitive conclusion. However, the development of a Psychothotonix^SM camera (PTC) resolves this issue, forever! Consider the first image of an electron on a time line (figure 2.0, following page) which was created by collecting photons (light particles) scattered off the electron over a small time-frame.

Dr. Richard's Extended Image Wave Equation

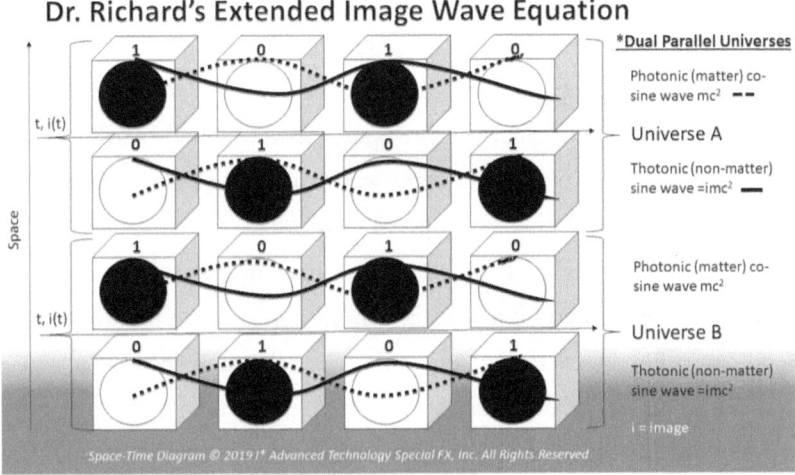

The first-time frame image (black circle in a box) shows the electron was processed by the camera and displayed by the PTC. The second time frame shows that the electron was not seen by the camera (empty box) – it somehow disappeared, but where? Again, the third time frame shows that the electron was again processed and displayed just as in time frame 1. The advantage of PTC is illustrated by superimposing Schrödinger's equation on top of the images. Notice the peaks and troughs show 100% correlation with the PTC images captured in time. The second image of the next time series (row two) shows that the electron that disappeared in frame one was replaced at the same instant in time but a different physical space point. Details of the camera image taken by the PTC image processor show that the electron in frame two of time series one gradually fades out, disappearing (as indicated by the empty box) and then fades back to 100% matter form in the third frame. Our special PTC image processor showed the same kind of process in the second time line of images. In time frame one the electron had disappeared, slowly faded back into full matter in frame two, faded out again and so forth – the times series keeps repeating itself forever.

It is visually obvious, that overlapping Schrödinger's wave function (dashed line) shows the math equivalent of this strange electron behavior of fading in, disappearing and fading out. But only the first (dashed line) time series is the Schrödinger wave, the next solid black line is my extended invention of Schrödinger's wave, called the Dualetonian wave. It is mathematically the dual opposite in peaks, troughs, descending and ascending behavior. The Chinese and Russians don't have the PTC camera or the Dualetonian wave interpretation – Mak will love this! It leads to seeing dual action of any entity all at the same instant of time – the beginning of the discovery of quantum space-time control!

We did this with many different quantum size particles, and they all exhibited this behavior. So the question arises, why are the two time lines similar but yet apparently somehow dual opposites of each other? – when one electron in the time series line one, is 100%, in existence, it 100% doesn't exist in time series line two – where each frame in both lines were taken by the PTC camera at exact simultaneous times (PTC dual time channel mode).

I went back to my calculations and discovered by extending the Schrödinger's equation to fit time series line two, the dual opposite waves fit the pattern perfectly. This implies the intuitively obvious conclusion that the particles are dual opposites of each other and so are their images! The first line is an electron with negative charge and negative energy, $-mc^2$. The second line is a twin electron, but it has positive charge and positive energy, mc^2 – which is called a positron of positive energy. I call the electron annihilation a hole in space-time because the matter is gone. Notice also a very important point. When the electron annihilated itself, the positron created itself exactly at the same instant in time. This implies that the dual action happens at infinite speed because the two particles are in different physical places simultaneously. This also violates Einstein's equation – which says nothing can travel faster than the speed of light! Images move in physical space and time at an instant. At the same time it demonstrates conservation of mass energy – when one particle fades out the other fades in keeping the total energy a constant of the motion.

We found another interesting thing about the particles fading in and out. We adapted our PTC camera with a wave conjugator which can look at the particle behind the scene of it fading out or in. We found that there is a space-time cloud that cloaks/masks the particle – similar to a solar eclipse. As the particle is fading away, it is just becoming buried in space time. Our PTC camera can see behind the cloud and reverse the space-time cloak completely. That is what gives it the appearance of a massless hole. The rim of the hole is a very dense negative gravity field that protects the hole from collapsing into a singularity without physical dimension. The hole can be a tube behind the cloak, so that quantum particles can travel through the massless hole at infinite speed to another parallel universe. A particle can go in a hole and never come back. So, if the PTC camera was just looking at the particle without the wave conjugator it wouldn't see anything for every frame in its relative future. Pretty amazing!

INTERVIEWER. Wow! In one fell swoop the extension of all physics currently limited by issues of the Schrödinger/Einstein approach is made clear by your interpreting images as a wave. What does Universe B, represent in figure 2?

DR. RICHARD. Notice that in time line three and four (figure 2.0) the same kind of thing happens, but now the particles created and annihilated are double dual opposites of lines one and two – an electron with positive energy and a positron with negative energy. This can only mean the existence of parallel mirror image type universes. So, we have two universes in this set of PTC camera images – A and B. The dashed and

solid lines show the extension of Schrödinger/Einstein space time –
when the electron has zero probability of existing its twin positron has
100% chance of being in matter form at a different physical point but at
the same instant in time.

INTERVIEWER. What about the images of let's say myself as I move
in time?

DR. RICHARD. Ok, consider (figure 2.0) again and picture an image
of yourself sitting in a chair in each of the four time lines. Time line
one shows you popping in and out, sitting in your chair as you move
through space-time. Time line two is the same but your chair is now
at a different point in space, all at the instant in time that your image
disappears in time frame one.

Time line three shows you in a dual opposite state (one of an infinite number that you can be in at the same instant of time!) The
state that you are in is illustrated in the novel as Time Smith travels
to Atlantis, remember? I can bring back the image of you now because
thotonix time can be created at any time by using the PTC technology.
The blank holes are just you being cloaked out; we can see you if we put
the wave conjugator back on the PTC. The wave conjugator can even
take pictures of you faster than the quantum shutter speed of the universe– the time the hole stays in the zero-view state – the zero in the
probability wave function. You move in time on a non-linear random
curve in an expanded space-time diagram as illustrated by the Time
Smith in the novel see (figure 3.0, following page).

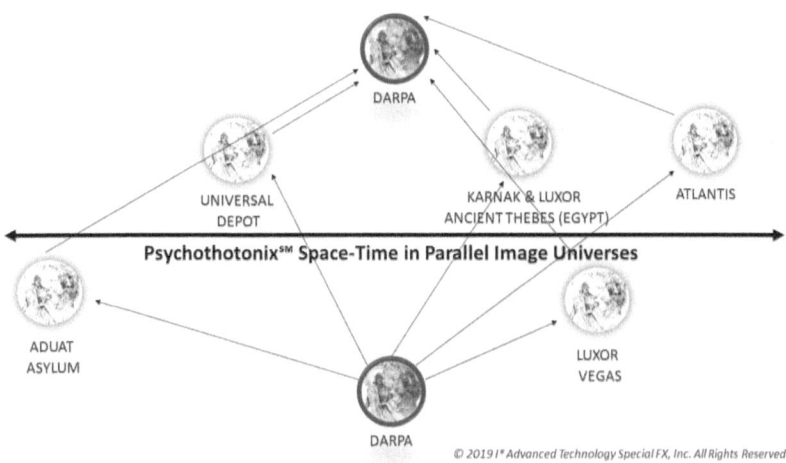

DARPA

UNIVERSAL
DEPOT

KARNAK & LUXOR
ANCIENT THEBES (EGYPT)

ATLANTIS

Psychothotonix[SM] Space-Time in Parallel Image Universes

ADUAT
ASYLUM

LUXOR
VEGAS

DARPA

INTERVIEWER. How does my brain process photons of myself or anything external?

DR. RICHARD. Think of an electron in the external world. As an external photon scatters off it and enters the brain it is processed by knocking off or exciting an electron in the brain itself. The brain electron jumps to a different energy level and emits a virtual photon, or what I call a thoton, that is processed by the brain's equivalent of a PTC processor/display. It is the process of consciousness or cognition where the image of the electron is projected into your internal view. Now think of taking an image of you in a mirror. All the quadrillions of photons scattered by the mirror back into your brain cause an avalanche of quadrillions of electrons jumping in harmony to each frame in the time line, thus projecting an image of you. But the image also has an interpretation because your brain has its own-form of an atom.

After the photons turn into thotons, they trigger a point on your spherical shaped thotonix atom which in turn creates you to have a response – I like the way I look, I hate the way I look (dual opposites) any of a quadrillion points of view (all of which have dual opposites). The internal process is complicated, but we can map it on our PTC and create a chart of each point and collected viewpoints of some external event. We call this the thoton atomic periodic chart in analogy to the physical atomic periodic chart of atoms.

INTERVIEWER. You incorporate many interesting special effects in *Tetrastatum*. In several places you mentioned that there may be many universes. Can you explain what that means?

DR. RICHARD. Many great philosophers and scientists (like Newton and Steven Hawking) have suggested that we live in a giant sphere-shaped universe (like a crystal ball) filled with all the planets, stars, black holes, particles, people....

INTERVIEWER. So, if the universe is this huge sphere, then is it finite in physical size?

DR. RICHARD. Some experts say that the universe is a huge sphere that is finite in size relative to the matter content, but it could be infinite anyway. In any event, for this fictional novel we use the idea that it is a sphere of finite size, because it is easier to visualize. So, even if it is finite it is really big! It takes photons emitted from stars at the edge of this giant sphere billions of years to get to us! However, this would still translate into a finite physical size universe.

INTERVIEWER. Then what is outside the sphere?

DR. RICHARD. Many scientists have been speculating about this for years. Einstein developed his general relativity equations based on the assumption this universe is a sphere of finite size, called a big bang universe. But others have said that since the total universe itself could be infinite in size, then there could be other big bang universes floating outside this one in some sea of infinite size. That is where the term mini big bang universes comes from. Intuitively, these giant spheres would also be moving at different speeds relative to each other.

INTERVIEWER. Could these spheres collide and create a huge explosion?

DR. RICHARD. Yes, but I have not seen any articles written on this topic. If that happened, it would be complete destruction. All the matter and the stars would collide in each of the two mini big bang universes, and probably all that would be left would be infinite photons (light particles) moving at the speed of light all over the rest of the infinite universe. Possibly, these light particles could puncture other mini big bang universes and create some huge lightning bolt-like action that could blind other inhabitants.

INTERVIEWER. Is there any evidence of such mini big bang universes? Can we invent an experiment that discovers these?

DR. RICHARD. There is no experimental evidence of known credibility relative to the scientific world. However, there have been some great scientists who have derived mathematical models to describe this possibility. I would propose a fiction-based physics experiment where one could place two detectors separated halfway around the world. Then, if there were particles that traveled at infinite speed, any one of these would hit the two detectors simultaneously! Both highly accurate clocks (called atomic clocks) would record this simultaneous action at a distance at one instant in time! The lab directors could then send these results back to each other at the speed of light because this is data that is already documented in their labs and the speed of light transmission of data is not relevant to the outcome. The interpretation of the data could be presented as definite proof that other mini big bang universes must exist—that could be a special effect in a movie.

INTERVIEWER. You use the word fictional physics and physics at points in the book. What is the difference and implications of these terms?

DR. RICHARD. Physics is a subject area where equations are derived about some physical process, like electrons interacting with each other. Then we go out to the lab and create an experiment—with the physics equipment—and measure the expected results that the equations tell us. If we get the same results repeatedly, then we say that the scientific principle has been achieved; it is based on observed facts, not imaginary ideas. This is what is so powerful about physics. Before physics was created, people could use their imagination and invent any possible thing—like any kinds of gods, demons, ghosts, or whatever they wanted—to explain unknown phenomena. However, my fictional physics effects are a logical extension of some physics principle with an equation that I have derived. I then invent some sort of technology (also as a logical extension of some known equipment that exists now). This is a form of Psychothotonix[SM]—the images created in the novel have a unique interpretation to each observer.

INTERVIEWER. So, this is sort of an extension of the scientific principle? Are there scientists who have issues concerning Psychothotonix[SM]?

DR. RICHARD. Yes, there are some, but most agree that is better than some totally non-believable extension of physics. Besides, the fact that it is just a special effect in a movie makes it more acceptable to those types of thinkers.

INTERVIEWER. My position is that it sounds like a good way for people to learn some physics in an entertaining way. Can you give me an example of this?

DR. RICHARD. Yes, in the movie "Interstellar" there was one key relativity equation that was introduced as a special effect. In physics parlance, we call this the twin paradox. Einstein invented it as one of the results of his relativity equations. The equations express the idea that if two identical twins highly accelerate away from each other and then deaccelerate back—now being together in the same physical space and time—then one twin will be less in physical age than the other! A paradox indeed. The reason is that their clocks run at different rates under these conditions. So the total elapsed time will be different for each. This math equation has never been tested in this manner, but it is expected to be what would happen based on other experimentally valid results. This was also one of the effects that I described in my first book called *I* star physics*. I suggested that this would be one of any number of entertaining physics effects that could be described prior to the movie being made. Consequently, the audience did indeed learn some physics that most of them did not know.

INTERVIEWER. One of the other special effects that is a major theme in the novel is that universes could have no matter, just pure images made of thotons. How would that happen in a fiction physics perspective?

DR. RICHARD. I coined the word thotons in one of my first academic articles in the late 1990s. The fact is, when our brain looks at some external photonic scene it somehow processes these external images into images in our brain. In photonics we say that the photons scatter off the scene objects and enter our brain via our eyes. The brain then in some miraculous manner image processes these photon images into an internal image. I call this process photons transforming into thotons—a logically extended word to include the thought process involved in the interpretation of the external photon image. It is important to note that the thoton image processing also adds at least two additional "dimensions" to the external photon image—emotional and behavior interpretations. That is any external photon image is interpreted by the brain's emotional and behavioral "thotonix processors," which I call tixels (to contrast with pixels as it relates to photons). Consequently, the external image is internally an image void of any real matter, at least in appearance—an image without matter. Of course, most scientists would say that the matter of the brain is somehow inextricably involved in the external matter image. So even though you can't "touch and feel" any matter within the internal image, they would say that it is still the result of interaction (touch and feel) of the external image. In any event, that was my first somewhat fictional example of thoton, non-matter universes. That is to say, that each person has an internal universe filled with thoton images that are recorded in space-time.

This also means that persons of the past had internal universes that were recorded in space-time and can be accessed, at least in the special effect of a movie. Now, when you combine the effect of other matter universes that I describe above, then it is a logical extension that we can put other people in other matter universes (each with a thoton universe within their brain). That is just one type of thoton universe. In the book we used the idea that Atlantis itself may be a thoton universe without being in a matter universe—just floating "out there somewhere." That is what is good about thoton universes: you can create an endless number of different types of special effects and even ways for people to think about the possible meaning of reality itself.

INTERVIEWER. You also mentioned, as a main theme in the novel, dream states as a series of thoton images.

DR. RICHARD. Yes, I expanded this into a fictional physics interpretation, a kind of Psychothotonix^{SM} effect. When we think about our dreams, most people would probably agree that the dream is really void of any matter. You may interpret the dream with matter forces involved, like someone physically hurt you, and you felt an emotional response and some sort of behavioral response to take action against your perpetrator. Dreams are strange indeed. Another example of a dream that we can relate to is the time travel aspect of a dream. We can dream that we are in some past point in time, some place in time of unknown origin, the future, a distorted view of the day's activities. There are infinite thoton states, internal universes of unknown real origin. So I use this as a fictional physics-based concept of a non-matter universe without any real defined physical space in time—you are a being in time without time.

INTERVIEWER. At another stage you mentioned scenes about travel to other non-matter universes via dream travel at infinite thoton speed? How did you come up with this concoction?

DR. RICHARD. Well, in general, my background in physics and philosophy certainly helped me think of this kind of fictional Psychothotonix^{SM} concept. However, some of my personal dreams helped me as well. For example, some of my own personal dreams involve me doing things that are completely out of my talent zones, such as playing and teaching Flamenco guitar, or conducting an orchestra. I have many advanced music-oriented dreams yet have no background knowledge in my mind. So where does the information come from at an apparent instant (without study)? I doubt that I would be able to memorize such details from a show and rerun these in my sleep. In any event, the dreams gave me the idea that such dreams could be connected to some other sphere of knowledge—something inexplicable. If that is the case, then the information must travel to my dream instantly. So the idea of thotons came about via reflection of my own dreams. The fictional idea is that if there are thotons, then they most likely travel at infinite speed via some unknown channels in space-time that are void of matter, because dreams are essentially non-matter images in fictional physics terms. It is abstract, but still a somewhat logical possibility.

INTERVIEWER. You mentioned that the Psychothotonix^{SM} and photonic images are points on spheres. Can you give me some examples?

DR. RICHARD. Yes. Most people know what a sphere is. The earth is basically spherical in shape. A basketball is spherical in shape. You can look up spheres online and get all kinds of images of a sphere with the related mathematics of a sphere: equations about their diameter, circumference, the length of arcs, spirals on a sphere, etc. As I mentioned, the model of the big bang universe that Einstein derived is that our physical universe is spherical. Atoms, electrons, photons—all kinds of physical entities—are spherical in nature and modeled mathematically as spheres. In calculus a point is an infinitesimal sphere and any object is thus an infinite number of spheres added together.

Photonix is about making images of some external event relative to our brain. This is done fundamentally by using spherical lenses that consequently collect photons from a cone of light that is a circle (a reduced-down version of a sphere) at its entrance pupil. So the camera image is basically a sphere of photons at some depth of focus. Clearly, there are many other forms and shapes in the field of view, but these are immersed in a sphere of spherical photons. You can imagine a sphere in your mind very easily because it is a fundamental image of the macroscopic and microscopic universe. I use a sphere for photonic (external to your brain) or Psychothotonix^{SM} (internal to your brain) modeling because it is the basic form of images.

INTERVIEWER. In the novel, you have a military tribunal put "reality" on trial where you talk about images as points on photonic and

Psychothonix[SM] spheres. Will you expand on this in a more general case?

DR. RICHARD. Yes, in the math model section of this appendix I derive a detailed courtroom example by expanding on quantum logic. I can make this very simple to visualize, at least in terms of the basic concepts.

Consider a defendant, four jurors, and two lawyers. Let's say that we don't have a clear set of evidence of the defendant's state of guilt for the murder of someone. The lawyers present convincing evidence of both dual opposite states (100% guilt is the dual opposite state of 100% innocent). The jurors are given a computer where they can pop open a sphere to mark points on it relative to their perception of judgement. A new sphere pops up every so often so that they can change their judgement points on the sphere. They are instructed to just point and click on the sphere when asked to. The spheres then are lined up chronologically, sort of a set of spheres evolving in time. Consider each point on the sphere as a degree of the judgement of guilt or innocence. The North Pole is the judgement point of 100% guilty as perceived by the juror. The South Pole on the sphere is the judgement point of 100% innocent as perceived by the juror at some moment of required decision-making ordered by the judge. The East point on the sphere is representative of 50% perceived guilt and 50% perceived innocence based on some set of images/conditions presented by the lawyers. The West point on the sphere also carries the same perceived values of the degree of guilt and the degree of innocence, but based on some dual opposite perceived images or conditions. Mathematically, all points on the equator would be points of judgement that are 50/50% of each state, but based on different perceived conditions. So the North and South are dual opposite states, the East and West are dual opposite states, and each point on the equator has a dual opposite state of conditions.

To make it simple, the jurors are asked to point and click on one point of judgement at the required time. They are instructed to pick East as a 50/50% degree of judgement, but they perceive the situation as moving toward the South Pole. They are also instructed to pick the West as a 50/50%

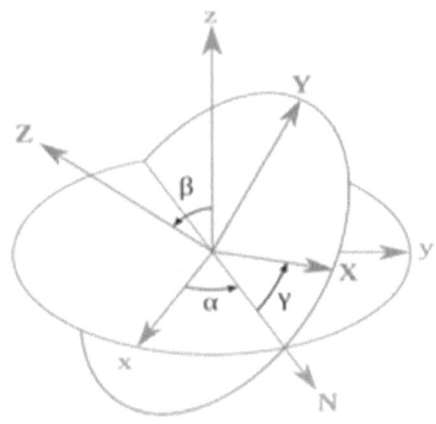

degree of judgement, but they perceive the situation as moving toward the North Pole. So the condition of dual opposite sub set conditions is the way they see their next decision most likely moving. In order to simplify, they just have four points to choose from. If they see the defendant in some mixed probability state, such as 25% guilty and 75% innocent, they are asked to just pick one closest to the four points on the sphere.

Mathematically, when they pick a point of judgement there is an arrow that points from the center of the sphere to the point on the sphere they have chosen. These are called phasors in mathematics; they serve the purpose of assisting the jurors to have a mental image of how the judgements move in time—sort of like the hands on a clock. Of course, a computer program can keep track of all of the arrows relative to points of judgement. Each sphere consequently represents a mental image at a moment of judgement. This is what I call a Psychothotonix[SM] image sphere on a computer, which is actually a photonic image device. Notice that the size of the sphere can be any unit on the screen. You could adjust it to suit your visual state. However, the values stored in the computer are always one unit of judgement. That is, the arrow stays the same length anywhere on the sphere (because the spheres don't change shape), but the computer program knows the point judgement value chosen by the juror. The adjacent image is a sphere, a thotonic or photonic sphere of anything. The angles shown by phasors represent different perceptions of any single person or a group of people at a given time. As time evolves the phasors move around. Clearly, there can be an infinite number of thoton spheres "floating around in people's brains," streaming through time-forward, moving in the present or in the past!

INTERVIEWER. Okay Then I assume that at some point the judge asks the jurors to make their final decision, and that is the final judgement by each juror.

DR. RICHARD. That is one way to do it; however, because the juror most likely changes his points of judgement as time moves on—statistically, the most objective way to come up with a final point of judgement is to weight all of his points of judgement in time and come up with an average, an expectation value of the degree of guilt or innocence. The computers are linked together, and all the jurors' decisions are weighted, summed together to get an average value of all the jurors' judgements (their mental images of the degree of judgement). A computer could easily calculate this type of data, so this represents a new way to model perception of jurors in a courtroom trial.

INTERVIEWER. Interesting. So when you talk about thotons, then each point on the sphere is a thoton value?

DR. RICHARD. Exactly that, a thoton value! The thoton value is of course based on images from the external world. For example, the lawyers might show images of the crime scene (taken from a camera, which is a photonic technology) or they might use a laser to scan the blood on the scene (a different type of photonic technology). They move about, talk, and express a spectrum of emotion-packed statements. All this courtroom action adds up in the juror's mind with the final outcome of the juror picking a thoton value of judgement. Remember, the external images are called photonic images, so in this case the photonic images turn into one thoton point. Quadrillions of photons turn into one thoton point on a Psychothotonix^{SM} sphere! That's the whole point! All photonic images end up as just thoton non-matter points on a sphere.

INTERVIEWER. You used many scenes of duality in the book. Can you give me the spherical math model of the tigers, for example?

DR. RICHARD. Yes, I invented the four image states of a potential threat as another example of points on a Psychothotonix^{SM} sphere. Clearly tigers are a potential theat. Think of the North Pole as a point where someone in a tiger situation views the potential threat of the tigers as not a threat at all! This is because he sees (thotonically) that he can tame the tigers, get the tigers to work with him cooperatively—maybe putting a leash on them making them pets. Let's say another person in the scene perceives that the tigers are a 100% threat and has the thotonic image of running away, fleeing from the scene altogether! That point can be thotonically described as the South Pole on the sphere—exactly the dual opposite of the North Pole. Now consider a third person who perceives the tigers to be a threat, but he can beat the threat by removing himself from the scene. He can sit in a tree above the tigers, a tree that tigers can't climb. Symbolically, this has the connotation of being calm and content, so we can call this the East Pole on a Psychothotonix^{SM} sphere. Now consider a fourth person, who sees the tigers as a threat that he can conquer. He views himself being able to club the tigers to death, all of them! This is the dual opposite to the above point and is the West Pole on a Psychothotonix^{SM} sphere.

INTERVIEWER. I see. This is a different kind of Psychothotonix^{SM} sphere but with the same mathematical representation.

DR. RICHARD. Yes. In fact, I have proven that any situation can be modeled this way. This makes it a powerful new way to model human behavior—emotional, mental, decision-making, physical reactions—anything.

INTERVIEWER. The book dealt with many types of defense-oriented concepts (control of Atlantis, etc.). Can you give me a typical example involving military action where your Psychothotonix^{SM} modeling methodology could be applied?

DR. RICHARD. That is a very good question because there are unlimited applications of this Psychothotonix^{SM} technology in military scenarios where the laser and electro-optics technology are viewing a potential threat. In photonics there is a standard that people use to analyze the images, called the Johnson criteria. It is complex, but in a simplified way we can say that any image has a degree of resolution from zero% up to almost 100%. For example, the details of a threat such as an enemy tank could be close to 100%. The Johnson criteria would then say that the object is a close match to its image. Clearly, in this scenario the image is used to decide about what to do. One of the obvious choices is to blow it up. But with Psychothotonix^{SM} sphere mathematics there could be an infinite number of possible actions that need to be considered. There could be ways to tame the situation, to use it as a negotiation tool to save many lives. Another option could be to just keep it at bay until action could be taken. The Psychothotonix^{SM} sphere could be linked to an artificial-intelligence neural network that learns best-case decisions over time (based on the degree of success of its history of decisions). Each point on the sphere is then a probability-amplitude phasor connected to the origin. The equations of motion of the probability amplitude are then derived using similar logic to quantum mechanics. The change of the points on the sphere evolves in time.

INTERVIEWER. In the last chapter of the book, "The Resurrection of Reality," you mentioned (in the trial of reality section) how the Time Smith moves in Psychothotonix^{SM} space-time via quantum teleportation. How did you derive this concept from physics as a special effect?

DR. RICHARD. Quantum mechanics has some very strange effects that are outside of being intuitive—in fact, counterintuitive. One of these is that a particle can go from one point in space-time to another via an infinite number of possible paths! We can't see this with a camera (a photonic device that takes matter images in space-time). Nevertheless, the quantum mathematical machinery says that all paths between two points in space-time need to be part of the final destiny of the particle in space-time. You can view this in your mind as a point in time—say, at exactly twelve noon a quantum particle (perhaps an electron or its dual opposite, an anti-electron) leaves its "gun," and then we have some advanced detector that sees the particle hit its screen. If we solve the Schrödinger equation of space-time motion (which is the key equation of quantum mechanics) we have to consider that the particle did not go in a straight line of a "space-time diagram"; rather, it went via any one of an infinite number of curved lines that stretch from the space-time point at the gun's exit-point to the final entrance into the detector.

As a fictional special effect, think of a Psychothotonix^{SM} sphere where the South Pole is the trigger point of the electron or its dual opposite anti-electron (which is also a real particle in physics). Consider the North Pole as its final point—hitting the detector. The path connecting the North Pole to the South Pole is the "matter path" of the particle. This is the path that we would measure if we had a camera that neglected the infinite possible quantum paths, since this is the most intuitive to an audience. I call this the matter universe path in general terms. Let's say the camera can take as many images as the brain—about a billion times a billion per second—and we can go back to any time and look at the quantum size particle on its path on the Psychothotonix^{SM} sphere. We can pick any point of its journey and display its point on a laptop computer screen. So this means that the camera and the laptop work as an image processor, recording the flight of the particle image-by-image, a billionth of a billionth of a second per frame!

Next, let's say I set up this demonstration for an audience. I send an electron from a gun to its detector and display the electron hitting the detector at an exact time, which is then displayed on the laptop screen. I play it back to other points on its matter path. Everyone is then asked to agree that this is true reality—it really happened in the matter universe! It turns out that they all agree. So what is that matter point on their own laptop Psychothotonix^{SM} screen? Exactly the same thoton value for all the jurors in the court room. They all agree that the particle did move across the room on the same identical path, and that it hit the detector and showed up on the screen at the exact same moment. Yes, that means there are now two Psychothotonix^{SM} spheres. The particle sphere and each juror's sphere on their own laptop.

In Chapter Ten of *Tetrastatum, Resurection of Reality*, I brought in my tame dolphins as an exhibit to annihilate reality. We explain in detail in the book that I discover that the dolphin is capable of traveling to other Psychothotonix^{SM} spheres while it is sleeping and simultaneously wide awake—that the dolphin can travel in Psychothotonix^{SM} space-time on this planet. The dolphin can travel on other space-time curves on the Psychothotonix^{SM} sphere simultaneously! Wow, kind of like the Schrödinger curves in quantum relativity! The dolphin can Psychothotonix^{SM} time travel!

I hook up the dolphins and Dr. Smith with electrodes to prove all of this. I call this my Biological Quantum Teleportation Image Processor "BQTIP" in the novel. I capture the Psychothotonix^{SM} images of the dolphins and Dr. Smith's space-time travel, clearly beyond any path of a camera in the DARPA matter universe. From the monitor, beyond any reality that we know of, the dolphin can see everything in the courtroom in DARPA and in Aduat as Dr. Smith converses with Erwin Schrödinger. Dr. Smith can see both matter and non-matter image paths simultaneously! In fact, I demonstrate that the BQTIP could create images of faraway places at an instant—thus showing that thotons travel at infinite speed and have no mass! The panel concludes that we are guilty of annihilating reality, demonstrating that reality is infinite in imaging dimensions of time travel. Images of everything can be created at an instant. Finally, I connect this to the case of Dr. Tim Smith/Time Smith. The novel demonstrates that his family indeed died on one curve of Psychothotonix^{SM} time travel but did not die on the one matter time path of the universe in the DARPA court room.

I explain that the DARPA project changed after my work with the dolphins, which provided a solution to an impasse with my calculations using standard relativity, quantum mechanics, and current technology. I conclude that a matter time travel machine can never be created. It would be locked into one matter path of images and could not go forward or backward in time, with our current technology and current laws of physics. The dolphins provided an opportunity to employ a fictional Psychothotonix^{SM} effect.

INTERVIEWER. What are the areas of product applications that use Psychothotonix^{SM}?

DR. RICHARD. Laser and electro-optic technology that can measure/control human perceptions and related human behavior patterns can be used to model human interpretations of images in any field using Psychothotonix[SM] methods. I Star Advanced Technology Special FX Inc. is the only company that utilizes the proprietary technology in the following application areas:

- Photonix and Psychothotonix[SM] Special FX Concepts for Screenplays, Books, Movies, VR, Gaming
- Psychothotonix[SM] Research & Product Development
- Photonix and Psychothotonix[SM] Application Media Tools for Defense, Biomedical, and Entertainment Industries

ADVANCED PSYCHOTHOTONIX^{SM} *TOPICS*

P*SYCHOTHOTONIX*^{SM} *AS A TOOL* to maximize image interpretation and decision-making using the I* mathematical model and related AI software tools is not limited to the basic areas discussed in Appendix A. The list below provides a summary of key photonic areas and advanced topics that Dr. Richard routinely discusses in his seminars. These topics can also be used for designing a limitless number of highly advanced applications and entertainment special effects. (The list of topics assumes the reader is an advanced photonic expert.) In general, the following photonic topics develop very complex interpretations and decision-making methods that are essential for the success of Psychothotonix^{SM} applications.

Dr. Richard's Key Topics: Quantum Optics/Imaging, Laser Quantum Field Theory, Speckle Wave Interactions in Application to Holography and Nonlinear Optics, Fourier Optics, Electro-optic Imaging Systems, Dynamic Light Scattering, and Computer Imaging.

INFORMAL DISCUSSION NOTES—A FEW KEY POINTS TAILORED FOR PHOTONIC EXPERTS

QUANTUM OPTICS/IMAGING/NONLINEAR QUANTUM ELECTRODYNAMICS

+ Starting with Maxwell's equation in a dispersive anisotropic material and using the slowly-varying amplitude and phase approximation for the polarization, one can show that the amplitude is driven by the imaginary part of the polarization and gives rise to the absorption and emission. The real part is associated with the phase and thus the phase velocity index of refraction, dispersion, and self-focusing. This gives rise to the standard Lorentzian Bell Curve which is the sum of space-time integrals of the convolution of susceptibility and the electric field. Consequently, the polarization induced at each point within the nonlinear material is a tensor-based function (each component of the polarization then having some combination of electric field components for each electromagnetic wave). Typically, only the first through third order terms are of current application interest.

+ The Hanbury Twiss experiment demonstrates the coherence of light via the autocorrelation function, which varies from 1 to 0. It can also go to below zero when photon anti-bunching occurs, which means that no two photons can reach the detector simultaneously. This has no classical counterpart, only a purely quantum solution.

+ The nonlinear dipole oscillator equation of motion of a response to a monochromatic electric field can be used to describe the expansion of the polarization in a power series. This process can be used to develop various wave mixing phenomena, such as four wave mixing, the Ker effect, side band resonances, sum and difference frequency mixing, phase conjugation, etc.

+ The solution of Schrödinger's equation demonstrates the quantum wave packet and probability density harmonically oscillating in time. In addition, the Fermi Dirac solution shows the probability of transitions to build up, which can be used to explain the constant rate proportional to the intensity of the incident light, which in turn explains the photoelectric effect.

+ In general, for nonhomogeneous, nonlinear, temporal dispersion, and anisotropic media with n fold quasi-monochromatic waves interacting at a point in space-time, the polarization of one component can be expressed as an n fold integral of the convolution of the susceptibility tensor with each electric field vector. Thus, the polarization picks off different combinations of the n electric field components (the tensor nature).

+ The probability density matrix is the key tool for modeling most of the nature of photon atom interaction. In general, each atom has its own line center, creating inhomogeneous broadened Lorentzian—each atom experiences different Stark shifts.

+ The Bloch Vector is a good tool for visualizing the equations of motion of the probability density matrix components. For central tuning the state vector processes clockwise around the U axis at the Rabi flopping frequency. Off resonance is seen as elliptical action in one quadrant.

+ One can visualize the Schrödinger picture of this nonlinear behavior by visualizing a delta function that oscillates harmonically along the z direction. This is the probability amplitude solution to the standard Schrödinger equation. The squared version gives the actual probability density.

+ The quantum mechanical harmonic oscillator can easily be solved from the Hamiltonian picture. The solution is Hermite polynomials. If we introduce the creation and annihilation operators, the solution can be put into state vector relationships. The product of these operators gives the total number of quanta of excitation for both stimulated and spontaneous emission in a two-level atom. The process can be expanded to a many-level atom.

+ A single state vector is called a pure case, while an incoherent sum of pure-case contributions is a mixed case. Thus, the density operator is typically the best way to describe this quantum action. The density operator is easy to visualize as a bilinear combination of probability amplitudes. The time derivative of the density operator gives the equations of motion of the quantum states of a two-level atom. Typically, we deal with the population matrix, which is the integral across the homogeneous or inhomogeneous Lorentzian for each line center and pump rate per unit volume to each level.

+ Spectral hole burning of the Lorentzian occurs in many media. In the case of many media that have a population inversion from a Maxwellian distribution we can solve the population difference equations, which reduces to the plasma dispersion function (the convolution of a Gaussian and a complex-valued Lorentzian). In the special case of the convolution between a real and imaginary-valued Lorentzian, we can use the residue theorem to easily solve for the spectral hole burning. It is intuitively obvious that this leads to just another Lorentzian with a dimple in the middle of the population difference versus the normalized frequency difference. This reduces to the homogeneous and inhomogeneous broadening limits.

+ Spatial hole burning for counter propagating wave interactions can induce a grating that couples the waves together. By solving the population equation of motion, we arrive at the spatial hole burning case.

+ Two photon two-level models describe a typical second harmonic generation where two photons create one photon at twice the energy (as in 1064 to 532 nm processes). Also, the sum of the momentum vectors is conserved. In addition, intermediate Stark level shifts play an important role. Further, we can have a complex-valued polarization scattering off the induced two-photon coherence.

♦ Polarization of semiconductor gain media. Here the use of Fermi Dirac distributions for electrons and holes in terms of the density matrix (which is the sum over all dipole matrix elements multiplied by the density matrices and divided by the volume of the semiconductor media). For carrier densities sufficiently high to give gain, the media is homogeneously broadened as in the two-level model. This linear gain is very simple (even though the summation is over a wide range of transition frequencies).

♦ Light forces and atomic media: every time an atom interchanges energy with the electromagnetic field, the momentum of the absorbed or emitted light must be compensated for by the mechanical motion of the atom. This is the way light influences the center of mass motion (in contrast to the above responses of light to the internal degrees of freedom of the atom). Expanding the Hamiltonian to include the kinetic energy operator and working out the algebra leads to a simple equation of motion for the probability amplitude, which is interpreted from the particle view as constant motion of the free particle from the photon momentum transfer. In addition, we can calculate the gradient force and the scattering force (the real and imaginary parts of the change of the expectation-value of the momentum operator (i.e., the same form as Newton's equation). Thus, this leads to many applications because the atom is diffracted by the light, as opposed to the diffraction of light from the edges of sharp media, such as atom mirrors, lenses, gratings, and interferometers. The Raman Nath approximation shows just this: the atomic spread of the transverse momentum increases linearly with time and Rabi frequency.

+ Quantum theory of a laser is first calculated by assuming the polarization is a superposition of polarization components when substituted into Maxwell's equations yield the amplitude and phase temporal changes as functions of the imaginary and real parts of these polarization components. This solution leads to the important difference between the gain problem and classical absorption problem, namely in that it is the oscillation frequency, rather than the wavelength that is shifted by the medium. Plotting the solution of the real and imaginary parts of the susceptibility for a homogeneous Lorentzian gain also shows the effect of mode pulling.

+ Mode Locking: Plotting the average frequency difference relative to the beat frequency parameter shows that the relative phase angle change in time is proportional to the rotation rate of the laser gyroscopes.

+ Three level system: The applied field (assuming the rotating wave approximation) causes transitions between levels a and b while level c (the ground state) acts as a reservoir connected to levels a and b via the decay and pump rates (from level c to a and b). If the pumping rates are significantly less than the decay rates, the three-level system reduces to the two-level system.

+ Coherent Dips and the Dynamic Stark Effect: pump and probe interaction create side band Stark-shifted frequencies (Raman shifters). In degenerate probe and saturation pump conditions with level lifetimes long compared to the dipole lifetimes, a coherent dip in absorption versus probe detuning caused by the inability of the population inversion to follow the probe-saturator beat frequency much larger than its decay rate is observed. Hence the coherent contribution to the probe absorption coefficient falls off as the beat frequency is increased. This quantum phenomenon allows one to measure population decay times particularly important for non-radiative (pico/femtosecond) decays in liquids and semiconductors.

- The Ti-sapphire and Quantum cascade lasers (as pumps) in combination with such Raman shifters allow for optical parametric oscillators (tunable over MIR). Other types of OPO allow for tunable lasers over most of the visible and infrared spectrum.

- Phase Conjugation: Two and three-level phase conjugation can be created via multi-wave interaction in a nonlinear material, including double phase conjugation and many spin-off applications. All events happen via two opposite pump waves creating a grating where the probe scatters to create a conjugate wave (reversed in space-time), thus duplicating the image of any object prior to its distortion due to some medium.

- Time-Varying Phenomena in Cavities: Multimode mode locking is typical, which differs from mode locking because here the coupling of the modes is between multi-mediums and can be used to create side band and combination tones. In some nonlinear processes, such as hydrodynamics, strange attractor chaos can be created—where the polarization is random but fits to a macroscopic pattern unique to the buildup of the multimode behavior—effectively, the strange attractor point in phase space.

- Coherent Transients: The pulses start out coherent but become incoherent in time—typical useful examples exist in Optical nutation, Ramsey Fringes and Photon echo.

- Field Quantization: A full quantum mechanical treatment requires quantizing the semi-classical multimode electromagnetic wave, using creating and annihilation operators representing the numbers of photons interacting. Coherence in this representation can be modeled with correlation functions like the semi-classical situation. For example, a coherent state is described by a Dirac delta function, but with uncertainties.

- Interactions between Atoms and Quantized Fields: Lays the foundation for more advanced problems such as spontaneous emission, resonance fluorescence, squeezed states, and narrow line width used to minimize the quantum noise.

FOURIER OPTICS

+   In all cases the optical transfer function (incoherent light) is the intensity convolution integral. The OTF is the integrated normalized autocorrelation function of the amplitude transfer function (coherent light) in the image plane where the optical transfer object can always be considered a black box with an entrance and exit pupil.

+   Talbot Images: Bar target diffraction – take the Fourier transform of the amplitude transmittance function, inverse transforming and squaring this gives the intensity distribution – yielding a perfect image of the grating under certain imaging distances and longer ranges one produces phase shifts (contrast reversals – black to white etc.)

+   Focusing Error Aberration: When a system is diffraction-limited, the amplitude point spread function is seen to consist of the Fraunhofer diffraction pattern of the exit pupil centered on an ideal image point. When wave-front errors exist the wave-front is distorted; thus, we can calculate the path length error (the curvature of a spherical wave-front) converging toward the image of an object point-source, which lies to the left or right of the image plane. Solving for this and placing it into the integral for the OTF aberration integral gives the OTF as a function of the spatial frequency. The MTF (the absolute value of the OTF) can then be plotted for various spatial frequencies— which shows the gradual image attenuation and contrast reversals.

DYNAMIC LIGHT SCATTERING

+   In all cases, we are looking for the temporal Fourier transform of the autocorrelation function of the dielectric constant fluctuations, which is the spectral density.

◆ The laser light is focused onto the sample. The scattered light is frequency-shifted do to the fluctuations of the polarizability constant. The scattered field can be considered a superposition of individual scattering centers which fluctuates in response to the molecular motions.

◆ Optical mixing (heterodyne or homodyne spectroscopy where no filter is inserted) is typically used for fluctuations less than a microsecond. Otherwise, a Fabry Perot filter is used. The scattered volume can be a NLO or any type of physical entity, and this technique can work for any fluctuating physical observable: velocity, mass, energy, temperature, concentrations, vibrations.

ELECTRO-OPTICAL SYSTEM PERFORMANCE -MEASUREMENTS OF PERCEPTIONS AND IMAGE INTERPRETATIONS

◆ The performance of all electro-optical imaging systems is measured by the product of the modulation transfer functions of each subcomponent to include (MTF optics, MTF motion, MTF detectors, MTF temporal response, MTF amplifiers, MTF filters, MTF LEDs, MTF lasers, MTF display, MTF psychophysical (eye plus brain interpretations).

◆ In all cases, the temporal Fourier transform of the autocorrelation function of the psychophysical MTF fluctuations of a person will give a measurement of how the person interprets any given special scene, bar target, and/or any image.

◆ Computer Image Processing after the electro-optical image processing can be performed to create further image enhancements. For example, processing in the frequency domain a light micrograph of a cross section of a skeletal muscle: a. thresholding does not delineate the fibers – b. applying a top hat filter by subtracting the brightest pixel with a five-pixel area [also by the spatial Laplacian of the brightness], which improves the ability to threshold the gold particles – c. the power spectrum from the Fourier transform shows the broken ring of spots corresponding to the average diameter of the fibers – d. retransforming the ring of spots with an annular filter selects just the spacing of the gold particles, adding this back to the original image increases the contrast and thresholding the image delineates the fibers.

♦ Speckle Wave Interactions in Applications to Holography and Nonlinear Optics: Speklons can increase the storage capacity in 3D holograms by orders of magnitude. Spatial and temporal speklons can be imaged processes similar to dynamic image processing to yield acoustic holography images of blood flow, material vibration, and many other fluctuation phenomena of any physical observable. Other topics include the instability of the phase conjugated speckle waves in Kerr-Like Media which can show compensation for distortions just like four-plane wave interactions do.

QUANTUM MECHANICAL LOGIC FOR PERCEPTION WAVES

♦ The mathematical machinery of quantum mechanics is based on probability waves. This has been validated by measurements for many years. However, all human factor-based measurement theories and methodologies have always been based on classical probability statistical-based models. It may be of some utility to develop a model of perceptions that is based on logic similar to quantum mechanics.

♦ To demonstrate this concept, consider the following simple example. A perception of a piece of art is interpreted in a different way by each of any number of observers. It is one entity with many different perceptions. Any given perception drives one to make some sort of decision. It is possible that a hyperspectral imaging tool can create the facial recognition of decision states. (The scope of this process is outside of this exploration.) However, imagine that this technology exists. As an example, consider some crime case where a juror's initial position is 100% influenced by the defense attorney. Thus, he perceives the probability of innocence is 100%—the juror is 100% certain of the state of the defendant at this moment in time—and the hyperspectral imaging device captures this state as a unique pixel pattern, or simply a 3D picture of this state. In the next series of time events, the prosecuting attorney provides an equal weight of evidence, therefore moving the juror in the direction of this position. If both "forces" are of equal weight, then at some point the juror will have equal "interference" from both lawyers and decide that the defendant is 100% neither guilty nor innocent (for a set of conditions presented)—the juror is 100% uncertain of the state of the defendant at this moment in time. Clearly, as time evolves the juror then sees the defendant 100% guilty (the driving force of the prosecuting attorney will dominate for some moment in time)—the juror is now 100% certain of the polar opposite state. Once again, the defense attorney force moves the juror toward the 100% uncertain state based on some polar opposite set of conditions. In the last round of lawyers' arguments, the juror naturally returns to his initial position—the juror is again 100% certain of the defendant being 100% innocent. The juror has gone one full circle of the position of probability over some frequency in time. This example contains the basic kernel of all perception measurements which is called the duality principle*, which means there are an infinite number of possible perceptions of the defendant at any given time.

+ We can also devise another dramatically simplified hyperspectral imaging application that demonstrates this fundamental property of duality in the world of measurement. Imagine that an infinite number of parts are being inspected by a hyperspectral imaging device. The first part is "perceived" by the hyperspectral imager as 100% perfect, the next part is very slightly less than perfect (a small amount of uncertainty), and going one-fourth of the way around the circle of duality results in a measurement of 100% uncertainty. The process continues (within the logic of the above circle of duality)—half way around the circle is a part that is 100% imperfect and the imaging device perceives it as such. Thus, one full circle represents one cycle of duality.

PERCEPTION MATHEMATICAL MODEL

    ✦   For those of you who know the basic quantum theory, we can show that quantum theory is in fact just a special case of this duality principle*. In addition, note that the above events clearly fit on a unit circle in the complex plane (with time as the central coordinate) and a "phasor rotating with amplitude" always equal to one – as some perception must occur at any given moment, a unit metric measurement in Hilbert space. In this model, $x = \cos \theta$ function is called the certainty coordinate, and $y = i* \sin \theta$ function is called the uncertainty coordinate. This is Dr. Richard's modification of the wave function in quantum mechanics, but the results will be the same.

    ✦   For example: $i*y$ is defined as the uncertainty coordinates; five observers (dots) separated in physical space would represent five different observers' perceptions in physical or temporal space. The harmonic amplitude along x (at theta $= kx$) is a non-physical Hilbert space coordinate. The certainty coordinate is ninety degrees out of phase with the uncertainty coordinate. The same wave amplitude mathematical machinery is used for the theta equaling the evolution of the wave in time.

THE DUALITY PRINCIPLE

    ✦   The conceptual-based examples covered in this material suggest that a modified version of the mathematics of nonlinear optics and quantum laser (two-state) systems can form a solid basis for a new paradigm in modeling human perceptions as waves in nature. The key tool for such modification would be the duality principle which can be stated as:

"There are always an infinite number of dual opposite views of any one physical object or any one entity at any given time. This also implies conservation of duality."

+   Many different types of special effects in movies and other modeling processes can be created using this model of duality in perceptions. When a movie that has advanced scientific concepts and technology embedded within the script is made, it is important that the movie viewer understand and be stimulated by various effects. Two of the critical components are:

+   How does the movie viewer perceive how physical objects and entities move in space-time?

+   How does the movie viewer perceive the principals of duality—the degree of love or hate, the degree of pain or pleasure, the degree of right or wrong, the degree of conflict or cooperation, the degree of noise or coherence, the degree of quantum wave or quantum particle, the degree of space or time contraction, the degree of one universe or its parallel opposite, the degree of the influence of past and future, the degree of the "external" forces of good and evil, the degree of the forces of physical chaos and order…?

INFORMAL TOPICS IN PSYCHOTHOTONIX^{SM}

Informal presentations by Dr. Richard—creating "new universes" with *i*∗physics and computer automation (2011)—created the *i*∗movie methodology, a new dimension in filmmaking where the laws of physics and *i*∗physics ("which are modified laws of physics") are introduced along with related, endless special effects to immerse the viewers into new realms of cognitive inspiration. On the following list are topics developed by the author and presented to Cal Tech and Dream Works:

INFORMAL TOPIC 1: *BASIC TYPES OF LIDAR MEASUREMENTS*

Lidar is very useful in many types of technology applications. In this section, we will review some of the mathematical concepts related to using lidar. In addition, perception space-time is a derivative of physical space-time. Consequently, reviewing the basic ideas of physical space-time and related lidar measurements will be useful. Measurement of space-time often involves a basic four-dimensional model of flat space-time defined by using world maps, world pictures, lidar maps, or Euclidean maps. The highlights of these manifolds are reviewed below. It is assumed that the reader has enough experience to visualize the graphic equivalent of these brief outlines.

WORLD MAPS

All objects are points on a space-time grid of physical space on one axis and time on the other. This concept originated from Newtonian theory but was not practical until the invention of radar and laser technology. In this world map, all objects are viewed as occurring at an instant in time (on a surface of simultaneity, time, $t = constant$). Consequently, each point on a surface of simultaneity is some event at a precise spatial location. As the observers move in time (along their world lines) the spatial points intersect new surfaces of simultaneity at points that coincide with their relative velocities. Vertical lines thus represent no velocity, other lines of curvature represent velocity space-time functions. World maps are limited in practical terms (for large astronomical distances) because events farther out along any surface of simultaneity require sending lidar signals at successively earlier times so that one can receive the echo pulses at some future world line point. Consequently, this method requires sending and receiving a vast array of lidar pulses to create an observationally meaningful image of astronomical phenomenon. Clearly, however, world maps are practical when the spatial distances are small compared to the distance that light travels in a few seconds (on "our" world space-time geometries).

WORLD PICTURES

In contrast to world maps, a world picture is a view of objects in space-time on the past light cone of the point of observation. The collection of light from distant objects via: a photograph, lidar picture, telescope, or direct observation of the sky in our "mind's eye" is a representation of the objects from our past light cone. Spatial image formation therefore necessitates associated time delays that are inherently imbedded within the medium of representation. Consequently, a two (or even a three-dimensional lidar) image of the distal objects (no matter how far away) are all projected onto the same plane, making it difficult to ascertain actual spatial details (metrics of the data). For astronomical-based world pictures this often requires special techniques, such as determination of distances by measuring apparent sizes, apparent luminosities, or redshifts. By incorporating these methods an observer can construct "his world picture" at any time in his history. Therefore, the key advantage is that a world picture developed with these special techniques allows one to measure extremely large distances.

RADAR AND LIDAR MAPS

These types of images are created directly by electro-optic technology typically used on airborne, land, or seaborne platforms. Pulses are directly sent out, reflected from the object as echo pulses delayed in time according to the limits of the speed of light and collected by the elctro-optic imaging instrument, thus enabling the creation of an image of the position of each object on the future light cone of the event.

This image processing technology has the advantage in that the image is directly obtained and immediately displayed, but it is limited to relatively short light travel times—consequently, not a good technique for astronomical distances.

World maps, world pictures, and radar/lidar maps are conceptually quite different representations of positions of objects in space-time. However, these maps differ substantially only when the objects depicted move appreciably on the relevant time scale. That is, when ordinary units are used to describe occurrences in our everyday world, the light cones are extremely flat, and the three views are very similar.

EUCLIDEAN SPACE (E3)

When the velocities are small compared to the speed of light for all relative observers, the space-time metric, or invariant, becomes the metric in E3 space. In such cases, the first and second fundamental forms can be used to describe the motion of objects in E3 space. A curve in E3 is uniquely determined by two local invariant's quantities, curvature and torsion, as functions of arc length. These are defined by the Fernet equations. Along with any curve, the tangent normal and bi-normal derivatives are simple differential equations. In a similar way, a surface is uniquely determined by local invariant quantities, called the first and second fundamental forms. Defining a coordinate patch on a two-dimensional surface of the three-dimensional object and defining differentials of the mapping leads to the first and second forms. If the metric changes in its local basis then one must also use Christoffel symbols. The mathematics is derived in any graduate level book on topology.

The first fundamental form is used in lidar applications to calculate the length, angles, and surface areas of the topology of examination. The following example demonstrates how this is accomplished. The following steps highlight how to use lidar with the first and second fundamental forms. This method works in many defense applications where decisions need to be made relative to calculating the best probability successes of the necessary actions.

1. Consider the image of an object in motion on the unit sphere.

2. This curve starts at the equator and winds like a spiral about the North Pole. To determine its length, we first must calculate the derivatives as defined by the first and second fundamental forms.

3. The first fundamental form and the arc length are easily calculated.

4. The surface area can then be calculated using the second fundamental form.

5. Any topological surface can be used for mapping the object's trajectory along the surface. Another common example is the motion of an object along a toroid. Most other surfaces can be computer-generated by matching the topologies from conic sections (hyperbolic sheets, hyperboloids, ellipsoids, spheres, circles, elliptic paraboloids, hyperbolic paraboloids, and quadric cones), embedding the appropriate spirals or arbitrary curve of motion.

Where the addition of spirals can be added as necessary, the degree of pitch of the spiral can be changed from the above example of a spiral on a sphere. For example, in the above instance of a toroid, a circle rotated about some z axis will generate the toroid and the addition of the spiral will have the motion of the given object at some "frozen point in space-time." Then the first and second fundamental forms can be calculated to yield the imaging data required for the application. Of course, very complex geometries can be generated directly from image data; then regions of interest can be developed from some mix and match of the above conic sections and spirals to generate the motion of the object of interest. Naturally, the mathematics of some situations requires significant detail and can go beyond the systems-level picture described here, but the concepts are still the same. Basically, this is all one needs for most lidar applications that use hyperspectral imaging, sum and difference mixing, or any type of laser/ electro-optic imaging techniques. Hyperspectral technology is an advanced form of lidar, yielding significantly more data than other laser or CCD instrumentation.

INFORMAL TOPIC 2.0: PERCEPTION OF SPACE-TIME WITHOUT PHYSICAL COORDINATES

Now that we have reviewed the basic concepts of physical space-time, we can start to derive the perception of space-time mathematics. Effectively, this model combines the physical space-time model with quantum mechanics and psychophysics concepts. At a first glance, the essence of perception space-time is: At any moment in physical space-time any person has an infinite number of possible ways to perceive any given event. Consequently, instead of one event in a physical space-time diagram (such as a photon ejecting an electron as one point in a space-time diagram), a person could see one of an infinite number of possible events at a given point in physical space-time. For example, (as described earlier) a juror would perceive the defendant in one of an infinite number of degrees of possible guilt or innocence at any given time. This logic is like quantum mechanics in the sense that the juror has an "amplitude" to perceive one of an infinite number of possible states of the defendant. Again, this can be modeled as amplitude points on a complex-valued circle at each point in physical space-time. The logic is similar to modeling possible states as "amplitudes" of polarization for a particle at a given point in physical space-time—that is, a quantum-limited laser can only see an infinite range of possible states because the laser linewidth is limited to a small, but infinite, range of possible "views" of the particle's state of polarization.

We can put this view into a mathematical machine: we can say any state of perception at a given moment is one of an infinite number of phasors in the complex plane—a sphere, or in simplified cases, a circle. There are different types of spheres, as will be discussed. There are also conditions of "interacting spheres."

Where the "positions" of the phasor are perception states of any given observer, clearly, each element of the position is non-physical—a thotonix state. For example, the observer perceives the defendant 20% guilty (the juror's position on the defendant) and therefore 80% uncertain of the state of 100% guilty under the conditions presented by both lawyers. As explained below, the juror here will also be 20% uncertain of the state of innocence, or 80% certain about the state of innocence. Consequently, the perception is at an angle with unit magnitude (a phasor) on a unit circle in the complex plane of the sphere or circle.

Notice that the duality state can also be set up orthonormal to one another. For example, 100% guilty is orthogonal to 100% innocent. If one wanted to use bra-ket notation, as we do in quantum mechanics, we would say that the inner product of 100% dual opposite perceptions is zero. That is, what is the probability amplitude of perceiving someone 100% guilty and at the same moment 100% innocent? Clearly, this fits with common sense. This logic (which is why we need a sphere or a circle to describe perceptions) will be expanded upon later in this text.

INFORMAL TOPIC 3: CASE STUDIES

The following case studies were developed to further define the nature of a perception space-time diagram that presents perception spheres moving on a physical space-time diagram. This is easy to view by drawing a sphere or circle at each point in the usual physical space-time diagram.

Again, the points on the sphere or circles are nonphysical coordinates. So mathematically speaking, you need to remove it from the physical space-time diagram. Hence, the center of the sphere or circle is a point in physical time and the perception phasors are abstract Hilbert space imaginary numbers. This is true for all perception types of spheres or circles. I call it the perception space-time diagram. Clearly, the spheres/circles move along their proper timeline (which is consistent with the fact that the perceivers are moving relative to each other physical space and time). This also introduces an interesting perception topic: an observer of some event moving at relativistic speeds will perceive the other spheres as contracted in perception—contracted spheres/circles relative to the observer, say, in the fixed lab frame of reference—an expansion of relativity principals.

These following general concepts are for informal conversation and are thus not in any particular order:

CASE 1.0: CLASSICAL HARMONIC MOTION AS PERCEIVED BY AN OBSERVER WITH A QUANTUM-LIMITED LASER

Consider some macroscopic physical entity oscillating in the x plane of an (x, iy) plane with $x0$ the center of the harmonic motion. It is conventional to draw a circle in the complex plane (x, iy) to illustrate this motion—namely, calling A as *the amplitude of motion.* As the particle moves from one extreme point, $x\ maximum$ on the right, to another extreme point on the right, $-x\ maximum$, it clearly executes simple harmonic motion. At time equals zero the physical entity is at some point on this circle, which can be represented by a phasor. Let's say that at time equals zero the phasor is all along the cosine maximum direction on the right of the circle. As time proceeds, the entity goes back and forth along the (t) axis. In a space-time diagram this would be a wave of space-time motion. The (it) component is just a mathematical generating function creating the accurate wave action in a space-time diagram, a complex-valued wave on a Hilbert space-time circle that is stationary on the initial surface of simultaneity. As the phasor moves around the circle the projection onto the x axis describes a wave in a space-time diagram; the center of the circle represents a stationary point in the space-time (world-line) point of view. We can always normalize the amplitude of any harmonic motion. Thus, we can define this wave as a perception wave that is being tracked by a quantum limited laser (with a line width that is limited in quantum noise when the uncertainty principle is equal to h bar using quantum squeezing techniques). This is really a single physical oriented perception of the particle's harmonic motion, not a perception circle or sphere (like the court room case) moving as described above. It is a typical way we describe this in wave theory of physical particles, etc. However, it is clearly a somewhat thotonix-oriented way because this kind of mathematical modeling creates an image in our mind of the physical particles motion. In the extreme condition, where we are talking about non-visible quantum particles, this mental construct also applies. It is part of the basis of my derivation of the more general nature of the Psychothotonix[SM] model.

The above non-quantum-based example is common sense basic physics, where we conclude that the macroscopic physical entity is always visible (perceived by the observer of the laser reading) as being at every position in time along its journey from its maximum right and maximum left positions—the only limitation being the longitudinal line width of the laser. For a slow light laser, the position can be tracked to the order of the wavelength spread of the laser, or sub-nanometer in wavelength—very exact at every moment in time. It is a Hilbert space circle because the complex valued iy coordinate is a non-physical coordinate, just functioning as a mathematical generator of wave action.

However, this fits with the standard solution of the simple harmonic equation of motion, where macroscopic physical entities can be observed at every moment in time.

CASE 2.0: PERCEPTION OF THE HARMONIC EXCHANGE OF KINETIC AND POTENTIAL ENERGY

We can also have a realistic perception of the Hilbert space circle if we add kinetic and potential energy to the wave equation. The kinetic energy and potential energy are oscillating back and forth where we can define the potential energy as (x) and the kinetic energy as (t). For example, at time zero the entity is all potential energy at the right of the circle. After a quarter of a cycle it is all kinetic energy. The (x, iy) energy curve (world line) is just a helix in a space-time coordinate system. In this example the (x, iy) axis gives us a mental view of energy transfer—a perception of harmonic motion of energy states that is a different kind of perception than the previous example.

CASE 3.0: QUANTUM SPIN-STATE PERCEPTIONS

We can extend this simple mathematical idea to the more general form of a perception of a state harmonically moving in space-time. Consider an observer recording (using a quantum limited laser) some spin-based particle moving along a stationary world line of a space-time diagram—a vertical line if the velocity of the particle is zero relative to the observer traveling with the particle. The state of the physical particle is the spin at each point in the vertical line of the space-time diagram. Assume the particle starts out with spin up and has a full 360 degrees of precession. We can get a mental picture of this state of precession by considering the same circle of unit amplitude in Hilbert space given above, except the physical x coordinate is replaced with the non-physical coordinate, $x*$. For example, $x*$max, the maximum non-physical position of the circle on the right, is the mental picture of the particle being 100% in the spin-up state. So, $x*$max is just a phasor of unit amplitude—the general phasor being $\cos \omega t + i* \sin \omega t$ at any point of this imaginary circle, in the imaginary plane, embedded in the physical space-time diagram. Thus, a phasor drawn to a point on the circle just represents a perception of the view of the spin. For example, (ωt = 90 degrees, 180 degrees and 270 degrees are just the spin left, spin down, and spin right states, respectively). Generally, the magnitude of the sum of the squares of both state coordinates (the amplitude) is always equal to one which has the meaning that each state coordinate gives the degree of spin up or down. For example: at 45 degrees the particle is half spin up and half spin to the left. Again, mathematically this is just a helix in a space-time diagram, or each state coordinate is a wave when plotted in time. This type of perception, without the use of physical space coordinates, is new to the math/physics world and is thus given a special function identity: $i*$. Clearly $i*$ has the same mathematical machinery that the imaginary number i has, but the conjugate connotes the motion of non-physical coordinates; in these cases $x*$ and $y*$ are non-physical coordinates tracking purely physical states. We can (as shown below) use $x*$ and $y*$ to track "non-purely" physical states, like the decision states of a human or any other type of entity. Notice in this example, the sum of the squares of $x*$ and $y*$ is always equal to one. We can say that the probability of the spin particle being in a state is always 100%—like the idea that the wave function amplitude in quantum mechanics is always equal to one, meaning that the physical entity in question must be in some state at every moment even if it has zero probability of being at some physical space point!

CASE 4.0: *REPRESENTATIONS OF AN ATOMIC TRANSITION*

In quantum mechanics we can represent the transition of an electron in an atom with amplitude mechanics equations. To perceive atomic action in terms of the, perception equation, consider the following: a two-state atom absorbing a photon and emitting a photon exactly on resonance—no lost energy per cycle of absorption and emission. The same $i*$circle above is used to describe this action. The maximum x^* co-ordinate is the mental vision (a point on a Psychothotonix^{SM} sphere) of the atom absorbing a photon, and the $-x*$ maximum coordinate is the mental vision (a point on a Psychothotonix^{SM} sphere) of the atom emit-ting a photon. The value of $x*$ is thus, 1 (standing for the 100% chance of the atom absorbing a photon) and for $-x^*$ the value is -1 (standing for the dual opposite condition, which is also 100% because we set up our hypothetical system that way). What is the value of y^* at 90 degrees? It is, i^* (standing for the fact that the "transformation energy" is exactly half way through its cycle). It is 100% in the magnitude of $y^*= i^*$. The first thing that is interesting is that we can only see the $-x^*$ maximum condition in terms of a physical perception state; it emits a photon that hits our detector, but all the other states are "just in our minds" because we must assume that the physics is happening in some exact harmony (harmonic state)—but nothing can be visible because we can't see in-side the atom! Again, the x^* and y^* coordinates track a helix in a space-time diagram.

CASE 5.0: DUALITY

The basic idea presented thus far shows that harmonic perceptions are based on the concept of duality. As described above, duality means that all observations have dual opposites. Simple examples include: degrees of conflict, degrees of cooperation; degrees of pain, degrees of pleasure; degrees of right and wrong, spin up, spin down, degrees of order, degrees of disorder, etc. Notice that the basic equation can also be expressed at a moment in time. The center of the circle is some value of physical space and time, a space-time point. The $x^*$and y^* axis are just values of the degree of perception of some duality state, the degree of potential energy and kinetic energy at some moment in time of a harmonic cycle: dual opposites. We can then have the circle in the complex perception move along a harmonic space-time curve. In general, we can place the circle at any physical spatial point, point in time, or any span of space-time.

In the court case mentioned above, the center of the circle could be some short span of time where several jurors decide about the degree of guilt and the degree of innocence of the defendant—which are the x^* and y^* coordinates, or phasor coordinates. Notice here that these are amplitudes of a phasor which imply perceived probability of guilt or innocence of each juror (each phasor), but these are not components of a probability amplitude because each juror is making a perception of the degree of guilt or innocence. A probability of perception would be trying to predict how a given juror might respond at some moment. Also, in this case the center of the circle need not be associated with the physical space coordinate of any juror, because it is typically not relevant. Even if we thought of an example where people around the globe voted (on the Internet), then the spatial coordinate may not be the important coordinate. For example: because the speed of light puts all of the voters on approximately the same surface of simultaneity—what they voted, not where they voted, is the important parameter in this example.

CASE 6.0: REGIONS OF CONFLICT AND COOPERATION

Consider a case where the center of the circle is some point in time. The state coordinates could represent degrees of conflict and cooperation in some region of geography. The (x^*) and (t) coordinates representing degrees of cooperation or conflict at the points $*(t) = 1 \ or -1$ and $y*(t) = i^* \ or -i^*$ implies 100% cooperation in some region, 100% conflict, etc. In this case the measurements would be on some internet sphere application.

CASE 7.0: *INFINITE PARALLEL UNIVERSE*

Consider a case (as a special effect in this novel) where the center of the perception sphere is the initial point of the big bang. Any other sphere is just another universe. One can visualize infinite spheres floating around in an infinite physical space-time region as infinite mini big bang universes, each of which is finite in size.

CASE 8.0: *THE QUANTUM PROBABILITY AMPLITUDE WITHIN AN INFINITE POTENTIAL WELL*

Consider an example in quantum mechanics. Solve the Schrödinger equation for the probability amplitudes of, say, the ground zero energy state within an infinite potential well, then square these for the probability at any physical space point in time. Now draw an $i*$circle around any of these physical space-time points. The state coordinates: $x*(t), y*(t)$ are just metrics of probability. For example: an $i*$circle at the physical space-time center of the well (for the lowest energy state) yields $x*(t) = 0; y*(t) = i*or - i*$ because the probability of the electron is zero at this point and thus is also completely uncertain, as mentioned above. As mentioned above, $x*(t)$ and $y*(t) = Asin(\omega t)$ can also be called the degree of certainty and degree of uncertainty coordinates. This is a good idea related to perception harmonic motion. A thotonix sphere in this case is just a mental visualization of the event—we use this kind of mental view in physics all the time. Much of quantum theory is understood by having a mental image of some solutions to Schrödinger's equation.

CASE 9.0: *PROBABILITY AMPLITUDES AND PERCEPTION PROBABILITY AMPLITUDES*

Reviewing the basics of quantum logic is necessary to understand the logic of perception phasors, perception waves, and perception probability amplitudes for any kind of Psychothotonix^{SM} application.

In order to do this simply, create a basic space-time diagram with the horizontal x coordinate as the physical space axis, and the vertical axis as the time axis. In quantum logic the wave function is a modification of the above classical wave function, which can be visualized by imagining you are looking down the x axis. The quantum mechanical wave function would therefore be an infinite set of Hilbert space unit circles (one for each physical point on this surface of simultaneity). So at each physical space point the probability amplitude of some physical state (like the spin-up state) is simply defined as the cosine function squared—the sine function just creates the circle (or amplitude of a phasor in the circle). So an amplitude of 1 means that the state of something (like the quantum particle is "there") is 100%—the quantum wave-function collapses and all Hilbert space circles disappear because the energy of the particle would be completely defined (actually, a non-quantum possibility—just a visual for the reader). This is very similar to our $i*$circle diagram. In fact our $i*$unit metric Hilbert space circle is just rotated by 90 degrees, which changes the meaning of its functionality ("re-engineers" the quantum wave function). In fact, this rotation allows us to bring meaning to the sine function being the uncertainty axis of any physical or non-physical state. Consequently, at each physical space-time point there is one circle with an infinite number of possible phasors, one for each observer, because in this case all observers can view the same state in a different way (unlike the probability amplitude in quantum physics where all observers see the amplitude and probability at any given physical point) as the same value! Careful analysis of this quantum logic of probability amplitude waves shows that these won't work relative to explaining all the different types of perception states. The quantum wave-function is limited to explaining nano-particle quantum states only. Basically then, quantum logic just spreads the energy of some state over a region of physical space at some instant in time, surface, or simultaneous views of all observers within a light cone.

To obtain a more detailed view of the above description of the differences between wave functions consider the following three-dimensional sphere of probability amplitudes for a two-state system. This was developed as a two-state physical state for two spin half-states. The spin up state can be considered the z axis and the spin down state the −z axis. In fact, this was first derived to describe the Stern Gerlach experiment for the probability of observing spin up or down states between two observers, $O1$ and $O2$. Probability observations for $O1$ are the (x, y, z) axis, and probability observations for $O2$ are the $(x'y'z')$ axis—the rotated coordinate frame. The rotation of the coordinate frames by (α, β, γ) can be derived using quantum logic (the details are left for the reader's reference). The angles of rotation correspond to actual physical angles (unlike the angles in the $i*circle$, which correspond to different perceptions of the same event, as will be discussed later in more detail.

The probability amplitude for an observer in the prime system (rotated around the $z\ axis\ by\ \theta$) to view the spin up state relative to an observer fixed in the unprimed frame, (x, y, z) who sees the particle in the spin up state is: $C'+ = exp(im\theta C+)$. (This is perception language. In quantum language these two amplitudes are described as two Stern Gerlach apparatuses at some angle relative to each other and at any angle as a system of two units in a space-time diagram.) The + sign stands for the spin up state as viewed by the fixed observer and the primed observer.

The same logic applies for the spin down state, which is: $C- = exp(im\theta C-)$.

The value of m, according the quantum logic must be ½, which is described in a vague and uncertain way (of creating opposite phases per 360-degree rotations around any z axis). Thus, the experiment is called a spin ½ coordinate representation. Below it can be shown that this value really has to do with the fact that all events have duality (polar opposite) contributions—a result of the derivation of the perception wave function.

Working through all the possible quantum states for any angle represented by the Euler angles (α, β, γ) is straightforward. We start with (x, y, z) and rotate the primed coordinate system through an angle β about the z axis, bringing the x-axis to a line $x1$. Then we rotate by α around this temporary x-axis, to bring z down to z'. Finally, a rotation around the new z-axis (that is, z') by the angle γ will bring the x-axis into the $x' - axis$ and the y-axis into y'. The transformations for each of these can be derived. The final total rotation of probability amplitudes are described by the Bloch Vectors as mentioned above.

An example couched in the perception language, will refresh our memory on how to interpret these functions. First, consider a particle in the spin up state with the up state along the z axis at time zero. We could say the fundamental observer is along the z direction. Now consider an observer "aligned with" (as in the case of two Stern Gerlach devices at a physical angle relative to each other in some arbitrary special orientation) the particle state. So α is zero. The first equation states that $C+ = 1$, which means that the observer has a probability amplitude of 1, and probability of 1, of perceiving the particle in the spin up state. Both observers thus perceive/measure the orientation of the spin up state the same way. So, in this case the probability amplitude is like the possibility of perceiving a physical state. It is comparable to the possibility of the visibility of some physical state as seen by two dual observers. This can be thought of as the "angle between their perceptions."

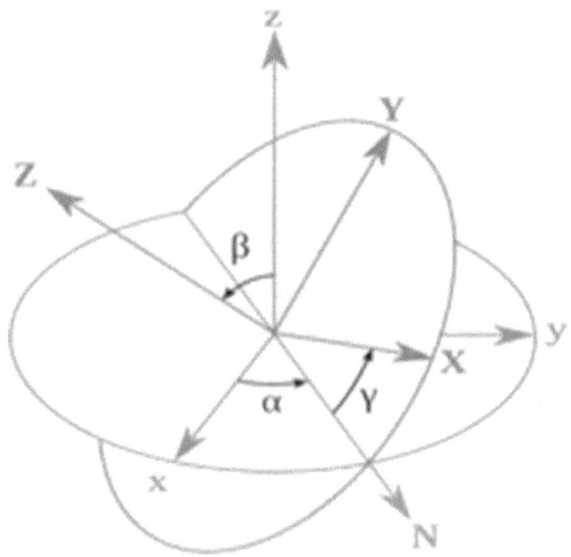

Perception angles between observers of physical phenomenon

CASE 10: HARMONIC PERCEPTIONS OF HUMAN DECISIONS

In case 1.0 we examined the action of a classical physical harmonic oscillator with normalized unit amplitude. After that, we investigated harmonic motion as a probability amplitude between two dual opposite physical states that included mixed interference-oriented probability amplitudes. With these ideas in mind it is intuitively obvious to derive the equations of deterministic and probability-based perceptions moving in the i^*space-time. The court case is again one of the easiest (most visible) two-state human decision-based systems that illustrate these processes.

First, we can describe the duality state of harmonic motion of perceptions with words that connote the underlying logic that will naturally fit with the method to derive the equation of motion of perceptions. Finally, we can connect a visual aid to demonstrate how hyperspectral imaging systems can actually measure deterministic, and even probabilistic, duality states in motion—the "how to" of turning perceptions into photon bunches!

Suppose that, at time equals zero, some juror perceives (judges, in this case) a defendant in a court case as 100% innocent—and the juror's only influence (driving "energy") is the defense attorney, who will be assumed in this imaginary court case to be 100% successful at driving and maintaining the juror to the 100% innocent state (judgement of the degree of innocence being 100%). Because we have not yet introduced a prosecuting attorney to this courtroom drama, the juror would simply maintain his position at time and into the future (until the driving energy of the prosecuting attorney is introduced). Consequently, there is no harmonic motion of the juror's decision state. The change of the perception in time is zero and therefore a constant in our $i*$ circle—it is a phasor all along the $+x*$axis, with $(x*, t*) = (1,0)$ as the center of the circle, which also corresponds with some (x, t) physical space-time point. Consequently, the perception equation is simply:

$dP(t) / dt$ = zero, $P(t)$ is a constant value in time, $\cos \theta = 1$ at time zero.

Consequently, in our $i*$ space-time, this is the $i*$ circle moving up a vertical line—the center of the $i*$ circle simply being some point in physical space at each time (a physical surface of simultaneity).

Now simply reverse the logic and say that at time equals zero the juror has only the prosecutor to influence his decision, and the prosecutor is 100% successful at convincing the juror to judge the defendant 100% guilty. All the other logic is the same, so the equation of motion is the same, except we have the duality state equal to -1, which is the dual opposite (polar opposite) of the previous example.

$dP-(t) / dt = zero$, $P-(t)$ is a constant value in time, $\cos \theta = -1$ at time zero.

This is the same perception i circle moving up the same vertical line, except the perception phasor is of value in this Hermitian space of, -1. The value of the perception is defined as the minus state as indicated by the lower scripted minus value. It is the dual or polar opposite of the previous example.

In both cases we have assumed a deterministic scenario (where the juror has stated his position of judgement at the initial moment). If this were probabilistic, we would not know what the juror's initial state was. Because there is only one lawyer, the defense lawyer, introduced in this scene, the juror would be of one of either of the two states.

In summary, thus far, we have defined a situation where there are two juror perception states that don't change in time. In fact, the perception states defined here are the same as the lawyers' perception states, because the lawyers are the only driving forces creating the juror's perception state with their persuasive (100% influential) presentations.

Now let's expand this logic one more step. Repeat the above two situations, except assume that in each case the lawyers are driving the juror's perception state into harmonic motion. So in the first case, we have:

$$dP+(t) \, / \, dt = Re \, \exp(i*\omega t) \, P+(t)$$

And in the second case:

$$dP-(t) \, / \, dt = Re \, \exp(i*\omega t) \, P-.$$

Clearly, these are just two simple harmonic states of motion, which we assumed are not connected to each other. The amplitude of the wave, or the magnitude of the phasor, are dual opposites at time equals zero in each of these two cases. So we have two perception waves, or equivalently, two perception phasors oscillating back and forth in time (over one cycle, ω). Effectively, we have called the driving forces of the perceptions (the lawyers) as (1, -1). Again, these are deterministic (as assumed in the description of the situation). The juror in each case starts out by saying, "Yes, I have determined, based on the lawyer's input, that the defendant is 100%" ('guilty,' 'innocent,' respectively)—a perception of judgement, and clearly not the actual probability of the actual state of the defendant (which would require a different set of equations).

Taking the derivatives of these equations yields:

$$dP+(t) / dt = i*\omega 11 P+(t)$$
$$dP-(t) / dt = i*\omega 22 P-(t).$$

Clearly, each value of ω is proportional to the driving "energy cycle" of the lawyer—doubling the energy cycle double the value of ω cuts the cycle time in half, etc.

Now, to make these probabilistic perceptions (where we are guessing what the juror is deciding) all we must do is say that at time equals zero the juror was in one of these two states, but we don't know which. So the juror is swinging from amplitude 1 over one cycle in time, or from amplitude -1 over one cycle in time. Whichever one it is, it is assumed it is not coupled to the other one, but still just one of two possible probability waves of perception. If there was another juror his/her equation would be the same. In general, if there were N different jurors, then there would be 2N probability equations of harmonic motion of amplitudes. The amplitudes are polar opposites—which we have called a fact of all perceptions due to the duality of perception in nature. These equations just say that the change of each dual opposite perception is proportional to the driving energy influencing the perception at any moment in a space-time diagram view.

Now we need to consider yet another term, because each lawyer could be coupled together in a way that creates interference of the juror's simple harmonic motion view. Effectively, the juror would pick up a "piece" of each lawyer's view at each moment in time, which can be called the values $\omega 12 \omega 21$.

Rearranging the terms (to fit with the quantum mechanical counterpart equations) we have, for each juror, two duality equations to describe their probabilistic perceptions moving in time:

$$dP+(t) / dt = i*\omega 11P+(t) - i*\omega 12P-(t)$$
$$dP-(t) / dt = i*\omega 21P+(t) - i*\omega 22P-(t)$$

The diagonal terms relate to simple harmonic motion of probability
amplitudes of perception, and the off-diagonal terms relate to coupling
terms that modify the perceptions at any time depending upon the
driving terms. If we want to generalize these equations, we can say that
the lawyers are just "operators" who generate perception states of the
juror. We can then intuitively invent the duality operator (two lawyers
generating some mix of two dual states for each juror). The equation in
operator notation is thus:

$$dP(t)/dt = \Sigma Di,jPj$$, the duality equation of motion of perceptions, or $$(t) = \cos\theta + i* \sin\theta$$, its dual opposite as a phasor.

The first equation is exactly the same form as the Hamiltonian
equation in quantum mechanics, except we now have the "Dualitonian".
The value of *j* is a running index because, clearly, there could be any one
of an infinite number or driving energies, or influences, for each part
of the duality equation (i = 1,2, or here +/–) of motion for each juror.
The second equation again says that no matter how complex the duality
equation is, to solve it all reduces to a simple phasor at a given point in
time ([a point or interval] in physical space-time where appropriate)—
where the real axis is the observer's perception of the degree of certainty
and the imaginary axis is the observer's perception of the degree of uncertainty within the arbitrary event map, the *i** circle.

The "Derivation of Quantum Mechanics"
With this background we can now make the quantum connection. To
start "assume we don't yet know quantum mechanics," and derive a

perception differential equation for the change of perception in time with time-dependence only—with a non-physical entity like the judgement in a court case. Then do the same for space dependence only. Finally, we can then reduce these equations to the perception of a physical entity (as in quantum mechanics). The general perception equations should then correspond to the physical-based perception equations.

CASE 11: TURNING PERCEPTIONS INTO PHOTONS/DUAL SCHRÖDINGER EQUATIONS

If we carry these concepts further, we can readily see that there should be in fact dual Schrödinger equations for perception at any time. For example, if an electron is oscillating in between two charged mirrors and the probability of the electron being in the middle is zero, it is not logical that it disappeared! We can just invent the dual opposite condition. When the electron disappeared, then an anti-electron was created. This is consistent with the Dirac interpretation in relativistic quantum mechanics, except he did not invent a dual Schrödinger equation, that Dr. Richard calls "The Dualitonian."

The process of duality is common to all human interactions. Here it was also shown that quantum mechanics is inherently a language of duality of physical states. The quantum mechanical uncertainty principle and the quantum limit of the laser linewidth are indications that no entity can be pinned down to 100% certainty. The $i*$ circle can be a useful visual aid to describe the basic concepts of duality in all observations including quantum theory. It was shown that basically every point (or interval) in a physical space-time diagram "pops out" into a Hilbert space unit circle ($i*$ circle)—the only mathematical way to describe the nature of duality. This leads to a different kind of space-time wave function in Hilbert space rather than physical space-time, a "hole" in the space-time network (as originally introduced by the author). It was demonstrated that the i^* classical harmonic motion maps one perception at each space-time point for all observers—all observers agree with the unique motion of the harmonic oscillator. In quantum physics, the waves, $exp(ikx)exp(i\omega t)$, give one answer for all observers (for example, with $t = 0$ and some point $x0$, say, the probability amplitude is $\sqrt{2}/2$ for the electron to be "there")—one number for all observers (in this case a probability of $1/2$). The $i*$ circle approach would suggest that there would be at least two possible (amplitudes) for the electron to be at $x0$ at $t = 0$ (the center of the $i*$ circle) one for each possible, dual opposite spin state (in this case $\theta = 45$ degrees and $\theta = 125$ degrees)—that is, there must be duality conservation in this case, 50% probability of being at $x0$ with 50% probability of being in one of two possible spin states. In general, there are an infinite number of possible perceptions (points on the $i*$ circle) at a given physical space point in time, or quantum limited interval (which are, again, represented as the center of the $i*$ circle). Of course, the circle concept can be expanded to a sphere, or an "$i*$ universe."

A basic concept of using a hyperspectral imaging device to measure perceptions is straightforward. For instance, consider the above example where the juror moves in some simple harmonic state over some cycle of time. At each of the major points (say—0, 90, 180, 270, and 360) on the harmonic cycle, a hyperspectral image (which is just a sophisticated pattern of colors over a spectral range) is created. At each time segment over the interval $\omega = 1/\Delta T$ there are N photons in the hyperspectral image pattern, or, $\omega = NE/h$, where E is the energy of one photon and the N photons fit within a 3D hyperspectral cube at each short time interval (shutter speed). These images can be correlated with pattern recognition software identities and many other emerging spectral image sensor technologies. So, the general equation at any moment in time is given above.

CASE 12: ANHARMONIC PERCEPTIONS

As a secondary note, perceptions in general satisfy the nonlinear harmonic oscillatory equation of motion.

The first terms are just the harmonic perception equation of motion mentioned above. The other terms create non-harmonic terms (combined frequency of motion). In general, the solution is a Lorentzian function when the driving forces are harmonic. The important connection is that the change of perceptions in time can be technologically created as photons from a quantum laser source, therefore also a Lorentzian function satisfying the laser quantum field equations.

A perception and the spin-off decision in the court case can be modeled as a two-state system with a Hamiltonian that is mathematically analogous to the two-state system of an atomic transition in a laser—consisting of N different cloned atoms. Refreshing our memories about this solution which is easily verified:

CASE 13: RELATIVITY PERCEPTIONS—THE $z*$ AXIS FOR SPECIAL EFFECTS IN MOVIES

In *Tetrastatum*, there are several special effects created from using the logic of the $i*$ circle. If the principles of duality are universal, then it is also necessary to answer questions about "purely" physical objects (for the purpose of physics or just as special effects in movies).

As mentioned above, a $i*$ circle maps harmonic motion of a macroscopic object as $\cos \theta = 1$. That is, if we place the $i*$ circle at any point on the wave, $\cos \omega t$ (generated by the $(e i \omega t)$) with its center at the physical spatial point of the physical object—the associated time—it means that all observers would agree that the object is there (which translates to $x* = \cos\theta = 1$)—but then one would ask: "What do the other points on the circle mean?" One of the main answers is that other observers could arrange the object to rotate in time as it moves, either by some optical element (like imaging it with one prism), or actually just creating it to move. In other words, there is always the potential for the object to be viewed as rotated at the same point in physical space-time. In this case, for example, points (θ =0 90, 180, 270) means that an object is 100% "upright," 100% rotated by 90 degrees, 100% "upside down," and 100% rotated by 270 degrees, etc. Points on the $i*$ circle represent the possible macroscopic orientation of the physical object relative to an infinite number of other possible observers. Again, duality is a conserved object.

We can use $i*$ logic to describe relativity effects as well. We know from relativity theory that an observer moving at some velocity past an observer who is stationary alongside some object will measure the size of the object differently according to his/her speed. In fact, the object will "shrink" as he/she moves faster, and "disappear" when he/she reaches the speed of light. In terms of $i*$ logic we can say that the first observer sees the object 100% of its size, or $\cos\theta = 1$. (From the above logic a different observer could use optics to view it as 100% of its size but rotated by 180 degrees, or $\cos\theta = -1$.) If the observer is moving at a speed where the object reduces in size by 50%, then we could define this as a $i*$circle of half its size. Consequently, the size of the circle represents observers moving at higher velocities. So the relativity contraction equation is expanded in meaning. The amplitude of the circle is equivalent to the size of the object as viewed by different observers. A stationary observer sees the object as 100% in size as compared to an observer moving at the speed of light who sees the object 0% in size, and thus the duality is still two observers who see dual-size objects! In this case the polar spatial opposites of any diagonal fit 100% in the stationary CCD "grid" (the first case) and less than that for the velocity dependent image (sent from the moving observer grid to the stationary grid).

Putting this concept into mathematical terms yields:

$P'(t') = \gamma Pi(t) =$ Relativity of Perceptions.

Now we can invent a $z*$coordinate—an infinite set of perception circles, one for each $\Delta z*$. The image of the object exists in an infinite number of 4D parallel universes—a special effect illustrated in the novel.

CASE 14: INTELLIGENT HOLOGRAMS AND THE SHUTTER SPEED OF THE UNIVERSE

Currently, movies can be made in 3D. There are many applications for making movies based on advanced concepts from nonlinear optics and laser quantum field theory. Most of these can be derived from the basic four wave-mixing formulas generated by Amnon Yariv at Cal Tech.

Consider the following overview of the process: When a nonlinear such as BaTio3 (Barium Titinate) is driven by two pump fields in a Kerr-like medium in counter propagation directions (dual opposite polarization directions) an index of refraction is created, causing a perturbation of the dielectric medium. This is true even if the pump waves are speckled in nature. This interaction, in terms of the Maxwell or quantum mechanical equations, creates the possibility of 512 relevant tensor-based mathematical terms. However, for holography and other special nonlinear processes, only a few terms are current, practical examples. These terms are called phase conjugation and lead to many of the effects mentioned above.

In linear, homogeneous, isotropic, non-dispersive atomic laser mediums the polarization in any given space-time point is simply a product of the applied electric field and the material polarizability function at that point. In the nonlinear medium this general product is conceptually similar for many waves interacting at a space-time point; except one must integrate the products of the material tensor with tensor components of each electric field to include conjugate waves (time re-versed). (The tensor product just picks off components of the fields at a given time and all retarded (past) times.) The general form is, conse-quently, intuitively obvious. Polarization of a two-level laser medium is a modification of the above. The polarization equation above can be modified to fit various kinds of nonlinear optics and laser quantum field theory applications and scenarios.

In terms of holographic and phase conjugation applications, the fol-lowing nonlinear polarization terms, which are reduced versions of the more general polarization equation above, are important.

We can envision a simple security device where the user creates a unique perception (as a modulated conjugate wave) by tuning the phase conjugate mirror. (Some cloak in front of the mirror can add ad-ditional security because only the user can remove the cloak via phase conjugate waves.)

CASE 15: TWO-STATE PERCEPTION STATES IN BLOCK VECTOR VIEW

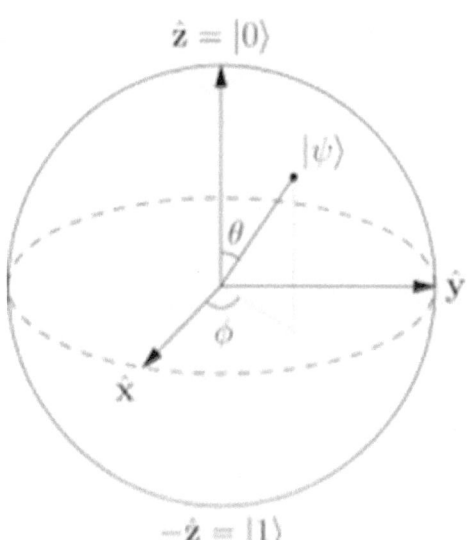

Our two-state court case can be placed in Bloch Vector notation, which is similar to our $i*$circle. On resonance the state just circles the y axis, and off resonance it cir-cles some ellipse with-in a quadrant—never transitions.

CASE 16: *THE MOST IMPORTANT TOOL FOR MEASURING PSYCHOTHOTONIX^{SM} EVENTS—THE SLOW LIGHT LASER OSCILLATOR*

The most important tool for measuring Psychothotonix^{SM} events is the slow light laser. Because of its extremely narrow linewidth, we can maximize any interpretation of an image. The following is Dr. Richard's brief description of how slow light lasers work.

Laser Oscillators have always been promoted as sources of single-frequency coherent optical radiation, thus implying quantum limited performance. However (until the invention of slow light) the reality is that all laser oscillators have frequency and amplitude noise orders of magnitude above quantum limited performance! The underlying physics of our slow light fiber laser oscillators involves creating a traveling wave virtual ring laser (in contrast to a ring laser) and slowing the intracavity photon group velocity to below the speed of light. This action translates into a dramatic increase in the number of stored stimulated-emission photons while simultaneously quenching the spontaneous-emission photons, resulting in quantum-limited ultra-low noise, high power laser oscillators. Slow light lasers also open doors for unprecedented measurement accuracy and better systems performance in many laser technology applications, including: Acoustic Sensing; Lidar; Quantum Cryptography; Coherent Communication; RF Microwave Photonics, and Wind Energy.

Virtual Ring Laser
There are three main categories of fiber lasers: the distributed feedback laser (DFB), the distributed Bragg reflector laser (DBR), and the Fiber Ring Laser. The linear cavity DFB and DBR fiber lasers operate in a standing-wave configuration where the electromagnetic field is zero at the spatial nodes of the field at any given time. This means that at

these points no stimulated emission can occur, lowering the laser power overall and allowing higher spontaneous emission. This so-called spatial hole burning also contributes to the growth of side modes, which results in significant mode partition noise. A ring laser eliminates these problems by creating a traveling wave oscillation so that the wave travels without manifesting in places where the electromagnetic field vanishes. Consequently, the ring laser has higher power and much better noise performance. Indeed, in the last two decades, the NPRO ring laser was the supreme laser and set the benchmark for high-power laser oscillators. However, this technology can't be replicated in fiber. In addition, Fiber Ring lasers require many external components (couplers, narrow band filters, and isolators)—long cavities that produce frequency instabilities. The propriety "Virtual Ring Oscillator" (VRO) architecture creates a traveling-wave oscillation in a compact linear all-fiber cavity. In addition, this configuration (as described below) also enables slow light laser oscillation—another big step in quantum-limited performance.

As can be seen in the diagram below, the VRO laser cavity is formed by the composition of a high reflector, the output fiber Bragg gratings and wave-plates. The gain media is highly-doped fiber (Er/Yb for 1550nm, or Yb at 1060nm) producing up to 450 mw of power in a several-centimeter cavity.

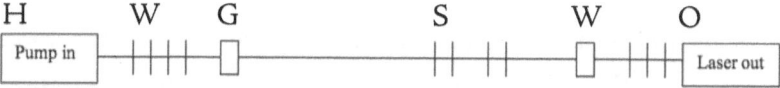

The "virtual ring" structure. The laser is made entirely out of fiber which includes (H) Frequency selective high-reflector (G) gain section (S) slow light element -(W) polarization mode transformers (wave plates) (O) PM output.

The wave-plates and the Bragg gratings produce counter-propagating circularly polarized waves (which sum to a linearly polarized wave without spatial nodes; thus eliminating spatial hole burning). In addition, the wave-plates also provide isolation of the light-slowing filter from the Bragg mirrors, hence eliminating problems associated with having multiple embedded cavities. Furthermore, the proprietary highly dispersive and high Q in-fiber filter precisely defines the laser frequency, without the need for an external reference temperature control or complex electronics. The all-fiber configuration also allows control of the laser frequency against temperature variations (by more than three orders of magnitude.) All this technology is packaged in a novel vibration isolation unit. These factors synergistically combine to yield laser action with the smallest linewidth, the highest signal to noise, and the lowest noise (the relative intensity noise, the frequency noise, and the side-mode noise) in the world!

The Quantum Physics of Slow Light

The virtual ring laser not only creates a traveling wave but is also designed to slow the photons' group velocity. To better understand the consequences of this, let's consider the quantum physics of laser linewidth. It is well known that the fundamental laser linewidth, given by Schawlow Townes limit, is inversely proportional to the laser cavity quality factor. The Q factor, in turn, can be expressed as the (photon) cavity lifetime. The role of the photon lifetime in the laser noise dynamics can be understood by realizing that as the time is increased, more photons are stored in the cavity. Therefore, the higher intracavity laser power reduces the relative contribution of phase diffusion due to spontaneous emission into the lasing mode. To achieve narrow linewidth, one can increase the photon lifetime simply by using a longer cavity or by increasing the cavity mirror's reflectivity. However, with small output coupling, the laser can't produce high-output power, and a longer cavity can introduce mode instabilities—due to the smaller Free Spectral Range FSR (given by c/2nl). A long cavity is also more susceptible to technical noise induced by temperature variations and mechanical vibrations. Using slow light to increase the photon lifetime offers a solution to this conundrum. If a spectrally narrow long delay (slow light) resonator is placed in the cavity, it can extend τc while suppressing the side modes, even as the FSR of the cavity becomes smaller. Such suppression is not trivial and is a consequence of the spectral shape of the slow light narrow resonator. Furthermore, the slow light allows one to tailor the laser's output mirror reflectivity to maximize the output power, while maintaining a high Q.

Slow light lasers increase the Q by a factor of thirty, thus suppressing the FM noise due to spontaneous emission by close to three orders magnitude, as well as significantly reducing the (1/f) FM noise.

i* Quantum Mechanics

There is an easy way to visualize slow light action in a virtual ring cavity. Consider placing an imaginary spatial plane in the cavity. At any point on the plane (and at any moment in time) there will exist places where the electromagnetic field is zero due to standing wave phenomena—call these the "zero states." The other points on the plane will have stimulated emission—call these the "one states." In the slow light traveling wave configuration, the zero states are essentially eliminated, thus providing more one states. Now imagine that the plane is moving at less than the speed of light. This effect will naturally create even more photons in the one state (as there is more time for stimulated photons to clone). Combining these two effects (one states are the "good photons," and zero states are the "bad, or noisy, photons") means more laser power with less noisy photons. It's all about 1's and 0's.

Conclusion

The dramatic laser noise reduction (as seen in figure 2.0) achieved by slow light lasers is a scientific and commercial breakthrough because laser noise in many photonics applications is the defining factor for better system performance. Ultra-stable coherent slow light lasers can enable more information to be extracted in imaging, create better sensitivity of sensor systems, and provide higher spectral efficiency in data transmission. For these reasons, slow light semiconductor lasers will be the core component for virtually all photonics-electronics driven technology of the future.

The slow light laser development and its commercialization have been supported by DARPA, the US Navy and NASA.

* From Dr. Richards book: i* physics (the physics of imaginary surfaces)

Parameter	Semiconductor Laser	Slow Light Laser
Power (mW)	40	>500 mw (without amplifier)
SNR (0.05 nm RBW)	50 dB	>85 dB
SMSR (3MHz RBW)	50 db	>85 dB
Linewidth	1 MHz	<10 Hz
RIN @1 MHz/10GHz	-145/-150 dBc/Hz	-150/-175 dBc/Hz

The above table gives typical specifications of a slow light laser. There are several laser vendors who build such technology. It is a key tool for Psychothotonix[SM] research.

CASE 17: THE CONSERVATION OF PSYCHOTHOTONIX^SM IMAGE IDENTITY IN INFINITE PARALLEL UNIVERSES

Clearly, to experience a parallel universe involves being able to interact with other people/entities in some modified space-time universes. The following has been theorized:

+ Any matter form expresses itself as a time series of images on Psychothotonix^SM image waves that go on for eternity.

+ Any matter form equivalently can be expressed as image points on a Psychothotonix^SM sphere that evolves forever.

This process can be mathematically derived, which is the expansion and interpretation of the Schrödinger equation. Photons scatter off matter and are processed into the image of matter via a camera or brain. This process is called the Psychothotonix^SM equation of image motion. It may be expressed as matter photons raised to the power of their own image (in the brain or camera) creates matter images (that can then be transmitted to other parallel universes in perpetuity). Any matter form can be expressed as the power to the image in an infinite time series.

$$\text{Matter Forms} = e^{-ih\Delta w\Delta t} = e^{-i(\Delta E/h)\Delta t} = \text{The Images of Matter Forms}$$

Where, (is the shutter speed of the camera or brain for one image, so the series continues forever). Mathematically this is equivalent to an infinite series of image formations on different space-time paths.

Figures (1-3) in Appendix A illustrate that matter can transform from 100% down to zero percent, but the thotonix images go on forever. Either the image can be uncovered from the space-time cloud/cloak or manifest in another image parallel universe. This all happens via photons (limited by the speed of light in any given matter universe) or via virtual photons (that travel at infinite speed and can travel to any universe instantaneously). In any case our identity keeps evolving without degradation/entropy.

| APPENDIX **C** |

TIM'S NOTES
IN ADUAT

TETRASTATUM

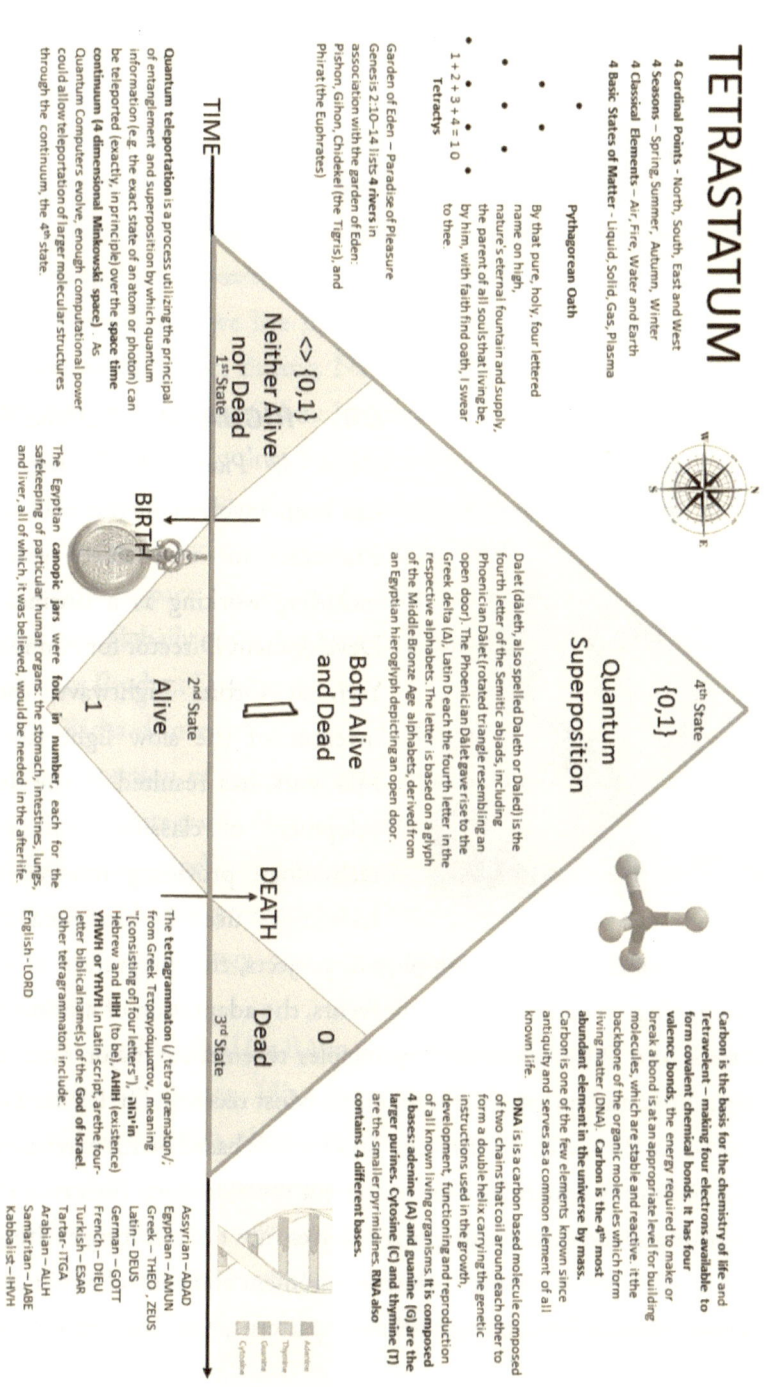

4 **Cardinal Points** - North, South, East and West

4 **Seasons** – Spring, Summer, Autumn, Winter

4 **Classical Elements** – Air, Fire, Water and Earth

4 **Basic States of Matter** - Liquid, Solid, Gas, Plasma

$$1 + 2 + 3 + 4 = 10$$
Tetractys

Pythagorean Oath

By that pure, holy, four lettered
name on high,
nature's eternal fountain and supply,
the parent of all souls that living be,
by him, with faith find oath, I swear
to thee.

Garden of Eden – Paradise of Pleasure
Genesis 2:10–14 lists 4 rivers in
association with the garden of Eden:
Pishon, Gihon, Chiddekel (the Tigris), and
Phirat (the Euphrates)

Quantum teleportation is a process utilizing the principal
of entanglement and superposition by which quantum
information (e.g. the exact state of an atom or photon) can
be teleported (exactly, in principle) over the **space time
continuum (4 dimensional Minkowski space)**. As
Quantum Computers evolve, enough computational power
could allow teleportation of larger molecular structures
through the continuum, the 4th state.

TIME

**Neither Alive
nor Dead**
1st State
<> {0,1}

BIRTH

**Quantum
Superposition**
{0,1}
4th State

Dalet (dāleth, also spelled Daleth or Daled) is the
fourth letter of the Semitic abjads, including
Phoenician Dālet (rotated triangle resembling an
open door). The Phoenician Dālet gave rise to the
Greek delta (Δ). Latin D each the fourth letter in the
respective alphabets. The letter is based on a glyph
of the Middle Bronze Age alphabets, derived from
an Egyptian hieroglyph depicting an open door.

**Both Alive
and Dead**
[]

2nd State
Alive
1

DEATH

3rd State
Dead
0

The Egyptian **canopic jars** were **four in number**, each for the
safekeeping of particular human organs: the stomach, intestines, lungs,
and liver, all of which, it was believed, would be needed in the afterlife.

Carbon is the basis for the chemistry of life and
Tetravalent – making four electrons available to
form covalent chemical bonds. It has four
valence bonds, the energy required to make or
break a bond is at an appropriate level for building
molecules, which are stable and reactive. it the
backbone of the organic molecules which form
living matter (DNA). **Carbon is the 4th most
abundant element in the universe by mass.**
Carbon is one of the few elements known since
antiquity and serves as a common element of all
known life.

DNA is a carbon based molecule composed
of two chains that coil around each other to
form a double helix carrying the genetic
instructions used in the growth,
development, functioning and reproduction
of all known living organisms. It is composed
**4 bases: adenine (A) and guanine (G) are the
larger purines. Cytosine (C) and thymine (T)**
are the smaller pyrimidines. RNA also
contains 4 different bases.

The **tetragrammaton** (/ˌtɛtrəˈɡræmətɒn/,
from Greek Τετραγράμματον, meaning
"[consisting of] four letters"), **יהוה**
Hebrew and **IHIH** (to be), **AHIH** (existence)
YHWH or YHVH in Latin script, are the four-
letter biblical name(s) of the **God of Israel.**
Other tetragrammation include:

English - LORD

Assyrian – ADAD
Egyptian – AMUN
Greek – THEO , ZEUS
Latin – DEUS
German – GOTT
French – DIEU
Turkish – ESAR
Tartar- ITGA
Arabian - ALIH
Samaritan – JABE
Kabbalist - IHVH

optical design; and other advanced certifications in fiber optics, computer programming, technology business development, financial products, dance, anatomy, and physiology.

Marcus Rodriguez (*Nom de Plume,* "Tim Smith") is Chief Operating Officer of Gramarye Media, Inc., an Atlanta-based cross-media studio complete with content development, production, and distribution. Marcus enjoys creative writing, collecting/researching historical financial documents, crypto-currency mining, and alternative investments.